SIFRI

THE GHOST OF

HANNAH MENDES

A NOVEL

Naomi Ragen

 SIFRI

This book is a work of fiction. Names, characters, places, and incidents either are products of the author's imagination or are used fictitiously. Any resemblance to actual events or locales or persons, living or dead, is entirely coincidental.

Designed by Ruth Lee

 SIFRI LTD.

P.O Box 526
Tel-Aviv 61004
ISRAEL
Tel: 03-5775766 / 5783216

This book was originally published in hardcover by Simon & Schuster, 1998
First Printed in Paperback: Sifri 1999, Reprinted 2000

ISBN 965-7100-19-4

I would like to emphasize that while I have made every effort to be true to historical facts in a broad sense, this book is a work of fiction, and all characters and events described are works of the imagination, including those based on true historical material. Any resemblance to actual persons or events is purely coincidental.

The true descendants of the house of Nasi-Mendes are numerous, and include many distinguished members all over the world, who continue to do credit to their remarkable legacy.

NAOMI RAGEN
JERUSALEM, 1998

For my dear mother and father,
Ada Fogel Terlinsky and Louis Terlinsky.
May their memory be forever blessed.

Man comes forth like a flower and withers,
He flees like a shadow which fades. . . .

But there is hope in a tree,
That if it be cut down, it will sprout again.
Its tender boughs will not cease
though the root grow old in the earth,
and its trunk dies in the ground.

Through the scent of water it will bud again,
Putting forth leaves like a sapling.

JOB, 14:2–9

Gracia (Hannah) Mendes Family Tree

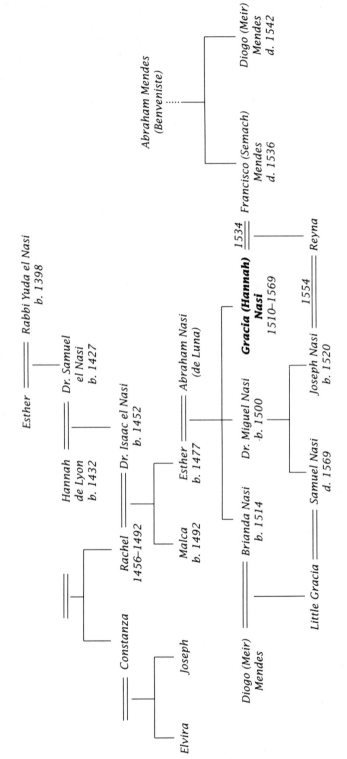

NOTE: There is only one Diogo Mendes, brother of Francisco and husband of Brianda.

Catherine da Costa Family Tree

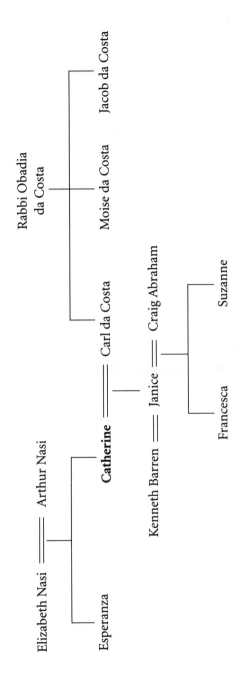

PROLOGUE

From: Carl Mershwam's *Tagebuch einer Reise nach Konstantinopel und Kleinasien*, 1553–1556. (Munich, 1923.)

I n 1553 a Portuguese woman came from Venice to Constantinople
with her daughter and attendants. The Jews seemed to feel she
was a very important person, and she has that difficult race
practically bowing to her. The Hebrews are not in agreement as to
who her husband was and what his name was; some say that he
was called Diego Mendes and his brother was Francisco de
Anversa, some claim the opposite. She is reported to have escaped
with great wealth from Portugal to Venice after her husband's
death, which she flaunts shamelessly; she is said to have a sister
who was supposed to come here, but has somehow been jailed or
detained in some way. The Jews are very proud of this woman and
call her Señora. She lives in luxury and extravagance; she has
many servants, serving wenches also, among them two from the
Netherlands. Like all her kind, she is reported to be gluttonous,
lawless and godless. She is said to have been formerly a Christian
who defiled herself with Mosaic depravities, profaning the
sacraments of the Holy Mother Church, and performing
witchcraft, until finally openly declaring herself a Jewess. The
Venetians are reported to have arrested her and to have refused to
let her go. She is then said to have intrigued with the Sultan's

*physician, who had a son and hoped she would give him her
daughter. The Sultan is then supposed to have taken the part of
the señora and they had to let her go from Venice. They allege they
have left much wealth behind them, and also that some is
following them by sea. They gave the pashas a lot and distributed
several thousand ducats to the poor Jews and their hospital. . . .*

Manuscript pages, memoirs of Doña Gracia Mendes, circa 1568.
Handwritten, India ink on parchment. Private Collection. 1–10,
23 x 33 cm. Isle of Naxos (?).

> *Caminando de vía en vía*
> *Penando esta alma mía*
> *esperando alguna alegría*
> *que el Dio me la de a mi*

My *days of wandering are over. I can allow my feet to rest on silk
footstools, exquisitely shod in gold embroidered slippers that
hardly touch the ground these days. And many times, as I look at
the calm waters of the Bosphorus dappled in brilliant sunlight
outside my palace window in Galata, it seems to me that I have won.*

*Then why do I force my old and weakening hand to take up
quill and parchment, to write this full and passionate accounting
of my days? The reason is this: I do not wish my enemies to own
my history. I know what they will write: that I betrayed my religion
with the worst blasphemy. That I bartered my people and my king
for wealth. That all that was ever dear to me were riches. I can see
their portrait now: the rich Jewess weighted down in gaudy gold
trinkets, riding in her golden carriages toward her ill-gotten
palaces of wealth. . . .*

*Like the worst lies, that description too contains its truths.
Although the priests who baptized me in my mother's arms in the
great Portuguese cathedral of São Vincente de Fora would be
outraged to hear me described as a Jewess, for me, it has always
been a fact as well as an honor. Nor can I deny that I am rich. I
was—indeed, I am—the richest and (many would accuse me) the*

most powerful woman in the world. Kings borrowed from me and were loath to repay. Thus the royal penchant for playing matchmaker, inundating me—the helpless, beautiful young widow in need (they assured me) of male protection—with their asthenic cousins, their effete courtiers, and greedy Old Christian aristocrats; anyone, I am sure, who pledged their monarchs a generous portion of their future dowry. . . .

They did not know with whom they dealt. There has been only one, passionate love in my life. Even death could not separate us. The only other who came close to finding a place in my heart was a man very different from those chosen by kings and princesses. But enough. This is for later on. I shall write of this later on.

Although I was bothered frequently by suitors, each one in his turn was thankfully brief. Sooner rather than later, they tired of their impossible task, as did their royal go-betweens. Instead, they began to pursue my daughter, my Reyna.

I do not think it would be a mother's foolish pride to insist that, in this pursuit, desires other than wealth took part. Reyna possesses a beauty that is forbidden for me to describe, as the Evil Eye lurks waiting for such boasting to free it to its task. I will say only this: Even I, so practiced in the ways of human deceit, believe that at least some of those who professed love for my daughter were sincerely enamored of her delicate young charm and loveliness, rather than her heiress's dowry. With some, I even sympathized. They were heartbroken.

Nevertheless, a marriage is more than mutual desire. It is a union of interests, a partnership in which every member of the family, living and dead, takes part.

She was and is my only child. G-d gave her to me and Francisco to carry on not only the family name, but its honor, all that was dear to us in this life. I knew exactly the kind of man she would marry. I plotted it to the last detail. But, as it is written: If the counsel be made in heaven, no wisdom or wit on earth can prevail.

Nothing I planned came to fruition.

And I succeeded beyond my wildest dreams.

I also achieved full victory in routing lovers and fortune-hunters. For there never was a personage—royal or otherwise—

possessing so little sense and such excess of foolish courage who dared pursue either me or my daughter once I put it to them plainly that I could envision a coffin with far more joy than I could themselves inside a marriage bed.

When the monarchs didn't succeed in laying their hands on my wealth and person through the delicate slavery of marriage, they sent the Reverend Inquisitors, hoping that the grasping arms of the Church would succeed where their own had failed. That, too, was a courtship of sorts. Except the Church had no wish to bed me, simply to burn me. Had the black-robed ones succeeded, the yellow Sanbenito would have been my bridal costume, the torture rack my marriage bed. I imagine consummation would have come quickly in the body-licking flames of the auto-da-fé. Brideless, the Papal Office would no doubt have consoled itself handsomely with the bride's matchless dowry—gold castellanos and precious stones enough to choke even the deepest papal and royal coffers.

Oh, in what beautiful guises you all pursued me, my enemies! Courting noblemen in the richest garments of gold brocade; religious mentors in holy black robes; lovely queens, princesses and duchesses in your beautiful partlets and graceful, wide farthingales. . . . How noble, how gracious you were, wanting only to help me, to befriend me! I was beautiful, you told me. Desirable. I listened to your whispers and read your notes sealed with the finest wax and the most royal of insignias. Oh, how clever and persistent and cruel you were! And how you very nearly succeeded.

I have not, nor will I ever, forget Venice. The icy wetness of the filthy dungeon floor; the stinking smell of the rancid water outside the high, barred windows; the shadows, like dancing demons, brought up by the foul, smoking tapers. Not knowing what you had done to Reyna, where my sweet child slept, if she wept for me. And yes, despite everything, my heart ached for my Little Gracia, too. After all, she did not choose her mother. And worst of all, knowing Brianda was in the next cell, knowing it was she who had betrayed me and the children. . . .

And yet I, a pampered girl whose tender feet had known only the most delicate of gold-embroidered silk slippers; a young, inexperienced widow with one precious child managed to outrun

you all: informing traitors, soldiers, priests, kings. . . . I had a
secret, a weapon, that was stronger than any you brought against
me. Something so powerful it was beyond your comprehension.

Witchcraft, some of you called it.

I called it something else, as did my parents, who bequeathed it
to me.

You never understood what it was. Which is why I succeeded
and you failed.

How I should like to lay my hands on you now, my enemies! To
bring you here to Constantinople, to Galata. How I should like you
to rest your heads a moment on the exquisite softness of my beds
and on the sofas of rare, carved woods and Florentine lapidary; to
feast your eyes on the portraits painted by Raphael, Bellini, Titian,
and Bronzino; to ogle my jewels and my gowns, which have always
been so richly envied and so poorly copied by your tasteless queens
and their noblewomen.

Often, I allow myself to dream of you standing out there among
the crowds of ordinary folks who doff their caps respectfully as I
pass in my beautiful carriages. I imagine the arrogance in your
eyes fading to despair as you begin to fathom how thoroughly you
have been routed and foiled, not only in your greed, but in your
creed—the gospel that it is G-d's will that unconverted Israel
wallow in tortured poverty and unspeakable degradation; a gospel
you have spared no effort to realize.

But because you are not out there and cannot see, I must ask
you then to picture this: As I write these lines my head rests on silk
harem pillows, my hands heavy with bracelets and rings of
priceless rubies, diamonds, and sapphires. Around my neck is a
string of glowing matched pearls the size of pigeons' eggs.
Cocooned in unimaginable wealth, luxury, and happiness, the
India ink in my quill flows easily over the pressed parchment as I
write these words: I, Gracia (Hannah) Nasi Mendes, falsely known
to you as Beatrice de Luna, did wash the baptismal waters from
my daughter's head, as my parents washed them from mine. I
observed the Sabbath on Saturday and donned clothes worthy of a
holiday and took my ease that day and went to visit kinsmen.
During Lent, I ate meat of sheep whose throats were slit by a

Jewish scholar. I kneaded and baked and ate unleavened bread during season. I cooked my food on Friday for Saturday. And in the books in my home the words "Adonai" and "Merciful One" appear, and not Jesus Christ. I did these things, knowing full well that for each such act you have torn tender young girls apart on the rack; serrated the flesh of mothers with iron combs; filled the lungs of living men with putrid water, and then, finally, burned them.

And what then, shall you do to me? I am beyond the reach of your torture chambers, your holy acts of faith now. My life has been my trial. G-d has judged me.

I have described to you His sentence.

But I am no fool. I understand that every triumph is temporary, and that the terrible game of pursuer and prey never really ends. Nor can one ever predict which lull following what battle signals the end of the war, not simply some regrouping of the enemy.

As I near the end of my life, I find I have no great fear of death. But what I do have is a vision of hell which terrifies me more than all the burning pits and screaming damned of the Pope's creation. This is my vision: my body turned to dust in my beautiful marble sepulcher, while above my enemies, born anew, break through my barbicans and drawbridges, climbing over my castle walls to destroy my unsuspecting progeny.

My soul yearns to protect them!

Wealth, cunning, powerful friends—many have possessed all three and been annihilated, root and branch. There is only one thing I can leave behind to defend you. In these pages, I reveal and bequeath it to you, my children. Guard it well.

Thrice now the physicians in my antechamber have sent in my lady's maid, importuning me to end my labors, to lay down and rest. Good advice, I know, which of course I shall ignore. I must finish, and quickly. While I still can.

Do not confuse this with commendable industry. I am a spoiled old woman, used to her luxuries. There are two reasons for my haste and diligence. The first, I am loath to admit, is simply this: Of late, my mind begins to break down. Not in the sense of vapors or fits, but simply like someone on a pleasant stroll, enamored of field and sky, unaware of a small hole in the pocket through which *belongings silently toss themselves to the pleasant decay of earth and wind. It is very pleasant, this fading of details, colors, dates, sounds, smells. I—who for so many years felt my past was a series of highly finished oil paintings, each detail vividly in place—find the images and colors blurring like watercolors, becoming lovelier still.*

This is not to be permitted. We do not want to leave the prettiest picture behind. For the artist who straightens protruding teeth— who flattens stomachs and paints on priceless jewels when the fat, buck-toothed matron wears none—does no favor to later generations, who will not understand why the child is overweight with bad teeth and where the diamonds are.

Who embroiders the truth to enhance it becomes a liar. And that I have never been.

The second reason is that by month's end, I must leave here, probably forever. I know I may not survive the journey—but it is one I have waited for all my life, and that can be put off no longer. It is, therefore, my duty and obligation to leave behind this document, fully finished, and as truthful as I can make it. For as our sages say, truth is a tree of life. From it shall you be nourished all your days.

Let then these pages be my true resting place, my ineradicable epitaph. Even as my body is trapped beneath the earth, its powerful truth shall wander free, entering the hearts of all my children's children, as far into the future as G-d shall grant me offspring.

> *Just as the rain or snow comes down from heaven*
> *and does not return to it without accomplishing its task . . . so*
> *shall be this good word of mine. . . . It shall not return to me void,*
> *but shall accomplish everything that I want it to do, and shall*
> *make you, to whom I sent it, prosper.*
>
> ISAIAH, 55:10–11

This is my story.

1

New York City, March 1996

The street felt cold after Dr. Emil Weinsweig, Jr.'s elegantly overheated offices on Fifty-fourth Street and the Avenue of the Americas. Catherine da Costa crossed her arms, hugging her coat around her. It was soft, brown suede lined with shearling and very warm. But somehow it did nothing to stop the chills that ran up and down her spine. It was early afternoon. The Manhattan sky was a pale gray mist with no hint of sun. Almost instinctively, she raised her arm to hail a cab, then thought better of it, burrowing her hand into her warm pocket. It clenched into a fist.

It wasn't fair, she thought, a single tear sliding down her cheek. She dabbed it with her glove, then rubbed the makeup off the black kid.

There was no point in hurrying home. Only the phone was waiting for her, staring with a dozen menacing, insistent demands. Call Janice. Call your lawyer about the will. Call your broker.

Call Suzanne. Call Francesca.

She crossed the street like a dreamer, falling behind the brisk crowd who almost ran across, New York style, like people on their way to pick up long overdue checks. Cars honked at her, pulling up short. One taxi driver, his hair disheveled and matted to his forehead, even leaned out and shouted, "Move it, old bag!"

She hurried then, her heart pounding as she reached the sidewalk, shocked with insult.

She was a woman who for more years than she cared to remember had been spoken to in the deferent, low tones of Harvard-educated retainers, men who wore expensive suits and combed their hair in front of crystal mirrors in the bathrooms of beautiful old houses. Men who flattered her and overruled her only in the most solicitous, charming way.

Old bag.

She reached up and adjusted her warm mink hat, carefully patting down the hairspray-armored gray curls, immovable on her forehead. Old but still rich, she bristled, walking indignantly down Fifth and pushing open the doors of Cartier with a strange defiance. She was met with the delighted smiles of all and a familiar surge of power ran through her, electric, as she sat down and pulled off her gloves. What would it be? A ring, perhaps? Ruby with diamonds? Or maybe a bracelet? Or perhaps that watch she'd had her eye on for some time. What was it called in those lovely ads with the famous opera singer? The "Diamond Flame"? Deciding she was in no rush, she leaned back comfortably and asked to see all three.

The gold was forgiving against the veiny whiteness of her skin. She held up her hand and peered at herself in the mirror. The bejeweled hand of a rich dowager empress, she thought cynically, even a bit amused. The hand of a woman whose expensive doctor has just gently, and with many protestations, informed her that she is going to die.

She stared at herself in the mirror, then thanked the salesman and took off the jewelry, laying it carefully back on the thick velvet tray.

Back outside, she hugged herself against the mannerless wind and walked toward Central Park. A dirtied snow still smeared the pavement, but up ahead, she noted with a faint, hopeful stir, some of the trees were already in early blossom. She walked toward them.

When she got there she stopped a moment, shrugged, then walked inside.

She couldn't believe it. Catherine da Costa, seasoned New Yorker wearing a mink hat and carrying a purse, risking a walk through Central Park! Might as well wear a sign, "Available for muggings, wildings, and all sorts of other inner-city sports," she thought, pulling up her glove to hide her watch and shaking her head in amazement and disapproval. But then another wave of feeling washed over her, half bravado, half despair: Do whatever you want. Who really gave a good goddamn now?

Lifting her chin bravely, she continued on her way.

She walked slowly until her toes began to tingle with the cold of the pavement. Stamping her feet, as if in protest against the worthless thin soles of her expensive designer boots, she suddenly felt the pain. It ripped up through her bowels, slicing through her stomach and chest, worse than any mugger's blow.

She laid her palm against her chest in a gesture that was at once impatient and importunate; a gesture which said: Please, all right, that's enough now. I get the point.

If only I could bribe it, she thought, groping for the nearest bench. Give it my watch and my wallet and ask it to go away and not bother me anymore. If only I could make it ashamed of itself, and demand it have a little mercy, a little decency for a good, elderly woman who had lived a perfectly respectable, harmless life, who, indeed, had even done some good. . . .

She sat down with dignity, her arms trembling. Far too cold to be sitting, she thought irritably, fumbling in her purse for the green pills that might discourage the rude stranger pressing into her flesh, or at least mollify it. With some difficulty, she swallowed one.

Seventy-four years old. It was a reasonable age, she reminded herself, thinking of her sister, Esperanza, dead of influenza at nineteen, and of Carl, dead of a heart attack at sixty-eight. And even Dr. Emil Weinsweig, Sr. with his decades of exercise and lectures on the evils of smoking, red meat, and sunshine, long gone.

How much easier it would have been to hear the news from Dr. Emil Weinsweig, Sr. than it had been to hear it from his son! There would have been no lowered eyes, no pen tapping nervously against the side of his stethoscope. And no encouraging litany of statistics followed by a recitation of recommendations phrased in such a way as to convince a fabulously rich, spoiled old lady that she would live forever if she spent enough money and endured enough medical tortures. Emil, Sr. would have spared her that, at least.

She had no intention of suffering. None whatsoever. She shook her head adamantly, as if attempting to impress some unseen power with her firm negotiating stance. No operations. No horrible chemical poisons. She touched her hair nervously.

How many months, weeks, days, hours to go, then? she wondered with an odd sense of detachment. And how would she spend them? It was a strange idea. Time had always seemed like those bank accounts she could never seem to empty no matter how much she withdrew. Her father's and grandfather's trust funds, Carl's endless investments, and her bankers and brokers had seen to that. She would leave a great deal behind.

But . . . to whom?

She thought of her daughter, Janice, and her husband, Kenny. They would expect, no doubt, to move into her apartment on Fifth. Not, of course, before turning loose some deranged decorator with instructions to spare no expense (they would assume her money would see they didn't have to) in making it over into a perfect showcase for their hideous collection of fabulously overpriced, bad modern art. She shuddered, imagining the results.

They'd ask Suzanne to move back in. And her granddaughter would be insolent and stubborn and never agree. Why should she? Janice had never understood Suzanne, even though everything that had happened to the girl, every nuance of her life, had been predictable. Indeed, she herself had predicted it.

She closed her eyes, made breathless for a moment by another stab from the stranger who had moved from rudeness to brutality. Despite the green pill, the pain chopped like a machete through her delicate nerve ends. But this time, it was accompanied by a sensation that, for a woman like Catherine da Costa, was much rarer and even more painful: guilt.

She was not a person to rehash old decisions. Usually, she viewed anything she'd done in the past as not only perfectly correct, but quite inevitable. "What else could I have done . . . ?" was one of her favorite mantras. Seldom did someone come up with an answer that convinced her there had been a viable alternative.

Yet, thinking about Suzanne, she found her confidence shaken. She'd been as responsible as the rest of the family for what had happened to Suzanne, as relentless and wrongheaded. For a moment, she thought impulsively about leaving her granddaugher everything—the apartment on Fifth, the stone country cottage, the bank accounts, the jewels, the rare books and other priceless heirlooms. . . .

Oh, yes. Now the blame. Make it up to her. Let's not skip that cliché, either, shall we? she thought irritably, taking off her hat and letting her carefully manicured fingernails ruin three hours at the hairdresser's. In that case, why not give it directly to the rainforest-savers? Or the whale-defenders? Why not send the sables and minks straight to the animal shelters to keep stray cats warm? In fact, might as well turn it all into cash and throw it down from the rooftops of the South Bronx myself. Why burden Suzanne with it? So she could confuse giving away money with living? So she could keep bouncing around trying to find something to believe in?

Well, if not her, then why not her sister? Why not sensible, honest, practical Francesca?

Francesca. She closed her eyes, envisioning the result. The computer printouts of sensible money market funds and stock options. The commodities futures. The thrifty purchase of on-sale designer showroom samples at 50 percent savings. The vacation package tours to the over-crowded beaches on the Costa del Sol. And perhaps, perhaps, a husband, a fellow systems analyst at the bank. Someone just as level-headed and earthbound as she.

Janice and Kenny would show it off. Suzanne would give it away. And Francesca would probably double it.

But who among them, she wondered, would truly cherish what she had to leave behind and find in it true joy? And who among them would understand that to be an heiress was not just a question of easy money or material possessions to squander or hoard, but a responsibility—burdensome in many ways—that demanded tutelary vigilance?

She sat quietly, feeling suddenly quite drained and ready for sleep. A sound, like the chatting of old ladies at a bingo night, made her raise her eyes to where tiny, fawn-colored birds conversed on a brown branch completely bare of buds. She stared at them. They'll be here next year, she thought. And I won't.

For a fraction of a second, the crazy idea of somehow trading with them entered her mind. The idea of giving up everything simply to re-tain some connection to the world, to still feel the sun, the cold, even the pain. To be part of the only kind of existence she could imagine.

Yes, a bird, she thought. She considered it with all the weight and seriousness of a true option. A small, brown bird on a green branch, soaring with unconscious life, warm in the sun. And then she thought of the heavy, cold earth, and the unproven tales of heaven.

Yes, she nodded, emphatically. Yes, I would trade.

How strange, she realized, studying the tree. Not a single bud, not a hint of green when all the trees around it were bursting with new life. Was it simply a late-blooming species, she wondered, or was it dead?

It was a terrible thought: a large, many-branched tree suddenly dying like that, especially when all the trees around it were budding and full of new leaves, flourishing and young again. And what happened when a tree died? Did you cut it down and turn it into ash in the fireplace? Or simply leave it there among the others until its dead roots gave up and it collapsed of its own weight?

A woman wheeling a shopping cart filled with old canvas bags tied with pieces of filthy string passed by. The smell was overpowering and awful, even on such a cold day. Fat and ungirdled, she wore torn slippers and many sweaters and scarves. Her face, badly wrinkled, was both stoic and cunning.

Where was her family, Catherine wondered. Why was there no one to take her in, to care . . . ? And then she looked again at the brown, bare tree and shuddered.

Suzanne, she thought. Francesca.

2

Later that evening, Catherine eased back into the luxurious down pillows of her favorite easy chair. Propped carefully on the side table next to her were invitations to benefits for the New York City Ballet and the Metropolitan Opera; an engraved reminder of a special meeting of the Friends of the Forty-second Street Library; and two tickets to a Picasso preview at MOMA for major donors.

She glanced at them listlessly. Dance, literature, art. Was there anything worthwhile in all these things, she wondered, in all her clean, easy, antiseptically correct good works? Should she have worked in soup kitchens or clothed poor children instead?

Just . . . she really loved music and books. She got up and stared sadly at the glass wall unit holding hundreds of compact discs, tapes, and records. For a terrifying moment, she imagined interplanetary silence—dark, endless, and absolute. But then the phrase "music of the spheres" came into her head, and she felt slightly comforted. There was no way of telling what the afterlife would be like.

Besides, she was still alive.

Choosing her favorite disc, she sank back into her chair and abandoned herself to Dvořák's matchless *Eighth Symphony.*

There was the *allegro con brio:* birds singing, spring rampant, the theme soaring on youthful energy. And then the *adagio,* the theme returning, but echoed, almost mocked, by the deep despair of experience.

27

Still, the lilting, youthful tune kept coming back, like the annoying "But why?" of a sweet, innocent child who refuses to be ignored. The adult answer, by the deep bassoons and the horns, the painful counterpoint to the strings, did its best to disillusion—but the child refused to believe. There was an argument, louder and louder, the soaring transcendent theme a battle between youthful joy and the painful middle age of experience.

As always, she waited for the *allegretto grazioso,* where the battle would turn into a dance, the reconciling waltz of two lovers. When it came, she sighed, envisioning old, bitter age embracing youthful optimism, carried away and made young again with the soaring joy of it.

Was such a dance possible? she wondered. Could partners, so mismatched, ever synchronize their steps and glide together in harmony? She mused on the idea, watching the firelight throw flickering shadows over her beautifully appointed rooms, her well-polished antiques, her china and crystal, until gradually she felt her mind empty of thought. It *was* magnificent, she considered, allowing herself a brief stab of happiness. The high ceilings, the elegant moldings, the rich, polished woodwork. Yet, years ago, when the wife of one of Carl's business acquaintances had compared it to one of the stately homes of England, she'd been appalled, thinking of those huge, cold, lifeless rooms so meticulously maintained by descendants with a boundless reverence for the past that bordered on stupidity. All that useless, ugly bric-a-brac gathering dust in crumbling palatial estates and dusty museum corridors!

But now she wondered if the woman (who had never been invited back) had been right, after all. Was her home lacking in the animating spirit of life, like the well-preserved—but meaningless and quite useless—merchandise of an antiques store?

She found the idea devastating.

It was a home, with character and life, she protested, her eyes nervously darting from the simple beauty of the William and Mary gateleg table to the handsome pair of Gainsborough armchairs to the richly carved seventeenth-century Spanish chest. Scandinavian-crystal vases filled with bouquets of spring flowers were everywhere. There was nothing chintzy. Nothing just for show, she bristled, fighting a bit frantically against the idea that she was hardly in a position to judge.

After all, it was all so beloved, so familiar.

And yet, she could not ignore the strange feeling that she had already left it all behind and was now viewing it with the critical, envious, and slightly adulatory eyes of the tourist. Why, then, should she feel so defensive, so vulnerable?

So guilty.

The word popped into her head unbidden, a balloon in a comic strip injecting a thought into a cartoon character's head. She put down the glass and walked slowly over the thick, beautiful Persian carpets into the hushed quiet of the library. She stopped at the threshold, breathing in the masculine scent of teak oil and heavy leather bindings.

It had been her grandfather's, and then her father's, favorite room. Carl, too, had loved it and spent many hours there. She ran her fingers over the dark, worn leather of the reading chair. She had been held in many arms and sat on many laps in this chair. She stared at the collection of valuable rare books, and then her eyes focused on the huge desk with its dozens of family photographs in pretty silver frames. She picked up one and then another, rubbing off the smudge mark of her slightly damp fingers with a caressing thumb.

Carl. He'd been dead six years, yet she could still feel his presence in the room, smell the pipe smoke and the warm, pleasant scent of his Scottish wool sweaters. She hugged herself, almost feeling the pressure of his arms around her shoulders and back. Young people thought youth and beauty were necessary for passion. They didn't understand. . . .

She walked to the wall behind the desk, swinging out the portrait that cleverly concealed a safe hidden deep inside the wall. She turned the combination lock, pulled back the heavy metal door, and carefully removed a large glass container. Inside was the priceless Bible that had been in her family for more than five hundred years, along with several other rare, handwritten manuscripts.

Ever since she could remember, the Bible had filled her with feelings of deep confusion. On the one hand, it was one of those heirlooms that infuse memories with a particular form and substance, without which the past becomes as amorphous and characterless as smoke. She could not imagine the family without the Bible. Just its dark, tooled-leather cover was enough to evoke reminders of a real, solid world shrouded in mysticism, attuned to an older, wiser order of things. A world rough with physical deprivation and harsh discomfort, yet suffused with meaning.

Yet, on the other hand, its very preciousness made it a burden. One was afraid to touch it, to look at it or show it. Not only because of its physical fragility, which was understandable, but because of the potent, yet indistinct power it held over the present. She had never been able to quite define that power—what it was *supposed* to mean to her, other than its simply existing. She existed, and it existed, and they were inextricably intertwined; this she had always accepted and understood. But what she was supposed to do with that connection had always eluded her. More—it had been frightening and guilt-producing. It had been burdensome.

She lifted out the Bible carefully. Published in 1475 in the tiny Aragonese city of Hijar by Eliezer ben Abraham ibn Alantasi, physician, scholar, and businessman, it was one of the first Hebrew Bibles ever printed, one of only ten copies. When Ferdinand and Isabella banished the Jews from Spain, printer and press had disappeared, along with thousands of other refugees and their belongings. As far as she knew, this was the only one of Alantasi's Bibles to have survived.

She gently caressed the brown-leather binding with its rectangular central panel and rosettes. Then, with extreme care, she opened it. Around the printed Hebrew letters, the loving craftsmanship of illumination still glowed: acanthus leaves painted in blue, green, and magenta curled around peacocks, dragons, and royal lions. On other pages, green scrolls with blue and green flowers opened to show their pistils of gold on backgrounds of wine red or Prussian blue. She feasted her eyes on the skilled handiwork, turning the pages until she reached the shimmering gold tree that held the family's long history.

Sketched in tempera and gold leaf, it had always seemed to her, even as a small child, to be a remnant of some enchanted forest, leaves thick on its golden boughs, where Midas and Danae walked arm in arm. At the top of the tree was Rabbi Yuda el Nasi(b. 1398), and his son, Dr. Samuel el Nasi (b.1427), and daughter-in -law, Doña Hannah de Lyon el Nasi (b. 1432). They in turn had had Isaac (b. 1452), who also became a physician. Isaac and his wife, Rachel (b. 1456), who died on the day of the expulsion from Spain, had had two daughters, Esther (b. 1477) and

Malca (b. 1492). Esther had one son, Miguel (b. 1500), and two daughters, Gracia (b. 1510) and Brianda (b. 1514). And so it went, on and on,
uninterrupted for hundreds of years. Until now.

She sat quietly, turning page after page holding the rich history of
her family—births, deaths, and marriages, the golden boughs growing
barer and barer with time. She stared at Suzanne and Francesca's
names. Two golden leaves left, she thought, and then—the dead, bare
branch.

She felt a chill, like a cold piece of steel, tap across her forehead.

They were both in their twenties—beautiful girls—with a trail of
broken relationships behind them. Suzanne considered herself a
widow, even though she'd never been married. And Francesca had
some mathematical formula for deciding exactly which kind of man
she'd even deign to go out with. She suspected the right numbers did
not often come up for Francesca. Catherine had no idea if there were
any men in their lives now at all. . . .

In this obscene age, when middle-aged men cast off the wives of
their youth because their breasts sagged; when men considered marriage only in their late thirties, and then to high-school seniors; when
women began to consider marriage and children only after finishing
graduate school, working, and taking a trip around the world . . . what
were the chances of her granddaughters marrying at all? And even if
they did, what were the chances of their staying married?

And what could she do about any of it?

Why was it old people weren't respected in our society? she thought
peevishly, remembering the hateful face of the cabbie. It was a surprising thing, wasn't it? The wrinkles and the white hair were, after all, signs
of having accumulated knowledge and experience distilled into precious wisdom and insights that should be sought after and valued.
Some cultures did. She thought vaguely of the Chinese and Japanese. . . . But somehow the picture of a Japanese boy in a punk haircut
and earrings she'd seen near Bloomingdale's came to mind.

The Japanese had their problems, too.

What had Janice once told her and Carl soon after starting college?
"Practically, the old have no very important advice to give the young,
their own experiences have been so partial and their lives have been
such miserable failures . . . Old deeds for old people, new deeds for

new." It was from Thoreau, a text assigned to Janice in an enormously expensive college class at an enormously expensive university.

Thoreau. She imagined with distaste the bearded, disheveled young philosopher in his dirty clothes as he sat writing those lines in his unheated shed by some stagnant pond full of dreadful mosquitoes. You handed over thousands and thousands of trust-fund dollars for tuition, room and board, clothes, books, travel—and then they quoted you Thoreau.

She shook her head, thinking of Kenny Barren, second husband of her only daughter, driving his blue Porsche wearing English tweeds. He was a tall, blond Californian who'd grown up climbing pear trees in a little farming town in northern California where the biggest cultural event of the year had been the annual Pear Festival. His parents had once been farmers, good Methodists, who counted the Vikings among their forebears. After a brief fling in the theater, Kenny had finished his master's in business at the University of California. He was now a bank vice-president in charge of personal finance.

He was the kind of person who never missed an opening night at Lincoln Center or the Metropolitan Opera, but at home never listened to music and in his car had John Denver tapes. He was the kind of person who attended SoHo gallery openings whenever possible, but in Paris or Florence skipped the Musée D'Orsay and the Uffizi, preferring to shop for clothes or antiques instead. He was the kind of person for whom a family Bible would be as meaningful as a crèche in a department store window.

Janice had met him right after her divorce from Craig Abraham, at one of those art-appreciation courses at N.Y.U. She'd run off with him to the Caribbean for three weeks, leaving Suzanne and Francesca with Catherine.

There had been stormy, tearful, long-distance arguments that had ended with enormous phone bills and Janice's threats to get married in Las Vegas. Finally, someone had found a Reform rabbi willing to perform the ceremony even if Kenny didn't convert—which he had no intention of doing, and which Janice thought was stupid anyway, since both of them had no interest at all in (as Janice liked to call it) "mumbo-jumbo."

They'd been married—happily, as far as Catherine knew—for nearly fifteen years now.

Mixed marriages, diminishing births, broken families . . . It wasn't just her family. It was everyone's.

She thought of Carl and his three brothers, descendants of one of the most respected rabbis of the Sephardic Jewish community in Iraq, Rabbi Obadiah da Costa. One brother had died in World War II. A second had emigrated to South America and become fabulously wealthy in diamond mining. He'd married late—to a South American woman of Portuguese ancestry—and converted to Catholicism. They'd had one child, a daughter, who'd been killed in a freak waterskiing accident when she was only twenty-three. A third brother had wound up making films in Hollywood and never married. He was sixty-nine and living with a twenty-four-year-old starlet.

She felt her heart contract as she closed the Bible, replacing it carefully. There was one other book kept in the safe. It, too, was a rare, old manuscript handed down through the generations. She picked up the pages, winey with age.

Memorias de Doña Gracia Mendes

> Caminando de vía en vía
> Penando esta alma mía
> esperando alguna alegría
> que el Dio me la de a mi

She remembered her father's finger tracing the words as she sat on his warm lap, his arms touching her shoulders as he translated: " 'From town to town I wandered, my soul suffering within. Yet I hope still for the joy that G-d will give me.' "

"Who was she?" she'd asked him. Why had she suffered and where had she wandered? "It was the same Gracia as in the family Bible," he'd said. "Your ancestor. Very beautiful and very brave. A heroine, in fact, who'd risked her life to save the lives of hundreds during the Inquisition. She'd lived like a queen in beautiful palaces in Lisbon, Antwerp, Venice, and Istanbul."

"Then why did she suffer?" she'd asked impatiently, looking into his smiling face. But he'd only continued smiling, shaking his head.

· "All we have are the first few pages. The rest of the story is lost."

"But what do they say, these pages?" she'd persisted, tugging at his tie and undoing the knot. "Do they say G-d granted her joy?"

"They say that she has a secret, a secret weapon to protect her family."

"What's the secret, *Padre?*"

"I would love to know," he'd told her, smoothing down her hair.

She'd touched the manuscript, her childish finger tracing the flowery script, thinking, My hand touching her hand.

Often, she'd dreamed of finding the rest of the manuscript hidden somewhere in the archives of some medieval library or on the shelves of a rare bookseller's. She'd dreamed of learning the answers to her questions. And Carl had actually made several unsuccessful attempts to track down the missing pages. But then both of them had somehow lost interest.

One thing was clear—Gracia's weapon must have been potent. Despite the wars, the expulsions, the pogroms, the family had survived for hundreds of years, the tree flourishing, its branches thick with leaves. They'd managed to pass down the precious Bible, spice boxes, menorahs, *etrog* holders, silver candlesticks.

She had never forgiven Janice for marrying out. Probably never would. But now, looking down at the precious, fragile parchment, she somehow felt she had no right to nurse any anger toward her daughter.

After all, I raised her.

And what has my family's long history ever meant to me? How many arguments did I have with my own mother over outlandish, empty rituals?

She remembered the bitter family fights just before her wedding, culminating in her refusal to immerse in the *mikvah* or to attend her mother-in-law's traditional *bogo de baño* party that preceded immersion, or her mother's *cafe de baño* party afterward, scandalizing them both.

Carl had been more cooperative, enduring the *salidura de boda,* making wearying rounds with his friends from house to house, in deference to the tradition that insisted the groom was never to be left alone before the wedding, lest the demons from the north, jealous of his happiness, spring upon him unawares.

Yet, I've always known who I was, where I came from, and to whom I owed my loyalty, she bristled, as if in an argument with a nasty and unreasonable foe. I've taken good care of every single one of the family's precious heirlooms! Look, just look at what wonderful condition they're in! I had the silver polished; I kept the books in climate-controlled cabinets, I kept the embroidered linens fresh and immaculate. . . .

The anger suddenly left her, replaced by a terrible emptiness as she thought of Janice and Kenny and her granddaughters ransacking her things after she was safely buried. Janice might behave herself at first, but eventually that husband of hers, with his bespoke suits and custom-made shirts, would simply unload the silver and the books at Sotheby's or Christie's. He'd no doubt use the spoils to buy more bright red canvases with handwriting and bits of old china or plastic bottles pasted all over them.

She felt her whole body rise up in revulsion.

I could leave them to a museum, she considered. She looked at the Renaissance display cabinet of rare, carved walnut that held the silver and gold heirlooms. For hundreds of years these items had been carefully used by some blood relative to sanctify the Sabbath, holidays, weddings, bar mitzvahs, and circumcision ceremonies. She imagined them in her grandmother's and great-grandmother's hands. And then she tried to imagine them mummified and lifeless inside glass cases surrounded by little typed-up informative notes, tended by indifferent guards in gray uniforms. With horror, she envisioned the dusty, long museum corridors filled with bored adults and rowdy children.

For the first time since hearing the results of her tests, hot tears stung her eyes.

She moved unsteadily across the room, settling herself once more before the fire and refilling her glass. The reflected firelight, blood red yet full of gold, lapped with an angry tongue against the cold glass.

Suzanne had asked about the silver things once or twice when she was little. And Francesca had asked even more often, pointing curiously at the china closet and the bookcases, patiently sitting on Carl's knees while he smoked his pipe. She distinctly remembered Carl telling them they must learn all about it when they were older. All about the family's history . . .

And do you remember what *you* told them?

She fingered the cold, sharp grooves of the cut crystal. Yes, I remember.

I told them not to touch.

It doesn't matter now, it's the past! There was always the future. Each one of her granddaughters might eventually have a child. She tried to envision her great-grandchildren: pale, chubby replicas of Janice who would whine their way through F.A.O. Schwarz as toddlers, watch television through to adolescence, and then proceed to think about sex and money the rest of their lives.

It was terrible, terrible, she thought, not sure if she meant the vision itself or the meanness of spirit that had conjured it. Maybe they will be perfectly darling! she cried out silently. Intelligent, polite, serious. The kind of people who cherish family heirlooms and family histories; who read family Bibles with pride, and found societies. . . .

She walked into the living room and peered through the glass at the lovely, priceless keepsakes. The problem was, it would be too late. The shelves behind the glass doors would be emptied long before her great-grandchildren had a chance to be curious, no matter what she wrote in her will. They would never see the magical, shimmering gold tree thick with leaves, or their place on it.

IT ISN'T MY FAULT THAT THERE IS NO ONE TO LEAVE THEM TO!! I MARRIED, I HAD A CHILD. I DID MY BEST!!

She threw back her head and drained the glass, completing her thorough disregard of Dr. Emil Weinsweig, Jr.'s careful orders.

A drowsiness born of exhaustion and a certain deep melancholy washed over her. She felt her eyelids droop and the crystal glass grow suddenly unbearably heavy in her hand.

A wind, like a gust from a door left rudely open in winter, chilled her hands and shoulders like falling ice.

"Freezing," she muttered, pulling her shawl more tightly around her. "Carlotta, there's a window or a door open," she protested to her unseen housekeeper.

When she looked up, a woman stood in the doorway. She was dressed in a magnificent gown of russet, black, and cream brocade with an elaborate design that resembled paisley, but was far more imaginative and bold. A thick gold braid covered her shoulders on either side of her long white neck, and a matching gold hairnet restrained her thick, curly, reddish-brown hair. She wore enormous drop-pearl earrings and two strands of the largest pearls Catherine had ever seen.

She stared at the woman, speechless. The woman stared back. She had a broad, clear forehead; a graceful, almost Roman, nose; and a sweet, small chin. Her eyes, large and dark, looked out from half-closed lids with curiosity and a profound sadness.

"How did you get in? Are you one of Carlotta's relatives?" Catherine finally asked her.

"My feet are very cold," the woman replied, lifting her skirts and sitting down in the second easy chair before the fire. She wore delicate slippers embroidered in gold thread.

"Well, if you insist on wearing those kinds of flimsy, useless shoes in this weather, I'm not surprised. . . ."

"Where I came from, it was lovely and warm."

"Have you come straight from Tijuana, then? Legally, I hope. Is the dress Mexican, too?"

"I wear nothing. Your eyes deceive you."

"Who let you in? How did you get in?" Catherine repeated, with a faint stirring of fear.

There was silence. The deep, dark eyes looked out at her, pityingly. "You did. You let me in."

"I don't recall doing any such thing," she said hotly, thoroughly frightened and defensive. "What is it you want?" she almost shouted.

The head tilted, the eyes turned quizzical. "The question is: What is it *you* want?"

"What I want? From you?"

"You asked for something. I heard you clearly. I saw your tears . . ."

She wiped her eyes, embarrassed. "I never cry."

"Yes, you do."

"This is a dream, isn't it? I'm dreaming. All that wine, and the painkillers . . ."

"You have no reason to cry, you know. There is fate, and then there is destiny. It is foolish to cry over fate when you can plan and work toward changing destiny."

"Are you a dream, or are you real?"

"Your tears are not for the unborn," the woman continued, ignoring her. "They are for yourself. You thought your mother was a fool with her rituals, prayers, and incantations. And now you're going to die, and you're afraid. Your daughter, whom you think you don't like, is just like you."

"Janice is nothing like me! Is that it? Did she send you? To check up on me?"

"You could not have kept me away. Everything's been squandered. Everything our lives were for . . ."

"A bad, bad dream . . ." Catherine wept, covering her eyes. "I'm sorry, so sorry . . . It's all too late. There is nothing I can do now. My life is almost over."

"No, Rivka. It isn't."

Her mouth fell open. "Why did you call me that? Who told you that was my name?"

Rivka. The name she'd been given in the synagogue the first Sabbath after she was born.

"Tears are like little self-indulgent diamonds. We decorate ourselves with them to charm our way out of scandals and accidents. My sister was a great crier. I, on the other hand, cried only in secret, after I'd made my plans. There is always a secret way, a secret power, a plan that twists its way around enemies and obstacles."

Catherine wiped her face. "Do you have a plan? For me?" she suddenly asked.

The woman nodded, as if that were exactly the point. "Here it is."

It was an old map, as dark as calfskin, with elaborate cursive lettering. London. Toledo. Córdoba. The Bay of Biscay. Balearic Islands. Aix-la-Chapelle. Ragusa. Ferrara. Ancona. The Duchy of Naxos.

"Where are these places?"

"This is where we start. In London."

"Start?"

"The journey."

"I am too old to travel. Too sick. Too tired."

"I thought that once. But my last journey was the best one of all."

"Was it?" Catherine looked up hopefully.

"It was for me." She nodded, the dark eyes shining, all sadness gone.

"I can't go," she repeated.

"You must. And you must take the others with you."

"The others?"

"The young. Suzanne, Francesca."

"How do you know their names?"

"They belong to me, too."

"They are too busy to take trips."

"All my life I traveled. I am still traveling. . . . You must make them, then. They have to get married. You have to help them find husbands."

Catherine snorted with startled laughter. "Match them up! Like Yentl in *Fiddler?*" She closed her eyes and shook her head. "Dream or ghost, go away now! I'm a sick woman. I can't have this! Carlotta!"

"You're afraid they won't listen to you. That you have no power over them."

Catherine felt her heart freeze. She wrung her hands.

"They will go. And at least one of them will find a husband, a good one. You will persuade them. You will hold your gold above their heads. Gold is a great persuader, I've always found."

"You don't understand. It's not like that. No one listens to parents or grandparents anymore. It's too late." She shrugged. "Their characters are set. A trip won't solve anything. At best they'll sightsee, buy some trinkets, and sip champagne with my money."

"A shroud has no pockets, Rivka."

A chill went up her spine, the chill of the nightmare-spinner alone and helpless, smothered by night.

"It's too late to visit me. Visit *them*. Convince *them*."

"Send them to me."

"Where is that? Where shall they look for you?"

"In the book, of course. My book. I wrote it for them."

"We looked for it. Rare-book dealers, collectors. It's never turned up. I've got only a few pages."

"They'll find it."

"You don't understand! They have jobs, apartments. Money won't be enough. They won't go off just because I tell them. They don't care about me."

"Then you must hold your death above their heads. Use their pity, their greed. Tell them you are dying, tell them about your will."

Catherine was shocked. "That isn't fair! It's emotional blackmail! It would be appealing to their worst instincts . . . !"

"It is all of that, and more." She nodded. "Do it."

She hesitated. "And if I don't?"

The woman shrugged. "Have you ever heard the thud of a large tree in the forest when it dies? It's a terrible, blasphemous noise, like the crack of a small child's skull hitting the hard pavement, or the slam of a body thrown against a wall. Everyone who hears such a sound, be they living or dead, can never forget it, or forgive."

"*No!* It isn't fair! You haven't told me enough! What should I convince them to do? Where should I send them? What should I tell them?!" She felt a rising hysteria.

"Missus, missus. Are you all right, all right, missus?" Carlotta shook her. "You sleep so long. You moan. I think you not feel good."

Catherine blinked, looking around the empty room. "I slept?" She let out a deep sigh. Her back was sticky with sweat, almost clinging to the chair. She wiped her forehead, trying to calm down. "You probably thought I was drunk."

Carlotta—who, seeing the open bottle, had wondered exactly that—blushed furiously. "*No!* Señora. S'not true!"

"It's all right. I'm sorry. I'm just a bit cranky. I'll go to bed now."

"I help you."

"Oh, don't fuss! I don't need any help to get up." She waved her away in exasperation. Not yet, anyway, she thought grimly, pushing herself out of the chair.

There was a wineglass on its side under the coffee table. It must have rolled out of her hand as she slept, she thought, bending to retrieve it. A tiny thread was stuck to its side. When she removed it, it glinted in the firelight like gold.

3

Handwritten manuscript, author unknown. Constantinople, circa 1574 (?). Microfiche. Guenzburg Library, Moscow.

I will begin with the dream that has always been for me the true beginning of my adult life. It is not even my own dream, but my mother Esther's, whispered to me in the cellar of our beautiful family mansion in Lisbon, on the eve of my twelfth birthday; whispered with the strangest and most glorious pride and the deepest of sorrow.

This is what she told me:

She was walking through the forest with her mother, my grandmother Rachel, a tall and queenly woman. Her mother's head was lifted proudly, her reddish hair coiled thick beneath her cap. But as she walked, her cap was stolen by the branches, the hair tangling in the sharp, leafless limbs. She stumbled, falling to her knees and my mother saw her velvet dress and overmantle covered with brambles. And as my grandmother lay there in the forest, the branches gave birth to dark birds that swooped down and filled her mouth with coals that sank through her body, swelling her feet. She fell prostrate on the rocks, her swollen stomach splitting, the red blood pouring to the ground like wine from an unfit gourd. My mother screamed for my grandfather Isaac, for all his physician's tools, his medicines and books. But he *was far away, tending to the long line of marchers who snaked through the hills out of Spain; thousands and thousands of them, my mother said, like some weary caterpillar with a million weak and broken feet.*

When my grandfather finally did appear, to my mother's great shock, he did not rush to heal grandmother's wounds. Instead, he put his arms around my mother's waist, lifting her. I imagine his thick mustache must have tickled her young skin, his strong arms banished her childish fears. For she told me that at that moment, she forgot about her mother and leaned into his warm arms, complaining; "Where are the wagon, the horses? My feet are so tired." And he comforted her, singing a song about the Hebrews leaving Egypt, arriving in the Promised Land.

And they were Hebrews and Lisbon was that land. There would be no cruel corregidores *in Lisbon to take their coach and horses, he whispered to her. When they left the cursed Spanish border, the land of the demons Ferdinand and Isabella, they would ride in golden coaches drawn by white horses in bejeweled caparisons. He promised my mother her hair would shine like copper, washed clean with hot water and perfumed soap, and she would have little diamonds for her ears and thick gold chains to hang about her throat. There would be lamb, first stuffed with herbs, vegetables, and wine, then roasted slowly over a wood-fired oven lined with clay; tender onions and potatoes marinated in tarragon leaves and olive oil; grapes and almonds and apples dipped in honey for a sweet year; candles in their silver holders would light the Sabbath day and silver spice boxes filled with frankincense and myrrh would lend a sweet fragrance to each new week's beginning. They would drink almond water chilled by snow, and wine as thick and sweet as honey.*

Often, I imagine him standing there, hugging my mother, his face wetting hers with a mourner's tears, and my mother suddenly waking up and remembering her mother and all the blood. . . . He didn't try to comfort her, my mother told me, but wept aloud until his eyes turned milky and his dark pupils swam. When he had finished, he took out a Bible with a beautiful cover of tooled, dark leather and opened it to a page at the very beginning. There was a

tree with golden branches, each one with a name and a date. And
then he took a quill and dipped it into blue dye and wrote: Malca el
Nasi, born July 31, 1492, sister to Esther; and then, next her
mother's name: Rachel el Nasi, died, July 31, 1492.

And this is how my mother learned that her mother had died
while giving birth to her sister.

My mother was eight years old the day that her mother died,
the day all Jews were expelled from Spain. Many died that day and
the days that followed, falling down on the endless, hard road—
buried, as my grandmother was, in unmarked graves along the
way. So pitiful were they that even Old Christians went out of their
houses and stood crying on the roadside, urging them to spare
themselves, to accept baptism and remain behind. But the rabbis
urged them on, asking the children to play drums and cymbals, to
sing.

My mother wanted to go back to her beautiful house outside
Seville. So many nights, hard stones rubbing raw her back, she
dreamed of the polished steps leading to her zaguán, the smell of
the purple flowers and the climbing vines trailing up to the little
balcony off her whitewashed bedroom that was always filled with
red geraniums. She dreamed of her estrado with its soft pillows, of
her bed of down quilts and fresh straw mattresses, and of the spicy
breeze that wafted through the tamarind trees.

Many had stayed behind, her father told her later. They had
shaken their heads sadly at the foolishness of preferring the hard
uncertainty of exile to the soft rain of baptismal waters; waters,
they winked, that could always be washed away in the mikvah
beneath the synagogue. I can almost see my grandfather's face as
he explained this to my mother: his lips grim, his eyes touched with
black humor and contempt mixed with sadness.

But neither those who stayed, nor those like my stubborn
grandfather who risked all to leave, understood that both were
equally doomed. For in the end, I imagine, there was not enough
water to douse Torquemada's fires as they roasted the flesh of
those cunning pretenders. Nor could my grandfather, as far as he
wandered, succeed in escaping the flood of holy waters the Church
was determined to pour down upon his head.

My mother walked all the way to Lisbon, as my grandfather carried my aunt Malca, who was just a few days old. All the way, he searched for wet nurses, and when he failed to find them, he finally bought a goat and poured its warm milk through a sucking horn held between Malca's lips. When she gagged at that, he took lumps of sugar and bread and rubbed them in a piece of linen that he shaped into a teat that Malca sucked.

How my mother envied her infant sister—carried and fed in their father's arms while she trudged alongside, her tongue cleaving to the roof of her mouth in thirst, her stomach boiling with hunger. But even as a baby, Malca was never content, my mother recalled. At night, she never stopped crying, and during the day she whimpered and screamed.

I sometimes try to imagine what it must have been like for my mother: how long the road was, how hard on the uncallused soles of a small child; how hot the sun, how cold the nights! Isn't it strange, then, that my mother should also have remembered the beauty of the Spanish sky—turquoise and gold with sunlight? The lovely rolling hills and valleys, the sparkling waters, and the rosy brilliance of distant horizons? Spain's white castles with their moats and turrets? So that, when she finally reached the border, she could not help but look back with longing, like Lot's wicked wife as she was led by angels out of Sodom. She looked back and wondered if she, too, would be turned into a pillar of salt for her profane regret.

But she was not to be so stricken. G-d had a different set of terrible punishments selected for her, she told me.

The first was Lisbon.

The confusion at the Portuguese border was terrible. Thousands of people pushing and screaming. My mother remembered bobbing in the stormy human current, her only anchor her father's strong hand. But something was terribly wrong. They had walked over mountains, waded through streams, and been battered by rocks and branches to reach this goal. And yet, the cries were heartbreaking.

She asked her father what there was to cry about now. But something had come over him. His gentle voice turned suddenly harsh. "Say nothing," he demanded, his eyes burning like a devil's.

My mother grabbed on to him like a frightened animal, but he pried her loose, almost cruelly. Covering his eyes with both hands, she heard him say, "My sins have sapped my strength, Lord. Deliver us in your everlasting compassion."

Then she saw him crouch over his bag of medicines and instruments, taking out his mortar and pestle and crushing some herbs, which he then mixed with goat's milk and poured through the sucking horn into Malca's mouth. Slowly her cries quieted, but then, just as suddenly, her body flailed as if in a fit, until it went as rigid as a piece of wood.

My mother started to cry, but her father shook her so hard her teeth rattled like pebbles. She sat down in the dust and wiped her eyes in astonishment, watching as her father took out an old gunnysack and wrapped it around Malca so that even her face was covered. Wrapped so, he placed her in the bottom of a beggar's pouch and buried her in feathers of down.

Grandfather Isaac was a tall man with a broad forehead and large eyes that seemed always to be amused. She used to think of them as smiling eyes, mother told me. His lips were a calm, generous curve across his handsome chin. But that day when my mother searched his face for regret, kindness, even sorrow, she found only hot, burning coals that flashed through his narrowed lids, and lips that stretched like a jagged wound beneath his mustache. A horror washed over her as she began to understand what had really happened: Her father, her dear father, had been taken from her, and now in his body a demon dwelt.

For this she had several proofs. First, when she searched for his shadow—the truest proof he was no demon—she could not find it. And second, he took nothing to eat, his tongue rolling in his mouth like those that lap up fire, water, air, and slime. Terrified, my mother ran through the wailing women, screaming her father's name.

"Demon fed on fire, water, dust, and slime, release my father's shape!" she screamed back at the demon who pursued and overtook her. "You will dry up and return to nothing!" she shouted, wondering if she, too, was to be poisoned and wrapped in a gunnysack. But the demon in the shape of her father caught and held her fast, paying no heed to her hysterical cries.

"*All right,*" *he said in a whisper that was so strangely calm in her ear, a whisper that immediately made her tongue freeze in cold fear. "Maybe I am a demon. But the Portuguese soldiers are bigger devils yet.*"

My mother looked at the Portuguese. They were enormous, dark men in metal helmets that hid their faces. They held sharp swords and their horses snorted and stamped the ground, filling the air with a smoky fog of dust. Vicious packs of barking dogs snapped at their heels. She then decided that the demon was preferable, and held his hand and watched quietly as he counted out the head price to the Portuguese, who then allowed him to carry her and their belongings across the border.

As she crossed the border, she felt the dull ache of hopelessness fill her. Her mother and baby sister dead, her father possessed, she waited with stoic acceptance for her turn. She wasn't surprised when the demon began to run toward the forest, dragging her behind him. In the darkness, she waited for him to reveal himself, to see his clothes evaporate and his head go bald, hair sprouting instead over his face and body.

Behind each dark tree, she could see evil estries lurking, waiting to make a meal of her. Once, she was positive she'd seen the dark coiled hair of Lilith herself flashing among the branches. Lilith, Adam's first wife, who spent her time sucking away the breath of a hundred babies a day, vengeance against Eve's children.

Her heart stopped cold. Suddenly, she bit the terrible hand that gripped her, drawing blood, and ran ahead, hiding behind the pines. To her surprise, the demon-father didn't try to follow her. Instead, all his attention was riveted on her sister. My mother watched as he spilled out the down and unwrapped the gunnysack, taking out her sister's motionless form. He slapped the baby's face very hard, rubbing his hands roughly along her chest and back.

My mother always stopped at this point in the story, her face flushing red. "I must tell the truth," she would say. "I did not so much mind seeing my sister peacefully dead, all her nagging cries stilled. But I could not abide seeing her abused."

She ran to the demon and threw all her weight against him,

making up in swiftness for what she lacked in bulk, knocking her
demon-father over. Just at that moment, she screamed at him the
words her own dead mother had taught her to say at bedtime to
keep the night demons away: "Behold, the guardian of Israel
neither sleeps nor slumbers! The angel who redeemed me from all
evil, bless the children so that my name and the names of my
fathers, Abraham and Yitzchak be carried on. . . ." My mother said
that her demon-chasing prayer was suddenly interrupted by her
father's laughter and her sister's cries. She looked, startled, into the
demon's face and suddenly saw it was again her father's, whom
she loved. As she held his hand and he stroked her hair, he
explained how he had put Malca to sleep with mandragora and
opium in order to smuggle her across the border because he had
not had enough gold to pay her head price. He apologized for
frightening her with tales of devils. He hadn't known how else to
keep her from accusing him of witchcraft in front of the
Portuguese soldiers, who might have put him in a basket and
carried him to prison—the fate of witches.

There were no such things as demons, he told her. The only
thing one had to fear in this world were human beings who had
chosen evil over good.

My mother, Esther, always repeated these words to me with
pride, but I knew she herself did not believe them. She was
convinced her powerful incantation had undone the devil's work
and restored her father and sister to her.

I bless my mother in her grave for having passed such power of
belief down to me. For even as a small child, I, too, felt in
possession of a wondrous secret that would allow me to outwit the
myriad hosts of evil spirits that roam the world threatening me
and my family. For as far back as I can remember, I shared my
mother's unshakable conviction that I, too, had the cunning and
strength to save myself and those I loved. I must admit, it is a
feeling that has sustained me through most of my troubled life,
deserting me only on two significant occasions that I shall describe
in greater detail at a later time.

But the fool is half a prophet, she liked to say. And her
terrifying entrance into Portugal was a portent of things to come.

Once across the border, it took my mother several more days to reach Lisbon. If the inn she stayed in was horrible—filthy and overcrowded—then the streets were unbearable. My mother did not mince her words in delicacy and false modesty. The slop of chamber pots dumped, making dry roads into rivers of stink; people emptying their guts from all ends where they stood; the smell of dead animals and the rotting meat—all this a thousand times over as the city swelled until there were more people than stars for counting. And as if that wasn't enough, conditions worsened daily as thousands more arrived in the city.

The Portuguese king had allowed those who couldn't afford his fees to pay less on condition that they hire boats and leave for North Africa and Saloniki. And so whole families took up residence in the streets and hillsides, homeless and nearly penniless, for they had been robbed of all their worldly goods by the decrees of the Spanish monarch, and relieved of even the small remainder by paying the head price.

Years later, I understood that some who had paid for passage to the Levant never saw a boat; while others were put afloat in unseaworthy vessels without food or water, the captains refusing to let them disembark. Thousands died at sea from disease and hunger. And of those who reached shore, many were despoiled and murdered, robbers slitting open the stomachs of young women to search for swallowed rings. And those who survived lived to see their wives and daughters unbearably outraged in public orgies. One mother, having seen two daughters murdered thus, dug herself a grave and lay down in it until she died of starvation. Bereft of clothing, some even sewed together the pages of their holy books to cover their nakedness. Most were sold into slavery by the Moors in whose lands they had hoped to find refuge, although the King of Fez, in his kindness, took them in and gave them shelter in the "Valley of Blessing."

At the time, my mother knew nothing of such things, although I'm sure my grandfather must have known. All she knew was that instead of the roast lamb her father had promised her, there was pale bread soaked in rancid olive oil, and watery lentil soup. And for her bed, she had rags covering a hard, cold floor. And each day, the house took in more people, until even her small, thin body could no longer find room to stretch out.

They were the fortunate ones, her father would tell her each time she complained, pointing to the streets, alleyways, gardens, and mountaintops where miserable masses swarmed over one another like panicked ants.

My mother listened with a child's peevish unreasonableness, her father's words bringing her no comfort. All she knew was that her hair was matted and that her scalp and body itched beyond endurance. She scratched endlessly until once, examining her nails, she saw tiny creatures crawling over her hands. When she showed her father, his face blanched and he hurried her outside. But instead of washing her hair in perfume and combing it until it shone like copper, he shaved her scalp and threw the hair into a fire, over which he boiled her clothes in a large, stinking pot.

For a long time, my mother remembered, she hated him, refusing to speak to him at all. And each day, her father was called away for longer and longer hours. Only as an adult, a wife and mother, did my mother begin to fully understand how brave her father had been, how selfless, to spend his days and most of his nights dropping little boats of hope into that raging ocean of human misery. Or how close he, and all of them, had come to tragedy.

Instead of being a good, dutiful daughter, filled with the virtues of patience and forbearance, my mother became a little hellish estrie, waiting to pounce upon her father whenever she saw him. Filled with childish fury and consumed by jealousy, my mother played evil tricks on the poor woman who cared for her and her sister, pouring beet juice into her boiling pot of linens and feigning fainting fits to alarm her.

The woman responded by using the switch on my mother as often as she dared. "Poor woman!" my mother recalled. She was not unkind, but she had three children of her own who sat with pale, bloated faces crying with hunger, and no husband. My mother never did learn what had happened to him, but one day, wanting particularly to vex her, she told the woman's children, "Your father is a filthy apostate who has stayed behind in Spain to kiss the cross!"

She often thought that her childish barbed arrow had not strayed far from the mark. For instead of going for the switch, the woman simply flung her apron over her head and wailed. My mother always said this sight filled her with remorse. She waited anxiously for her father's return, hoping to corner him with a much improved picture of events before the woman could tell him the unpainted truth.

But when her father finally did appear, he seemed frantic, almost distraught. He quickly gathered them, their goat, and their other belongings together and loaded them into a small wagon pulled by a tired, ancient mule. A few lashes set the animal trotting at a pace which, for the aged beast, must have seemed like a jousting tournament.

Plague had broken out in the city. Before the year was out, thousands of refugees and their reluctant hosts would be swept away by that appalling and terrible sickness that even my skilled grandfather could do nothing to stem.

My mother must have been curious; she must have asked him questions, but somehow the only image that remained with her of that midnight flight was the wonderful silence of the long road once they were well out of Lisbon and its miserable crowds. My mother remembered, too, how she rested her head on her father's arm, her whole body one with the gentle rhythm of the mule's slow trot.

They traveled many days. And often, it was so intensely hot that my mother thought her limbs would melt and her blood turn to steam. They ate food from a basket my grandfather had brought with them—warm meat and stale bread and warm wine. Sometimes, if my aunt screamed too long, her father stopped the wagon and found a stream to bathe her. In the evenings, the cold mountain air turned their sweat to ice. Sometimes, her father would build a small fire and they would sit around the bright, warm glow. Often, my mother saw him read from his prayer books, the careworn lines on his handsome face relaxing for a moment, replaced with a calm and serenity that soothed her worries. She stopped asking him where they were going, content to have him to herself. And perhaps, too, she had despaired of explanations, and wisely distrusted promises. Like the Israelites, she was content to follow the Cloud of Glory and the Pillar of Fire wherever it took them for at least forty years. After the sojourn in Lisbon, the idea was not so terrible.

When my mother lost count of sunrises and sunsets and burning days and bitter-cold nights, and was almost reconciled to the idea of being a wanderer, her father abruptly drew in the reins and said, "We're home, child."

My mother remembered looking around but, in the pitch-blackness, could see nothing. She remembered the dull sound of her sister's crying, and her own drowsy complaints, and being impressed—even shocked—by the contrast of her father's cheerful whistle. He seemed overjoyed.

She heard him open a door, and felt herself cradled in his arms until she was lain on a bed of fresh straw and covered with soft down. And then something happened that in all her long life she never forgot, nor considered less remarkable, despite the passing of time: She felt her dead mother's hand caress her shorn head and heard her voice croon prayers as she tucked my mother in.

My mother decided that she herself must be dead. She closed her eyes, wondering why she had not thought to die sooner since it was so pleasant.

In the morning, she couldn't believe her eyes.

She was in a proper bedroom, with an estrado, and beds and chests and draperies. She went to the window and threw open the latch. She found herself high off the ground in a grand house surrounded by green fields and fragrant trees. There was a beautiful silence broken only by the joyous sounds of small, free creatures that live and roam the sky and earth as G-d wills them. The crowds were gone. The terrible noise, the stench, the milling unwashed, diseased, hungry people. The horror of Lisbon was gone, and my mother was, she must be, she thought, in Paradise.

And then, as if G-d had read her thoughts, the door opened and her dead mother walked in—beautifully alive. She ran to her and pressed herself against her, hugging her with small childish arms. "Madre, Madre," she wept, all the scalding sorrow within her boiling over and disappearing. Only a few times in her life, my mother recalled, had she ever felt such happiness.

But the woman pulled back from her, crouching, lifting up my
mother's chin in her soft palm. Her eyes, milky with tears, stared
at my mother in sorrow. It was then that my mother realized that
it was not her dead mother at all, but someone who looked
remarkably like her. At first she pulled back, heartbroken and
betrayed. But the woman gathered my mother in her arms and
held her fast. "The moon has died and the clouds have buried her,
and all the other clouds weep for her," she whispered, rocking her.

Her name was Constanza, and she was my mother's aunt,
Rachel's younger sister.

Grandfather Isaac had bought the house while he was still in
Spain, somehow transferring the money through intermediaries,
which was almost impossible to do. No one was allowed to take
money or valuables out of Spain. My grandmother had written her
sister's family to join her, but Aunt Constanza's husband had, at
the last moment, been forced to care for his widowed older sister
and her five children. He'd insisted that Constanza take their
children and go on ahead, promising to join her later. She had
arrived at the house a few days before my mother and
grandfather.

My mother had never met her cousins, as they lived far away in
the Extremadura. The boy, Joseph, was my mother's age, but
seemed older because of his great size and tendency toward
corpulence. But there was nothing of the bully about him, my
mother recalled mournfully, her eyes filling with tears. The
opposite. Perhaps because he felt he was taking his father's place,
he was fiercely protective of his mother and younger sister, Elvira,
who was just a baby at that time. Unlike my aunt Malca, family
legend has it that Elvira was a sweet, contented child with great
rosy cheeks and eyes the color of cornflowers.

Constanza tried her best. But she, like my grandmother, had
always had many servants to help her and was unfamiliar with
running a household. She burned the bread and left the linens
boiling too long, so that the material tore to shreds. My
grandfather never said a word, but one day he arrived with two
local village women, Alphonsa and Maria.

From then on, my mother recalled, there were clean clothes and

bed linens that smelled like sunshine. There were warm loaves of
bread and pies cooling in the breeze that flew through the kitchen's
great windows. And each night, a wild, warming fire burned in the
clean grate of the fireplace.

Constanza spent her time nursing Elvira and Malca, who—even
my mother admitted—nestled in womanly arms, began to take on
some of her cousin's charming peacefulness. After all the
upheavals of their lives, the family began to feel a certain calm.

My grandfather announced that it was time to resume the
civilized lives they had left in Spain. To Aunt Constanza's wonder
and to Alphonsa's and Maria's great horror, my grandfather
insisted everyone start bathing once a week. It was felt that one
should not expose more than a single part of the flesh at a time for
ablutions, and many felt not to bathe at all was even more
healthful. Constanza asked my grandfather many questions about
this until she allowed her own children to shed all their garments
and plunge into the wooden tub. But the two good servant women
asked nothing, simply crossing themselves and waiting, no doubt,
for the family to shrivel up and die.

My mother's hair began to grow back, and Constanza combed it
out in the sun, which was shining brighter and more benevolently
each day. They would take long hikes in the hills, feasting on
bunches of ripening grapes and filling their aprons with firm olives
whose first pressing gave them the most delicious oils. My mother
remembered lying back in the grass with her father and Aunt
Constanza and her sister and cousins, smelling the sweetness of
wild violets and jasmine, wishing for nothing more perfect.

My mother always spoke of Constanza with tears in her eyes.
"Ours is not to question the justice of the Holy One," she would say.
"Why the righteous must suffer the agonies that the wicked never
know."

I never knew my great-aunt, but through my mother she has
become part of my life. Her gentle kindness, the love she poured
over my mother and her sister, trying to make up for their terrible
loss—all of this has somehow seeped into my being, as if the act
were done to me as well.

I can see my mother holding her hand and walking through the

silky, warm grass, beginning to believe that it was possible the
terrible hole in her heart was going to heave together and close
somehow after all.

The days passed with gentleness. My grandfather started seeing
patients again, who came to the house at all times of the day and
night. Often, he took the wagon and was gone a day or two,
always bringing back toys or sweetmeats for all the children.

Before my mother knew it, the hot summer days of humming
bees and childish laughter drew to a close, and the New Year and
the Day of Judgment were upon them. My grandfather sent word
to his fellow countrymen that he would hold services in his home,
revealing the joyous news that he had brought with him a sacred
Torah scroll.

Renova sovre nozotros anyada buena i dulse del prensipio i
asta el kavo del anyo—*Grandfather blessed guests and family.*
"Send us again a fruitful year, sweet from beginning to end." They
feasted on dates, pomegranates, pumpkin pies, and leek patties.
The head of a fish graced the table, so that they should be the head
and not the tail, and move forward toward the future forcefully.

My mother always remembered that particular New Year's and
Judgment Day—the communal chanting of the prayers, the
dazzling white and black of the prayer shawls, the piercing sound
of the ram's horn calling the wayward Hebrews back to the fold.
Most of all, she remembered the way my grandfather hugged the
scroll to his chest and kissed it, his eyes full of pain, but joy, too.
She knew that her mother's death was on his mind, as well as those
friends and relatives left behind who, having chosen expedient
baptisms, were now vulnerable to the savage, tireless Reverend
Inquisitors, something we as Jews had no reason to fear.

My mother recalled the sweetness of her father's voice as it rose
with the soaring Hebrew melodies of Spanish Jews, and the sense
of pride that never left her, despite the inconceivable events that
were soon to transform their quiet lives beyond their wildest
nightmares.

4

The doorbell rang, followed by a polite interval of silence. It was the interval that caused Suzanne to lift her head off the strong, male arm in which it lay pillowed.

It couldn't be a friend. Her friends either knocked and whistled until she answered, or, failing both, leaned against the buzzer. Only the landlord buzzed once and waited politely. But he never came by unless she'd forgotten to pay the rent. As far as she remembered (although on these particular types of things she was never absolutely sure), she'd paid the rent. So who could it be?

"Don't get up, gorgeous!" her companion groaned.

She looked down at the man in her bed, pulling the covers over her breasts, making some quick calculations. He wasn't exactly a stranger—no, not exactly. She'd met him through a man she'd met at a Greenpeace meeting who'd invited her to a party in the Hamptons, where Julius (the man in her bed), and a number of other men, had taken her phone number. All of them had called her. But Julius had had the nicest voice and he'd invited her to a party at William Schrader's— the famous naturalist—back from two years in the Ivory Coast studying the influence of global warming on viviparous toads. So she'd accepted him and turned the others down.

This was their second date. And decent enough, although he wasn't actually someone she'd care to introduce to anyone she knew. Not quite yet, she thought reasonably, mentally apologizing to him, even as her mind racked up the deadly minuses: His saliva had an odd flavor and he tended to rush things and lay back waiting for compliments.

In addition, he'd made the fatal mistake of insisting on spending the night. She could tell he'd done it out of a desire to please her. And *most* women would be pleased, she admitted to herself. Unfortunately, she wasn't one of them. In the morning, she wanted her own space, time to look disheveled in her rattiest, most comfortable bathrobe; time to put on the TV and radio full blast, to spread the morning paper out on the floor and drink cocoa and suck the white centers from Oreo cookies. She didn't want to be cheerful and make breakfast or be nice to anyone. Most of all, if she felt like crying, she didn't want anyone trying to comfort her.

She gave him a friendly tap on the shoulder.

"Julius, don't you have a job to go to?"

"I thought I'd take the day off and spend it with you."

Uh-oh, she thought.

The doorbell rang again.

She threw her long legs off the bed, pulling a robe around her, pushing her curly, copper-colored hair off her forehead.

She really was a stupendously beautiful woman, the man in her bed congratulated himself, unaware that this was the end and not the beginning. Really stunning in a big, Cindy Crawford-ish, voluptuous sort of way. He lifted his head to get a better view, propping his chin on his palm, almost as delighted with her as he was with himself.

She walked, lithe and noiseless as a cat, to the armed fortress that was her front door. Beneath all those crossbars, bolts, locks, and chains, she knew there was a peephole. But with all the scratches and accumulated dirt, you couldn't really see anything through it anyway, even if you made the effort to unearth it. Besides, if she couldn't recognize the voice, there was no way she was opening the door.

There had been a time, she recalled, when—fresh out of her ivy-covered dorm in Boston—she'd never even asked who it was, happy to open the door and speak to anyone: Jehovah's Witnesses, Hare Krishnas, March of Dimes volunteers, salesmen, neighbors, strangers . . . It had taken only one bad experience to end all that.

"I'm going to look through the peephole, and if I don't open the door it means I don't want you, so just go away, got that?" she said, having found this statement very effective for most callers, and well worth the minor unpleasantness it sometimes caused.

She held her hand against the door, as if willing it to stay shut. The banging became more insistent.

"Who is it?"

"Suzanne, don't you recognize me? It's your grandmother."

She leaned her back up against the door, surveying the wreckage that was her living room, and beyond to where her naked new companion lay waiting for her imminent return. Her shoulders sagged.

"Well, well, perfect timing," she whispered to no one in particular, opening the bolts, deadlocks, chains, and assorted iron bars.

Neither woman moved.

What was called for here? Suzanne considered, the taste bitter in her mouth (her fault? her recent partner's?). Polite cheek-brushing? Outstretched arms? Full kisses, sighs of familial warmth and exhilaration?

"Please, Suzanne, I'm too old to play games. Are you going to invite me in, or encourage me to leave? Either way, I really want to know soon."

Suzanne opened the door wide, feeling an unreasonable sense of defeat as she watched the old woman invade her home. A few months ago, I *would* have slammed it in your face, she thought.

Catherine's steps were hesitant and contemplative, full of painful awareness of the transformation that had taken place since Renaldo's departure. All the posters were gone, those beautiful Impressionist prints from the Musée d'Orsay; the Bronzinos from the Uffizi; and the Italian Renaissance prints from Venice. Suzanne had brought them all home after her senior year at the Sorbonne, the way she'd brought back Renaldo.

Instinctively, she searched the shelves holding the glazed-ceramic animals from Mexico and Brazil that Suzanne had begun collecting under Renaldo's influence. They, too, were gone, the shelves empty and dingily bare. Even the large, bright canvases depicting healthy, brown women in Aztec splendor—Renaldo's specialty—were no longer visible.

Except for the photographs on the piano, anyone could live here, any Bronx shopgirl, any Flatbush Avenue secretary, Catherine thought, feeling a little heartsick.

"Here, Gran, sit down, you must be exhausted," Suzanne said suddenly, pushing a few scattered clothes to one side of the threadbare couch to create a small island.

Catherine nodded gratefully, looking for some sign of a thaw. But Suzanne's face was tight and silent as she leaned back against the wall, her arms crossed defensively, one leg swinging with nervous abandon.

She was queenly, Catherine thought with a touch of wonder, taking in her height and slimness. Those long, shapely legs flashing beneath the skimpy robe, those elegant cheekbones, that posture. . . . Nothing like me or Janice. The beneficiary of some long-lost DNA contributed hundreds of years before by some royal Gentile princess who had married into the Nasi clan at the height of its wealth and power.

"Really, Grandmother, you could have called!" she said peevishly. "I would have been happy to save you all the steps up here. And"—she hesitated, taking a deep, defiant breath—"if it has anything to do with all those things Mom and Kenny have been badgering me about, I wish you'd save your strength. I'm not going to change my mind."

"Badgering? About what?"

Her toes dug listlessly into the brown-and-red kilim rug beneath her. "The stuff about moving back home, socially correct parties, Junior League. The bribes: car, apartment, et cetera. I'm twenty-five years old. I've got a good job. I have my own home. I'm *never* going back to Scarsdale, so you can just . . ."

"What happened to your prints from Paris and those beautiful ceramics and the antiques? And where are all Renaldo's paintings?" Catherine interrupted her.

Suzanne surveyed her grandmother coolly, reaching for a pack of cigarettes. Without asking permission, she lit one and took a deep drag. "I'm redecorating," she said calmly, lips stretched tight over teeth.

"The bed's cooling off, Suzanne," a deep male voice called.

Catherine's appalled eyes caught her granddaughter's. She was surprised and grateful to see a blush creep up the young woman's cheeks.

Not completely lost. Not yet. "I've heard those temperature controls on waterbeds are so fragile. Is the repairman almost done?" Catherine asked innocently.

Suzanne stared at her, and then both of them broke into a grin.

"I'll go see, Grandmother."

He left, disgruntled, and with a distinct lack of grace that banished any sense of regret Suzanne might have felt. Actually, she felt relieved.

"Tea, Gran?"

"Actually, I was hoping to treat you to an early lunch."

"Well, uh, that's, that's very . . . but you know, I'm a strict vegetarian these days, and no milk or cheese or eggs either," she said coolly, waiting for a reaction. There wasn't any, so she kept going: "Rainforests are being destroyed. Food supplies are being squandered. Animals are needlessly suffering all in the name of cattle production, even though we no longer need meat for survival. Besides, with all those hormones they inject into beef, it's just poisoning us and the whole ecosystem," she argued, beginning to feel a bit cheated and inexplicably flustered, somehow, at Catherine's equanimity. "The only thing that's preventing us from moving forward is this stupid connection to the past. . . ."

Catherine listened patiently, swallowing hard. "What about a seafood restaurant, then?"

"Grandmother! Fish are living creatures, too! Besides, they boil lobsters live, and oysters are actually swallowed live! I mean, cannibalism!" She shook her head. "But there is this vegetarian Buddhist restaurant they just opened up a few blocks from here. The upstairs is actually a temple with these fruit offerings around an altar."

"Whatever makes you comfortable, Suzanne dearest," Catherine said with determined cheer and a distinct sense that strangulation was slowly settling in over her vocal cords from inhaling all that cigarette smoke.

"It's not a question of comfort, Gran. It's a question of the planet's survival!" Suzanne exclaimed passionately.

Catherine was about to bring up the issue of tar and nicotine pollution to the planet's (and her own) survival, but thought better of it. The young were so full of love for their own ideas, so oblivious to contradiction. They were sure no idea they'd thought of could possibly have been tried or thought of before. "You know, the rabbi of our temple once remarked that before the Flood all people were vegetarians and no one was allowed to kill and eat animals."

"Really?" Suzanne said skeptically.

"I remember it distinctly."

"But the Bible is so full of animal sacrifices, meat-eating . . ."

"Well, I'm not the one to ask. I only remembered that little bit. Is it far, your Buddhist temple?"

"No. Just around the corner. Wait here a minute and I'll throw some clothes on."

Five minutes later she was back, looking—Catherine admitted, amazed—more beautiful than ever, despite the strange outfit. The skirt, a swirl of blue Indian cotton, touched her ankles, and the top clung to her breasts like a dancer's leotard. And the silver jewelry! Where in heaven's name was that from? Calcutta? Afghanistan? "Come, child, help me get up. I'm feeling a little weary."

She was light, almost weightless, Suzanne thought, comparing her grandmother's white, clearly veined, and almost transparent skin to her own rosy, tanned arm. A tenderness and a strange feeling that was akin to grief welled up inside her as their hands touched.

She fought it.

5

A wind, gentle and warm enough to make them forget to button their coats, flapped their clothes against them as they strolled down Mulberry Street, creating a soft murmur that took the place of conversation.

Suzanne walked slowly, wondering at each step if she should turn back. But the thought of a carte blanche lunch was too tempting to pass up. She seldom ate out these days. Money was tight, now more than ever. Certain grants hadn't come through, and she and all the other counselors at the rape-crisis center had agreed to take a 30 percent pay cut rather than close down or fire staff.

Besides, there wasn't a scrap of food in the house. And she was hungry.

Still, the battle scars from the recent war with the family throbbed, threatening to rupture and bleed anew at the smallest jarring motion. If this was going to be yet another family onslaught—she brooded—another sea of whiny *mea culpas* and justified self-pity cushioned in vague threats, well, she just wouldn't stand for it, free lunch or no free lunch. There was *no way* she was going to sit back and listen to that crap. No way.

Did they even realize, she wondered, how thoroughly they'd destroyed her best (her only?) real chance for happiness? Or how deeply she sometimes despised them all? If it hadn't been for that little private chat among her mother, Kenny, and Renaldo a few months back, Renaldo would be up in her apartment right now, laughing and singing Spanish love songs, his strong brown arms splashing color magically over blank white canvases, instead of . . .

Her eyes misted.

Renaldo.

She glanced at her grandmother, her throat tightening, her eyes un-friendly. She had no proof, of course—Gran had been too savvy to broach the subject with her personally—but she didn't doubt for a sec-ond that her grandmother had been at least as guilty as the others for what had happened. Direct confrontation was seldom her style. She was The Matriarch, puller of strings.

It wasn't too late to send her packing.

She considered it, glancing at her malevolently.

But somehow, her grandmother's delicate, slightly bent frame with its silver crown did not play well as the proud, formidable opponent who had so infuriated her only a few months before. She felt her anger drain as she walked on, brooding.

Catherine didn't notice her silence, all her attention focused on hid-ing her own growing panic. Her brave and foolish foray into Central Park notwithstanding, her view of New York remained unchanged: It was a safari park, a place to be passed through in a closed, moving ve-hicle, windows tightly rolled up. It was seldom she found herself ex-posed to the city on any street below Madison and Forty-fourth. She looked around at the grungy streets and even grungier people, un-nerved.

"Perhaps we should hail a cab, dear," she suggested, trying to keep her voice steady.

"What for? It's just another block or two. Isn't this place great! All these little boutiques and outdoor cafes. And you have to see the Festi-val of San Gennaro."

Catherine glanced at her sharply. "You go to that, do you?"

"Sure. Wouldn't miss it for the world. All those holy statues and the flowers and music and great food. It's so colorful and interesting. Sometimes I wish . . ."

"Go on."

"It's just that the Italians seem to have such a great time. The stuff we do is so sterile, so boring. Like Passover, all those long-winded recitations and that inedible food, and the little groans from the men and the kids fidgeting and all the women left behind in the kitchen."

"Italian Catholic children don't fidget, and their fathers don't groan on the hard benches in church, and all that great food, why, it gets magically cooked while the women dance in the streets, I suspect."

"Just forget it. It's not possible to make you understand."

"Why do you say that? I understand exactly what you mean. I used to feel the same way." She shook her head sadly.

"You?" Suzanne looked at her, startled, waiting for some explanation.

None followed. Catherine looked ahead, clearly finished with the topic. Or perhaps, Suzanne suddenly wondered, taking in the slight trembling motion of her head, she'd simply forgotten what she'd meant to say.

The restaurant was an odd mixture of fake Chinese and genuine Delancey Street old-fashioned, its decor consisting of fringed red lanterns and a genuine pickle barrel.

"This used to be a kosher deli," Suzanne explained.

"I thought you said this place was vegetarian."

"It is."

"What's this, then?" she asked, pointing to the "sweet-and-sour pork" on the menu.

"Oh, it's not real pork, Granny! It's made out of bean curd, and I assure you it's just as delicious as I remember the real thing. Although, as a vegetarian, I haven't tasted that in quite some time," she pointed out with some righteousness.

Catherine supposed that was true, but it didn't please her. Eating vegetarian food on the ground floor of a Buddhist temple hardly qualified as a link with family tradition.

They ordered many dishes, although Catherine took no more than a spoonful of each, leaving Suzanne free to devour the rest. She did so, with gusto, then eagerly ordered dessert. It came covered with ice cream and a good number of flaming sparklers, which sent floating ash everywhere.

"Fried pineapple. My favorite," she said between bites, thoroughly enjoying herself.

"Are you all right?"

"What do you mean?"

"I mean, do you have what you need, dear, to get by?"

Suzanne put her fork down slowly, dabbing the corners of her mouth with a napkin. "Do you mean, do I have enough money for food?" she asked, suddenly amused. "Plenty. But when someone else pays, it does wonders for my appetite." She grinned.

"Well, at least you're not getting insulted. Young people these days think they have to prove something all the time, and even if they can't really manage alone, they foolishly refuse to ask their families for help out of some ridiculous pride."

Suzanne felt her jaw twitch. "Considering the recent past, I'd appreciate it, Grandmother, if you wouldn't bring up family help, caring, et cetera, et cetera."

"I don't understand . . ."

"Eleven months ago, when I wanted to marry Renaldo, Grandmother," she said, lifting her eyes from the napkin she'd been rolling into tiny balls. "The point is, last year, where was my wonderful, caring family then?"

"I don't remember you ever discussing Renaldo with me," she answered weakly.

"Okay. But Mom and Kenny knew we were planning on getting married. They must have discussed it with you. And I'm sure you didn't tell them to wish me *mazel tov,*" she accused, accurately.

"I had no idea it had gotten that far," she muttered, shocked, betraying herself. "What I meant to say was—"

"Just stop! It's done. Renaldo was an honorable man. Family was vital to him. He wasn't about to get into a relationship where people treated him like the sleazy Puerto Rican boyfriend of the girl in the nail parlor. He couldn't take it. But what's the point? He's gone."

The click of other people's forks against their plates became suddenly almost deafening.

"Suzanne, whatever else was involved, it was never personal. We never had anything against Renaldo *personally.*" She bit her lip, sorry to have said so much. "We were all devastated at how hard you took the breakup. Heartbroken, believe me. These things happen. Why do you insist on blaming your family, yourself . . . ? We never wished either of you any harm."

She saw Suzanne's bright face suddenly fade and darken, her lips twitching for control. She reached out impulsively across the table, taking her granddaughter's hand in her own. "Child, he was a married man twice your age, from another culture!"

"And another faith! Don't forget that!" Suzanne wrenched her hand away.

"Another faith," Catherine admitted. "But also a man with two grown children and a wife!" she went on doggedly, ignoring the sharp turn onto thin ice that the conversation had suddenly taken. "You were so innocent, so inexperienced."

"He was a brilliant, talented artist! A man full of life, of joy! He'd been separated from his wife for almost five years. Catholics don't believe in divorce."

"And *we* Jews," Catherine said with a strange defiance, "don't believe in intermarriage!"

"Oh, really? Does Mom know?" Suzanne added nastily. Then, seeing her grandmother's face blanch, she softened her tone. "Look, Gran, as far as I'm concerned, there is no *we*. What can you expect, after all those years of Hanukkah candles and Christmas trees, Passover seders and Easter candy? It's all garbage, just artificial gimmicks that separate people. It just causes hatred and misunderstandings." . . . 'Imagine no religion, nothing to kill or die for . . . ,'" she sang.

"And no Festival of San Gennaro."

Suzanne paused. "That's different. That's cultural," she said slowly. "I mean, we should all respect different cultures, customs, art, music . . ."

"Just not your own," Catherine said, her voice rising unexpectedly. To her great shock, she found tears rolling down her cheeks.

"Gran?"

Catherine took out an immaculately clean, hand-embroidered and monogrammed handkerchief from her bag and dabbed her eyes. "I have something to tell you, Suzanne . . ." she began impulsively, then hesitated. The conversation had not gone at all the way she'd expected. She'd meant to lead up to this subject tactfully, making it sound like a beautiful new beginning, or at least a chance for a decent last chapter. Now, it would sound like so much blackmail.

She saw the sand hemorrhaging inexorably through the aperture of an hourglass. There was no time for another such meeting, which might go more smoothly. It was either going to be now, or it was not going to be.

"Suzanne, I'm dying."

She watched the slow, predictable look of wonder and horror pass over her granddaughter's features, and then something less expected. A look of curiosity.

"I'm seventy-four years old, and my young doctor says that with the proper care I might reach seventy-five. Except that I don't plan to have the proper care, not if it's painful or ugly. . . ." She held up a hand as if warding off a potential flood of objections.

There were none.

She looked at her granddaughter, surprised and grateful. "You know I've always been a spoiled, cowardly woman, and I see no reason to change now."

"*Abuela.*" It was Suzanne's turn to reach out for her across the table littered with the cold remnants of the odd meal. She had not used that childish term of endearment for many years.

"Don't you dare cry, Suzanne! That's why I've taken you to this public place. You know how I hate emotional scenes. I have something I need to ask of you. Yes, it's blackmail, the worst sort of blackmail. A dying request. There is no way you can get out of it, so just set your mind on doing it."

Suzanne gulped down the last of her Chinese tea.

"That's right. Not a word. You're trapped, so just listen. I want you to do a job for me. A little research. I have in my safe a few pages of memoirs written in Portuguese by one of our distant Spanish ancestors. I want you to help me track down the rest of it."

"How distant?"

"It was written in the 1500s."

Suzanne looked at her speculatively.

"I know a little bit about finding rare books and manuscripts. Your grandfather Carl was a great collector, you know."

"What's it about?"

"Doña Gracia Mendes. She was a young widow with a small child when she inherited the greatest fortune and one of the most successful trading companies in Europe. She was an intimate of kings and queens.

And then, for no apparent reason, she just fled, and began openly declaring herself a Jew."

"So, you already know what happened?"

"Yes and no. I've read about her in some history books. I more or less know what she did. But none of the books explain why." She peered into Suzanne's face. It looked blank. "How can I can make you understand? It was like a rich German aristocrat in the middle of Berlin in 1936 calling Hitler and telling him that he'd decided to be a Jew! I mean, it was the height of the Inquisition. People were being burned for changing their linens on Fridays, or because no smoke came out of their chimneys on Saturdays, never mind praying in synagogues! And the Inquisition didn't just burn you—they tortured you until you implicated every last member of your family. Then they confiscated every scrap of money or property you owned and turned it over to the Church and King; they took your children away and put them into monasteries or convents. She had so much to lose. In some ways, it was insane for her to behave as she did, yet, incredibly brave as well. I don't know. I've never really understood. She had everything. Why did she risk so much? So will you do it for me?"

"Do what?"

"Travel to Europe to look for the manuscript."

"*Abuela*, I can't just pick myself up and . . . First of all, you can hire a dozen scholars to do this for you who know Spanish and Portuguese. Who are at home in the book stacks of old, nasty libraries all over Europe. Besides, if you're ill, I think I should be here."

Catherine hesitated. "I don't know if I can make you understand. But I feel I've let someone, something, down badly. I've betrayed some kind of commitment, some trust. I didn't have much else to do in life, and the little that was my duty, I didn't do it. I don't want to hire someone to give me a report, the way I hired maids to polish and dust my heirloom silver. Before I die, I want to understand where it is I come from, and what it's all meant. It's really a family matter, and not some archaeological dig. You're my family." She shrugged. "I'm asking you to help me."

Suzanne looked at her blankly, flustered. The whole thing was ridiculous: traipsing around Europe in the hopes of finding a few more pages of a manuscript that had been missing for hundreds of years. Trying to find motivations for a long-dead ancestor by cruising along the Grand Canal, or walking through the streets of London. How could you ever really know anybody's motives, even your best friend's, let alone someone who lived hundreds of years ago?

"I just don't know, Gran . . ."

"Listen, Suzanne. I haven't made up my will yet. Remember that!"

"Gran!" She was absolutely shocked. She looked across at her grandmother, watching against her will the light flash off the two large diamond rings she wore on either hand. She thought of the apartment on Fifth, of the stone country house in Connecticut, of the rare antiques and books, with a horrified and almost helpless fascination.

What the rape-crisis center, the ecology groups she belonged to, could do with funds like that! So much could be accomplished.

And then, quite unbidden, some other images came to her. Leisurely strolls through museums, libraries, and galleries. Good hotel rooms, fine wines. And maybe . . . (Her mind flashed the image of Renaldo, leaning on the railing of the bridge spanning the Grand Canal.) A trip to Europe. All expenses paid.

Blushing pink with shame and excitement, Suzanne looked into her grandmother's eyes. She looked all right. Maybe the doctors were just being alarmist. And if this would really make her feel better, if this was really what she wanted . . .

"Look, this is just theoretical, okay? But let's just say for a minute I agreed to all of this craziness. Then where would I need to go, and how soon?" she asked, smiling with more accommodating sweetness than Catherine had ever dreamed possible.

6

It was Vivaldi's *Mandolin Concerto*, Francesca Abraham realized as the radio alarm went off. Lively, unrelentingly upbeat, it was probably the perfect tempo in which to start the day. Covering her head with a pillow, she reached out blindly and urgently, desperate to shut the damn thing off.

Five more minutes, she negotiated with herself. Or maybe ten. Why was sleep such a delicious treat this time of morning and such a boring burden when she turned in at night?

Fifteen minutes later, she dragged her petite, shapely legs over the side of the bed and stood up. Her eyes felt heavy and her head spun as she crossed the floor. Mind over matter, she thought wearily, slapping on wrist and ankle weights and feeding a cassette into the recorder. It was a fifteen-day program guaranteed to reduce her thighs and firm her buttocks.

She didn't stare at Jane; it was too depressing. Instead, she looked at one of her backup girls, a blond Barbie who started like plastic perfection and then slowly began to melt, sweat dripping down her face and making big dark circles under her armpits. Fifteen minutes into the tape, and the girl's smile was gone, her breath was coming hard, and you could tell she was hating every minute. I love that girl, Francesca thought, her whole body crying out for mercy.

She was only on the fifth day.

The shower, set to the merciless massage setting, hit her like biblical punishment. When it was over, she sat on the cold edge of the tub staring at her pink, naked flesh in the full-length mirror. Everything about her proclaimed powerlessness and vulnerability, she thought, discouraged. Petite body, small face, little hands and feet. Like a china doll, her mother's friends used to exclaim over her, convinced they were paying her a compliment. Even her hair, she thought, running her fingers impatiently through the damp golden brown ringlets that curled romantically around her face. A Botticelli angel, a boy in college once called her, begging her to let it grow. Right! That was all she needed: wild curls cascading down her back like a doomed Shakespearian virgin, or a rock star.

She squared her slender shoulders, leaning forward. Only her eyes pleased her. Large, brown ovals with flecks of amber and gold around the irises, they dominated her delicate, narrow face, giving it a cool strength. She rubbed the sleep wrinkles on her cheeks and forehead.

In four years, I'll be thirty, she thought, rubbing harder.

She sighed, opening her closet and flipping through the hangers, mourning once again that she lacked the trampoline tautness necessary for the latest fashions. The tight, ass-hugging skirts that looked so chic on Bendel's window dummies underwent an alarming change the moment she tried them on, becoming indistinguishable from those Lycra creations long favored by Puerto Rican schoolgirls.

It was the old-fashioned stuff that looked best on her, she knew: the full-skirted girlish dresses, the heart-shaped necklines. No one wore that anymore, except as evening wear. It had been a year since she'd said "Fine" to anything as frivolous as "Why don't we have dinner?," and nearly two since she'd broken her engagement to Peter Aronson. Evening wear was not a justified economic expense for Francesca Abraham.

Peter, she thought, stepping into the gray, pinstriped skirt of a severely tailored suit. He was married now, to a girl she'd known from expensive, horsy summer camps. They'd bought a house in Short Hills, New Jersey. A charming Tudor with a Jacuzzi and a circular driveway, Mom had informed her accusingly. They'd just had a baby, too. A little girl.

She opened the drapes and pressed her forehead against the cold glass. The gray March sky was flattened against the hundreds of identical windows of her unknown neighbors. Far below, a hint of green winked against the silver branches of winter-shorn trees. She listened to the ceaseless city sound of vehicles conversing. My Rapunzel tower, remote and inaccessible, she thought. And me with short hair.

She'd made the down payment right after the breakup with Peter, using every cent she owned or could borrow. It was a tiny studio in one of several huge apartment towers near Lincoln Center, a place with a doorman and private, armed security guards who roamed the grounds twenty-four hours a day.

But it was hers, all five hundred square feet of it. Hers and the bank's, that was. Homeowner, she congratulated herself, her spirits rising bravely. Maybe it didn't have a Jacuzzi or a circular driveway, but it also didn't have Peter Aronson sitting on his butt complaining dinner wasn't ready, or waiting impatiently for ironed shirts and matched socks to magically appear.

She tried to imagine Peter's tall, manly body amid the delicate flower portraits hung with bows, the scented candles, and the gilded cherubs hovering over the doorposts. The vision dwarfed everything she owned, making it all seem make-believe and doll-housey.

That was the Peter effect, all right. He'd towered over her, an invalidating and overwhelming presence that sucked her in, taking away her separateness, relieving her of all responsibility. At first, she'd been attracted to his wealth and position, but most of all to his suitability. He was the quintessential "catch." But as time went by, she realized that it wasn't her he wanted, not really. She was simply raw material—a girl from the "right" family, an heiress, he pointed out to her on more than one occasion, no hint of amusement in his face. He had taken on the task of "redesigning" her, as it were, to fit the lifestyle he planned for himself.

He made her take tennis lessons—even though she had no interest in tennis—and helped her buy the perfect white outfit. He gave her books to read and told her what to think about them. Often, he laughed at her opinions. "Don't be childish" was his favorite phrase. He was constantly tutoring her on how to behave and what to say in front of his friends. Slowly, but surely, she'd felt herself growing smaller and smaller until she was afraid she'd disappear altogether.

No one had the right to do that to someone else. She shook her head as if once again reviewing the rightness of her decision. Even if there was some truly superior male out there, whose expertise and knowledge far outweighed her own, the most she would ever agree to do would be to walk by his side.

Still, a rich, handsome Jewish surgeon, and she'd said "No, thank you" a month before the wedding.

Her mother and Kenny had been furious, Gran sad. Only Suzanne had partially understood, and then in her own strange way. She'd called him "the ultimate consumer-boomer" to his face and laughed at his pretensions at serving humanity. "How? By performing unnecessary hysterectomies and milking rich patients and the health system?"

Francesca straightened up her clean, orderly house, then brought in *The New York Times*. Something else in Bosnia—those horrifying photos of senseless suffering. She turned quickly to the comfort of the stock pages. Nothing morally ambiguous or heart-rending here, she sighed, relieved. Her no-load mutual funds were blooming petunias, well watered; the interest on her money market funds a worm's crawl upward. High-tech stocks had wilted, though. But that could change.

She was all right, all right, she comforted herself, feeling suddenly lonely and tearful. I'm the piggy who built the house of bricks. I'll be safe and you'll be sorry. . . .

She took out her thick-leaved day planner, glancing through her packed schedule for the months ahead. Equity. Equilibrium. Calm waters. Days divided into predictable and manageable segments where nothing terrible could happen. My own apartment, my own job, my own investments, my own life. She lifted her chin bravely. And every month the victory renewed itself through the ritual of check signing: mortgage, credit card, utilities, Gran. . . .

Her grandmother had often offered to forget about the loan. But it seemed downright underhanded to Francesca to have asked for a loan for the down payment and then to renege somehow and turn it into a gift. The fact that family was involved shouldn't make any difference. Fair was fair.

Suzanne, of course, disagreed completely. "Not accepting it as a gift is hostile, even aggressive in a way," she'd argued. "I mean, it's family, after all, and you're denying her the joy of giving!"

Usually, Suzanne was big on the "joy of giving" when it came to strangers. With family, it was the "joy of taking" she was best at. Suzanne never had a problem demanding money from the family for the myriad causes she passionately supported as well as occasional "grants" for herself. But when it came to fulfilling her family obligations, well, that was another story.

Take the Passover seder, Gran's pride and joy and the sole annual family event left. Every single year, Suzanne attempted one excuse after another to avoid coming.

Poor Gran. Getting the family together was like herding cats. Every year, it took more and more of her bullying powers to pull it off. Still, she usually managed it. And then they'd all sit around with the *hagadah* in their laps (so it would be easier to hide it when the Inquisitors came knocking on the door!) while Great-Uncle Moise droned on in Ladino, Hebrew, and English about foolish, wise, and ignorant sons, the hand of G-d, and the plagues of Egypt.

But the meal was worth waiting for: roast lamb and prunes; *mazzah mojada, buñuelos,* and *sfongato;* brick-red apples, raisins, and almonds mixed with spices and sweet, red wine. And all of it served in *la loza Pascual*—as Gran called it—the stunning antique porcelain used only seven days each year. And all through the evening, the beautiful silver heirloom wine goblets were expertly replenished with the finest Chardonnays, Reislings, and semi-dry Rosés, in addition to the traditional *raki,* a liqueur distilled from dried raisins. Except for the unleavened matzoh— that inedible cardboard!—it was always a memorable feast.

She felt a sudden sense of guilt. Gran had left several messages on her machine asking her out to lunch, and she still hadn't gotten back to her. It wasn't right, she scolded herself briefly, glancing at her watch.

That late!

She grabbed a doughnut, eating it in little pieces so the calories would leak out; then she stuffed the thick wad of systems specifications into her expensive leather attaché case. She was going to convince those macho clowns that the new currency-trading back-office system had to be based on a PC peer-to-peer network, and not those antediluvian giant mainframes. If it was up to them, they'd still have punch cards safely tied with two rubber bands and paper tape all over the wall! Any new ideas, especially if they were being championed by a woman half their age and weight, were going to be resisted.

She squared her shoulders, turning on her alarm system, then hurried out the door before it began the Sing Sing wail of breakout that always put the nice old lady in 34E into incipient heart-attack mode.

The elevator paused on the nineteenth floor to allow two dark-skinned women in white uniforms to enter. One pushed an expensive carriage enthroning a pink-skinned baby boy.

The baby looked up at Francesca adoringly, his blue eyes sparkling. Francesca adored him back, feeling a sharp pain in her chest that dulled into a familiar ache. It was a pain she knew well; one she had had checked out medically. After a million tests, it came down to this: an irreducible side effect of living the life she'd chosen. A protest, as it were.

She had learned to ignore it.

But this morning, it seemed worse than usual, almost like a hysterical cry welling up from her gut; the cry of an unreasonable child in a shopping mall throwing a bloody fit.

Babies.

There weren't going to be any Third World ladies in white uniforms for hers. No, not for hers.

When the time came.

When the man came.

When marriage and home came.

When her turn came . . .

When . . . she thought, letting the single word dangle, almost feeling his silky hair and tasting the warm, fat curve at the back of his neck. She tapped her bulging briefcase nervously against her thigh. Tick-tock, tick-tock, she thought, wondering if that was supposed to be funny.

Petite was a problem in the New York rush hour subway crowd. Pushed and jostled as if she were weightless, she felt her arms and shoulders pull apart with the reach toward the overhead strap and the downward pull of her heavy attaché case. But outside, surrounded once again by the straight and logical forms of steel and concrete, her dignity and competence revived. She was part of this powerful machine, she thought, almost proudly, banishing irrational visions of soft, clingy things.

At the elevator banks of MetroCorp, she signed in at the security desk, smiling at the courteous greetings of the well-groomed guards. Lately, she had been looking them over with unforgivable interest. Of course, it was unthinkable. They were *high-school graduates*, for Pete's sake! Some had probably even earned *equivalency degrees* after *volunteering for the military!* Still, they were young and attractive. More important, they looked straight and (she scanned for wedding rings) perhaps available?

A young man in a uniform.

A young man in a suit.

A young man.

Or even, she thought, examining the middle-aged male who entered on the twenty-second floor, a man not so young, with nicely combed hair, an expensive sweater, and no wedding ring. A man who wasn't too tall . . .

She got off the elevator and made her way through the maze of six-foot-high partitions that divided the enormous room into tiny cubicles. As she rounded the corner, she was surprised to see people gathered in small groups, speaking to each other in low whispers.

"What's going on?" she asked, full of instinctive dread. It had to be something bad. Something good would have been louder.

"Francesca," Robert Murphy, her supervisor, greeted her somberly, putting a brotherly arm around her shoulder and refusing to look her in the eye. Without another word, he walked swiftly into his office and closed the door behind him.

She felt her amorphous dread solidify and sink down her windpipe to her knees. She stumbled into her cubicle, dropping her briefcase a little too high off the floor. The resulting thud seemed full of editorial content.

"It's not the end of the world, you know," Gilbert Odessa's voice intruded on her thoughts. He stood in the doorway. A large security guard stood behind him, holding a cardboard box.

She looked up, surprised. He looked visibly, humanly distressed.

In the two years that Gilbert Odessa's cubicle had adjoined hers, this was the first sentence he'd ever addressed to her that didn't contain the words *bit, byte, chip,* or *algorithm.* She had always considered him simply an extension of his hardware.

"I mean, it's not like a serious illness or anything. It's just a job," he said, in a tone of voice that reminded her of a small child who'd just found new underwear and socks in his Christmas stocking.

Francesca felt the rush of questions push up urgently, but somehow, looking at Gilbert and then at the guard, she didn't really want the answers. Instead, she nodded sympathetically, silent and wary.

Gilbert pushed his glasses up his slippery, glistening nose, and Francesca felt him lean toward her in a way that someone else—a woman of normal instincts who hadn't sat near Gilbert Odessa for two years—might have wrongly interpreted as an intimate gesture.

"My mother died at forty-four," he told her, undeterred by her lack of verbal encouragement and her slight recoil. "Massive stroke. Didn't drink, smoke, or do drugs. Married to the same guy for twenty-five years. Never worked a day in her life. Lived in the same house for twenty years. . . ." Gilbert looked at the guard, who'd just lifted the box and set it down meaningfully upon his desk.

He patted his balding head mournfully. "Life is totally unpredictable. Anything can happen to anyone," he said, devastated. Slowly, he began loading his personal belongings: the pictures of ducks, the duck ashtrays, the duck mugs, the wooden decoys, the Donald Duck stuffed toy, and the framed photographs of himself wearing a ducktail haircut. When he was finished, he came back.

"Good-bye, Francesca. It was nice working near you."

She took two steps toward him, gripping his hand with both of hers. "Good-bye, Gilbert."

He walked with the guard to the elevators.

And then he was gone.

Just like that.

Francesca sat down, her stomach gripped with a horrible queasy fear, as if she'd just witnessed an auto-da-fé. Better get to work. Fast, she told herself with a swift glance around to see if her diligence was going to be noticed. She took out the specifications and turned on her computer, reassured by its vibrant hum and the comforting flash of green words. No use worrying, she told herself, typing in her password. Just get the work done. It was important work, work only she, and she alone, was really expert at in her division. Indispensable work, she reassured herself.

ACCESS DENIED, the computer flashed at her poisonously.

Access denied.

She took a deep breath, rebooted, and tried again, typing her secret password in much more slowly and carefully.

"ACCESS DENIED!" it screamed.

Before she could dial her supervisor, her telephone rang.

It was Human Resources.

The interview took ten minutes, nine of which she didn't hear. She left with a letter in a white envelope and a tall, handsome security guard who accompanied her, unsmiling, back to her desk. He, too, handed her a carton.

She ignored him, sitting down in her chair and looking at the missive in her hands. Like an engraved invitation to Hell, she thought, taking out her letter opener and slitting its throat.

"Dear Employee," it began.

The bank has been MERGED WITH THE AMERICORP BANK GROUP, who are now STREAMLINING OPERATIONS. MOST REGRETTABLY, as a result, your entire division HAS BEEN ELIMINATED. In light of this, METROCORP DEEPLY REGRETTED its inability to continue offering you, as a VALUED EMPLOYEE, a position SUITABLE TO YOUR HIGH LEVEL OF ABILITY AND PERFORMANCE. On behalf of Metrocorp, please accept DEEPEST THANKS, a month's salary, and BEST WISHES ON ACHIEVING PERSONAL CAREER GOALS ELSEWHERE.

She slumped down, letting a small groan escape. Then she picked up her attaché case and swung it against her thighs once more. Bang! Bang! Bang! she thought, looking at the guard, who stood there patiently, waiting to make sure she did not steal anything, type anything damaging into the computer, or become verbally or physically abusive.

Bang! And you're dead.

Just like that.

Francesca stood up and walked to the water cooler.

"Fired, huh?"

It was one of the secretaries. Helen something. She looked almost gleeful, Francesca realized, staring at her styleless hair, her predictable polyester pantsuit. This same woman had greeted her each morning, smiled, made coffee, sent everyone Christmas cards, and regularly collected money for staff birthday gifts. Francesca glanced around the room, wondering how many other low-level employees of advanced middle age had been secretly wishing unemployment, as well as early death and dismemberment, upon the young hotshots around them.

The tempo of the day, she thought, was definitely not that of Vivaldi's *Mandolin Concerto.* More like Mozart's *Requiem.*

She packed her carton. "Can I just make one phone call?" she asked the guard.

He shifted uncomfortably, tugging on his cap. "Hey, I'm sorry. My instructions are not to allow any calls from up here. There's a public booth down in the lobby," he said, expressionless.

So that was it: from expert and respected hotshot to piece of burned-out waste material in twenty minutes! Gilbert was right. Life certainly was unpredictable.

Riding down in the elevator with the guard, who suddenly seemed more like a Fascist stormtrooper and less like tempting but unworthy husband material, she shrank with humiliation. Under his watchful gaze, she turned in her employee badge and walked out into the public lobby. Only when he was satisfied she was truly gone did he turn his back and return to the elevator banks.

She leaned against the cold marble wall, her hands trembling with anger, fright, and a feeling of terrible waste. She couldn't believe it! For four years, this job had been the steady, solid hub of her existence. Everything had revolved around it, been postponed or decided because of it. It had been like the ground beneath her feet.

She looked at her belongings: a few books and photographs. A silly teddy bear. Some manuals . . . All that effort and devotion, thought and dedication, reduced to one small, pathetic box. And it could always happen again with some other job.

Something else has to be the hub, she thought. But what?

She sat down in the phone booth, holding her head in both hands. Then she dialed.

"Gran, it's me. Is lunch still available? I suddenly have all the time in the world."

7

"*Abuela*," Francesca said, pecking both her grandmother's cheeks, European style.

"Francesca." Catherine allowed herself to be pecked.

They looked at each other and waited.

"You look beautiful, my dear, but a little tired, I think."

"Actually, I feel woozy," Francesca admitted, astonishing herself.

There was an ironclad rule that one never admitted weakness or misfortune of any kind to close family members who would simply tsk-tsk and find a way to blame you for your troubles before extending a reluctant, put-upon helping hand.

To her great surprise, instead of insisting upon immediate medical attention, vitamins, or lifestyle changes, Catherine simply murmured, "I'm not in the most dazzling physical condition myself these days, either."

Francesca took her arm, concerned. "I guess we'd both better sit down then, Gran."

The place was quiet and pleasant, the white-metal balustrade and greenery calming. From the next table, the tempting fragrance of a large plate of steaming pasta, redolent with sauce, wafted over them.

Francesca motioned to the waiter. "Could you bring me a double Scotch on the rocks as soon as possible?"

"Wouldn't you rather eat first, dear? That pasta smells lovely. And now they say if you don't load it with cheese and butter it's not actually fattening, either. . . ."

"Trust me, Gran. I need a drink."

The Scotch appeared. Then it disappeared.

"Francesca, dear, either you're not yourself, or we've been away from each other much longer than I remember."

"Actually, Gran, I've just been canned."

Catherine stared at her. "What in Heaven's name does that mean?"

"Oh, let's see, how would they say this in Britain? 'Been made re-dundant,' I believe is the proper phrase. In short, sacked, booted, fired. Disconnected from my only visible means of support."

"What did you do?"

She looked up and grinned, the alcohol giving her an irrational de-sire to giggle. "Me? Nothing. I'm a VALUED EMPLOYEE WITH A HIGH LEVEL OF ABILITY AND PERFORMANCE," she tittered, draining the last drop from the glass. She motioned to the waiter to re-fill it.

"So you're really out of work." Catherine clapped her hands to-gether, delighted.

Francesca stared, astonished. "You're pleased?

"It's wonderful! I thought that was going to be the most impossible task, prying you loose from your computer. I wonder how she did it."

"What do you mean, 'prying me loose'? And who is 'she'?"

"Never mind. Let's order some food. I'm famished."

"I'm not hungry at all," Francesca said, momentarily forgetting her questions, overcome by a churning in her stomach and ice water in her bowels. She wasn't a drinker, and her stomach was empty. The waiter brought the second drink. She eyed it with a newfound respect, sipping carefully.

Catherine cleared her throat, but just then a waiter appeared, pen-cil and pad in hand. They ordered and ate in companionable silence: large, steaming plates of fresh pasta tossed with basil and oregano and fresh tomatoes; steamed forest mushrooms with tiny, delicate pieces of smoked salmon.

Catherine thought of the meal she had eaten with Suzanne amid the pickle barrels and red lanterns; all the foods called one thing and actu-ally made with something else. Fake pork, fake shrimp, fake chicken. . . .

Something good for you masquerading as something that wasn't good for you, but which you wanted anyway. Like diet Coke, and Weight Watcher brownies.

She looked around at the simple white walls and the clean white tablecloths, the white plates with their simple, delicious food, looking and tasting exactly as you hoped and expected. Suzanne would no doubt find that boring, she thought.

Anything described as "new" was invariably something very old and familiar simply dressed up and plastered over with some kind of makeup. Food, the arts, ideas. It was all the same. All clever fakes. There was nothing new under the sun.

Take that phrase psychologists and anthropologists thought up for *Newsweek* in the late 1970s: The New Morality. They made it sound so revolutionary: open marriages, uncommitted but honest. Passionate, spontaneous, casual adult relationships. It had turned out to be nothing very new at all; simply a rationale (for psychologists and anthropologists?) to justify sleeping around, picking up one-night stands in bars. Of course, herpes, and then AIDS, had come along. No one was talking about New Morality anymore. Now it was all about the New Celibacy.

She chuckled.

Why is it when we're young, we are always convinced the world was born on the same day we were, its possibilities limited only by our imaginations? Why can't we connect to the past, see the patterns, learn the lessons? Why is mankind doomed to begin continually at square one and painfully repeat all the old mistakes?

"Dessert?"

Francesca shook her head. "Let's not add injury to an already insulting day."

"Insulting?"

"How would you describe being thrown out of your office with ten minutes' notice, and given to understand that you are superfluous and that the working world could get on just fine without you? Redundant." She shook her head.

"Well, instead of dessert, let me offer you this: a job."

"Sure, any systems analysis in C, Windows, or Motif you need taken care of, especially when it comes to a currency-trading back-office system, I'd be happy to do for you. But I'll only work with personal computers, not mainframes, I warn you," she said dryly.

"I'm not talking about your little computers, you know. The world doesn't rise and fall because of computers. We all got along perfectly well without them for thousands of years."

"Don't let Bill Gates hear you say that."

"William who?"

"Never mind."

"I'd like you to do some research on our family history. You'd have to do some traveling in Europe. I want you to find the missing pages of a manuscript that's been in the family for hundreds of years."

Francesca's head swam. She shaded her eyes, which suddenly watered from the light. "Whoa! I have no idea what you're talking about."

"You say you've been fired. Well, I'll pay you the same as you've been getting, plus all your expenses. All you need to do is make up a research report for me to read each week."

Francesca suddenly leaned forward. "You know, there are so many sources on the Internet I could look into—university libraries, the Vatican collection," she said, suddenly excited. With that and severance pay, she could last weeks, maybe even a few months! Surely she could find another job in a few months!

Then another thought hit her and her face reddened. "I don't need your pity, Gran."

"My dear, this was the very reason I invited you out to lunch in the first place. Ask Suzanne."

"You mean you were going to ask me to quit my job?" she said incredulously.

Catherine nodded. "Or take a leave. That's what Suzanne's doing."

"So, we'd be working together." She paused thoughtfully, her forehead puckering.

"Yes, side by side."

"I suppose the manuscript would be very valuable, a very significant addition to your collection."

"Child, I'm not doing this for any 'collection'! This is personal. It has been a lifelong dream of mine to read the rest of my ancestor's story. I'm not getting any younger. I feel now is the time to try."

"Have you contacted rare-book and manuscript dealers?"

"I've been in touch with many of them. Each and every one has a different theory, different leads. You'll need to meet with the most important of them and make some order out of it. They'll be willing to help you. But I think the search could use a new head, a fresh vision. So many great paintings and manuscripts were lost for centuries until some enterprising and persistent individual simply took a better look at what was there all along. Besides, you are one of her descendants. You have her genes. Perhaps you'll have an intuitive sense about where to look."

"Well, that's too mumbo-jumbo for me." She shook her head.

Catherine looked at her, surprised. There was a little of Janice in her curvy, petite frame. But otherwise, she had always seemed to take after her father's side of the family: the calm, reasonable, respectful Abrahams. The echo of Janice's favorite, insulting phrase gave Catherine goose bumps. Who knew what stores of hidden influence a bad parent had on a child? Was the cause lost before the battle had even begun?

"Well then, you agree?"

"Agree?" Francesca reached across the table and grasped her grandmother's hand. "It's like a dream! I was so depressed when I walked in here and now, it'll save my life!"

Catherine smiled at her. Surprise, surprise! No emotional blackmail, no threats, no funeral stories. Straight business. Francesca, whom she'd thought would be as impossible to disentangle from her job as a piece of chewing gum from a child's hair. "This calls for a celebration. Waiter, bring us two lemon-raspberry tarts and cappuccino."

"Why not?" Francesca thought, intuiting that tomorrow would not be the sixth day in her fifteen-day program to reduce her thighs and firm her buttocks. That it would be much, much more.

8

On the fourth ring, Janice Barren stopped propping up the sagging volume of her oversprayed hair, turning her attention from the hall mirror to the louvered doors leading to the kitchen.

"Imelda," she called pleasantly, maintaining that edge of modulation necessary to prove to the new maid she was demanding but not unkind.

The phone rang again.

"Imelda!" She raised her voice slightly, wondering if this was going to be a problem. The thought of indoctrinating yet another Third World stranger into the intimate mysteries of the elegant Barren household brought a sad droop to her recently uplifted cheeks. It was too awful to consider.

She sighed, picking up the phone herself.

"Hello. . . . Yes, this is Mrs. Barren speaking." She paused, listening, her eyes widening. "Who is this?" she demanded.

"Missus Barren?" the maid called timidly.

Janice looked up from the phone into the girl's eager, guilty eyes. She covered the mouthpiece. "It's all right, Imelda. I've got it this time. Didn't I explain to you? Wasn't I clear?" she pleaded. "Please, Imelda. Try to answer the phone no later than the second or third ring . . . "What!" she gasped into the phone. "What's that? Mr. Barren? Kenneth? WHAT . . . DID . . . YOU . . . SAY?" She slammed her palm over the mouthpiece."That will be all, Imelda! JUST . . . GO!"

The little, dark-haired woman lowered her gaze so that her new employer wouldn't see the tiny flash of hatred that lit up her meek, docile eyes. Swiftly, she dashed through the doors.

Janice stood there motionless, listening, a cold chill drenching her hot face, draining the color. She hung up, sitting down in the nearest chair and pressing her sweating palms hard against her knees to steady them. When she felt the shivers subside, she picked up the receiver to call Kenny. She stared at it in her hand, hesitating. Then slowly, and with infinite resignation, she replaced it.

Bastard, she thought.

She went back to the mirror and dabbed makeup over the tear streaks. She was almost out the door when the phone rang again. Let it, she thought, wondering what she dreaded more: some unknown female's disgusting revelations or her husband's slick, soothing lies.

"It's for you, Missus."

"I don't want to talk to anyone, Imelda."

"But . . . you said . . . when it ring, pick up . . . "

Gauging the height of the linguistic and cultural barriers she would need to vault to explain herself, Janice reluctantly took the phone, smiling with guilty haste as a flash of the previous housekeeper's unhappy face flitted across her memory. "Thank you, dear. You did that very well."

Ignoring the smile, the maid left.

To her surprise, it was Suzanne.

"Is everything all right?" she asked a bit apprehensively. Since the Renaldo fiasco, Suzanne had called her only twice: once to demand a list of her friends to solicit for a rape-crisis center fund-raiser, and another time to borrow rent money. "Lunch, today? Of course, darling. I'd be . . . it's been so . . . I've just got a nail appointment. I'm actually on my way now. Meet me there and I'll take you to lunch after? Suzy, I'm so happy you finally—" She didn't finish the thought, realizing Suzanne had already hung up.

Even from two flights away, it smelled like a toxic-waste dump, Suzanne thought, cringing as she climbed the steps toward the Art Deco doors of Nail Art Inc.

Her mother was already seated, her hands languidly poised above a basin of something looking vaguely like poisonous nuclear glop.

Suzanne watched her mother's dark head nod in deep concentration to whatever the woman next to her was saying. "She's such a good daughter," Suzanne heard. ". . . not only helped her mother find the apartment in Palm Beach, but hired a decorator to do it for her. All the rug and wallpaper samples were Fed-Exed straight to Scarsdale. Gloria didn't have to lift a finger. Could you imagine!" the woman extolled, lifting all of her fingers out of the glop and into the hands of an Asian beauty, who patiently wiped them dry.

"That's thoughtful," Suzanne heard her mother's peeved voice reply, in a way that clearly said that she—Janice Barren—would never experience such maternal joy.

"Mother."

"Oh, Suzanne!" Janice turned, half rising from her seat. Her eyes did a quick, critical loop. Moderately satisfied, she smiled. "Girls, my daughter."

Suzanne nodded at the sea of unfamiliar faces. They looked like those images in little girls' books of paper dolls, Suzanne thought: pages and pages of faceless, bodiless getups and *accessories* you wrapped around the cardboard princess, or the cardboard bride. What book would they be in? The *I Have Too Much Time and Too Much Money* book of cutouts?

"Sorry I can't hug you," Janice apologized, lifting her fingers in a gesture of contrition. The goop dripped a little down the sides of the bowl. "We'll be done any minute, won't we, Pearl? Pearl is the best nail technician. A wonderful stylist." Janice gave the nail technician a dazzling, gracious smile, which Suzanne couldn't help comparing to the dim one she'd received. Then, all of a sudden, out of the blue, Janice turned to her with a look of almost heartbreaking tenderness.

"*My little girl,*" Janice said, her heart suddenly lonely. "*My sweet little Suzy . . .*"

"Mother, please." Suzanne glanced around the room, as embarrassed as a high-school student saddled with a parent at the prom.

"Why don't you let me treat you to a set of nails, Suzy? It would look fabulous on you. Wouldn't it, girls? She's very busy and doesn't take care of herself, my beautiful daughter," she announced.

Suzanne felt her face grow hot.

"Come on. It'll be my treat."

Suzanne's eyes rolled ever so slightly heavenward.

Janice felt the warm milk of her maternal kindness turn to sorbet. *Little ingrate!*

"Don't take it personally, Mother."

"I'm just trying to help you, Suzanne."

"No, Mother. You're trying to give me what you would want if you were me. That's not the same thing."

"But just look at your nails, and look at mine!" Janice whispered fiercely.

Suzanne compared her own unpolished, perfectly clean (if slightly bitten down during rape-crisis phone-line sessions) nails to her mother's hard, glossy, Joan Collins ovals—perfect for ripping out the eyes of bitchy rivals.

"I think I'll keep my own, thank you," she murmured.

"Well, suit yourself. You always do," Janice said peevishly as she paid and walked out the door.

"Mom, do you actually like these claws?"

Janice peered down at her fingers, startled by the question. She shrugged. "I do it for your stepfather, really. He likes long nails."

Kenny and her mother. Her mother and Kenny.

Suzanne still found it . . . well . . . not exactly hard to believe, but predictably bad, like the plot of an amateurish movie. Just recently she'd seen a couple about the same age in the supermarket. Like Kenny, the man had had this dangerous kind of energy—sexual? emotional? He'd gone charging down the aisles with the cart, grabbing things nastily off the shelves—expensive things like Dutch butter cookies and gourmet coffee—while the woman hung back with helpless apprehension, staring at the ceiling. "If it was up to you, you'd never buy anything," the man kept saying.

Suzanne looked into her mother's face. You couldn't say she didn't try. Makeup, tons, and every little tube and wand costing twenty, thirty bucks, not to mention the creams, the little bottles and jars of oils, essences, hydrating, purifying, cleansing, anti-aging, vitamin, hormone-enriched . . . Hundreds of dollars, maybe even thousands, if you added it up over time.

She wasn't a woman about whom a man would say, "She's lost her looks," but more: "When she was young, she must have been a beauty." And it wasn't really anything as boring and predictable as wrinkles that had done her mother in. It was more the pinched, insistent look in her eyes, and the way her defeated mouth seemed to plead.

Suzanne glanced at herself in the mirror and saw the careless confidence, the sparkle, and, most of all, the energy. There was nothing you could smear over that to preserve it, she thought, tossing her head. Nor could wrinkles destroy it. She'd seen women of all ages—volunteers at the center—women in African gowns and turbans, or in old Bloomingdale's sweater sets, their faces creased with laugh lines, their gray hair hanging loose down their backs, retain some of that same feminine swagger. One woman weighed about two hundred pounds. A whole lotta woman. "My husband loves it," she told everyone. "He says I'm juicy." And you just knew it was true. All that beautiful, firm black flesh. She looked like a queen.

That was the secret: to have someone who loved you keep telling you how beautiful you were until you believed it. Someone who made you feel: G-d, am I ever worth it!

She looked at her mother, feeling a sudden pity. That was something you just couldn't buy, could you?

"Where would you like to eat? You're not still into that strange food, are you?"

"Why can't you just say 'vegetarian'? Lots of people are these days. Perfectly respectable *rich* people."

"I know, I know. But I find it all so boring when it's taken too far. I mean, fresh vegetables are fine, but on the side, you know, with lean roast beef, or turkey."

"Oh, Mom!" Suzanne said, leaning down impulsively and putting her arms around her mother.

Janice stepped back, startled, then gave in, collapsing against her. Tears stung her eyes as she tried to remember the last time someone had hugged her with affection. She composed herself, ashamed, aware of onlookers. "So, you've finally forgiven me?"

Suzanne stepped back, her body stiffening. No. She had not forgiven anything. Then how could she explain what had come over her? The sudden idea of Gran and Mommy, one of them dying and the other growing old and sad . . .

"Mom, let's just have a lovely lunch, shall we?"

"What about Pineapples? They have lots of salads, and it's green and pretty there. . . ."

"Fine. But is the service fast, or is it one of those places you sit all afternoon . . . "

"Why are you in such a hurry?" Janice protested. "We really *do* need to talk. I have no idea what's going on in your life anymore. And there are some things I'd like to discuss with you. Your stepfather, for example. I've got to tell you what happened this morning. . . ."

Suzanne held her hands over her ears and ground her teeth. Oh, yes, indeed-dy. This *was* going to be just as much fun as she'd expected. "Please don't!"

Janice stared daggers at her.

Suzanne looked straight ahead, humming until the waiter came. She ordered a huge salad, and Janice ordered lobster. Suzanne picked at her bean sprouts, watching her mother pick apart the red, horrible creature, fishing out the bits of white meat and dipping them into some oil-drenched sauce.

"Try some, dear? It's delicious. Just like chicken."

"As wonderful as that, huh?" She shrugged.

"You needn't look so disapproving."

"Sorry. My mind is . . . I was just thinking about Gran."

"What about her?" Janice said, concentrating on extracting yet another delicate morsel out of the hard shell.

"Has she spoken to you at all lately?"

"Well, of course. I speak to your grandmother almost every day."

"So, what do you think?"

"Think?" Janice looked up, confused. "About what?"

"Her condition, of course."

"What condition?"

Suzanne leaned forward. "You know . . . don't you?"

"Suzanne, can we stop playing games? Just say it."

"Mom, you don't have to hide it from me. She's already told me she's dying."

Janice's mouth fell open. "Don't be ridiculous."

Suzanne gazed at her, appalled. "Oh, my G-d! You mean to say she hasn't even . . . I'm sorry. I thought for sure you knew. Otherwise, I would never have . . ." She took both her mother's hands in her own. "She came over last week. We had lunch. She told me her doctor has given her a few more months at the most."

Janice pulled her hands away and pushed back her chair abruptly, almost overturning it. "I'm going to the ladies' room."

Suzanne watched her weave unsteadily through the crowded tables. Fifteen minutes later, she returned. Her eyes were red and dull, but there was new makeup on her cheeks and fresh color on her quivering lips.

"She told you and not me."

"I'm sorry. I don't know why. I'm not very close to her. You see her all the time."

"She doesn't like me." Janice shook her head emphatically. "Never has. And she'll never forgive me for divorcing your father and marrying Kenny. She hates Kenny."

"Well, I wouldn't go that far."

"The worst part is that she's right. She's always been right about him. He's having an affair."

"Oh, Jesus!" Suzanne winced.

"Why did you call me? Why are we having lunch?" Janice asked suddenly, her tone belligerent and betrayed.

Suzanne sighed. At least she'd be able to skip the bull and get to the point. "Gran is sending me and probably Francesca on a trip to Europe to research the lost memoir of some medieval relative of ours. She says she wants to read it before she dies."

"To Europe? And you're going?"

"Yes. I'm going. She says it would make her feel better. And frankly, I think it would be fun."

"And Francesca's going, too? What about her job?"

"She just got laid off."

Janice leaned back. "Nobody tells me anything."

"Look, Mom, this isn't about us. It's about Gran."

"It's all nonsense," Janice said dully. "Old people always think they're dying." Her vermilion fingertips touched the corners of her eyes, wiping away the moisture. "I'll call Dr. Weinsweig as soon as I get home."

"I suppose that's a good idea. But anyhow . . . well, I guess the reason I'm here is simply to tell you to watch over her. She's talking about not taking any treatment if it's unpleasant or painful! You know how stubborn she can be. Also, she's acting very strangely, talking about feeling guilty, and not having done her duty to her ancestors in passing things on. She's talking about her will."

Janice looked up sharply.

"Look, it's really none of my business, but I would hate to see those vultures on the ballet and museum boards get hold of her now. She's so vulnerable. Some of the places I work for, on the other hand, are really worthy causes that are struggling so hard right now. A bit in the right direction could do so much incredible good."

"You want her to leave her money to abused women and rainforests, instead of to her own flesh and blood!" Janice's voice rose.

Suzanne got up. "I've got to go. Listen, maybe none of this is true, and she's going to be fine and outlive us all. Please don't tell Gran I said anything, will you? If it is true, she has the right to break this kind of news in her own way. You will take care of her, Mom, won't you?"

The eyes of mother and daughter suddenly locked as they explored each other.

"As much as she'll let me," Janice promised, her eyes moistening once again.

$$9$$

Manuscript pages, handwritten, 23 x 33, unnumbered. Origin unknown. 1570–1630 (?). Bodleian Library Collection. Oxford, Great Britain. Attached to copy of Luis de Camoes's *The Lusiads* (1572).

A t the threshold of my memories there is a dark, taper-lit staircase. I skip down it quickly, unafraid, as I hold my mother's hand. She is not smiling but I see an indefinable pleasure in the lift of her head, a gesture distinct and positive beneath the heavy, festive headdressings.

I am four years old, perhaps even younger. Strangers call me by my Christian name, Beatrice de Luna. But amongst my family, I am called Gracia, the equivalent of the Hebrew name Hannah, meaning charm. It is the name that my parents chose; the name with which I was sanctified at birth: Hannah Nasi. It was my great-grandmother's name.

How I long to tell everyone that this is who I am! Yet I know I mustn't. I know that no one must call me by my real name.

The stairs seem to shimmer in the shadows, the way magical roads do in the enchanted forests of old wives' tales. I touch the dark walls to ascertain their damp, rough substance, proof I am still in a real place, the moist, lower chambers of our own home.

In the darkness, I feel the reassuring pressure of my mother's fingers. They warm me.

At the end of the corridor, a pillar of light stands blazing from ceiling to floor like some knightly sword. As I come closer, I see it is merely a slightly open door.

My mother pushes through. For a moment, my eyes are blinded by an explosion of dazzling light from a hundred candles. When the piercing shards recede, I see a long table laid with white linen at whose center are many small dishes arranged in the shape of a six-pointed star.

Searching the plates, I am suddenly hungry. But there is nothing there I would fain eat: bits of parsley and lettuce, burned eggs, and a burned lamb's shank. I search the table, disappointed and confused. Bottles of cool, red wine, beaded with moisture, catch and hold the light, paling to pink. At each place setting is a wine cup of beaten silver and a shiny brass dinner plate. Both cups and plates are empty of food.

I feel a surge of strange unease, almost of anger. At the head of the table sits my grandfather, Don Isaac el Nasi, hunched forward like a tree in a storm. Always have I waited for the wind to die and the storm to pass and for my grandfather's shoulders to straighten tall again. But it does not happen. The burden clings to him with the strength of Ashmedai himself, bending him almost in two.

His beard is dark brown still, with only one patch of the snowy white that will transform him into an old man just several years hence. It feels like spun wool against my face as he kisses me, twice on each cheek.

I like to think I will always be his favorite, more than my brother, Miguel, or the new baby still unborn. I fancy it is because of my copper-colored hair and my large, dark eyes, which my mother tells me are like my grandmother Rachel's. Often, my grandfather strokes the top of my head and rubs the back of his hand along my cheek, and I imagine that I see in his eyes a distant longing and love that swells his heart.

I have no such fantasies about my father. Miguel is his favorite. And this, I think, is the way it must be. He is the man-child, after all, the physician-scholar to-be, destined to bring honor to the family name. My father's face is teasing and amused when he *speaks to me, warm and serious when he speaks to my brother.*

His hopes and plans for Miguel are boundless.

And what does he hope for me? First of all, for good character, and then that the promise of early beauty shall ripen and bloom, winning our family an alignment with another of greater stature and at least equal wealth. And so, I must be neat and pretty for him. I must smile and watch the sauces do not soil my overmantle, and never raise my voice.

When I look at my tall father, who is preoccupied with the book before him and does not really see me, I realize again how low the ceilings are, and how thick the walls. And although no one explains this to me, I understand why: No one, I perceive, must see or hear us in this place, doing these things.

I do not know how I know this. Perhaps it is the strange whispers all around me, the air of forbidden pleasure. Or perhaps it is the sudden realization that we are in a room with no windows, whose walls and ceilings enclose us like treasures hidden in a box, or like prisoners.

(And I wonder, now, if I have added to this scene feelings and images that were not there. How much, after all, does a child really remember, and how much is he told later on that is then perceived as experience and woven into memory? And does it matter, then, that which is experienced and that which is dreamed, if the dreamer himself cannot tell them apart?)

We are below ground, hidden, our voices smothered. We see and smell nothing of the dazzling spring that above ground assaults all our senses: the blooming orange and lemon trees, violets, roses, laurel, and jasmine. It could be any season, and we could be anywhere, detached from all other living creatures that inhabit the earth.

For a moment, I feel a strange sensation of breathlessness, akin to drowning. This is a secret thing we do. Secret and—although no one says so—dangerous.

I am afraid. And although it is not clear to me if this is true memory (I am not a crier, nor can I imagine an age, however young, when I trusted in the efficacy of self-pity), I think I whimper.

Miguel lifts me off the ground and swings me in the air. I am ashamed and greatly pleased. My mother reaches up and taps him on the shoulder, chiding him with laughing eyes.

He is not as broad of shoulder as my father, but almost as tall, with my father's handsome Spanish eyes and his thick, dark, wavy hair. I remember, vaguely, that he used to play with me, but that he has not for some time. Shut up in the upper chambers with tutors and books, his face is habitually serious.

But now, in this place, at this time, he laughs, his eyes merry.

My astonishment grows as I hear his merriment echoed all around me. Aunts, cousins, uncles, and my immediate family, all in their Easter finery, sport with one another, and the laughter grows a bit wild.

We are not afraid. We are celebrating.

This amazes me, and I begin to smile, too, a little uncertainly, letting myself breathe. For the first time, I become aware of the tantalizing smell of spices: comino, karwiya, *cilantro. And the mouthwatering promise of food: sweet wine and apples, nuts, figs, dates, black raisins, and ground seeds. I sniff the air. Roast lamb, too, and great olives and pomegranates and almond water.*

As he lowers me, I throw my arms possessively around Miguel's shoulders. He is already betrothed. I saw her once. And although I contrived to pull her thick, black curls, she gave me sweetmeats and played ball with me.

As he sets me down, I look for her. Satisfied she is not here, I am filled with covetous happiness. I lift my arms to him, begging to be lifted again, but he refuses, smiling.

Everyone has taken their seats, I see. The men recline with kingly languidness on thick feather pillows, while the women sit alert and straight-backed.

I try to climb into my mother's lap and everyone bursts out laughing. I bury my head in her soft bodice, the velvet cool against my burning cheeks. But when I look up, I realize it is she and not I who amuses them. Big with child, her lap is too small for me! On the very edge of her knees rests a small prayer book filled with bright pictures. I touch the pages, curious. It is different from the psalter we take to mass, in which some of the letters are already

familiar to me. But these letters are strange, going from right to
left, rather than left to right.

My mother helps me to take my place beside her. Her arm is
around my shoulder, the book held between us.

My grandfather gets up and pours red wine into a beautiful
silver beaker. We rise with him, out of respect. And these were his
words as later I came to understand them: "Blessed be You, G-d,
our G-d, King of the Universe, Who has sanctified us by His
commandments and taken pleasure in us, and in love and favor,
given us His holy Sabbath and holiday as an inheritance, the
memorial of the work of the world's beginning. . . ."

At the time, of course, I understood nothing. My memory is of
unfamiliar words recited in unison like a song, until my
grandfather held up his hand for silence and began to recite a
story I had never before heard.

It was a strange tale that began like a fairy story. Once, once
long ago, in a faraway land called Egypt, our ancestors were
slaves and became free men. To loosen the bonds of tyranny, G-d
sent plagues down: blood, locusts, hail, vermin. . . . And with the
mention of each new horror, we pour drops of wine into a basin
that my mother forswears me neither to see nor touch.

And when all the plagues are mentioned and all the wine is
poured, my mother brings in a pitcher of water and washes the
hands of my grandfather and father. This, she explains to me, is a
pouring out of our sadness at the death of the Egyptians who
pursued us, the Children of Israel, because we do not rejoice at
any man's death.

And now the part comes that informs all my being, which is
stamped on my heart and mind so vividly that I know it cannot be
retelling, but true memory. "But are we not Portuguese, the
children of Christ our Lord and His Holy Mother!" I remember
protesting, astonished.

Suddenly a great murmuring breaks out all around the room. I
look at everyone. They are frowning, arguing with one another in
low, angry voices, until my grandfather slaps the table.

The dishes dance, then are silent.

"Come here, child."

*I bury my head in my mother's bosom. I do not know why I am
ashamed, or afraid; why I hide and try to escape. I know I have
made a terrible mistake, but not what it is.*

"Go." My mother pushes me gently.

*My grandfather holds his hands over my head and murmurs
words I do not understand. Then he takes me in his arms and
stares at me. I see an unutterable sadness in his face, as if his
heart were held together with fragile strands of meadow grass
that could tear asunder at any passing moment. When he finally
speaks, he says something that even now sears my memory,
something so astonishing that even now, in my old woman's head,
it clangs like all the bells of the great cathedrals of my childhood.*

"If you can forgive me, perhaps G-d can, too."

*I feel the questions crowd my brain, clogging it. They are like
pieces of dough kneaded together, one large, heavy clump,
inseparable into small, intelligent questions that can receive
illuminating answers that will turn the clump into something
familiar and digestible. And so I do not ask.*

*As soon as I return to my seat, I see my grandfather rise
abruptly. He throws a napkin with a piece of hard, flat bread in it
over his shoulder and leaves the room. When he returns, he has a
staff and a belt and a sack, and looks like a wayfarer.*

Everyone shouts at him: "Where do you come from?"

And he answers: "I have come from Egypt."

And then they ask him: "Where are you going?"

And he answers: "I am going to Jerusalem."

"Why do you cry?" I nudge my mother, terrified.

*"Sorrows enter in a flood and leave drop by drop," she answers
me, wiping her eyes. "But all the waters of Babylon cannot wash
the Jewishness from my soul."*

*Tomorrow we will celebrate Easter Mass. We will kiss the foot of
the Holy Virgin and take communion, drinking the wine that is the
blood of Christ, and eating the host that is His Holy body. We will
celebrate His death and resurrection with our neighbors in the
great Cathedral São Vincente de Fora, where my parents received
the sacrament of marriage and I myself was baptized.*

I do not know what thing this is my mother declares is in her soul. And I wonder if it is, without my knowing it, in mine as well.

We eat the hard, flat bread and burning, bitter herbs. I gag and my mother tries to wash it from my mouth with the sweetest of wine.

She does not succeed.

The bitterness and sweetness remain, one never canceling the other.

This was how I first understood that one can live two lives: one above ground, surrounded by fragrant gardens and fruit trees, in a place where one's father is a respected physician, where one's family sits in the first pews; the other below ground, in secret cellars lit by Sabbath and holiday candles, scented by wine and myrrh and frankincense, where joy is secret and celebration guilty.

And I knew, too, with a child's instinctive wisdom, that both lives were infinitely fragile and should one somehow touch the other, both would be destroyed.

All this I suspected long before my dear mother sat me down on my twelfth birthday and taught me my true history, as now, my children, I teach you yours. It must change your lives forever, as it changed mine.

10

The African violet, Francesca thought at the last minute, her hand on the light switch, her suitcases in the hall. She'd brought all the rest to her friend Paula's, but she'd forgotten the African. She stared at its dark velvet leaves and healthy purple blooms. An entire New York City apartment building—hundreds of people—and not a single one she could be certain wouldn't call the cops if she rang their bell at six in the morning, even if she did come bearing an exotic plant!

She felt a strange, teary tingle at the back of her throat. "O woe is me—O lonely me!" she said out loud, attempting a parody of self-mockery, achieving instead the real thing. It really *was* pathetic.

For a crazy moment, she considered taking it with her. But there were laws, weren't there, problems about little green flies that brought plagues to foreign lands? Besides, plants were not meant to travel. Even a short move from windowsill to tabletop could prove fatal, let alone a transatlantic flight.

She took a piece of paper from her desk and wrote: *For adoption. Please feed and water me sparingly (I hate water on my leaves) and place me in a pleasant, light spot.* She arranged the note carefully among the green leaves and placed the pot gently in the hall. With the uneasy conscience of a bad parent, she bade it a silent farewell.

It was the only good-bye she was likely to make that morning, she thought. She'd had dinner with her mother and stepfather a few nights before (scallops and pasta), a strange, almost silent meal, with Kenny sulking and getting up abruptly, and her mother stoic and preoccupied. On her way out, her mother had looked her over almost mournfully and said, "Get your hair layered, darling."

Ah, maternal wisdom.

Gran had called two days before, sounding as breathless and agitated as a little girl about to go to her first party. Was she positive she'd put the manila envelope containing the instructions in a safe place? Did she understand how important it was to follow the instructions to the letter? Had she met with Suzanne to discuss working together? It was so important, she emphasized, for the two of them to get along.

Suzanne. She pursed her lips and shook her head. On that score, her conscience was clear. She'd dropped in on her sister several times, dripping helpfulness and goodwill, bearing magazine articles on packing and sun protection, only to be laughed at. She'd arranged for a working lunch, only to have Suzanne show up late with some hard-luck case from the crisis center, whom they both wound up feeding and comforting for close to three hours, their original agenda out the window. And last, but not least, she'd attempted to coordinate their sharing a taxi to the airport that would get them both there in a timely and economical fashion. She'd left long, urgent messages on Suzanne's answering machine, which Suzanne still hadn't returned.

That had been the last straw. The girl was on her own.

Francesca lugged her suitcases down the hall, amazed at their weight. She'd tried and failed to imagine what she might need, and so had taken almost everything. Sweating with exertion, she pushed them into the empty elevator.

The taxi was waiting for her promptly in the driveway, as if anticipating her punctuality. She smiled, filled with a wonderful sense of competence. Traveling wasn't so bad, she encouraged herself, opening her day planner and giving her neat checklist a final once-over: tickets, passport, credit cards, and last, but not least, her grandmother's precious manila envelope containing her itinerary and a translation of the manuscript pages. With careful planning, you could keep things under control completely. She glanced at her watch. She'd arrive at least two hours prior to departure, as required by security checks.

"It's okay, driver. We can go now," she told the cabbie, leaning back comfortably.

Without any warning, she felt herself suddenly propelled with reckless speed into the unknown. This, she thought, clutching the seat, was the true problem with traveling: No matter how much you prepared for it, you were helpless against the selfish cosmic forces bent on moving you through sights and experiences at a pace not of your own choosing. An uprooting—even the smallest journey was that. Though we think we are taking ourselves with us firmly ensconced in the compact soil of our familiar containers—our luggage, our cameras, our pills and lotions, our shoes and stockings and prescription sunglasses. Still, our nourishment—our food and drink and even the amount and intensity of the sunlight itself—will change to something more or less than that to which we are accustomed.

And it is not just the fear of being hungry or thirsty, hot or cold, or sick without a doctor. It is equally (May I admit this to myself? Francesca wondered) a fear of experiencing a generosity and comfort that will cast their painful shadows over our normal life, making it seem drab and petty. It is the fear that we will not be able—or not want—to go home again.

She looked out the back window, watching her Rapunzel tower fade in the distance.

Suzanne stuffed two more unwrinkleable Indian skirts into her army duffel bag, her sole item of luggage. Her friend Jean, who'd just broken up with her abusive Haitian boyfriend, would be moving in that afternoon. She'd been thrilled to sublet. (Well, "sublet" was a bit optimistic. It wasn't really clear whether Jean would actually be able to *pay* anything. But at least the plants might get watered. Besides, what was the point of leaving it empty for weeks if someone could get some use out of it?)

She looked around the room. All the valuables (the opal earrings from Dad, her stereo and vintage Joan Baez recordings) were at her mother's for safekeeping. Only Renaldo's silver bracelet was left. She snapped it around her wrist, feeling a mystical certainty that she wouldn't lose it, no matter where she roamed.

In the distance she saw the buttery headlights of a yellow cab melt in the morning fog. She put out her hand to hail it. If it stopped, she'd have exactly enough time to make the plane. She slapped her pocket to see if she'd remembered the tickets and her passport. If they weren't in her pocket, then she was fairly certain they must still be on top of the refrigerator in that brown envelope . . . No, there they were! Good, she thought, slamming the cab door.

A strange feeling came over Francesca as she unloaded her luggage and watched the cab drive off. She felt as if she had somehow entered a different world, a place where water-cooler gossip and listless commuters had no place. A country of more intense feelings and heightened drama, where partings and reunions, beginnings and endings, were the norm and where even time itself—that dependable regulator of habits and bodily functions—had lost its authority. Planes came and went around the clock, crossing time zones, so that you might arrive even before you'd left!

"Smoking or nonsmoking?"

The question drifted down to her. Two more people to go and then she'd get to pick her seat.

"I always ask them right away for a nonsmoking aisle seat in front of the wing," a businesswoman just ahead of her turned around to say. She was wearing a fabulous trenchcoat, with an expensive leather attaché slung over her shoulder, both of which Francesca immediately coveted. "It saves time, and that's really the best place to sit. Personally, I feel like a prisoner when I'm trapped at the window. How many clouds can one look at, after all? And if one needs the lavatory, one has to climb over people, or disturb them, even when they're sleeping. I hate that, don't you?"

Francesca, who had been looking forward to looking out at the clouds and hadn't even considered the bathroom business, nodded. "Of course."

"An aisle seat in front of the wing in the nonsmoking section, please," she said dutifully when her turn came.

"Miss Abraham?" The clerk looked up. "You've already got a seat."

"But I just got here . . . "

"It's all been arranged by your travel agent. Have a good trip." She smiled, handing her a boarding pass. "Gate forty-six."

"Thanks, I think," Francesca mumbled, looking at the mysterious numbers and letters, trying to figure out if she was going to be a cloud-gazing prisoner for the next five hours.

Divested of her suitcases, her garment bag, and even her heavy hand luggage, which the amenable clerk had agreed to check in despite the excess baggage, Francesca felt a strange weightlessness. As she turned toward the escalators, the feeling grew, making her chest expand and her legs move with a dancer's lightness.

Away, she thought, looking out the enormous windows that framed the vast city of her birth. Gone was its familiarity, replaced with a strange, touristy kind of charm: the buildings reaching into the sky, which every New Yorker ignored after the age of five, the flashing hard light of a thousand windows.

She placed her purse on the X-ray machine and walked through the metal detector. The idea of strangers looking you over as if you could be dangerous, searching and X-raying you for hidden weapons, made her stomach lurch with a delightful sort of agony. She was almost surprised when nothing rang or buzzed or exploded.

Perhaps this *is* legal, after all, she marveled, stepping onto the moving sidewalk, and willing herself to be transported, luggagelike, into the hands of a fate both foreign and magical, full of pleasures heretofore missed, or simply undiscovered.

Over her shoulder, the city grew more distant. Lovely, in its way, she thought, catching sight of the man-made symmetry, the distant, almost bluish light. Strangely, it no longer seemed like home, but like some foreign place she had visited briefly and was now about to reduce to postcards and souvenirs. As if it were simply only one stop on some joyful, extended journey that would lead eventually toward her real home.

She felt inappropriately hopeful, almost ecstatic, without any reasonable explanation.

It was frightening.

An hour and a half to kill until boarding time, she thought, wandering restlessly through the duty-free shops with a bargain hunter's eagerness. But as she looked at the mountains of perfumes and soaps and cosmetics, and the outrageously priced designer scarves and purses, she felt a waning interest in the goods, and a growing one in the buyers.

Who are these people? she wondered. Imelda Marcos's cousins? The wives and teenage daughters of those Japanese moguls who buy Picasso paintings at auctions and hang them over radiators in their offices? And what does one do with a two-hundred-dollar red-black-and-gold scarf?

But if it makes them happy . . . she shrugged charitably. Hey, weren't mutually consenting adults entitled to waste their own or their husbands' or fathers' hard-earned money any way they pleased? Just to prove she wasn't a snob, she bought an Elizabeth Arden eyeliner in her usual shade, noting that the duty-free benefit had netted her a grand savings of about fifteen cents.

She wandered around listlessly searching for Suzanne, who was nowhere to be found. Damn! She really was going to cut it to the last minute!

A sudden yawn took her by surprise. She'd been up at five, not to mention half the night, waking at intervals with lists in her head of things she mustn't forget to take. From somewhere down the brightly lit corridor came the scent of freshly brewed coffee. She bought a cup, then hunted through the crowded cafeteria for a vacant table, hot coffee sloshing over her fingers.

"Are you looking for a place to sit?"

He was good-looking, clean, and clear-jawed, with a really fine set of blue eyes. A guy who—if he cornered you at a party or rang your bell for a blind date—would make your heart give a little *blam* of pleasure.

Nevertheless: New York City. Her eyes scanned the room looking for an escape. But somehow it didn't feel like the city anymore, with all its harsh, rigid rules of self-preservation. It seemed like a gentler country, calmer and more civilized. Besides, there really wasn't any other place to sit. She nodded gratefully, watching his long legs move aside to make room for her.

"Such a long flight." He shook his head. "Three or four hours, okay, but this—what, eighteen, twenty-four? And just for a week?"

"Where are you going?" she couldn't resist asking.

"Australia. Family wedding."

"That's some trip just for a week," she agreed demurely, afraid to encourage him with more than just a slight smile. She sat basking in his interest, in the expression on his face that seemed to say he'd found something valuable and unexpected.

"But, it's family, you know. Can't quite say no . . ."

"It depends, of course, on how close you are—"

"Yes, exactly." He was leaning forward, his elbows resting on his knees, his fingers clasped, pointing in her direction. His smile broadened and she began to feel a hot flash deep inside her stomach. Perhaps, she calmed herself, this is the way such things happen—the romances that life was supposed to throw the way of unmarried girls who kept all the magazine commandments: who dieted, exercised, and wore expensive clothes.

"I'd do anything for my family," he was saying. "Even travel thousands and thousands of miles just to be with them for a few days."

He had gray in his dark hair, which was short, except for a small braid hanging down on the right side. She stared at it. A little bohemian, yet not alarmingly so, she thought. An architect or an illustrator, perhaps? Something respectable, even if creative, and with a steady income.

"Are you traveling alone?" he asked, interrupting her husband fantasies.

"No. At least, I don't think so." She perused the crowds anxiously.

"Late?"

She nodded.

"Boyfriend? Husband?"

"Sister."

He took a deep, relaxed breath. "You're lucky. Traveling alone can be awfully depressing. In fact, it's no fun doing anything alone. Don't you agree?" His eyes were warm and smiling.

The boarding call for Quantas came through.

"Well . . . " He cleared his throat. "That's me." He stood up.

She studied his face, feeling unwarranted loss. "Have a good flight."

"You, too. I hope you find your sister."

She watched him disappear, sipping the rest of her coffee, which was cool and very sweet with just a hint of bitterness.

This is not like me, she thought, sweating lightly, trying to concentrate on her watch. The flight was going to board any minute. Where in heaven's name . . . ! She got up and wandered around, searching fruitlessly for a flash of coppery-gold hair, disappointment laced with panic shooting through her with surprising harshness.

Perhaps she'd simply changed her mind and wasn't coming after all. The idea sank like a stone to the pit of her stomach. It really was awful to travel alone. Whatever else Suzanne was, she was certainly never boring.

"Call for passengers boarding Flight three-oh-six to London. The plane is beginning to board."

The *beginning*, she thought, her heart pounding as she made her way toward the gate.

Bad water and unclean streets and surly strangers.

Romantic hideaways and brilliant, sophisticated men with charming manners, she argued back.

"Last call for all passengers boarding Flight three-oh-six to London."

Alone, she thought, handing over her boarding pass and walking heavily down the platform to the plane.

"Aisle or window?" she asked the stewardess, handing over her boarding pass. It suddenly seemed portentous.

"Oh, it's an emergency-exit row."

"What does that mean?"

"It's means you're very lucky, miss."

She hurried down the aisle. When she got to her seat, she knew it was true. It had both lots of leg room so that you could get out without making anyone get up, and a seat near the window with a clear view of the heavens. The best of all worlds, she exulted, settling back. Where divine cloud-gazing is not canceled out by the need to empty your bladder. A good omen. She glanced at the empty seat next to hers. If only . . . She gripped the handrest.

"Ten minutes to takeoff. Please fasten your seat belts and make sure that overhead compartments are securely fastened."

She strapped herself in, listening to the plane door slide shut. Then, to everyone's surprise, it suddenly opened again.

"One more passenger," the flight attendant apologized.

"That's cutting it close," someone behind Francesca complained. "Some people!"

She didn't even have to look up. She just smiled, waiting for Suzanne to slide in beside her.

11

"Incredibly predictable." Francesca shook her head.

"Made it, didn't I?" Suzanne grinned.

"I left you a message on your machine offering to share a cab. Why didn't you call me back?"

"Did you? That was very nice of you." She tapped her pale, chapped lip thoughtfully. "Actually, I haven't rewound that tape in quite a while, so . . ."

"I'm really glad you made it."

"Are you?" Suzanne looked surprised and pleased.

"Of course. You've done a lot more traveling than I have. All this makes me nervous."

Suzanne flung one arm around her sister's narrow shoulders. "Don't worry, I'll protect you from all the big, bad marauding men!" She grinned. "That's what you're scared of, isn't it?"

"I can take care of myself just fine in that department, sister!" Francesca protested. "In fact . . ."

The plane began its clumsy roll toward the runway. She clutched the armrests in a panic, tightening her seat belt, feeling like prey hoisted in the claws of some winged predator. Forgetting Suzanne, she concentrated on the perky blond stewardess cheerfully demonstrating what to do if the plane ran out of oxygen, lost sudden altitude, crash-landed . . .

"Oh, my G-d, let me out of here!" Francesca whispered, appalled, looking out at the clouds one met 35,000 feet off the ground. "I'll never remember all that!"

"Relax, Fran. If this toy stops working, you'll only have to remember one thing."

"Which is?"

"To put your head between your knees and kiss your ass good-bye."

So much for companionship, Francesca thought, glaring at her.

"Okay. Now that that's over, I think we should have a serious conversation," Suzanne said when the stewardess had finished.

"About what?"

"About this fiasco we've embarked on to please Gran."

"*Look*, Suzanne, let's get something straight. I don't view what we're doing as a fiasco. I look at it as a job. I intend to follow Gran's instructions to the letter, and I think it's perfectly reasonable that we might actually succeed. Furthermore, I'm planning to enjoy this flight. I'm going to watch the PG-thirteen movie, eat all the bad food, listen to the musical program on all nine channels, and read fascinating magazine articles about the queen. So please, don't be negative."

"Don't be negative? Don't you think Gran's condition is enough reason to feel a little *negative* about this whole thing?" Suzanne blurted out, amazed.

Francesca turned around slowly. "What condition?"

"Her medical condition."

Francesca looked at her blankly.

"Oh, please, don't tell me she hasn't said a word to you, either? All right, fine. If that's the way Gran wants to play this, then I'm not going to interfere. Let her do whatever she wants." Suzanne threw up her hands, exasperated.

"What's going on, Suzanne?" she demanded.

The drink cart rattled to their side.

"Tomato juice, two of those little bottles of vodka for me, thanks," Suzanne said, leaning back and ignoring Francesca's question.

"One minute," Francesca insisted. "Let's . . ."

"I'm sorry, but vodka's available only in first class," the stewardess apologized.

"Oh, couldn't you, ple-a-s-e. I'll get so airsick without it, and sometimes when I'm that airsick, I don't even have time to reach for a bag." Suzanne smiled sweetly.

The stewardess handed over the small bottles.

Suzanne poured them into the juice, gulping it down in one shot.

"And for you, miss?" the stewardess asked Francesca.

"Diet Coke, please," she said distractedly, taking the drink and watching the stewardess move away. "Really, Suzanne. Bullying stewardesses!"

"I don't believe in false class structures based on economic tyranny. Why should first-class passengers be the only ones to get smashed? Hey, better hold on to that drink before it baptizes your dress," Suzanne advised, closing her eyes and relishing the joyous alcoholic warmth spreading up from her stomach.

"What's going on with Gran that I don't know about?" Francesca repeated. "Don't play games with me, Suzanne!"

"She told me she had some kind of medical condition that was very serious. But apparently, I'm the only one she told. Even Mom hadn't heard anything. Mom, by the way, says it's nonsense—that old people always think they're dying."

Francesca stared at her in shocked silence. "Is Gran dying?"

"We're all dying, Francesca. The cells of every living creature begin to deteriorate the moment they're born."

"Don't give me this garbage! What do you know?"

"I know that Gran wanted me to go on this trip. She said it was a dying woman's request. She said it was the worst kind of blackmail."

"She admitted that?" Francesca asked, confused and a bit relieved. "You mean, she might have just made things out to be worse than they are just to get you to go along?"

Suzanne opened her eyes, looking with sudden kindness at sweet, clueless Francesca sipping her diet Coke. "Who knows why old people do anything? I agreed to go for my own reasons. I view it as a trip to Europe, all expenses paid."

"That's disgusting!"

"Disgusting? And why, pray tell, are you here? Out of filial devotion, no doubt!"

"This is a job. We're being paid a salary."

"And you're unemployed, right? You need the money. So why are you holier than I am?"

"It's not just about money! Well, of course it's partly that . . . Okay, even maybe mainly, but I want to do the job well. I feel a sense of responsibility. Which is more than I can say for . . ."

"So why'd the bank can you?"

"It wasn't me personally." She bristled, shifting uncomfortably. "My whole department was let go because of some stupid merger."

"Did you get a gold watch, at least?"

"No. I didn't get anything." Her eyes suddenly misted.

"Hold on." Suzanne chased the cart up the aisle. She returned with two minibottles of rum, which she poured into her sister's plastic cup. "Drink up, Fran. It's good for you."

"Stop calling me Fran! You know how I hate it! And this stuff is not good for you! It corrodes the liver and is full of calories," she said morosely, drinking it down to the last drop. She stared out the window. "Things are not supposed to happen this way." She wiped her eyes and crushed the flimsy cup in her fist. "I mean, one day you're this hotshot they can't do anything without, and the next day they throw you away. They treated me like some criminal, walking me out with my box and a guard. And I didn't deserve it, Suzy. I worked really hard for them. I did a great job. And I have my mortgage payments. . . ."

"And all that money you owe Gran, and no boyfriend, to boot."

"It's not funny. Since Peter, I haven't even been asked out by anyone financially secure enough to make it worth my while."

"*Mejor es tomar ombre sin paras, ke paras sin ombre.*"

"Huh?" Francesca opened her eyes in surprise.

"Better a groom with no money than money and no groom."

"Where did you . . . ?"

"Grandpa Carl, of course. I can't believe you don't remember!"

Francesca looked blank for a moment. Then her face lit up. "*La yave de oro avre todas las puertas!*"

"The golden key opens all doors." Suzanne giggled. "That's what Grandpa Carl used to say whenever he had some business problem he needed to solve. And what about Gran's favorite: *El mundo . . .*"

". . . *pertenese a los pasensiozos,*" Francesca continued. "The world belongs to the patient in spirit." Do you remember when she used to take us to Radio City Music Hall right before Christmas and there would be these long lines . . . ?"

"Or when she took us shopping for Passover dresses, and she could never find one she liked, and we'd get all fidgety . . ."

"*El mundo pertenese a los pasensiozos*," they chorused, laughing.

They were silent for a moment.

"She looked a little worn out last time I saw her. Did you think so, too?"

Suzanne shifted uncomfortably, crossing her legs and folding her fingers in her lap. "These damn seats are made for midgets . . . ! Oh, I don't know." Suzanne studied her sister. "If Gran really is ill, does it matter? I mean, would you have acted any differently?"

"I don't know," Francesca answered thoughtfully. "I really needed this job. But if Gran is ill, perhaps we should be there with her."

"Even if it's her wish to send us on this quest instead of having us by her side to witness her slowly, painfully fade away?"

"It's a horrible choice. But maybe Mom is right. Old people do tend to have exaggerated fears about their health. And she isn't getting any younger. . . ." She leaned back, alcohol and exhaustion dulling her senses, making her sleepy. "I just hope she keeps getting older! That's what I hope for myself, too. I mean, every year that passes and I haven't contracted some fatal disease, or been shot in line at the cash machine, or murdered in my bed, I'm grateful. I don't understand all these women who want to be twenty-nine forever. My goal is eighty-two, know what I mean? And every year I get closer to it, I'm grateful."

"I'm not afraid of getting older, either. We've got these beautiful women volunteers at the center who have done so much with their lives: raised big families, run businesses, traveled, helped out in a million worthy causes. Aging doesn't worry me. I just don't want to die. I never want to die."

"Never?"

Suzanne stretched her legs luxuriously into the aisle, looking at the lovely length of them, so young and full of strength. "Never."

"Not even if you got paralyzed and could only communicate by typing on a computer with a pencil between your teeth?"

"Look at Stephen Hawking! He managed to revolutionize physics—and even start a little romance on the side!"

"Even if you had this horrible, disfiguring disease and you knew you were going to die slowly in great agony?"

"Well, thank you so much, sister, for bringing that one to my attention. I hadn't actually *thought* of that one!"

"Okay, that was a bit extreme. But don't you think it's possible to just
live this great life so that when it's over—I mean, when you've lived
your seventy-eighty-odd years—you'll be able to say, 'That was good;
I'm happy with what I had and grateful, and now I'm ready.' Sort of like
what Gracia says in those memoirs. Pretty interesting stuff—the manuscript, I mean. Don't you think?"

"You honestly think so?" Suzanne sat up.

"Well, I mean, she was this beautiful, incredibly wealthy businesswoman. Her husband was dead, and she had all those enemies after her
money and her body. You've read the English translation Gran put in
with the other stuff in the manila envelope, haven't you, Suzanne?"

"Well, not exactly." She'd *meant* to, but kept putting it off. She had
no patience with anything musty and old. She never went to flea mar-
kets, and she found antiques stores bad-smelling and pathetic: all those
things hanging around when their time had passed, things no one really wanted or they'd be in some descendant's living room instead of
gathering dust, on sale to strangers. She'd imagined the memoirs to be
some boring, flowery, medieval tribute to child-love and husband-care.

"How can you take this job, *Gran's money,* and not bother to even
read it?!"

"I told you, I will, eventually. So, she was a rich businesswoman,
huh? And you're crazy about her. Figures."

"It's not just the wealth. It's . . . she took no crap from any quarter.
Kings, popes, princesses. . . . No, just think about it. Let's say Hillary
Clinton invited you to the White House and wanted to fix you up with
this powerful but otherwise undesirable friend of hers. I mean, would
you have the guts to say no? But that's what she did. She just had this
enormous sense of who she was, of having some mission. Talk about
liberated women!" She paused reflectively. "Her life had a solid hub that
no one and nothing could touch. Know what I mean?"

Despite her misgivings, Suzanne was intrigued. "Tell me more."

"Read it yourself!"

"I will. I guess I just figured . . ." She shrugged.

"What?"

"You know, all this stuff—family trees, ancestors—it's just stuff losers flaunt so they can tell themselves they're important, that their blood is redder than everybody else's. I mean, look at the Daughters of the American Revolution, and all those pathetic social registers."

"So if the past doesn't mean anything, why do you bother toiling away to change things? I mean, the minute you die everything you stood for and accomplished is going to become dusty and irrelevant anyway. I mean, why not just be like me? Get a good job, invest your money sensibly, buy a little place . . . ? You know, like most people?"

For some strange reason, Suzanne couldn't think of an answer.

"I'm falling asleep. That's the effect alcohol has on me. Wake me when the food comes, will you?"

"You wouldn't happen to have a copy of the memoirs on you, would you, Francesca?"

"Where's your copy?"

She had a mental vision of a brown edge sticking out over a white enamel surface. "It's in my luggage."

"How could you travel without the itinerary? What if the luggage got lost? You wouldn't know where to go or what to do."

"I hate living that way, anticipating disasters."

"You're the piggy who built the house of straw, all right. Fine. I'll give you mine, but don't crease it or get it wet."

"You're still mad about that miniskirt I borrowed from you when we were in high school."

"And the mohair sweater, and the silk blouse, and my Walkman . . ."

"All right, all right. I promise to take excellent care of it."

"Here. Enjoy." Francesca handed it over. "And now, if you don't mind, I think I'll just . . ." She yawned, folding her arms, closing her eyes, and twisting to find a comfortable place for her head. Her arm brushed Suzanne's. "Know what, Suzy, I think this might be fun, don't you? Like when we went to Niagara Falls, remember?" she said drowsily.

Suzanne looked at her. For all her competence and seriousness, and those uptight clothes, she was still a little kid.

"Sure. A barrel of laughs." She leaned back as far as the seat would go and began to read.

It didn't take her long. When she finished, she closed her eyes, her head pounding with a great avalanche of contradictory ideas.

As much as she fought it, she was strangely moved. Not just by the words, but by the whole idea of having a distant ancestor, who had lived, struggled, thought, and loved in a time so far past, in a world so very different. Someone who had passed down something of herself—at least genetically—to her and Francesca.

It was both predictably foreign (evil eyes, witchcraft, slitting of sheeps' throats by Jewish scholars) and, at the same time, surprisingly familiar: *Marriage is more than mutual desire—it is a partnership in which every member of the family, living and dead, takes part. . . .*

Obviously, it didn't matter when they lived. Jewish mothers were always the same.

Family.

Everybody had one.

Like ear wax and belly-button lint.

She straightened the pages and put them carefully back into the envelope, brooding over Francesca's question. If, indeed, the past had no meaning, why struggle so hard in the present, which would very soon became the irrelevant past?

The answer was, of course, that one's own past was important. That's all one had, really: what you'd thought, what you'd done. A person's life was the sum of all those things. And of course the immediate past of those around you shaped the world one lived in.

The question was whether there existed such a thing as a shared and sacred past. Did history, the words and lives of ancient ancestors, really have anything of value to impart? What did it mean that all those things that people had been willing to die for were now barely remembered?

Was that progress? Or a terrible desecration?

She wondered.

She had come to a strange place in her life. It was like a sun-drenched forest clearing surrounded by an overgrown maze. She knew what she was doing for the moment: her job at the rape-crisis center, her boyfriends, her women friends, her causes. But she didn't have a clue as to where it would all lead.

It would be something, she thought, to have a child, a grandchild—part of your own body and blood that would go on living long after you'd died. Perhaps that was the point: to direct your life's work toward the unseeable future, for the benefit of the unborn. To keep the world, life, going.

"Is it cold in here?" Francesca murmured fitfully.

"Freezing," Suzanne said, taking a blanket out of its plastic wrapping and tucking it tenderly around the almost childish breadth of her sister's shoulders.

Niagara Falls. The mist, the powerful, awesome rush of cold water, and both of them in yellow raincoats on the *Maid of the Mist,* that tourist boat that took you under the falls into an astonishing silver haze of billowing, wet clouds. The dizzying step back, the sickening sense of falling hopelessly into the depths. And then—the benevolent forces, unseen, pulling you back. Francesca grabbing one arm, Gran the other.

Family.

12

Manuscript pages, handwritten, 23 x 33, unnumbered. Origin unknown. Circa 1570–1630(?). Private collection, Mrs. Anna-Laura Salvio, part of Solomon Dubno collection, acquired through auction by Ernst Salvio, Amsterdam, 1814.

H*ow shall I make you hear it with my twelve-year-old ears, or feel it with the vulnerable softness of my twelve-year-old heart? I am not a poet, but a businesswoman, more comfortable with the simple grace of numbers that either add to profit or do not. Yet, even were I the most talented and sensitive of scribes, with words like shining orbs to illuminate all the dark corners of the firmament, still I could find no phrase befitting the wonder and horror of my family's history, the path that led us to hide in cellars and celebrate in suffocating darkness.*

I carry it with me always, the way one carries an unborn child, close to the heart. And, like a fetus, that knowledge, that history, rolls and kicks, keeping me awake when I am tempted to close my eyes and lean back, soft and vulnerable, to be charmed by dreams and confused by pretty faces and prettier words. It has kept my eyes and heart wise and sharp enough to perceive the outrage lingering in wait behind even the most skillful seduction.

When I was twelve years old, and thus responsible for my own sins, my mother—may her name and memory be blessed—led me

down the secret passageway to our hidden rooms. There, by the
light of a dozen candles, she gave me my history, beginning with
the journey from Spain, and leading to the very day of my birth.
Part of it I have already told you, my children. Here is the rest:

In 1493, Alvaro di Caminha was given the captaincy of São
Thomé, an island off the coast of Africa. Islas Perdidas, the natives
called it. And a cursed place it was! Burned by a pitiless sun, an
abode to giant lizards, poisonous snakes, and crocodiles; home to
criminals banished from the kingdom.

Wanting to populate his little kingdom, the captain proposed to
King João that all the children of the refugees be seized and sent
there to be instructed in the Christian faith. Undistracted by the
influence of their Judaizing families, they would have no reason to
question the truth of their teachings, and no opportunity for
backsliding. This seemed to the King a worthy proposal. Too many
of the children had failed to pay the head price, he claimed, and
brought pestilence to the cities and countryside, filling Portugal
with their graves.

My mother was not at home the day João's soldiers came to the
door. Through G-d's guiding, merciful hand, she had gone with
Alphonsa and Maria to gather olives in a far-off grove. Questioned
by the soldiers, those good and faithful women had declared her
their daughter and niece. And so she was saved from the fate of
her cousin Joseph, whom the soldiers tore from his mother
Constanza's arms.

Grandfather Isaac took on the dangerous mission of traveling
to Lisbon to enquire after Joseph and to win his release. But in the
end, he could only stand in the harbor and watch as the ship set
sail, little Joseph imprisoned with the others.

After that, nothing was the same. Peace, my family understood,
was an illusion for those forced to squat on the head of a sleeping
dragon.

All this happened years before my birth.

And yet, how often I have traveled with those motherless
children to that cursed isle! I have seen their fragile white skin
savagely burned by the sun, felt their bitter thirst and the aching

of their hearts for their mothers and fathers. With them, have I taken the last stumbling, small steps down the gangplank to the island. My nightmares are filled with the terrible sound of the feasting, the crush of the small bodies in the pitiless jaws, the horrible spurts of innocent blood.

How can one explain it, that feeling in the heart that things that happened long ago are not merely a story well told, but the secret experiences of one's own soul?

The ultimate retribution of our G-d may tarry, but is not to be denied. On the wedding day of Alfonso, João's only son and heir, the King lived to see the child of all his hopes thrown from his horse and killed. Soon after, the King was himself struck down with a strange fever, which racked his body for many days before killing him.

My people rejoiced, not realizing that his successor, Manoel, would only deepen the horror.

And this is what happened next:

King Manoel wished to marry Isabel, the daughter of the Catholic Queen. Before she would agree—may her name and memory be blotted out for her sins and the sins of the evil mother who bore her—Isabel insisted that, if she were to be Portugal's Queen, she could not abide Jews, Moors, or heretics in her kingdom any more than could her parents. Manoel, desiring both the dowry and the bride, complied, issuing his own Edict of Expulsion. It was no secret, though, that he was loath to lose the skilled newcomers and their wealth. Banking on their weariness, and on the terrors of sea travel facing them if they defied him, he expected the baptismal waters to fall gently on resigned heads.

He was, of course, mistaken. My grandfather bowed his head but not his back. Unlike Lot's wife, he cast no backward glance of regret upon all he was once more forced to leave behind. His plan was to head for Lisbon and board a ship for the African coast, as King Manoel had promised to provide ships for all those who wished to leave.

Grandfather was not alone. And when Manoel saw the thousands of refugees determined to take leave of his dubious hospitality, his greed gave him the devil's cunning, for only Beelzebub himself could have fashioned such a cruel and matchless snare.

[Next five pages unclear. Water damage.]

Gois, Damiano de *Cronica de Felicissimo Rei D. Manuel.* New edition according to the one of 1566. University of Coimbra. 1949.

Chapter XX: Of How the King Ordered That the Children of the Jews Who Were Leaving the Kingdoms Be Taken Away. And for What Reason He Did Not Do the Same to the Moors.

Many of the native Jews of the kingdom, and many of those who entered from Castile, took the baptismal water, and those who did not want to be converted immediately began to negotiate the things which befitted them for their departure and embarkation, at which time the King, for reasons which compelled him to do this, ordered that on a certain day the sons and daughters of these people under the age of fourteen be taken away from them and distributed among the villages and places of the kingdom where, at his own expense, they would be raised and indoctrinated in the Faith of Our Savior Jesus Christ.

This the King, along with his council, decided to do, being in Estremoz, and from there he came to Evora at the beginning of Lent in the year of 1497, when he declared that the assigned date would be Easter Day. Because of this lack of secrecy, it was necessary for the King to order that this execution should be immediately carried out throughout the whole kingdom, lest the Jews, by ways and means to which they could resort, secret their children out of the kingdom. [The decree and the haste of its execution] caused great terror mixed with many tears, pain, and sadness to the Jews, but also great astonishment and surprise to the Christians because no creature can endure, nor tolerate, to be separated by force from their children. Many Old Christians—moved by such compassion and mercy toward the screams, cries, and laments of the fathers and mothers whose children were being taken away by force—offered to hide the children in their houses so that they would not be taken away from their parents, saving the children even though they knew that they were doing so against the law and decrees of their King and lord.

The same law of nature led the Jews themselves to resort to cruelty. Many of them killed their children by throwing and drowning them in wells and rivers, and by other means, rather wishing to see them end this way than to be separated from them without hope of ever seeing them again, and by the same reason many of them killed themselves. While these executions were taking place, the King did not fail to take care of that which pertained to the health of the souls of these people, by which, compelled by mercy, he deceived them, without furnishing them with the boats he had promised for embarkation. Of the three ports of his kingdom which had been assigned for their departure, he closed two, ordering all to embark in Lisbon where he provided them with lodgings for shelter at Os Estaos and where more than twenty thousand souls were gathered. Due to these delays, the time which the king had assigned for their departure had passed, with all of them becoming prisoners there.

Many of the Jews, finding themselves in such a miserable state, entrusted themselves to the king [i.e., converted] so that the King returned their children, and promised them that for twenty years they would not be under official investigation about their beliefs. And to those who refused to become Christians, the King immediately ordered that they be given embarkation, ending the captivity imposed on them, and all of them crossed to the land of the Moors.

The reason that the king ordered to take away the children of the Jews and not the children of the Moors was that the Jews, by their sins, have neither kingdoms, nor domains, nor cities, nor villages, but they are—in all parts where they live—pilgrims and subjects, without having power nor authority to execute their desires against the injuries and evils done to them. But to the Moors, by our sins and punishments, G-d allows to occupy a great part of Asia and Africa and a good part of Europe, where they have empires, kingdoms, and great domains with many Christians living under their tributaries, besides many whom they hold as prisoners. For all of these [Christians] it would be very harmful to take away the children of the Moors. . . .

Suárez, Fernandez Luis, Documentos Acerca de la Expulsión de los Judíos, *Consejo Superior de Investigaciones Cientificas*, Valladolid, 1964.

Even after their children were seized, thousands of Jews persisted in refusing to be baptized. These were summoned to Lisbon by King Manoel, who pretended that he would allow them to leave on ships. Instead, they were herded into the barracks of Os Estaos, tortured, and starved. When after three days this still failed to win their consent to voluntary conversion, their bodies were tied up with ropes and they were dragged by their hair and beards to baptismal fonts. Many threw themselves into the sea, or into wells or from the tops of roofs. . . .

And that is how my grandfather, my mother, my father, Aunt Constanza, her daughter, Elvira, and all the Jews of Portugal took the baptismal waters. But being forced, their conversion changed nothing in their souls and they continued to practice the religion of their forefathers almost openly, for the King—fearing their endless enmity—had promised them they would not be disturbed.

This, alas, was not to be.

In the year 1506, there was a drought and famine in the land. On April 19, Passover night, a family was found conducting a seder and eating matzoh. Preachers claimed this was the reason for G-d's holding back the rain. To ask for G-d's mercy, they constructed a crucifix from hollow glass and placed a candle inside. They told the people it would produce fire, proof of the great miracle, and that G-d would judge the Jews by fire.

A voice in the congregation rang out: "Would it were water and not fire, for it is water we need in this drought."

The crowd, who recognized the speaker as a New Christian, and thinking he mocked them, tore him limb from limb, then burst from the cathedral, raiding New Christian homes, urged on by the priests who promised them one hundred days' penance in the World to Come for every heretic they killed. Three thousand died that night, including pregnant women who were thrown out of windows and caught on spears.

King Manoel put an end to it, and forty of the murderers were hanged.

But this was the end of the life aboveground for my family and the beginning of the windowless cellars filled with secret rituals. Children were sworn to secrecy and only instructed as to their true identity when they neared the age for marriage.

I try, sometimes, to imagine how it must have been for Grandfather. How his throat must have contracted when told to swallow the communion wine and bread! How his knees must have shaken as they crumpled beneath him, kneeling and bowing before figures of marble and wood, in bitter betrayal of all he held sacred!

The older I become, the more I understand the power of the wind into which he had lowered his proud, strong head. I understood the burden that had bent his back into a permanent curve of submission.

And yet, for all his weakness, he bequeathed to me a heart that remembers to beat with a steadfast pulse and eyes that cannot be deceived. And something of that unquenchable spirit that flowed through his veins flows through mine as well, sustaining the sacred, unshakable loyalty that has always informed my life and my deeds.

I know there are others who, sharing my history and ancestry, have nevertheless turned traitor. Indeed, they have become our people's most despicable enemies. To my shame, I must admit that I have always understood them. For at first I, too, shed bitter tears over being one of those lowly people whom all despised. Only with time did I begin to fathom what a treasure had been bequeathed to me, and at what fabulous cost.

Be wise: Remember this.

All things of utmost excellence are extremely difficult to obtain. The luster of gold is found only after the dross is burned away in great fires; the splendor of the diamond revealed only after leveling by the heavy, grinding wheel.

So, too, human beings—particularly the great, misjudged, and most unfairly condemned of peoples, into whom I, and you, my children, have been born and are irrevocably connected. Thus must we endure our suffering in order to emerge—all dross fallen away—to shine in the eyes of G-d and man. And then—what happiness awaits us!!

And with this as preface, I now reveal part of the great secret that I hold and which I bequeath to you:

Endure. Resist the importunate harassments of the Enemy with a marvelous constancy. Yet be not like those brothers who end their lives rather than carry their burdens. Let your head bend, your back sway from the heaviness of the unbearable load, yet survive! Breathe. Move. Live!

For ten years in chains are better than one moment in the ground.

This is wisdom.

I remember that Passover night when my grandfather begged my forgiveness. I regret that I did not then possess the knowledge to have granted it with a full and understanding heart.

He died before I came of age. But many times since have I seen him in that twilight hour where dreams become flesh, and past overlays present.

"Grandfather," I whisper, "the shame is not yours, but theirs. I, Grandfather, will never let them trample me. I will keep this back, these knees, this heart, upright, for your sake and for the honor of all those who came before me."

And each time I say these things, I see it happen: Like a miracle, his back straightens and his shoulders rise and span the sky.

13

"Oh, here it is! The last one. I really thought they'd lost it," Francesca said, peering anxiously down the luggage conveyer. She grabbed the handle of the enormous Pullman, attempting to dissuade it from its relentless momentum forward. It wouldn't budge.

"Ask one of these guys to help you, Francesca. Men love that."

"I can manage perfectly well," she insisted, breathless with exertion, the suitcase moving her, rather than vice-versa.

"Right." Suzanne sighed, joining her sister and pushing at the dead weight with all her might until it slid to the floor. Together, they lifted it onto a luggage cart. "Really, Francesca! First commandment: Reduce consumption," Suzanne complained, throwing her duffle bag over her shoulder. "This kind of *Grand Hotel* traveling went out with Greta Garbo. If you insist on traveling this way, get a husband! Oh, look! Tourist brochures."

She picked up a few and leafed through the various listings of restaurants, nightclubs, galleries, and services. "Listen: 'Mandeer. Old, atmospheric and famous Indian cafe and restaurant serving gourmet vegetarian food. Special diets—vegan and Jain—are catered to. . . .' "How does that sound for dinner?"

"How can you think about dinner? We just ate."

"It's never too early to think about dinner," Suzanne insisted, skimming the page, her eye suddenly caught by a listing for "Women: London Crisis Center." It would be great to compare notes!

She circled the number and stuffed the brochure into her pocket along with a few pamphlets about current West End hits: Sting was at the Palladium. *Cats* was still playing. *Blood Brothers.* She began to feel a heady wave of joy. London!

"Theater brochures? We're not exactly on vacation, Suzanne."

"But we're not in jail, either. I mean, on my old job there was such a thing as after working hours. Besides, if I were Gran, I'd want us to enjoy this trip. We are her granddaughters, after all."

"I know. The joy of taking. Especially from one's own flesh and blood."

"Why do you have to be so . . . so . . . uptight all the time?"

"Look, let's get something straight. We have a lot of work ahead of us, and that is what this is all about. We'll just have to see if we have time left over for other things."

"You're just afraid to explore, to open yourself up to new possibilities. To enjoy life."

"No, I'm not!" Francesca protested indignantly, afraid it was true.

"What is the nature of your stay in Britain?" the weary passport control official asked Francesca perfunctorily, holding the entry stamp paused above her passport.

"I'm here to work," she said, glaring at Suzanne.

He put the stamp down and peered up at her, alert suspicion and unfriendliness swiftly replacing his lethargy. "Do you have a work visa?" he demanded.

"No. . . . But. . . ."

"You aren't permitted to work in Great Britain without a work visa . . ."

"But I'm not really working . . . I mean . . ." She swallowed hard, glancing desperately at Suzanne, who rolled her eyes heavenward.

"You mean you didn't tell me the truth? Is that it?" His voice rose. Francesca watched, terrified, as he lifted the phone and began to dial.

"Look, I'm sure my sister didn't understand your question. She's a little . . ."—Suzanne was suddenly at her elbow, making sympathetic faces at her—". . . woozy from the flight. All that liquor in first class . . . you know." She winked. "What she meant to say was that we're both on holiday and plan to work really hard at it."

He looked at her. She tossed her lovely reddish curls and smiled her big, white, American cover-girl smile. "Maybe you can tell us what's worth seeing in the West End these days?"

Francesca's heart lifted in relief as the man's eyes softened, moving appreciatively down her sister's face and body. He put down the phone. "Vacation, what? Well, luv, tell your sister not to mix business with pleasure, will you?" he said, stamping the passports and pushing them under the glass.

"I'm sure there won't be any time for business for us girls here in London," she said archly, nudging Francesca, who managed an inert smile.

"You almost got yourself thrown out of the country!"

Francesca walked forward at a New York pace, her fists clenched. "It wasn't my fault! How was I to know?"

"Well, at least thank me for saving you!"

"Saving me? I'm sure if I would have just explained the situation to him, I would have been perfectly fine."

"Sure. In a few hours. Oh, let's not fight. Let's take a cab straight to the hotel and check in. Then you can take a rest, and I'll go down to Leicester Square and see if I can't get us half-price tickets for the evening. I really want to see *Blood Brothers*. My British friend Ian said it was fabulous, all about the evils of race and class."

"I really think we should make our phone calls first to all the places Gran listed."

"Sure, sure. But after . . ."

"I'll say it again—I really don't feel right about planning recreational activities until we see about the work that's involved."

"You are such a wet blanket!" Suzanne groaned.

"And you are such a freeloading, lazy, good-for-nothing sponge." Francesca fumed as the exit doors slid open.

"Girls!"

Suzanne and Francesca looked up, stunned.

"Abuela!"

"Isn't it marvelous." Catherine beamed, linking her arms through theirs. "All three of us here, together, beginning this journey."

"When did you arrive?" Francesca gave her a confused smile.

"Gran, are you really feeling up to it?" Suzanne asked, shaking her head in disbelief.

"Not another word!" Catherine placed her finger over Suzanne's lips, giving her a private little warning shake of the head. "We'll talk about it all when we get to the hotel. Here, give the driver your bags. Ah, we've got so much to talk about! I have such stupendous news!"

14

Taking long, slow sips of freshly brewed coffee that had come up on her breakfast tray, Francesca pulled back the heavy damask curtain and peered into the street below. She was charmed by the lovely, rich foliage of old trees, the fountains and the quaint statues. That, and the luxurious, old grandeur of her hotel room—its marble floors and bath, the polished antique furniture and big canopy bed—seemed to transport her back in time to a more leisurely and gracious era.

London was everything she'd imagined: regal, civilized, polishing the past to a fine patina that spread its glow over the present.

It had been so odd seeing Gran there in the airport, but almost immediately, it had become a tremendous relief. Having her around setting the pace and directing the whole enterprise took the burdensome feeling of responsibility off her shoulders. Dinner, for example, had been such a leisurely, warming meal, wine sparkling in firelight and everyone so calm and mellow. Gran had looked tired, but there'd been a pinkish glow on her face and a twinkle in her eye as she laid out all her plans for the coming weeks. She seemed like a girl again in her frilly dress with the long string of pearls. London, she'd told them, reminded her of the time she'd fallen "crazy in love."

Gran, crazy in love! Just the words, the very idea! She laughed quietly to herself. But then, as she looked out at the bower of thick leaves and the little romantic niches on every corner, it seemed less ridiculous. She'd have to remember to get Gran to give them the details.

She put down her coffee and picked up a slice of toast, spreading it thickly with marmalade and wondering if she would be able to resist the temptation to crawl back beneath the soft down covers. Aside from the mere decadence of the idea, she couldn't think of a single reason why not.

She took out her day planner and checked it. She was in no rush. They'd all agreed to meet at eleven at the offices of Serouya and Company, Dealers in Rare Books and Manuscripts, 48 Charing Cross Road. Gran had advised them not to bother following up any other leads until then.

And so, for the first time she could remember, there was not a blessed thing that duty, honesty, or responsibility demanded of her at the moment. She glanced at the inviting bed as she poured herself another cup of coffee and took small bites out of a buttery croissant. Maybe. Or maybe she'd run herself a bath and pour in the entire bottle of bath foam . . . She leaned back on the soft couch pillows and simply closed her eyes.

Crazy in love, she thought, the phrase running through her head like a show tune.

Nothing opens in this place before ten. It was dreadful, Suzanne thought, kicking off her shoes and picking at the cold remains of her breakfast tray, which she'd polished off long before. She'd been up and about for hours.

First, she'd taken an early jog. It was a great area: The British Museum and University of London were around the corner, and Dickens's house was down the block. After that, just on a lark, she'd taken the Underground down to the Women's Crisis Center, which was in a very unlovely part of the city. It had been closed, but there'd been a name and number on the door. When she tried it, an alert female had answered and, within thirty seconds they'd achieved the warm tingle of sisterhood. They'd agreed to meet at the center in the next few days to compare notes.

She leaned back on the bed. London. It really was so similar to New York, she thought, despite all its airs: all the gorgeous, rich people in their princely homes overlooking lovely, verdant parks, and then those horrible contrasting pockets of poverty right out of Dickens. Street crime, muggings, rapes, robberies, all just festering below the regal surface. And those housing "estates," full of dog shit and broken glass and depressingly dirty back gardens; it didn't fool her a minute, London.

Still, they had the best theater in the world, no question. Even the most minor British actor on any British stage made any Hollywood "legend" look like a high-school amateur. And they had Mayfair and Regent's Park, and Buckingham Palace, and those glorious mansions in Hampstead Heath and St. John's Wood, and the most beautiful art galleries and museums anywhere.

There was so much to enjoy, so much to learn, Suzanne thought excitedly. She hoped that "manuscript hunting" (or whatever it was they were supposed to be doing—it wasn't exactly clear to her) wasn't going to occupy too much of her time.

The truth was, she found it hard to take the whole enterprise seriously. Anyone with the slightest perception could see that it wasn't an old manuscript Gran was really after. She was just lonely, Suzanne guessed, and this was a perfect way to get them to spend some time together talking over the past, discussing the future. Why couldn't she just come right out and say that was what she wanted? All this game-playing was so difficult and demanded so much insincerity and double-thinking—not to mention wasted time. But that's the way old people were, especially Europeans. Frankness was not a highly rated virtue, if they put it on the list at all.

It was just as well, Suzanne thought, since she couldn't imagine they stood any kind of chance of actually finding anything. Even if it hadn't been in a fire or lost at sea, it could be anywhere: an attic in Moscow, an old bookstore in Istanbul. . . . Where in heaven's name would anyone even begin to look?

She turned over, picking at the pillow threads. There was only one thing she hadn't yet figured out and it bothered her immensely: the actual state of her grandmother's health.

She slammed her fist into a pillow. Damn! What in heaven's name did she think she was doing, flying across an ocean in her condition? Did her doctor know? Or maybe, just maybe, Mom was right. She wasn't really as ill as she'd let on and that whole pitch had been a giant con job. She certainly didn't look ill. In fact, she looked younger and more vital than she had in a long time.

Maybe the old girl was going to be all right after all, she thought hopefully.

Catherine gathered her pink silk bed jacket around her shoulders, lifting her chin to swallow a handful of pills. They came in all shapes and all uniforms, she noticed, a little army with the generals (painkillers, mostly) and then the corporals, sergeants, and foot soldiers, all slogging through her weary corpuscles, prodding the exhausted battalions longing to surrender to keep on fighting. It wasn't time to give up. Not yet, she thought, swallowing with determination. The water was invigoratingly cool in her throat.

The girls looked so young and so lovely. Yet, just beneath the surface, she sensed their unhappiness. What did anyone so young and so lovely have to be unhappy about? If only they knew what happens to you when you age. If only they understood that life could be measured in finite quantities that were used up and couldn't be replaced. Seconds, minutes, hours. You could calculate exactly how many were given to the average person. Twenty-four hours a day equaled 1,440 minutes times 365 days a year for, let's say, 80 years, gave you—well. . . . She took out a calculator: 42,048,000 minutes a lifetime. And no more. And probably less.

When your body was young and healthy and without pain or disease, and you had so many minutes, hours, days ahead of you to do anything you wanted, how could you feel anything but joy?

But no one is like that. I wasn't. I was always anxious, always unhappy because things were never perfect. I kept thinking: When I grow up and leave my family, then I'll be happy. When I meet my husband and marry, then I'll be happy. When I give birth to this child, then . . . then . . . When all the while my life had been streaming through me, generous and full and seemingly without end. So much it had seemed immeasurable.

I never knew it was so finite, that it could be weighed and counted and measured like diamonds. And I spent it so freely and so unwisely. How many afternoons wallowing in the fashion pages of some silly magazine, or lost in some crossword puzzle, or watching a slick, bad movie or reading a false, poorly written but amusing book? Waste, waste, and more waste. And so many minutes worrying about impending tragedies that never happened, or plotting to prevent those that couldn't be stopped. Only so many minutes, and no more!

If only I had known that then, I should have spent my minutes like the diamonds they were! I would never have been sad for a moment! I would have told myself: This minute, let me feel the warmth of the sun, the joy of learning, of being with my lover, my child, my grandchild, my dear friends.

It was odd that now, full of pain, with so little to look forward to, that she should have finally found joy; that it stared her in the face when she opened her eyes, and laid down next to her pillow each night she succeeded in forgetting the pain and falling asleep. Just the sight of her granddaughters filled her with it. And each minute seemed like a jewel and the spending so thrifty, so right.

No one understood, and you could not explain it without sounding like an old fool, or invoking those infuriating, indulgent winks: how a grandchild saved you, bringing you into a future you would never see or be a part of. How their young bodies and vital lives somehow relieved you of your tired hopelessness, giving you a new chance to correct all the old mistakes.

They were the most precious thing a human being had. You could understand that, the way you couldn't when you had your own children. A child was wonderful, but also burdensome. You were responsible, somehow, for all the grinding details: the food, the clothing, the baths, the cleaning behind the ears and the checking of bowel movements, and the lecturing about report cards.

But a grandchild was something quite different. Yours, without any burden. Yours in the highest, most beautiful sense of being part of your flesh and bones. I nagged them, she lamented, and I shouldn't have. That was their mother's job, not mine. But I did take them traveling. Niagara Falls. Oh, their faces when they saw that great rush of water, oh, their wonder. That was what grandparents were for, she thought. To teach them about the wonder, the beauty, the possibilities. To explain to them how to use that most precious and irreplaceable gift each human has in such finite quantities.

I've been such a bad role model so far, she mourned. What have I taught them except to care about manners, food, clothes? And the *right* people to know. And to invest all those precious hours in chic causes when things that really mattered, life and death. . . .

She touched her damp, hot forehead. NO! No more recriminations. Just joy. I have found the right teacher now. And it isn't too late for either of us, she thought hopefully. She couldn't wait to get them to Serouya and Company, Dealers in Rare Books and Manuscripts. To see their faces. Like Niagara Falls all over again, she thought with a thrill, pulling on her stockings.

And where would they eat dinner tonight? The River Room of the Savoy, of course. And the same table, too, where she had once sat with her fiancé, the heirloom diamond heavy and bright on her finger. The same seat where she had glimpsed for the first time that handsome, intense stranger with the large dark eyes who had transformed her life forever. . . .

Crazy in love, she thought, swaying a moment, almost dizzy with rapture.

15

(In a suitcase in the attic of a house in Grindlewald, Switzerland, found in the mountains on the German side of the border, November 12, 1942. Owner unknown, presumed dead. Fifteen pages, handwritten, Portuguese. Several pages water-stained and unreadable, bound in two pieces of old leather and tied in rags. As yet undiscovered.)

. . . As is it written: "My face is red with weeping and on my eyelids deep darkness."

And so, as I have written in those tear-stained pages that have taken up so much of my ink, my dearest mother died the most unexpected and unjust of deaths, leaving me and Brianda in the care of a father, who, nearly insane with grief, forgot me for a while.

To my misfortune, I was placed in the care of my Aunt Malca, my mother's younger sister.

Malca was childless and newly widowed, but not pitied overmuch, the consensus being that her poor husband had found the shortest and easiest route out of a bad bargain. It was whispered that having squandered her wealth during her husband's lifetime, his death had necessitated the sale of all their property to pay tax and debt collectors. She was now rather destitute, which is why my father—out of respect for my dear mother's memory—had taken her in. More than once have I pondered how the pure seed of such loving-kindness should have sprouted into such a bitter, poisonous weed!

Malca was not a soft bosom to cry upon, nor a pair of motherly arms. To Malca, I was a great, spoiled girl, untutored in the ways of the world, whom it was her awesome and distasteful responsibility to mold into a new image.

I was thirteen, and my sister Brianda eight, when Aunt Malca descended upon us from Evora. Before that, we had seen our aunt only once or twice a year, on holidays, and always her ridiculously gaudy, richly embroidered but tasteless gowns and sour, pinched face had made us giggle and call her "The Golden Lemon" behind her back.

I can almost see her now descending from the large, black coach my father had sent to fetch her. Her eyes, narrow, suspicious, and full of envy, peered up at the tall, curtained windows of our salon, catching my own. As she looked at me I saw a small, crafty, almost wicked smile flash out from the corners of her mouth. There we stood, locked in combat as I stared down and she up, until finally her gaze shifted to my father and brother, who had come out of the house to greet her. I saw her lower her gaze, transformed into the most fragile, modest, and almost embarrassingly servile of creatures.

With Brianda and me, however, she showed quite a different character. Very soon she made it clear who would rule.

Before our sleepy rooster had roused himself for his first triumphant song, Aunt Malca was already tapping at my door. "As it is written, 'slumber is the first step to failure,'" she called out, exhorting me to dress and begin learning my household duties. Thereafter, she used a different proverb a day to rob me of my sleep. "Love not sleep lest you be beggared"; or "Sleepiness will robe a man in rags." And when she wanted to be particularly severe (or when I was particularly tired), she would thunder, "Sleep on, then! Is it not written that: 'The sleep of the wicked is a benefit to them and a boon to the world?'"

There was nothing, it seems, I could do right. I ate too quickly, and *not enough, of foods that would not put the beautiful plumpness on my body she said men found so desirable. I was, she declared, jading my palate with unwholesome foods: garden vegetables meant to feed livestock and cheap fresh fish that was servants' fare.*

It was not long before she was in the kitchen insisting the cook prepare fried breads with honey frostings, almond-paste cookies, and egg-yolk confections called yemas. *In addition, she insisted that with my father's wealth, it was fitting for us to feast upon all the delicacies of the New World: coffee, cocoa, sweet potatoes, and maize. Of course, Aunt Malca never dared demand such fare for herself directly from Father, who, together with my brother, Miguel, continued to enjoy "merchant class" foods: roast capon, saffron-scented rice, and heavenly bean and lamb stews.*

Since Malca, Brianda, and I often dined together—Father and Miguel supping at the odd hours their medical practice required— Malca bullied our poor cook mercilessly into preparing the delicacies she fancied. When she saw that I would partake of no part of that rich, indigestible fare, she declared I was deliberately fasting, and even hinted that she had heard me whispering incantations over the food pots to ruin their taste.

She was not far wrong. For I found all her pretensions and demands mocking to the memory of my dear mother, who had exhorted us to live simply and give much to the poor. I would have gone to any length to thwart her. It was only Miguel's, and then Father's, intervention that stopped me from becoming a rattling bag of bones.

She never forgave me.

Or perhaps she was just one of those people I have encountered so frequently, particularly among women who lack the love of husband and child, who cannot stand to see another happy. She redoubled her efforts to somehow see me miserable.

My days consisted of endless lectures on house and husband-care: The rooms in a house were best kept dark and wet, with no tables or chairs, well sealed against fleas. And if, despite this, there be evidence of fleas, spread alder leaves and trenches smeared with turpentine and leave a candle burning in the middle so that fleas will stick.

To catch flies, tie bunches of ferns shredded at the edges across a room; or set out a dish of milk with hare's gall or crushed onions, which the flies will sip and then expire.

To keep clothes clean, she maintained, spread them in the sun, and brush with dry twigs. To take out spots, heat urine and soak the spot two days. Then squeeze out. If it wasn't gone, add more urine and fuller's earth soaked in lye (or ashes), and clean with a chicken feather soaked in hot water.

If one's furs got hard, take a mouthful of wine and spit on them. Then throw them on the floor and let them dry.

As for the care of a husband, my aunt declared, one should treat him like a good groom treats a valuable horse: unshoe him, give him good feed, and bed him down!

For hours she would keep me in the kitchen, teaching me her wearisome recipes. The worst, I remember, was her compote. For this dish, I had to shell five hundred new walnuts before their shells hardened, and soak them in well water until they turned black. Then they were boiled and drained and added to pots of honey. This had to settle for three days. On the fourth, we added ginger and cloves, quinces boiled in red wine and strained, powder of hippocras, grains of paradise, galingale, a pound of sugar, and a quart of wine. . . .

It tasted like G-d's gall!

And then she showed me how to make sweet barley soup, a watery horror made with licorice and figs; as well as Flemish broth, a nightmarish confection of water, egg yolks, and white wine.

All this, instead of letting me attend my lessons!

Again, I complained bitterly to my father.

"Try to be gracious, child! Can you not see that I have more important things to do?" he said with impatience.

Fearing his wrath, I could do nothing.

One day, however, he unexpectedly (or had he actually repented and come looking for me?) walked into the kitchen, where I was stirring a pot of boiling beet soup, my sleeves rolled up and my face red hot, as smeared and sweaty as a kitchen maid's. My aunt was ensconced on a kitchen stool eating sweetmeats.

Surveying the scene, my father's face registered a new understanding. "Dear sister," he addressed my aunt politely but firmly, "the poor tutor complains that Gracia has not been to class for several weeks."

"Please forgive me, Don. I am trying to instruct her in the ways of running a household, of which she is scandalously ignorant!"

My father clicked his heels together and bowed. "Nevertheless, good sister, her absences waste the good teacher's time, and my good money. Most of all, it wastes her precious mind."

I was absolutely thunderstruck. Never had my father expressed such a feeling to me.

"To give her religious instruction in the sacred Hebrew texts is foolhardy and dangerous," Malca protested vehemently.

"It is a risk, true. But ignorance is a greater one, or so my dear wife convinced me. So we must trust in G-d's benevolence," he whispered back, equally adamant.

"As you will it. But a woman who learns to read will never wed a nobleman with a great estate or find any husband!" she declared. "She is already too old!"

This was too much for my father.

"Hold your tongue, woman! I have received many offers for Gracia's hand. I do not warrant she is yet ready to choose among them. Noblemen have a way of disappearing for months on business. I am preparing our Gracia to keep his accounts, fight his lawsuits, ransom him if he is kidnapped, and collect his taxes. In addition to that, if she knows how to read and write and think, she will also be better equipped to oversee the servants, who will bake bread, salt and store meat, spin cloth, and sew clothes, and"—he paused, his mouth tight—"stir soup."

My mind could not take it all in. Suitors had come. For me! Again, my mouth went dry. I had not even suspected!

"I never learned to read!" Malca said haughtily, as if that were all that was needed to substantiate the rightness of her claims.

"Ah, but I am sure your dear, late husband had you to thank for his prosperity nevertheless." My father grimaced, turning on his heel and leaving.

Aunt Malca's face took on an eerie resemblance to my soup.

From then on, the war between my aunt and myself took a different course. Instead of torturing me, she began to spoil my sister, Brianda.

Unlike me, Brianda had no patience for quill and paper. Numbers, she said, gave her a terrible ache at each temple. As for her religious instruction, she declared the Hebrew language unlearnable by anyone who was not sixty years old with a great white beard. She never did try to reconcile this opinion with the fact that I, her sister, had easily mastered the Hebrew aleph-bet, whose sounds and letters were so close to our own. She declared that she would pray in Portuguese, so at least she would know what it was her mouth was saying, and imitate those things she remembered our mother doing. Formal instruction wasn't necessary if one had piety in one's heart.

I knew she slept until ten and never performed her morning devotions, unless attempting to impress our father. I scolded her, but she tossed her head and went to Aunt Malca, who accused me of undermining her authority.

Day by day, I saw Brianda change before my eyes. Whereas before she had always been satisfied with the fine weave and simple cut of her dresses, she now whined and demanded that new clothes be ordered for her with fine gold embroidery and real pearls. She had always had a slight tendency to fill her plate overmuch and transfer the damage to her stomach, but now she increased her portions twofold, declaring that her cheeks needed plumping and her bosom ampler padding. Her favorite foods became fried breads and yemas. Very soon, new dresses for Brianda were not a choice, but a necessity.

I could also see my aunt's influence upon her in other ways, some petty and vainglorious, and others quite dangerous. We were on our knees during mass, saying our psalters, when I heard Brianda whisper gloria patri *with the others, instead of keeping silent and thinking, as we always did, "In the name of our Lord, Adonai: Amen!" And then, even more incredibly, I saw her take the Host, chew it, and swallow it instead of leaving it whole in her mouth to take out discreetly once we were alone in our carriages.*

I glared at her, but it was too dangerous to say anything. She gave me a smile of such smug superiority that I felt myself like some great cathedral bell that has been yanked with such force it is nigh to splitting. "Why have you done such things?" I fumed once we were safely on the road, out of earshot of milling eavesdroppers.

She tossed her head at me like a silly brat and stuck out her tongue. I kicked her hard and heard her squeal like a little stuck pig. "Aunt Malca says it does no harm to believe in two Saviors, and as the Host is His body, then I will have all His glory within me should I swallow it," she sobbed, rubbing her leg where the red welt spread like a rash.

I was dumbstruck. "And do you believe, you little fool, that the body of the Lord G-d is in the bread that goes down your throat and is then wasted in the chamber pot!?"

"Aunt Malca says it is very dangerous to believe otherwise, and that one must be sensible, even if others are fools," she declared.

"Does she mean, then, that Mother, Father, Grandfather, and Grandmother—all of our ancestors—were fools?" I screamed at her, pinching the fat, self-indulgent flesh of her white arms, folded so calmly and stupidly over her chest.

She wept and howled and rubbed her arm and her leg and threatened that she would make me pay. That someday, somehow, I would be sorry for how I'd treated her.

Truth be told, I was already sorry. As it is said, if you chew iron, you will swallow nails. I should have befriended my sister and turned her into an ally. Instead, I pushed her closer to Aunt Malca, who continued to feed her far more damaging things than yemas.

But little did I know then how much sorrier I was destined to be. My sister, it seems, had started down a bad path. And a bad path cannot lead to a good place.

16

"This can't be it!"

"Why ever not, Suzanne?" Catherine replied, puzzled.

"But, Gran, it's so . . ."

"Dumpy? Dingy?"

"Well, you'd think they'd look a little more like Sotheby's. . . ."

"What, with posh lighting fixtures and mahogany wainscoting, smelling like wax and brass polish?" Catherine chuckled, leading the way slowly up the rickety old stairwell. Halfway up, she paused, her breathing heavy, her hand outstretched in a speechmaker's gesture of emphasis: "Never be deceived, my dears, by packaging."

On the first landing, metal signs indicated a trading company of some kind; and on the second, old cartons overflowed with long tongues of computer printouts, almost blocking their way.

"Are you sure, Gran?" Francesca shook her head.

"Yes, of course!" Catherine declared, horribly winded and not at all sure. "Keep going. I'll catch up."

When they reached the last floor, there were wooden doors with milky glass inserts on which the name *Serouya* was painted in fading black letters.

"It looks more like some 1950s TV detective agency," Suzanne grumbled.

"And what is a rare-book dealer if not a detective, my dear?" Catherine smiled, relieved, a small shiver of excitement crawling up her spine as she slowly caught her breath.

"A pirate, perhaps?" a deep male voice suddenly answered.

He'd crept up behind them as silently as a mugger, or a person well exercised in the hushed etiquette of libraries.

The women turned and stared.

He wore dark jeans stretched loosely over long, muscular legs, a wide-sleeved Greek fisherman's shirt, open at the collar, and a weathered brown-leather vest. His shoulders were broad, and his forearms as muscular and tan as a dock worker's. His hair, a rich, loamy brown, still bore faint traces of a no-nonsense haircut by a barber who had never heard of mousse or hairdryers. His dark beard was severely trimmed, giving him the gentlemanly, yet slightly rakish, appearance of a sea captain.

Francesca stared at him. There was something aggressive, almost offensive, in the way his broad male body had suddenly insinuated itself between them. She looked into his eyes: they were dark, vital, full of inspired humor.

"Excuse me, but I wasn't aware you were part of this conversation," Suzanne said coolly, thinking that he looked like a depiction of Apollo she'd once seen engraved on a Greek coin.

"Pardon me!" He clicked his heels together with a slight bow. "But I believe that I may be the *only* one here qualified to make any statement at all on this subject."

"Who are you?" Catherine demanded.

The milky glass doors suddenly opened.

"Catherine!"

They saw a girlish blush that startled them creep into their grandmother's pale face.

"Alex," Catherine whispered.

"My dear."

He was an elderly gentleman with impeccably cut silver hair and a dark bespoke suit. They watched in utter astonishment as he bent over Gran's trembling hand and kissed it with courtly affection.

"Long time, Catherine . . ."

"Yes, so it is. . . ."

"Do you two know each other?" Suzanne blurted out, glancing from one to the other.

There was an awkward silence as the two looked at each other meaningfully.

"Yes, we are very well aquainted," Alex Serouya murmured, still holding their grandmother's frail, white hand.

Catherine looked down, overcome.

"Grandmother?" Francesca probbed.

"Don't they know, Catherine?" he asked softly.

She shook her head. "There didn't seem to be any point."

"Give us a hint, will you, Gran?" Suzanne urged, dying of curiosity.

Alex Serouya cleared his throat. "I see that you and my nephew Marius have already met."

"So that's David's son," Catherine said, grateful he'd changed the subject. She looked the young man over more forgivingly. "I wouldn't have suspected it."

Alex laughed out loud. "His mother's Italian, from the Benvenida family in Trieste. He's got all their brilliance and their impulsive charm, as well as those impossible Italian manners. But it's made him one of the best rare-book hunters in England."

"Please, Uncle! In Europe. In the world." Marius shrugged, a slow, impudent grin spreading across his face.

It was impossible not to grin back.

He was the classic heartbreaking male, Francesca decided. The foreign-correspondent or news-photographer type: rootless, coasting on charm, relentlessly in search of wonders. The stability of wife and children, family and friends, would be a chain around his neck, she judged, going into husband-material-assessment mode. All males over eighteen and under sixty were candidates, she finally admitted to herself, embarrassed yet helpless.

Suddenly, he turned to her with a knowing grin. She looked down, confused, wondering if he was a mind-reader. To her dismay, his smile broadened, white and disarming, his large brown eyes narrowing in amusement and an alert intelligence that was at once flattering in its intensity and almost insulting in its presumption of intimacy.

Francesca felt suddenly strangely warm, as if some electric current was passing through her, making her skin tingle and her throat dry. To her utter mortification, there, at the center of her body, some uncouth, savage organ, with no manners and little discipline, began throbbing away. She turned away, cupping her hot cheeks in both palms.

"Ah, yes, one of the best and one of the most foolish in the whole world!" Alex shook his head. "Last winter he took a car across the Carpathian Mountains because of a rumor that hidden in the woods was a small farmhouse attic filled with medieval manuscripts!" He sighed. "It was tantamount to suicide. There were no roads, and if the car engine had broken down, he would have frozen in thirty-five minutes."

"Sounds like fun," Suzanne said, laughing.

"No, actually, it was the stupidest thing you could possibly imagine," Marius admitted genially, rubbing his hands together with vigor. "I'd met some Russian emigrés in Belgium in November who told me about it and offered to go with me in the spring. When I told them I planned to go right away, they ran down the steps of their apartment house and after my car halfway to the border, begging me not to do it. But I, of course, knew better. What a fool! I was lucky to get out alive!" He threw back his head and laughed, his face taking on the irresistible gleefulness of a ten-year-old boy showing girls his bottled spider collection.

"It was most imprudent," Alex remonstrated severely, "but he also brought back three manuscripts that caused a sensation in scholarly circles all over the world."

"Imprudent!" Marius exclaimed. "Why, Uncle, it was bloody suicide, and I was an idiot!"

"Really, Marius, your language!" Alex frowned. But then he smiled. "Quite so."

Francesca smoothed down her hair, watching Suzanne give Marius a sidelong glance of curiosity and admiration that he acknowledged. Her heart sank.

Suzanne. Always Suzanne.

"That, of course, wasn't the worst," Marius continued, "the worst was that time I'd hidden this manuscript in a tin can in the forests outside Bucharest. The secret police let their dogs loose, thinking it was drugs. My leg looked like Russian borscht."

"Ahem!" Alex cleared his throat, laying a restraining hand on Marius's shoulder. "I'm sure the ladies would prefer to hear about the marvelous find you've made for them."

"Oh, Alex! I still can't believe it! After all these years. It's like a miracle."

"Miracle?" Suzanne interjected, still looking Marius over.

"Grandmother!" Francesca blurted out. "Please tell us. . . ."

Catherine patted their arms. "I haven't said anything to my grand-daughters about this, either. I wanted to surprise them!"

"Please, come in, all of you."

The three women followed him through the old doors. The sight took their breath away.

"I'd forgotten," Catherine marveled, sinking into an easy chair and looking around her. Old books in beautiful leather bindings were arranged in ceiling-high bookcases all around the room. Hundreds, even thousands, of them. She had a sudden, strange desire to experience their actual weight in her hands, to feel the tangible remnants of ideas and work that had outlived the physical existence of their authors.

Francesca took a deep breath. There was a certain, indefinable scent, she noted. Not just the old calf-leather bindings or the parchment—but something more, something indefinably mysterious, almost mystical. Like incense on an altar. "How old are they?"

"They range from good first editions of early twentieth-century classics—Conrad's *The Secret Agent,* Forster's *A Passage to India,* Lawrence's *Women in Love*—to medieval Latin and Hebrew manuscripts dating back to 1210."

"Actually, Uncle Alex," Marius interrupted, "we had one scroll that was a Greek translation of the Bible dating from 900 A.D."

"Ah, yes. How could I forget? That was a find! Marius got it from an Egyptian trader who'd found it in the *genizah* in Alexandria . . . but that's a different story. We didn't have it long. Museums all over the world began contacting us as soon as the rumor got out."

"*Genizah?*" Francesca inquired.

"Hebrew books, which contain the sacred name of G-d, cannot be thrown away when they get torn or old. They must either be buried in a cemetery, or put in a safe resting place, usually the attic of a synagogue. Such a repository is called *genizah,* and it is a gold mine for rare-book hunters."

"It must have been quite valuable," Francesca mused. "Was there an auction?"

Alex nodded. "Of sorts. Auctions aren't always necessary. There are just a small number of rare-book dealers and collectors in the world. We all know one another, and even the rumor that a rare book is hiding somewhere will cause an avalanche of activity. It's impossibly competitive. Yet, most of the time, we are aware of which collector has been yearning for a particular book or manuscript. It is only fair to offer it to them first."

"Unless, of course," Marius broke in, "it is a really flashy find that even rich businessmen and rock stars would be interested in. Then it becomes like the jewelry of dead duchesses and presidents' widows: Sotheby's. Bidding wars. Ladies in black dresses and diamonds. Then, of course, whoever spends the most money gets it," he added contemptuously.

"It sounds a little like Indiana Jones. You don't kill one another over old books, do you?" Suzanne chuckled.

"Of course, we stay within the law," Alex hastily assured her with surprising seriousness.

She looked at him in wonder.

"What my dear uncle means," Marius interjected, "is that we *try* to keep within the law, when the laws are *just* and the competition feels obligated by them as well."

"Marius!" Alex shook his head warningly. "He loves to cultivate this swashbuckling image."

"Alex, I really *can't* wait another moment!" Catherine burst out, twisting her rings around her white-knuckled fingers.

"Of course, my dear. Forgive me."

He took a stepladder and climbed almost to the top, unlocking a sealed cabinet and taking out a large folder. He clutched it to his chest, carrying it down the way a fireman might carry a newborn from a burning building. Laying it gently on the desk, he untied the strings.

"Here it is. Fifteen pages of the memoirs of Doña Gracia Mendes."

The pages were scrolled up, but surprisingly white, rolling slightly as the gentle breeze from a ceiling fan wafted over them.

Suzanne stared, thunderstruck. They'd found it! Actually found it. After all these years. It was almost—no, not almost—it *was* a miracle, like a ghost suddenly taking on flesh.

It had a certain scent. They were all struck by it, breathing it in slowly. Pungent. Fragrant. It overwhelmed the teak oil wax and London smog, the Giorgio and Chanel No. 5.

Myrrh? Suzanne thought, or sandalwood? Ambergris?

"It's like an Oriental bazaar," Catherine said softly, feeling lost in a dream as she stared at the pages. "Only fifteen. I was hoping for so much more," she whispered. "For all of it . . ."

Alex squeezed her shoulder comfortingly. "This is a wonderful, wonderful beginning, Catherine! It means it's survived. It's out there."

"Or under there," Marius murmured, looking down at the floor.

"What?" Suzanne looked at him.

Francesca watched his eyes very carefully as he raised them to meet her sister's. Here it comes—she thought dully, her heart already heavy with rejection—that inevitable stare of panting male approval that would begin at Suzanne's long thick hair and move slowly down her milky complexion, high, firm breasts, narrow waist, and long, long legs. . . .

"I mean it could be buried. In graveyards. In suitcases under Jewish houses in Saloniki. Under the canals of Venice. Or under the streets of London, for that matter," he said, his eyes amused and boyishly frank, never roaming from her sister's face.

Francesca looked down, almost giddy with relief.

"So, you think it's hopeless?"

"It's hard to tell," he admitted. "But I have some ideas about where it would be worthwhile to look."

"We were thinking about calling Sotheby's and Christie's next."

He waved his hand disparagingly. "I wouldn't bother. They have what people bring them. They don't have a clue how to track anything down. And frankly, if they find out someone is desperately seeking this particular manuscript, it would give them a good reason to raise their prices."

"Indeed," Alex interjected, nodding. "It's best to be discreet."

"Can I touch it?" Catherine suddenly asked.

"Of course." He smiled. "It's like a newborn. Not as fragile as it looks, despite its age."

She held the pages tenderly with the utmost care, tears springing to her eyes. She tried to gain some control, but it was hopeless. It was as if someone she dearly loved and had not seen for decades had suddenly come in through the door and embraced her.

"Beautiful, beautiful friend," she whispered, running her fingers along the edge. "Girls, would you like to hold it?"

"Yes." Francesca nodded. "Yes, very much."

She traced the lines of script, feeling an odd sensation of warmth that made her head swim. Was it the scent or the heat of the room? Or, perhaps, the man? she admitted reluctantly. Or perhaps, perhaps, it was something else, something quite different . . .

Years ago. In the synagogue on Yom Kippur. Grandpa Carl's strong hands beneath her armpits, lifting her up so that she could reach out and touch the sacred Torah scroll. The dark, unfamiliar letters had seemed to dance off the white parchment and flow toward her face. She'd held out both hands, as if trying to catch drops of some magic elixir. Her fingers had tingled and burned.

"It's magical, no?" Marius said softly, standing next to her. She nodded, handing it to him. The reverence in his big, muscular hands as he handled it touched and surprised her.

"What about me?" Suzanne interjected, feeling left out.

Marius handed it to her.

Gracia Mendes. Suzanne studied the handwriting, wondering at the clean, handsome script. There was nothing flowery or pretentious about it. In fact, it was something like her own, she thought, startled.

Chromosomes and DNA. Part of me, like it or not? She handed it back quickly.

Marius looked her over curiously.

"Do you wish to take it with you now, Catherine?" Alex asked.

"No, not to the hotel. . . . If it's all right with you, Alex, I'll arrange to have it shipped home from here. But I will take the translation with us, if the work is done."

"Yes, of course. We had copies made." He handed her three envelopes.

"Why, I think I'm almost a little afraid! I've waited so long." Catherine smiled, taking them reverently. "Thank you, Alex! Come, girls."

"Wait a moment!" Suzanne held up her hand. "Aren't you going to tell us where you found it?"

"Ah, we never disclose the secrets of the trade." Marius grinned. "But maybe I'll give you a hint next time we meet." He shook Catherine's hand warmly. "I'm happy for you. And for the manuscript. It's very gratifying to be able to return it to its rightful owners, people who will cherish it always."

"Yes, always." Catherine nodded, looking hopefully at Suzanne and then at Francesca, her hands shaking slightly with fear.

17

"Gran, who is he? How do you know him?" Francesca burst out as soon as they emerged into the street.

"More important, did Granpa Carl know about him?" Suzanne added wickedly.

Catherine looked pained. "Please, girls. Don't ask me anything now. I promise to tell you everything tonight, over dinner. It'll be easier then," she pleaded. "Now, what shall we do with the rest of this lovely day?"

"Well, we could try to get down to Oxford and the Bodleian Library. That was the next thing on our itinerary, Gran," Francesca suggested, leafing through her day planner and studying it earnestly.

"Oh, Oxford is such a long drive. Shall we be very wicked and simply take the rest of the day off? How about a stroll through Hyde Park to feed the ducks? Or . . ."

"Actually, Gran," Suzanne cut in hesitantly, "if we're going to have a little free time, there's this Women's Crisis Center I'd like to visit. You know, to exchange information about services. I've already spoken to them on the phone." An idea suddenly struck her. "How about joining me! It's really very . . ."

Francesca coughed. "I'm going with Gran to take care of the duck-food crisis."

"Very funny!"

"Now, now, girls." Catherine shook her head tiredly. "Have it your own way. But don't forget, we are having dinner together this evening."

Suzanne fingered her silver bracelet nervously. "That's another thing, Gran. I'd love to, really. But I'm not sure when I'll be finished at the center, and the woman I spoke to sort of invited me to meet with some other activists tonight . . . to, you know . . . sort of talk about joint projects."

Not another family dinner!! Jesus! The whole thing was beginning to feel like the plot of some old *Twilight Zone* nightmare: guest at family get-together becomes eternal prisoner when the party never ends. "You wouldn't mind, Gran, if I excused myself just this once, would you?"

"Yes," Catherine said stonily, "I would."

Suzanne looked at her grandmother's implacable face and swallowed hard. "Well, then, I suppose I'll meet you there. Time? Place?" she murmured with a hurtful lack of enthusiasm that cut Catherine to the quick.

"Seven-thirty. The River Room of the Savoy hotel."

"Come, Gran." Francesca took her grandmother's arm and tucked it possessively beneath her own, glaring at Suzanne. "Don't be late, Suzanne," she warned, shaking her head.

The Women's Crisis Center was packed. Amber-skinned Indians in graceful flowing saris, deep brown Africans in colorful flowered prints and regal turbans, tan Pakistanis, and blond Anglo-Saxons sat side by side on the worn benches. Many held small children in their arms. It was way too crowded, and the queues for financial, social, or medical advice seemed endless.

Yet, there was an atmosphere of womanly camaraderie, the mothers trading toys and offering candies to one another's unhappy toddlers; pregnant women leaning forward, deep in discussion. Only a few women sat silently apart—the youngest and prettiest—listlessly flipping through old magazines, not really seeing the pages.

"We've got plans to expand into the storefront next door," explained Regina, the director, her mellifluous Caribbean accent making every sentence end on a note of optimism.

Suzanne was both excited and appalled at the sheer diversity of problems under one small roof. Child- and wife-abuse cases; rape and incest victims; malnourished toddlers and unemployed immigrant parents on the verge of desperation; unwed mothers and panicked teenagers seeking a quick, safe way out of recreational pregnancies. . . .

"How many on staff?" she asked.

"You mean *paid* employees?" Regina paused, counting on her fingers. She didn't need, Suzanne noted, to use both hands. "I'm not really sure. Our funding is so erratic. Foundations and wills and then some government ha'pennies raining down from heaven now and again. We used to pay our doctor, because he was so important to all the women—health issues are connected to everything we do. The stress of poverty is the most unhealthy thing there is. About two years ago, he got married and moved to Birmingham. We were bloody desperate for a while, until the Baron saved us."

"The Baron?"

"Dr. Gabriel. It's a nickname he hates. He just walked in one day and rolled up his sleeves. After a few months, we actually begged him to take some money, but he just waved us away like were mosquitoes. He's a godsend. The women adore him, and so do the kids."

"Sounds lovely," Suzanne murmured, imagining some bald, pot-bellied old dear retired from the National Health Service come to do some good works before showing his time card to St. Peter. Well, better late than never, she sighed.

"Could I see some of your informational handouts, especially the ones to abused women?" she asked.

"Sure." Regina started opening drawers and pulling leaflets out of cubbyholes.

"Number fifty-six," the nurse called out, and there was a momentary hum of consternation in the crowded waiting area as the women anxiously pulled out their numbers and compared them.

Suzanne glanced through the open door to the clinic. She blinked, then looked again, long and hard.

He was sitting casually on his desk, a tall young man in his late twenties with the clean, bold shine of the golden college boy. His hair was shoulder-length, thick and blond, held back neatly in a ponytail, And in one ear, she saw the unmistakable shine of a small gold earring. Just before the door closed again, she glimpsed that beneath his white doctor's coat he wore a Spanish vest embroidered in elaborate and beautiful colors.

She looked down listlessly at the brochures offering sensible advice and numerous useful phone numbers to London's most fragile inhabitants, all the while waiting for the door to open again so she could make sure the vision wasn't a mirage.

The next patient, who looked like a sixteen-year-old who had been married for twenty years, was cradling a baby and had a two-year-old clinging with awesome tenacity to her milk-stained sari. But as hard as the mother pulled, and as vociferously as she insisted, the terrified child would simply not budge.

"Problem?" The doctor leaned against the door frame, his upper-class elegance incongruously framed by its peeling, chipped wood. He looked at the mother and child with slanting blue eyes full of gently amused concern. Then he crouched, holding out large, beckoning hands to the child, whose fright had already mellowed into uncertainty. The doctor was saying something in low, coaxing tones, his face all the while serious and respectful. The child suddenly smiled. Magically, Suzanne watched him take small, but eager steps forward, finally placing his hand in the doctor's.

She found herself staring, mesmerized by the sight of the long white fingers wrapped around the small brown ones. And when the door closed behind them, she had a strange sense of emptiness and loss, as if she'd been somehow shut out.

"So that's the Baron?"

"Who?" Regina murmured, still sifting through the papers.

"Your Dr. Gabriel. Is he young, blond?" Suzanne finally asked, point-blank.

Regina grinned knowingly. "Love at first sight, eh? Well, my dear. Take a number. Around here, we queue up for that, as well," she said, laughing.

Suzanne did something she hadn't done since Gran had caught her with a naked stranger in her bed. She blushed.

She said her good-byes soon after, curiously disturbed and eager to be alone. Outside, she noticed a red Alfa-Romeo convertible with a sign in the window: PHYSICIAN ON DUTY.

She went straight back to the hotel, where she roamed aimlessly around her room, fingering the wallpaper and twirling her silver bracelet around her wrist. She paused in front of the mirror, staring. My eyes are desolate, she thought, frightened, getting into bed and hugging herself long and hard against an almost unendurable ache of loneliness.

Lost, she thought, picking up the phone and dialing Paris.

"Thierry, bonsoir! C'est moi. Suzanne. Ça va . . . ? Moi? Bien, bien!" she said, trying to muster a little sincere enthusiasm. *"A Londre en famille."* She got tired of the French. "Have you seen Renaldo lately? Really, how is he? . . . Good, good." Tears sprang to her eyes. "What's he teaching? . . . Ah, Impressionists. He'll be in Paris, then, all summer. . . . Brazil? To see his children? Are you sure? . . . Oh, not definite. . . . No, no reason, I just wondered. If you see him . . . no. Nothing. Give Artur, Sylvan, and Cecilia my love. Tell them to call me? Here's the number." She read it to him quickly. "I'll be here a few days at least, and then, I don't know. . . . Thanks, Thierry. *Au revoir, chéri.*"

She put the receiver down and held her face in her hands, squeezing the temples. Lost, she thought. Lost, lost, lost.

She laid down and pulled the covers over her head, trying hard to picture Renaldo's large, dark head, his unruly hair, and deep, laughing eyes. But the picture wouldn't hold still. It kept getting displaced by long, thick, blond hair and gentle, white hands that beckoned with the promise of kindness.

18

They turned down The Strand, a busy London street lined with stores selling computers and cellular phones. Set back, and almost as removed in time as it was in space, was the Savoy hotel.

A doorman in a gold-braided uniform opened the doors and tipped his cap. Inside, one expected to see Winston Churchill, or to hear a radio announcing the latest news from the front. Time seemed simply to have stopped in 1940.

Overstuffed sofas and mahogany bookcases filled with leather-bound books framed a warming fireplace with blazing logs. Elsewhere, ladylike chairs clustered around small tea tables spread with pink-linen tablecloths and fresh flowers. In the center of the room was a white, trellised gazebo surrounded by baskets of fresh flowers.

"Wow!" Francesca whistled.

"Wait," Catherine smiled.

The restaurant was at the far end of the lobby, set off by etched glass. It was almost dark, lit by flickering pink candles and a few wall sconces that bathed the room in a delicate, almost magical light. Pink-marble columns with gilded capitals divided the room, and gracefully draped mauve-satin curtains framed the windows. In the far corner stood a small silver gazebo beneath which a band played swing music.

But the true beauty of the room was the stretch of windows overlooking the Thames. The lights of the National Theatre and Royal Festival Hall danced over the calm waters, joining the wall sconces and candles to bathe the large silver dessert carts and the enormous silver chafing dishes in a soft, charming glow.

"There used to be a terrace," Catherine said, suddenly remembering. "On a summer evening, you could sit outside and watch the boats along the Thames. There were fewer lights then—just Waterloo Station and the docks."

"But otherwise, is it really the same as you remember, Gran?" Francesca marveled, eying a slender woman in a backless black evening gown, wishing she had one just like it.

Catherine nodded. "The most romantic place in the world. A perfect setting to talk about the memoirs." She turned to them, her face suffused in a lovely, joyous glow. "Have you read it?"

"Couldn't put it down! It was . . . mesmerizing," Francesca said, her eyes wide. "She seemed so near, somehow. Her problems, her attitudes. And what a love story! Fabulous!"

A short, distinguished waiter with graying hair seated them immediately.

"I'm glad." Catherine nodded, very pleased. "What about you, Suzanne?"

Suzanne picked up a fork and tapped it lightly, first the handle, then the prongs, in an irritable rhythm. She was wondering if she should be nice and lie, or tell the truth and get into enormous trouble. The former, probably. But, somehow, she couldn't muster the necessary energy. She hadn't read it and had only the slightest curiosity about what someone five hundred years dead had to say.

Humanity was entering a new stage. The old ways of thinking were dismal failures. Just look at the world! All the old mechanisms that had separated people for so long had to break down. The answer was to cast off our failed history, the useless traditions that weighed us down, preventing us from coming together to ensure our survival on the planet. . . .

She looked around the room. After spending the afternoon listening to the problems of single mothers and new immigrants, crushed by Britain's antediluvian class system, such a place made her want to sock someone in the mouth.

"You know what's the matter with this place?" she said, ignoring the question. "It hasn't changed, but the world sure has. This is a dinosaur. I mean, evening gowns? And the prices. You could feed a family of five for two weeks." She shook her head, staring at the menu.

"A dinosaur," Catherine repeated. "That's what anything preserved out of the past is to you, isn't it? Some useless old fossil to be buried, or used for fertilizer? I suppose it would be better if they'd renovated the hotel with the times. We could all be eating fast food out of Styrofoam containers, standing up by Formica counters, for the cost of a McDonald's burger."

"Gran, really. I just meant . . . what has all this got to do with me?"

"That's really how you feel about the manuscript, too, isn't it?" Catherine asked evenly.

"In a way," Suzanne answered defiantly.

Catherine felt the waves of a monster headache begin at the back of her head. It was all such a farce, she thought hopelessly, just as she'd secretly feared it would be.

"'What does it have to do with me? Me, *me, ME*?'" Catherine mimicked in a rising crescendo of indignation. "That's all you ever hear nowadays! Women living alone because they can't find the perfect man for 'me'; married women refusing to put aside the 'me' for even a little while to care for others. Men out grabbing whatever's dangling from the branches of Eden, no questions asked and anyone else but 'me' be damned!"

"Look, Gran, I didn't mean to upset . . ." Suzanne began contritely, startled by her anger.

"No, let me finish! A generation of the damned, you all are! Everybody out for themselves, because 'me' is the only thing that matters. You've all forgotten . . ."

"Please, Gran, calm down," Francesca begged, glaring at Suzanne.

"Forgotten what?" Suzanne demanded, sick and tired of the whole thing.

"That you're a link. And a link cannot pick itself up and walk off."

"Shackles," Suzanne muttered to herself.

"Yes, shackles. But also a golden chain, a lifeline that'll keep you from stumbling off the cliff and falling into the vat of sleaze that some people are calling their lives these days!"

"Hmm. So let me get this straight: vats of sleaze, that's what you automatically dive into when you break with family tradition. Interesting. Let's take this to its logical conclusion," Suzanne continued with mock reasonableness, tapping her chin mildly with the tip of her finger. "Let's say you're from a tribe of headhunters and you decide you don't want to follow Granddad's footsteps and decapitate your neighbors and feast on their livers . . ."

"Be serious!" Catherine demanded.

She shrugged helplessly. "I *am* serious, Gran."

The rising tones were gathering odd stares around the room, Catherine noticed, taking a deep, calming breath. "I was once at a lecture given at Cambridge. 'Christianity and History,' I think it was called. I have no idea why I went, except perhaps to keep your grandfather company. And there was this marvelous, articulate don—Butterfield was his name, I believe—standing there very calmly presenting his learned case. For some reason, what he said made a great impression upon me. He said that there were many things you could do with the past. You could sing songs about it, or tell tales. And there were some people, like the Germans, who romanticized it until it became a national disease, and a terminal one at that. But what every person had to do, he insisted, was have an attitude toward it. He said, 'You've got to examine *your* past and make a decision. Because it's going to affect how you see the world, and your place in it.'"

She felt hot tears sting her eyes as she looked at both her granddaughters. "And I'm telling you both," she said fiercely, "that when you look at *your* history you're going to be glad and proud. And if you've got any heart or intelligence, you're going to want to do exactly what Gracia did—pass it on to those who'll come after. She understood what I just recently learned, that it's really the only way to protect them."

"Protect them from what, Gran?" Francesca asked, intrigued.

"From the bottomless pettiness of an unattached and unexamined life! From waking up one morning and finding you're seventy-odd years old and there's nothing! Nothing in your life worth having or preserving or passing on! That you might as well not have been here at all," she whispered, swallowing hard. "My two beautiful, precious grandchildren. . . . How can I make you understand before it's too late? You think your life is your own, that you're free to do anything, think anything you please, unconnected to what came before and what will come after. And you believe that it is a good thing, a wonderful thing, that freedom.

"It isn't. It's a terrible illusion, the temptation to completely waste your life. Because if you're not connected, your life is a fragment: a bit of cloth, a random page torn out of the middle of a book, useless, meaningless. We're meant to be connected! We're conduits. The past is supposed to pass through us, to connect us to the future.

"Like trees," she murmured, her mind suddenly focusing, her hands clasped hard in her lap. "We're planted in old soil enriched by the lives and deaths of so many who came before us. The nourishment is meant to flow through us, on to the newest branches, so that every branch grows a little taller, and blooms more beautifully still. If you refuse to understand that, if you act as if the world began the day you were born and will end the day you die, then the branches wither, the tree dies. . . ."

She leaned back in her chair in utter exhaustion, closing her eyes.

"Do you want to go lie down?" Suzanne suggested gently, wanting nothing more than to climb back into bed herself. She, too, felt suddenly exhausted. Nothing had been said that she hadn't heard a million times, yet, nevertheless, she felt a particular anguish. It was the fright in her grandmother's tired, almost desperate voice; the wretchedness in her fiercely loving eyes.

I love her, she understood with sudden clarity.

And she really is dying.

Catherine opened her eyes and leaned forward with a brave, but weary, smile. "I don't think bed rest is actually necessary right at the moment. But an aspirin would be helpful." She reached into her purse and took out a vial of pills, popping several in her mouth and swallowing them with ice water. The thunderous crashing at the nape of her neck subsided into the lap of water at the river's edge.

Francesca cocked her head and rested it nervously on her fingertips. Those were no aspirins. Anyone could see that. And Gran suddenly looked terrible, the pink blusher almost comical on her floury-white cheeks.

"I'm sorry I got so upset. I suppose you're right, Suzanne. This place is rather an extravagance. But I'd wanted this to be such a memorable occasion. A celebration." Catherine smiled ruefully, looking around the

warm, glowing room. "And it had to be here. You see, this is such a special place for me. The place I fell in love."

The girls looked at her, startled.

"There," Catherine said, pointing across the room at a table near the
windows. "Right there. That's where he was sitting the first time I saw
him."

"Saw who?" Suzanne asked.

"Why, Carl, of course."

She didn't say "Grandpa Carl," they thought, surprised and oddly
disturbed.

But it wasn't their elderly, beloved grandfather Catherine was seeing
as she stared across the room. It was a young RAF pilot, impossibly handsome, full of dash and charm, whose slanting black eyes peered at her
with mesmerizing intensity from his lean, dark face. He smiled at her, and
waved his jaunty wave. Her face lit up and she almost waved back when
the vision suddenly vanished. She felt her skin rise in small, cold bumps.

"Were you here alone?" Francesca asked, trying to picture it.

"No." Catherine passed her palm over her welling eyes, baptizing the
vision now lost to her. "I was here with my fiancé. It was three weeks before our wedding."

There was a stunned silence.

"Do you mean to say you broke your engagement three weeks before your wedding and ran off with Grandpa instead?" Suzanne tittered
with glee.

"There is no reason to laugh!" Catherine frowned. "It was wildly romantic and—I would have to add if it all hadn't worked out so well—
impetuous and foolish. I was sitting here with Alex Serouya . . ."

"What?" Francesca gasped.

"But you just said that you were here with your fiancé. What does
Alex Serouya have to do . . . ?" Suzanne interjected. "Wait a second! You
can't mean that you and Alex Serouya—"

"YOU WERE ONCE ENGAGED TO ALEX SEROUYA?!" Francesca
exclaimed, choking on her wine.

"Quiet, Francesca, manners, please!" Suzanne mocked, doing a perfect imitation of Francesca the Level-Headed.

"Sorry." Francesca gasped, trying to catch her breath.

"Yes. Alex Serouya and I were once engaged to be married." Catherine paused, the light in her eyes deepening. "We'd known each other since we were children. Our families were very close. It was always assumed that he and I would marry. And it wasn't as if I didn't love him. He was—is—a very intelligent, warm, kind-hearted person. And he loved me." She looked down into her lap, where her fingers were twisting a napkin into knots. "As I was saying, we were sitting here, Alex and I, discussing our wedding plans, our new home. I had his beautiful engagement ring on my finger—a family heirloom over two hundred years old, little rubies surrounding a perfect three-carat diamond—when I looked up and saw Carl.

"He was sitting with my cousin Blanche on the terrace. It was summer. He was in uniform, the handsomest man I'd ever seen in my life," she said dreamily, winding a lock of gray hair idly around her finger.

The contrast between that gesture, so young and girlishly sweet, and the drooping, creased flesh of those aged arms made Suzanne want to weep. And she would have, were not the lecture on the joys of tradition and adherence to the hallowed past now coupled with her grandmother's sudden admission of flagrant disregard for both not so deliciously amusing.

Way to go, Gran! Seize the day! Suzanne thought, exhilarated. But could it be seized? Any more than you could seize a wave and prevent it from turning into mist? she wondered, studying her grandmother's sagging chin.

This, she realized, not death, was her deepest fear. This slow, irreversible decay where your young, vital self simply vanished irretrievably into tired layers of aging flesh. . . .

"I just can't picture you doing it, Gran. Dumping a fiancé and running off with a stranger right before your wedding!" Francesca declared, unsettled.

"I . . . uh . . . suppose one might put it that way," Catherine admitted, squirming. And then, strangely, she giggled, her eyes sparkling. "I know it sounds shocking. How can I make you understand?"

She closed her eyes.

There was music, wasn't there? Violins? No! That's old movies. A pianist in a white evening gown. Chopin. An étude? And Alex's warm hand cupped over hers. And then her eyes suddenly looking up as the music filled the room like sparkling Champagne.

"It was the middle of the war. Pilots were dying every day, every day. And houses all around us were getting bombed, everyone dead in a minute. And he looked so carefree, laughing, a cigarette dangling from his lips." And suddenly, with no warning, the urge to touch him, to press her fingers into the thick dark hair, to hear his heart pump the good, strong lifeblood through undamaged veins, and the sudden knowledge of her own young blood throbbing and warm and fragile beyond imagining. The idea that she, too, at that moment, was alive and full of passion, and that the next bomb could end that in the blink of an eye . . . And then, as if he'd read her mind, Carl walking across the room until he was standing in front of her.

"He came over with my cousin. . . ."

Polite words, barely heard, and then his sitting opposite, the warmth of his body somehow already part of hers, and knowing, just knowing that this connection was going to be forever.

For an instant, Suzanne and Francesca had the startling sensation that they were sitting with someone else, someone younger whose body radiated feminine power. The blue eyes, clear and tender, flashed with excitement in the center of her lovely heart-shaped face. For the first time in their lives they sensed the woman in her, the peer, someone a strange man could fall desperately in love with by simply glimpsing her across a crowded room.

Perhaps then, Suzanne thought, our youth always breathed still within us, contained, not lost? Conduits, she thought, startled. "How did Alex take it?"

"He was devastated," Catherine admitted, gripping a spoon with white-knuckled fingers. "But there was nothing I could do. How can I make you understand?" She struggled, overwhelmed by the task. "It was . . . it's like . . ." Her features suddenly relaxed, serene. "It was like hearing something you had always known was true, something that matched exactly all the information stored in your heart. There was no question of disagreeing, of finding reasons to resist."

"But Gran, what about the 'family'?" Suzanne mocked, her face full of theatrical opprobrium and wicked humor.

Catherine flinched. "It was very painful for them, in the beginning."

Harsh and demolishing, the pain. But like childbirth, so necessary and unavoidable that in advance one had to forgive and plan to forget.

"But everyone got over it. Carl was Jewish, also from a good Sephardic family."

"Oh, now I get it! How convenient for you! I suppose if he hadn't been, the family would have had a little talk with him and he would have simply vanished! Excuse me. I'm going to powder my nose," Suzanne said with a bitterness she herself found startling. She grabbed her purse and walked out of the room.

Catherine watched her, devastated.

Would she have given him up if he had been from the wrong family, the wrong religion? Or run off with him anyway, abandoning her family forever? There was no point in pretending she knew the answer. Either act required a kind of courage that had never been asked of her.

She faced the humbling thought that it was neither courage nor virtue that allowed her to now sit before her granddaughters championing all the traditional values. It was simply luck. Or the guiding, providential hand of some *memuneh*.

That old word! Resurrected from memories long past of her own grandmother's artful tales. A word connected to summer evenings and rocking chairs, her head resting on her loving *abuela*'s broad, soft lap. Everything had a *memuneh*. Every blade of grass, every tree, every human. A guardian angel who helped arrange your future by guiding you through the present; celestial lawyers who pleaded before the heavenly court when you erred, convincing G-d to give you another chance before assigning your sins their just desserts.

She looked down at her own white, blue-veined hands. Had she the right or the skill to play her granddaughters' *memuneh?*

Francesca—who had not been able to get beyond the news of her grandmother's wild, passionate fling—sat there thinking: Did that mean that the unbearable cliché sometimes actually happened? Eyes meeting across a crowded room. Instant love that lasts forever? And how ironic, the memoirs, too . . . !"

It seemed unlikely. After all, what could you really know about such a person? Appearances were so untrustworthy. The moment you got into bed with a man, it wasn't his attractive face or the strong shape of his body that was important, but simply the tenderness of being touched like a cherished thing.

Case in point: tall, handsome Peter. He had never made her feel cherished, only used. He hadn't loved her. That was the short of it. *Her* story as opposed to her grandmother's, who had had the luxury of sitting with an adoring, diamond-bestowing fiancé while a handsome stranger fell madly in love with her. Who had had two men who loved her, simultaneously.

I still haven't found one, she mourned, smiling at the absurdity of her jealousy. Well, if such a thing were going to happen, this certainly was the right setting for it, she admitted, looking across the elegant, crowded spaces of the magical room. She blanched.

"It's him!" she exclaimed.

"Who?" Catherine looked up, not quite sure of her own eyes anymore.

"The guy with the beard. The manuscript hunter."

"Marius?"

Francesca nodded. He was suddenly looking across at her, smiling—a wide, beautiful smile of great vitality that seemed to blaze across the floor.

"He's getting up and he's bringing someone with him!"

He took long strides, deliberate yet leisurely, as if every step were bringing him pleasure.

"Mrs. da Costa, Francesca." He bowed, looking at both women meaningfully.

He remembers my name, Francesca thought, embarrassed by how much it meant to her. He looked remarkably different in a suit, even though his shirt was still open-collared and he wore no tie. Like a diplomat from a small, informal country, Francesca thought. Distinguished and somehow more mysterious than ever.

"May I introduce my friend, Dr. Gabriel Fonseca."

Catherine looked up at the young man, examining the ponytail, the earring, and the embroidered Spanish vest. She was not fooled by the lapses in his appearance. He was a British aristocrat, scion of a distinguished Church of England family, one of those champion Cambridge rowers who slide along the Cam with the graceful, steady strength of those born to it. She was sure of it. She bit her lower lip furiously.

"I'm afraid I can't ask you to join us. We'll be leaving shortly," Catherine said coolly.

Marius seemed surprised by the rebuff, but his companion looked positively relieved.

"It is just as well, as we would be tragically unable to accept, having a train to catch and an appointment to keep," Gabriel Fonseca said, nudging Marius.

"And where is Miss Suzanne?" Marius asked with determined politeness, ignoring them both, his eyes restlessly searching the room.

Francesca fingered her rib cage, rubbing away what felt like a physical stab of pain. Suzanne, always Suzanne.

"Oh, powdering her nose, I think she said," Catherine replied, her eyes darting around the room with panic, praying they'd leave before she returned. There was just too much mesmerizing male power in this blond Adonis to introduce him to her impetuous granddaughter. "And there's no telling how long that might take. Please, don't let us keep you," she said with a firmness bordering on outright rudeness.

Francesca stared, bewildered.

"Then perhaps another time. How long do you plan to remain in London?" Marius inquired stubbornly.

"Only another week, I'm afraid."

"What! I had no idea you were leaving so soon! I have so much still to tell you. Gabriel has the beginnings of one of the finest rare-manuscript collections in London. His father—the Baron of Avernas de Gras—has one of the most valuable eighteenth-century collections of French first editions in England. I'm sure both of them could be quite helpful to you."

Avernas de Gras, Catherine mused, as if trying to remember something. She studied the blond stranger more carefully. "And do you share Marius's passion for the past?"

"The first time I went manuscript hunting with Marius, we came across a leather-bound book in the attic of a condemned old building in a Polish village. Something about the smell of the books—so old and full of the scent of so many different hands—hooked me. I can't even explain why. As for my collection, I'm afraid I owe that to the prudence of forebears who left me with the means to indulge quite a few private passions."

"And his good fortune has been my good fortune. He's a delightful partner, and he often pays the bills," Marius laughed. "If we had time, we

could tell you all about our trip to the jungles of Brazil. But unfortunately . . ." he glanced at his watch and tapped it, annoyed at the information it gave him. "Can I talk you into extending your stay? I promise
it will be worth it. Here, take my card. Call me whenever you can and I'll
arrange something. Please do!" he pleaded. "Uncle is wonderful, but his
methods and advice are a bit too . . . conservative. Let me help you to
find the rest of it. If it's anything like what I've already read . . ."

"So, you've gone through it . . ." Catherine looked up, her face
brightening.

He nodded. "I think," he said, bending over Catherine's hand and
kissing it gallantly, "that I am a little in love with your Gracia."

Francesca felt her own fingers tingle.

"Can I hope we will be able to get together soon?" he said, his voice
filling the words with significance.

Both women nodded, watching the young men's straight, handsome backs as they turned and walked past the etched glass into the
lobby.

Charming, Catherine mused, studying their handsome, masculine
movements as they crossed the room.

Suddenly, she saw Suzanne.

She was walking back toward the restaurant, her strikingly lovely
body making small dips and curves as she navigated her way around
the tea tables. Her hair had been brushed out from its chignon and fell
like a glowing sunset to her bare shoulders, framing her face. The dark
green Chinese silk of her elegant, form-fitting dress caught and deep-
ened the color of her eyes, making them sparkle like jewels against her
pale, flawless skin. She looked, Catherine thought, like a queen.

With a sense of helpless déjà vu, she saw the blond stranger stop and
stare for a moment, then take slow, deliberate strides in her direction.
Suzanne's shoulders stiffened in surprise, her limbs assuming an odd
stillness, as if she'd just received shocking news. They stood facing each
other for what seemed to Catherine like an amazingly long time. And
then, without speaking a single word, both of them turned and disappeared.

An hour later, as the tea cooled in the cups, and the remains of
chocolate éclairs dirtied the dessert plates, Suzanne had still not returned.

Francesca threw down her fork. "Of all the inconsiderate, selfish things! But I guess that's to be expected. After all, we haven't been abused and aren't starving in the street. We're just her family!" She reached out to her grandmother, patting the wrinkled old hand, dreading looking into her face. "*Abuela,* don't be upset! You know Suzanne. She's always got better things to do!"

Catherine made an odd noise.

Francesca looked up in alarm. Her mouth dropped in astonishment. Gran looked absolutely radiant!

"Avernas de Gras," Catherine said, shaking her head in laughter. "The grandson of Antonio da Silva! Yes, I would agree. Much better things to do!"

19

Manuscript pages. Circa 1600–1660. Purchased by Ruiz Martínez of Librería Antiquario, Barcelona. Provenance unknown. Sold to Serouya and Company, London, for private collection of Mrs. Catherine da Costa.

P*assion.*
 I hold my quill in fingers gone stubby and pale with age and write this word, knowing full well that it will shock you, my children. That you will feel ashamed that I, a woman fading into that haggard precursor of death, not only still remember such things, but feel the joy of her remembrances.

Yet I will say its name. Did not our wise and most G-d-fearing King Solomon write: "When I found him whom my soul loveth; I held him, and would not let him go/Until I had brought him into my mother's house . . . Let him kiss me with the kisses of his mouth/for his love is better than wine?" And did he not write further: "To every thing there is a season, and a time to every purpose under the heavens"?

Before I knew such a season existed, it was upon me—ravishing all my senses with the mesmerizing heat of summer, the fecund richness of fall, and the dangerous wildness of a winter storm.

I thought I should surely die.

It began on a bright, cool autumn day. The smell of old leaves drying in the sun, the moist and fecund earth filled my nostrils as I walked into the forest with my family to secretly celebrate the Feast of Tabernacles.

It was in the aftermath of Diego Vaz de Oliverca and Andres Diaz de Viana, the converso *priests who slew the despicable apostate Henrique Nuñez as he kneeled in the Church of Valverde dedicating himself to barbarous treachery against his brothers.*

For Nuñez had been brought from the Canary Islands to begin that fearful process of inquiry and torture meant to destroy those among the New Christians who had kept faith with their heritage. His death had ended for the moment the prospect of the Inquisition's horrors being exported to Portugal. But the incident, and the execution of Oliverca and Viana, had cast its terrifying shadow, making us conversos *doubly cautious.*

We'd prepared our sukah *in a forest clearing far from prying eyes. It had three sides of wood over which we draped fine rugs and tapestries; and a ceiling of green branches from which we hung pomegranates, apples, grapes, and sweet, baked* biscochos. *The scent of myrtle twigs, willows, and hyssop filled the air.*

Though I knew that the sukah *was meant to be a humble shack, reminding us that, however fine our solid homes, we were wanderers like our forefathers, dependent on G-d's providing hand, it made me feel like a fairy princess, reigning in her sylvan bower.*

The only irritant to my joy was my appearance. I felt childish in the long-waisted amber gown with the high white-lace collar, because my aunt had refused to let me wear a farthingale, declaring it was not fitting for an unbetrothed girl of thirteen to sway and show her hips. My hair was even worse: Plaited and drawn back beneath my barbette and fillet, it made me look like some pious young novitiate.

While the women took out the pot hooks, the pipkins, and porringers to prepare our festive meal, I longed to join the men as they gathered to discuss matters of holy ritual or the profane intrigues at court. But I knew my aunt would not allow it. So I leaned listlessly against a tree, trying to think of some way to amuse myself, when a beautiful small doe darted past. I cannot tell

THE GHOST OF HANNAH MENDES 169

*you why, but something in her loveliness and her movement
beckoned me to follow, and I did, chasing her deep into the forest
until at last I was snared by a well-hidden root. I felt a sharp
wrench to my ankle, and fell into an ignominious heap upon the
damp ground.*

*Stunned, I lay there unable to move, realizing with fright how
far I had drifted from the others. Thoughts of bears, wolves,
snakes, and bands of cutthroat scavengers inflamed my
imagination. I closed my eyes and called to G-d and to my
memuneh to help me win the heavenly battle against demons of
rock and tree, animal and human, now ranged in battle against
me! And just when my terror peaked, I heard the sound of hooves
beating their way through thick foliage.*

*I lay there, frozen with horror, awaiting some terrible outrage
to my property or, worse, my person. But when I looked up, two
well-dressed strangers looked down upon me from the saddles of
their beautifully caparisoned horses. I looked frantically from one
to the other, searching their faces for my fate. And the more I
searched, the more convinced I became that His blessed hand had
reached out to me, for neither seemed inclined to strip me either of
my finery or my honor.*

*"Are you hurt, child?" one of them asked me kindly. There was a
powerful strength of character in his sharp features, which might
have frightened me had they not been softened by a refinement
that lent them a quiet kind of nobility. He had dark hair and the
swarthy complexion of an Italian prince. His attire was royal-
looking, too: a striking black doublet of rich, patterned velvet with
a scabbard of beaten gold, embedded with tiny jewels that
sparkled like a thousand small stars.*

"Say something, muchachica!*" his companion added
impatiently. He was blond, with the smooth and ruddy color of a
happy child and the gay attire of a young nobleman: a* cote hardie
with trunk hose and a high, feathered hat.

"I'm not a muchachica!*" I cried childishly, forgetting all about
highwaymen and being terrified, remembering only the argument
I'd had with Aunt Malca that very morning on the same subject. "I
am a young lady from a very good family!"*

I saw a strange transformation come over the face of the dark-haired prince as his companion threw back his head and roared with laughter.

"Forgive us, Doña. We have been to sea so long we have forgotten how to treat young ladies, particularly gente grande," the dark one said seriously, but with an infuriating merriness about the eyes he could not hide.

But as I glared at him, I suddenly realized how ridiculous my haughty words must be in light of my vagabondish appearance. For my dress had been muddied by matted wet leaves and my hair disheveled, escaping its hated confines and streaming wildly down to my waist. I looked like a scullery maid. Or worse.

"But it is not as it appears," I protested, stamping my foot in frustration. I let out a sharp moan.

In one swoop, the dark prince lifted me up and I found my cheek resting against that rich, soft material stretched over his broad shoulders. "Where is your family, señorita?" he asked, without a hint of mockery this time.

Impulsively, I pointed in the direction from which I had come. I regretted it immediately, realizing the danger of exposing our secret forest rituals to strangers. I demanded to be put down and let go in peace.

"You are injured, child. I must see you to them safely," he said, ignoring my frantic entreaties and spurring the horse to a gentle trot. And then he leaned over me and whispered close to my ear, "Never wander, child. Such loveliness is prey in this world. One in possession of it must guard it closely."

I stopped struggling, feeling a burning tingle that began in my forehead and streamed through my body. And as I peeked at the dark rim of his eyes, the rich thickness of his manly beard, I felt a clap and a sharp, white-hot wrench to my heart.

It was the moment where one's soul enters into another's and emerges, dazzled.

I sat erect, my back frozen so as not to touch his, my eyes staring ahead stupidly. It was a reaction, I thought, perfectly in keeping for anyone struck by a thunderbolt.

Already I hear the clammering of my grandchildren's sweet,

questioning voices rising urgently: "Why?" they shout. "What
happened?"

How can I tell you, my children?

I can describe only the details: the facts of our meeting, his
hair, clothes, eyes, body. I can describe it all, but cannot explain or
justify a hundredth—nay, a thousandth—of the mesmerizing
charm that bewitched me. Still, I will try.

He smelled of the forest: clean and richly honest, the scent of
cool wind and dry, pleasant sun. His dark beard was soft against
my cheek and his arms warm around my waist. I had seen how his
eyes could turn caring and humorous, intelligent and kind. I had
felt the strength of the muscles in his arms, which magically had
not overpowered his gentleness. And those lips—which had come
so close to my ear—how well formed they were, not thin or stingy
or tightly closed; perfect for the deep, commanding voice that
breathed between them.

I had never in all my life been so close to any man except my
father and Miguel. And thus—may the Lord forgive me for my
boldness—when finally I heard the voice of my father calling my
name and saw him running toward me, I felt my heart ache with
loneliness at the thought that my body should soon be separated
from his.

My father's face was filled with fear and wonder.

"I am Dr. Luna," my father said formally, taking me from
Francisco's arms. My cheeks burned in shame. "Can you tell me, sir,
what I am to make of this?"

"I'm afraid your daughter was interrupted in her innocent
pleasure by an unfortunate—but praise G-d, not serious—mishap.
She seems to have twisted her ankle. My brother and I were
happily able to see to her safe return." He bowed formally in the
saddle.

My father, perplexed, bowed back, then laid me on a bed of soft
leaves, dressing my swollen ankle with a poultice of herbs and wet
roots. When he had finished, he turned to my rescuers.

"I beg you to receive a reward as befits the deed," my father
pleaded.

Both bowed and shook their heads. "The pleasure of your

family's acquaintance is our reward," my rescuer said graciously.

"And may we beg, then, at least the same?" my father said.

"I am Francisco Mendes, and this is my younger brother, Diogo. We are traders newly arrived from Venice and Amsterdam."

"Will you then at least join us for a meal?" my father continued. "We were about to sup in the forest."

I could not believe my ears! I thought my father would do everything in his power to hide our secret, and instead, he invited them into it!

I saw the two strangers glance at our sukah and then at each other. The strange light in their eyes filled me with fear.

"With pleasure," they acceded.

A hut in the forest. Why should they guess it was anything more than an elegant way to protect wealthy people from the harsh sunlight? Perhaps, I thought, this was why my father had invited them in, to show we had nothing to hide. It was a bold move, and one I hoped he would not live to regret.

When we were all gathered around the table, my father prodded them gently for greater details about themselves.

I did not understand the conversation, which centered around trade, and Vasco da Gama, and the sea route to India. I sat dazed all through the meal, not tasting anything, my thoughts a turbulent river, rushing streams intermingling in a startling dance that thrilled and frightened me.

I heard no other voice, but his. Saw no other face, but his.

"But are not the waters dangerous and hard to maneuver?" I heard my father question Francisco. I looked up, startled, thinking he read my mind.

"I've built the best carracks in the world: four-masted square rigs with a sail on a yard under the bowsprit and flush-laid carvel planking that will hold six hundred fifty tons."

There was a loud gasp of surprise around the table at so many sails and such enormous tonnage. "And what do you plan to bring back?" my brother wanted to know.

"What else?" Aunt Malca interrupted. "Gold and silver, and precious gems, I warrant, to choke the coffers of kings!" She simpered, reaching for her jeweled necklace and caressing it.

"Ah, Doña, something far, far more wonderful!" Francisco Mendes laughed.

"Really?" Her eyes narrowed greedily. "Could you show us a sample, then?"

"With pleasure."

He put his hand into his pocket and took out a small pouch.

Aunt Malca, no doubt expecting pearls or diamonds, leaned over so closely she nearly fell flat-faced upon the table.

"This is much better," he insisted, opening the pouch and pouring its contents into his palm.

They looked like tiny black seeds.

"You sport with me, Don Francisco," Aunt Malca complained sullenly.

"Indeed, dear lady, I do not. What you see is far more precious than any jewel known to man." He took out a small mortar and pestle and placed the seeds inside, crushing them to a fine powder.

"Here, you be the judge," he said, sprinkling it over the venison.

Aunt Malca took a forkful and began to cough violently. "Water! I'm on fire!" she screeched, fanning herself.

My father tasted the meat with its magic condiment and offered a piece to Miguel. Both of them sniffed cautiously, chewing slowly.

"It has a pleasant scent, and a heavenly, warm taste," Miguel admitted. "I should like some more!"

"Ah, it has more than that, sir. It has magic properties that keep meat from rotting, and flies from landing. And it improves the taste of all food, however stinking foul!"

"Keep meat from rotting? Can it be?" Father asked wonderingly.

"It is well known in the Indies. I have flung it over our sea victuals, and the men say they never ate so well," Diogo swore.

"What is it called?" my father asked.

"Pepper," Francisco answered quietly. "And it will make Portugal the new Venice."

"And my brother and I richer than kings!" Diogo slapped the table impetuously.

Aunt Malca looked at the powder again, sniffing and tasting a little on her finger. She sneezed violently.

"May the good Lord bless you with health, Doña," Francisco said politely, a gleam in his eye.

She blew her nose. "As rich as kings, you say?" she scoffed.

"May I taste it as well?" I finally got up the courage to ask.

Francisco Mendes leaned across the table and sprinkled some on my roast capon. And when I ate it, a heavenly sword of fire touched my lips. I wanted to run into the forest and put my face in the cool running water of a stream and drink for days.

I got up abruptly, but Malca pulled me down. "Here, drink this," she muttered, handing me some almond water. "No more running after wild forest estries for you today!"

"You are too harsh, Doña Malca," Francisco interrupted her. "The child was lured by angels, not estries. It took the form of a beautiful doe, did it not, child? I, too, followed it," he said. "But like most precious and beautiful things, chasing after her only encouraged her to run farther. Sometimes, it is wiser to simply sit patiently and wait."

As he said this, he leaned back, looking at me strangely, his eyes sparkling and full of mysterious light.

The brothers stood and bowed.

"We are grateful to you for your hospitality," Francisco began, "just as we give thanks to G-d the Father for having given us his Divine Son as Brother in the Incarnation, Teacher of Divine Truth, and Savior on the cross. Whatever we might accomplish, may it be the object of His delight, and for the Glory of our Divine Jesus."

I saw my father and brother stare at each other tensely. They crossed themselves and rose to see the visitors out.

I started from my seat. The last glimpse of his beautiful dark head, together with the echo of his fervent Christian prayer, crashed together in my brain, plunging me into a chasm of despair.

In the months that followed, I saw my body change, losing its childish angles and taking on the soft roundness of womanly beauty. New gowns were ordered for me, simple undergowns and overgowns over conical farthingales that showed my tiny waist and my newly rounded bosom to advantage.

I saw Francisco Mendes several times at court weddings, and then again at Easter at the great cathedral São Vincente de Fora. And he was always kind, but in the teasing way fathers treat their daughters' friends. And always, at his side, were bejeweled court women wearing fur-lined capes and dresses embroidered with precious stones. My heart ached with longing and pangs of jealousy.

I was ashamed of my dreams. He was completely unacceptable, not only to my family, but to myself. And yet, I continued to dream the same dream: I was in his arms again, my cheek against his broad shoulder, and I was asking him to marry me.

The good Christian Mendes does not intend to marry now. He is gone to India with four carracks. It will be several years before he returns. You must forget him, child, my father told me in my dreams.

I wept, stunned, and my father touched my face in kindness.

It is G-d's will, he tried to comfort me. Your intended will be another. Your pain will pass.

And in my dream, I looked at my father for the first time without the awed reverence of the child and with the objective intelligence of an equal: He was wrong, I thought. I will never take another man for my husband.

And my pain would never pass.

Reality followed close on the heels of my dreams. Francisco Mendes did indeed leave Portugal on his carracks for India, and he did not return.

In the years that followed, any number of matches were proposed to my father among our fellow conversos. *Most, he rejected. As the Lord Who Sees All and Judges All knows, I never blamed him. His responsibility was a heavy one. For it was his task to see that no weak or ugly graft find its way to the beautiful tree of the House of Nasi.*

For from the time when the Israelites wandered through the desert, the title "Nasi" was not merely a surname, nor even a royal title bestowed merely by inheritance. Moses himself had called upon each family and each tribe to choose its most worthy. Those chosen were called Nasi, "Prince," by the people.

It was a title quickly shorn from those who proved undeserving.

And so, each potential bridegroom had his ancestral roots traced back five, even ten, generations. If no apostates, heretics, lunatics, or simply bad-natured villains were uncovered, then the full light of inquiry was turned upon the present. Was the family New Christian in name, or in spirit as well?

Those matches which survived all these hurdles resulted in a meeting between myself and the prospective bridegroom. In this we differed greatly from our Christian neighbors, and from many of our brethren, who betrothed their daughters without their consent at age five, and even younger, forcing them to marry men they had never even met before they took their conjugal vows.

While some of our Jewish brethren imitated their Christian neighbors in this foul practice, my father always insisted our faith forbade such things and that a father must gain his daughter's free consent to any match. I took advantage of his piety. Again and again, I rejected the selection of his lean gleanings.

My father was chagrined, disturbed, and, finally, sad.

My aunt was utterly furious. "She who does not know how to rejoice in her youth, will find no peace in Paradise, either!"

I could not think of the matches proposed to me with joy. Those scrawny young men, pale and mute. Or the ruddy, arrogant ones. And even those dark of eye and fair of form.

What did it matter? None of them was Francisco Mendes.

In short, as I sorted them, I could picture myself quite well ensconced as the virgin daughter and spinster aunt for the rest of my days. Indeed, I was well nigh reconciled to it, and had been for five years, from the very day I had first set eyes on the man I had wanted and could not have. The man who had not wanted me.

And so my life flowed on.

I was almost eighteen years old, and my time to marry, as my aunt so cruelly but accurately pointed out, had seemingly passed me forever. It was a Sunday in April, Easter Mass, or some such Christian holiday. (I admit—we were painfully ignorant of even the rudiments of the religion in which we professed to believe. We avoided mass and never went to confession, and did our best to avoid kneeling and kissing crucifixes.) But as my brother, Miguel, had recently been appointed royal physician, my father felt that the family had no choice but to put in more frequent appearances at mass.

I dressed for church. I was wearing a dress of simple damask in dark green with a plain gold locket around my throat. My only vanity was the delicate rete of spun silk and gold entwined with small pearls that held the thick coils of my red hair. It was a beautiful hair covering, but—as Aunt Malca scolded me—much too revealing and flimsy for mass. I tossed my head and ignored her. All the ladies at court wore their hair thus, I declared. Upon which she answered me spitefully: "The brazen-faced go to hell, and the shame-faced to heaven."

I thought no more of it until after the service ended and I was on my way out of the cathedral, my arms linked through Miguel's and his pregnant wife's. Suddenly, I felt a long golden-red lock impudently escape, falling down to tickle my nose. I quickly untangled my arms and stood perfectly still, working to tuck it back out of sight, as the crowd pushed my brother and his wife forward toward the doors.

For a reason I cannot explain, I felt something directly behind me, a presence solid and unmoving that pulled at me like a magnet. "Gracia!" I heard my brother call from up ahead. But instead of hurrying forward, I turned around.

There he was, that dark prince of noble birth and more noble feelings I had seen for so long in my dreams.

Francisco Mendes.

I stood there immobilized, all the blood rushing wildly though my veins, the hammers of a million urgent thoughts clamoring at my heart.

He stood relaxed, his hands clasped behind his back, making no attempt to circumvent the obstacle of my person. Instead, his dark eyes studied me with a look I had never before seen in all my days; a look of purest longing. It blazed from his whole being like a summer sun in a midday sky. I was consumed, bewitched, by its mesmerizing power.

All this happened in a magic instant, making the whole breathing and unbreathing world fade into a mist, until there was only he and I standing alone, our hearts clanging as urgently as steeple bells.

How long we stood there, I do not know. But long enough, I recall, for me to have seen our wedding, our life together, even our children, pass before me like shades. I was almost in a swoon when Miguel took my arm and led me past the Capella de San Gregorio and the Altar de la Asuncion through the Puerto Principal.

I knew without looking that he was following close behind me. When I turned to enter my carriage, he stood only footsteps away, his whole body in an attitude of expectant longing, his face suffused in an almost celestial light in whose reflected glow I felt myself transformed. It was not a passion based on knowledge or reason. For what did I know of him except what my eyes could see? Yet, I was like one of those novitiates who wear a wedding gown and marry themselves to the spirit of an unseen god.

"I must talk to him!" I implored my brother.

"A wealthy Christian nobleman who sups at the King's own table?" Miguel hissed in fury, steering me firmly away into our carriage.

"He is as rich as Croesus! It is told that the King himself is sorely in his debt!" my sister-in-law exclaimed.

Miguel, whom I had never before heard raise his voice, roared, "Enough! Never speak of it again!"

All the way home I felt dizzy and slightly ravenous, as if the churning in my stomach could be stilled by food. When we sat down to dinner, I piled my plate with rice, lentils, fish and stewed capon, sweetmeats and almond cakes. I ate and ate until I felt faint. But the churning, the hunger, continued to gnaw.

I took to my bed and wouldn't get up for days, refusing my brother's potions and ignoring my father's warnings that he would bleed me if I did not come back to my senses.

I knew it was hopeless.

It was clear to me where my duty lay. Ever since my twelfth year, I had been told of how only my marriage to the right man would ensure the continuation of that passionate faithfulness to our most treasured way of life, a way of life our ancestors had struggled and died for.

Were I to defy my duty, then one of two things would happen: I would need to hide my practices, and that of my family's, from the

*man I married, lest he turn on me and those I loved in hatred,
betraying us to the priests. Or, far worse, I could truly become one
with my husband, accepting his beliefs and thus heaping scorn on
my secret self and burying it in ignominy.*

And yet, my whole being yearned for him.

*The madness lasted near a fortnight. When it finally passed, I
felt weak and fragile, yet purified.*

I had made my decision.

*Happiness in the love of one man could never overcome the
sorrow of so large a betrayal of all I and my family held sacred.
Young as I was, I understood the difference between the joy of the
moment and that of eternity. True, lasting happiness had a spark
of divinity. Unless we could create a place in our love in which G-d
could dwell, sanctifying us both, it would decay into ugliness. And
if ugliness and sorrow were to overcome me in the end, I would
quarantine it upon myself now, before it spread like the plague to
all those I loved.*

*My father entered my bedchamber, agitated and about to
lecture me again, I assumed. I cut him short, apprising him of my
return to sanity. To my surprise and perturbation, this did not
seem to comfort him in the least. His eyes restless, he bade me to
dress and join him for dinner.*

*I still remember how my maid bathed me in water filled with
rose petals. How she washed my hair and rinsed it with henna and
lavender water, then brushed and dressed it in thick coils around
my head, covering it with my rete of pearls. I remember the dress I
wore: shot silk and brocaded velvet of heavenly blue with simple
gold embroidery and heavy, gold chains.*

*When I was dressed, Aunt Malca suddenly appeared. She
examined me with intense interest. I was pale, she said, offering to
rub my cheeks and lips with the dye of pomegranates.*

*I remember well not lodging any of my usual protests, and
being curiously willing to submit to her ministrations, so shocked
was I by her inexplicable interest and kindness. After she'd slipped
satin slippers upon my feet and led me down to join the others, she
squeezed my fingers and looked searchingly into my face. "Smile,
child," she urged me.*

And I, not knowing why, did.

When I entered the dining room, a tall stranger was standing between my father and Miguel.

My heart fainted within me.

My heart rose up and danced in my chest.

Was this some terrible test, I wondered, stricken, looking at my father's tense and weary face.

It could mean only one thing, I thought. That the King himself had requested this hospitality from my father.

A warm rush of deepest elation washed over me. Was it possible, then, that Francisco should have thought of me, demanded something in connection to me, from the King himself? The idea filled me with such intense happiness I could hardly breathe. Ah, how all my sensible decisions flew up the chimney like smoke from the hearth fire. Oh, the stupid, unreasonable happiness I felt at that idea, the idea that he and I would be together somehow; that he had the power to smite the monstrous Goliath that stood in our path, letting us walk over the dead giant and into each other's arms.

Yet, at the same moment, the icy fingers of a most horrid fear laid hold of me, squeezing me almost senseless. For, if that was the case, what else had this dear stranger the power to demand and accomplish?

What wretchedness filled me as I considered never again being part of those joyful rituals, those bejeweled hidden moments in which my family and I had always lived our truest lives. Never again allowed to find my way to those secret chambers deep within my own heart.

It seemed so wrong that this unknown man, this sudden passion, should succeed in wrenching me free of my blessed moorings, where all the brute force, the wiles and rewards of King and Church, had failed.

I was angry then, at him, at myself, my head bent silently over my plate, my bosom heaving in its tight lacings. I saw how all my mooning and nighttime fevers had led down this Stygian path toward a future of a single, false life lived openly yet in endless shame.

*"Will you have some fish, or beef, or perhaps some fowl?" my
father inquired of him. "I regret we can offer you no pork, as my
constitution is poorly equipped to digest it."*

*"I confess, my own stomach prevents me, too, of enjoying that
delicacy," Francisco Mendes murmured. "It is a weakness inherited
from my father, and his father before him."*

My father and Miguel exchanged odd glances.

*"Will you be settling down in Lisbon in the near future?" Miguel
inquired.*

*"This is a question to which I do not yet have the answer,
although I find the city and its inhabitants exceedingly fine," he
replied, glancing boldly in my direction.*

A thrill flashed through me.

*"Right now I am equipping my ships for their next voyage east.
But I do not expect to leave before the twenty-fourth of April."*

Again, I saw Miguel and Father study each other in amazement.

"And why is that?" my brother inquired.

*"I have been invited to a special dinner at my aunt's home. It is
a family obligation, and one I fulfill every year."*

*"The victuals must be of a unique savoriness and the meat of
wondrous tenderness if on their account you delay a venture worth
thousands of cruzados' profit." Father smiled, his eyes searching.*

*"Nay. The opposite, Don Luna. My aunt is a terrible cook. The
bread is stale and hard, the meat roasted burned, the herbs bitter,
and the condiments as salty as tears."*

*A startling change came over my father's face. "That will be all!"
He clapped his hands, curtly dismissing the servants. "Sister Malca,
would you take Brianda upstairs to her bedchamber, as I believe
she is looking poorly again," he commanded my aunt, giving her a
look she dared not defy.*

*Only when the servants had closed the doors behind them,
leaving the four of us alone, did my father turn once again to
Francisco Mendes.*

*"Gente da nação?" my father whispered. I could see the fear in
his face as he waited for Francisco's reply.*

"Gente da nação!" Francisco nodded with pride.

How strange it was! That phrase, uttered with the utmost

contempt by the Portuguese to indicate Judaizing conversos *like ourselves, had been adopted by us to convey the utmost honor and distinction. One could tell another brother simply by how he pronounced it.*

"Your true name, my son?"

"Semach Benveniste," Francisco answered.

Three hundred years before, Isaac Benveniste had been body physician to the kings of Aragon. His descendants included the most pious and distinguished members of the Jewish community of Spain. Abraham Benveniste, who had died in 1452, had been the Crown Rabbi of Aragon.

There was a stunned silence. "And which of your two names do you prefer?" my father inquired.

"I am the grandson of Abraham Benveniste." Francisco lifted his head with dignity. "In all that I do, I never forget that."

"And why, then, have you prevailed upon the King to press your suit of marriage to Gracia? Why did you not simply go to the converso *matchmakers? Or even your aunt, whom I am sure is well known in our community. It could have been done without any of this," my father protested in vehement whispers.*

Francisco turned to me. The passion in his eyes would have been frightening was it not so fully reciprocated. I raised my eyes to his and drank him in, all the long, princely length of him, the fullness of his physical beauty, the unexpressed strength latent in those well-formed bones, wanting to have him . . . to swallow him whole.

His answer stunned us all.

"My seeing Gracia at mass was no accident, Don Luna. For many years I have searched for a wife worthy of my family's name and lineage. When I came across her in that happy accident years ago and was invited into your sukah, *my heart had already made its decision. But I did not want to marry a child; someone who would quake in her slippers at my command and bow her head like a trained pet. I sought a woman fully grown, learned, intelligent, and pious.*

"All these years, my aunt has kept close watch over Gracia, informing me of the progress of her education, as well as the

efforts to find her a suitable marriage partner. Had one been selected, I should have come forward immediately. But as she remained unwed, and I myself was obliged to be absent from home so many months, I felt it would be better for her to benefit from the companionship of her family and continue her tutoring."

"Why have you come forward now?" my father asked, perplexed.

"Unfortunately, I was not the only one of the King's acquaintances to have noticed Gracia in church."

I looked up, shocked, blushing to the tips of my toes.

"My spies at court informed me that Rodrigo Olivi requested that the Queen act as intermediary to arrange a match between himself and Gracia."

"Olivi!? The former ambassador to the Holy See? The man who begged the Pope to bring the Inquisition to Portugal?!" my father exclaimed, disgusted.

"The gray-haired old devil!" Miguel spat out with contempt. "He's almost sixty!"

I imagined the old man's eyes upon me, his vile thoughts and malevolent power trained in my direction.

I felt near to swooning.

"Olivi is very powerful," Francisco continued. "It would have been extremely difficult, if not impossible, for you to have refused the Queen, Don Luna, without bringing great injury down upon your family. And so, begging your pardon, I had to think quickly. I thought the best way to stop Olivi would be for me to go directly to the King—who is now somewhat in my debt—and to ask him to intervene on my behalf."

My father came around the table. With one arm, he gripped Francisco's hand, and with the other, his shoulder, saluting him on both cheeks with brotherly warmth. "I am in your debt!" my father said, trembling with deepest emotion.

"I did not act, Don Luna, out of any motive more elevated than pure self-interest. I ask you now to forgive the shocking impropriety of my proposal and beg you to consider the extraordinary circumstances that brought it about."

"Yes, of course. And with the greatest gratitude," my father told

him. "But now, Don Francisco, let us rejoice in each other's
company, and continue our meal."

Continue our meal! I thought, outraged, wondering if at any
moment I might, like hot milk, boil over. Was this, then, the end of
it? A brotherly act of kindness acknowledged on all sides? And just
as I thought I should surely burst, Francisco stood up and turned to
my father.

"I cannot wait a moment longer, Don Luna, until the matter that
has brought me here is put to rest either way. I beg you to consider,
despite all my obvious flaws, allowing your daughter Gracia to
marry me, according to the laws of Moses and the G-d of Israel,
may His name be blessed."

My father turned to me. "And what is it you answer, my
daughter?"

"Father, I will do as it pleases you," I murmured piously, knowing
it was mummery, and that inside I was howling as wantonly and
desperately as any woman who ever stood in shameless need
outside a tavern door.

"It pleases me to ask you again, my daughter, and to receive an
answer, as our holy Torah does not allow a father to betroth a
daughter over the age of twelve without her full consent. Will you
have this man for your betrothed?"

I looked again at Francisco Mendes, amazed that such joy could
exist and could be mine for the taking.

"Yes, Father. With all my heart."

My father kissed my forehead and took my hands, lifting me
out of my seat. "Go now, child. We have many things to discuss that
do not concern you."

I knew the final test was coming now. The last obstacle. I had
lulled myself into the indulgent dream that my father might
somehow overlook it just this once.

I should have known better.

This was the final hurdle put before all my prospective
bridegrooms: He would now test Francisco's knowledge of the
sacred texts. If Francisco showed ignorance, there would be no
wedding after all, as it is written: "He who marries his daughter to
an ignoramus is as one that binds her and throws her to a lion!"

*With a frightened and heavy heart, I dutifully turned and left
the room. How many times I walked to and fro in the garden, my
heart diving and swooping up like some hungry bird, I do not
know. It seemed like eternity. But when, finally, I saw my father
walking down the path toward me, he was smiling. Behind him
was Francisco.*

My father put his hands upon our heads and blessed us both.

*Francisco looked at me and I at him. He made no attempt to
take my hand. He smiled and bowed and bid us both good-bye
until the morrow.*

*I watched his back as he left, realizing with a shiver I would be
connected to him, body and soul, until the day G-d saw fit to
cleave us.*

We had not exchanged a single word.

20

Dearest Grandmother,

By the time you receive this I will have already left. Please don't be alarmed, or sad. I am not running away. Actually, it is a far, far better thing I do, etc.

Acting is just not my vocation, nor can I shut my mouth and swallow my opinions for any length of time. As last night proved, another few weeks of this kind of "togetherness" and we will probably never speak to one another again.

Most of all, I find that I can't stand the idea of your being in pain, and my contributing to that in any way. I don't know why I am such a compassionate listener to strangers who are in need and such a complete failure when it comes to those close to me. Perhaps because strangers will take whatever you give them and swallow it with thanks. Relatives and friends are a bit more choosy.

I hope you'll forgive the abruptness of my departure. I did not plan to leave quite this soon. But something happened last night that changed all my plans and all my expectations. I know you're going to be aching with curiosity, but it can't be helped. I myself don't know what's going to happen next. Perhaps it will be the best thing that has ever happened to me in all my life. Or perhaps it will be a strange and temporary interlude of no significance whatsoever. Time will tell.

But in the meantime, I did want you to know that I read the

manuscript. The coincidence of just this part of the story turning up at just this point in my life . . . Well . . . If I did believe in magic, that's what I would call it. It's gone beyond coincidence in a way that even I find mystical: I am actually beginning to feel a strange attachment to this long dead ancestral fossil of ours, and an embarrassing tenderness as well. I'm sure it will pass. But in the meantime, she is even invading my dreams.

Last night, I dreamed she came to my room. She was wearing a paisley dress of rich brocade and large pearls. There was a golden net holding back her thick red hair, and gold-embroidered slippers on her feet. She sat down on the corner of my bed and looked at me, shaking her head. She couldn't approve of my behavior, she said, which was most inappropriate. Nevertheless, she wasn't discouraged. In fact—and she was pretty definite about this—she assured me that it was all going to work out for the best. It didn't really matter which route I followed, I'd wind up in the same place in the end.

She wouldn't answer any questions, so I can't elaborate.

Anyhow, when I woke up, I found a gold thread on the carpet. At least, that's what I think it was. Or maybe it was just a blond hair. And there is a very reasonable explanation for having found one of those. . . .

Nevertheless, I find this quite spooky, I am chagrined to admit.

I can't tell you where I'm going, or what I'll be doing. But I have this strange, inexplicable feeling that I am about to explore the things you really had in mind when you sent me on this journey.

You know what I mean, don't you, *Abuela?*

I will write you via your lawyers in New York, who I am sure will be able to track you, if not me, down.

Please, *Abuela.* GO HOME AND TAKE CARE OF YOURSELF!

As for Francesca, she can carry on with the official agenda alone or hook up with Marius. My advice: the latter. He seems to know a great deal more than he is letting on. Besides, wouldn't they make a lovely couple? So what if they are total opposites: finally a Serouya would marry a Nasi.

I happen to know he is quite attracted to her.

Before I shove off, there is something else I want to share with you. Do you remember that summer Mom ran off with Kenny and dumped me and Francesca with you and Grandpa? It was a boring Sunday, and Francesca had a bad cold. Just on the spur of the moment, you decided to take me to the Brooklyn Botanical Gardens. I remember I ran off and picked a whole bunch of lilacs and brought them to you, hoping to get us both into serious trouble. Sure enough, the guard ran after me, yelling, and I pretended I had no idea what I'd done wrong. Instead of slapping me, you told the guard—in your most polite and aristocratic way—to get lost. Then you took me back to the lilacs. We watched them for a while. They were so fresh and gorgeous. You showed me the place in the ground where the roots were buried in the soil, and the veins in the plant that carried the food and water to feed the blossoms. You made me understand that it was a living thing.

"Respect the separate life of things," you told me. "Don't insist on grabbing them for yourself. Don't insist on owning."

When I think about how I got interested in preserving all the beauty of the world, of protecting and helping women damaged by men grabbing at them, wanting to possess them, I think I can trace the beginnings back to you. I know you don't consider me, my life, or my values much of an accomplishment, but I, of course, shall have to disagree. So when you say that you never accomplished anything in your life, according to my way of thinking, you lie.

You've made me what I am today.

Take very, very good care of yourself, *Abuela.*

And try to explain all this to Francesca so she won't think any less of me than she already does (if such a thing is possible).

> Your wayward granddaughter,
> Suzanne

Suzanne sealed the envelope and addressed it. Then she picked up her bags and headed for the lobby.

She handed the envelope to the clerk at the reception desk, then looked outside. It was still dark and damp with drizzle. But out of the stillness, she heard the hum of the Alfa-Romeo.

She waited patiently for it to pull up to the curb.

She didn't see him immediately because he'd put the top up. But then he opened the door and got out.

It was like the sun coming out, she thought.

He touched a wisp of her red-gold hair, curled from the dampness. "I've missed you."

And though they'd only met ten hours before, and had been apart since then for only two, she had no reason to doubt him.

She threw her bag into the trunk, and got in beside him.

The car engine gave a burst of thrilling energy.

And then the journey began.

21

Francesca looked down at the Pyrenees, mountain passes steeped in snow, with tiny houses clustered together at dizzying altitudes. Informative, this G-d's-eye view of the earth and mankind, she thought. Everything so small, reduced not only in size but in significance. Whole mountain ranges becoming backyards; whole cities, little piles of pebbles by some tiny stream. And people, nonexistent specks of dust. She pursed her lips, thinking of Suzanne.

Of all the low-down, self-centered, grubby, impulsive things to do! A "far, far better thing . . . Let Francesca carry on." Leave it to Suzanne, she thought furiously, to make a virtue out of dumping the whole project to run off with some sexy stranger. And all that stuff about Marius being interested in her, the two of them making a perfect couple! The nerve! Was that any of her business? Besides, it wasn't true. Marius hadn't even called her to say good-bye. . . .

Gran herself had taken the letter much more stoically. For a few days, they'd carried on as if nothing had happened, visiting libraries, auction houses, and booksellers. But no promising leads turned up, and Gran's strength seemed to ebb moment by moment, like a tide moving inexorably out to sea.

And that morning, just hours before they were scheduled to leave for Spain together, Gran had announced she was going home. She'd looked drained, but not as defeated as Francesca would have expected. In fact, there'd been a strange sort of resignation, almost relief, in her manner.

"You can rest a few weeks, then join me later," Francesca had urged her, without much hope.

"Thank you, child, but I think my traveling days are over," she'd answered with a brave smile.

"*Abuela!*"

"Promise to write often, and to call." Her eyes had been bright with tears.

"I promise."

They'd embraced, Gran holding on to her with surprising strength as they'd kissed good-bye.

And then she was gone.

Francesca looked at her watch. She'd be over the Atlantic now, just approaching Halifax. Perhaps she'd be sitting next to someone pleasant, someone she could talk to.

She felt her eyes misting. So many times she'd been on the verge of confronting Gran about Suzanne's story; of insisting on knowing the contents of the little green pills and the blue capsules; the reason behind the sudden trembling and the terrible pallor. And each time, she'd pulled back.

If it wasn't true, then why rub Gran's face in the natural ravages of age? And if it was . . . She touched her suddenly dry lips. Who would it benefit to turn the harsh spotlight of truth on her grandmother's delicate deception, mocking her brave performance?

It must be unbearable to be old and ill. And there was no way to ensure it wouldn't happen to you. Everything human was so fragile and vulnerable and out of control.

She looked down at the beautiful puzzle in shades of brown and green that was Spain: clouds like mountain cliffs above fertile plains, plowed fields, barns, farmhouses. What magic power was down there? she wondered. What sorcery? How was it that five hundred years after the last Jew had been expelled from Spanish shores, their descendants still spoke its language, sang its songs, and decorated their homes in ways that did homage to its sense of beauty? How was it that she, Francesca Nasi da Costa Abraham, who had never set foot in Spain, called her British-born, Americanized grandmother *Abuela*?

The seat belt sign flashed on, and her ears already felt the pressure of the descent. She took out her day planner, looking over her schedule: two days in Madrid at the library and a few rare-book dealers; then Seville and Barcelona. She checked off her list, highlighting the phone numbers and ordering the days ahead as efficiently as possible.

It was a smooth landing. Madrid. I'm in Madrid, she tried to impress upon herself. It didn't work. Every place looked the same inside an airport terminal. And if you arrived alone with no one waiting to welcome you with flowers and open arms, it was always the loneliest place in the world, she thought, looking for someone who could help her with her luggage. But everywhere she turned, she heard only Spanish. She felt too embarrassed to try to make herself understood.

With every ounce of strength, she hauled her suitcases off the carousel and dragged them to a luggage cart. Overloaded, the cart veered wildly down the corridor, dragging her behind it. Clammy beads of perspiration sprouted all over her body.

Get a car, a map, find a hotel. . . . I can do it, no problem, she encouraged herself, wiping her forehead with the back of her hand. Didn't backpackers travel the globe solo with twenty dollars in their pockets and manage just fine?

Yes, she *could* do it. But she didn't *like* doing it, she admitted, her straining arms beginning to ache. Being in a country where you didn't know the language was like being two years old again: vulnerable and completely at the mercy of "adults" who could converse secretly behind your back.

As much as she hated to admit it, she missed Suzanne.

She parked the cart. There was one other person ahead of her at the Avis counter. Idly, she glanced over the rental agreement, translated into English, hanging on the counter: "There is a band of thieves operating in this area who puncture tires, then offer their assistance, meanwhile stealing your suitcases. If this should happen, or if your car should develop problems, DO NOT ROLL DOWN YOUR WINDOWS! Continue on until the nearest garage or police station. . . ."

Her heart began to pound.

"Does anyone here speak English?" she asked the two dark, good-looking men behind the counter.

"Yes, of course," they answered.

She felt immensely relieved. "I've got a car reservation. Francesca Abraham?"

They began to argue with each other, gesticulating and pointing.

"I don't understand!" What was the problem? *"No en tee yen doh!"* She looked in her guidebook, starting to panic. *"Por favor, señor!"*

"Señorita Abraham!" one of them said. "You are waiting for someone?"

"No." She shrugged, setting off another wave of excited debate.

One of them made a gesture of the utmost exasperation and left, while the other continued to converse with her in Spanish in the friendliest possible manner, as if his knowledge of the language was adequate for them both.

"Problems, *señorita?*"

She looked up in shocked surprise, the blood rushing with a warm, tingling jolt through her body.

It was Marius.

He looked tan, fit, and ruggedly charming in a pair of jeans and a clean, striped shirt open at the chest.

"How are you?" He smiled.

A change quickly went over her face. The closeness of his body, his warm, dark eyes assumed some right, some knowledge of her that it almost hurt her to recognize. She was afraid. "What are you doing here?! I mean, is this a coincidence, or . . ."

He shook his head, laughing. "I asked you first."

"I'm fine, I guess," she said, all the while resisting his bright confidence, the protective mantle his presence threw around her. She was almost ashamed of her relief, almost pained at the depth of her need and the electric flow that charged the air between them. She took a step backward, flustered, excited, and happier than she could bear to admit to herself. "I don't speak any Spanish, and I was trying to explain about my reservation."

"You can relax now. I'm here to rescue you," he teased, his eyes caressing, tensely alive.

"I don't need rescuing, thank you," she retorted, resisting his advance, the slow encroaching assumption of male power over her female will. She pushed her sweat-dampened curls off her forehead.

"Aren't you hot? I mean, with all those clothes?"

She looked down at her tailored suit, feeling suddenly matronly and overdressed. "It's a very lightweight material," she said, defending herself.

"You'll have to change into something lighter or you'll melt. This is the Mediterranean. Come. Let's get you to an air-conditioned hotel room. I know just the place." He reached for her wayward cart, moving it out the door. "Leave everything to me!"

She squared her jaw. "Please take your hands off my suitcases," she said with slow, deliberate calm. "I am not hot. I do not need to be rescued, and I'm not taking another step until you tell me what you're doing here."

He clicked his heels together and bowed, sliding the cart back to her. "Just part of our complete service, m'lady. But maybe we can talk about this in our car on the way. It's parked right out front. Come."

She stared at him. "*Our* car?"

"I didn't think we needed two."

She shook her head in disbelief. "Whoa! One second. Are you telling me that this isn't just a coincidence? That you're here because of me? And that you think we are going to be doing something together?"

"I've come to join you," he said simply, shrugging.

He had come looking for her.

Her whole body took on a new alertness, as if tensed for an invasion. The robber climbing over her high, hard walls. Or the prince, scaling the tower? Could Suzanne be right, then, after all? "But how did you know where I'd be?"

"Your grandmother. My uncle. They agreed it would be best."

Her face grew hot. Not his own idea at all, then. It had to do with the manuscript. It had to do with business. She felt like a complete fool. "Grandmother and Uncle decided, did they? Why didn't anyone bother to tell me to expect you, then?"

"It wasn't definite. I wasn't sure I'd be able to make it. You were scheduled to be in England another week or so, weren't you? Your leaving took me by surprise. I was actually scheduled to go to Bucharest. . . . So I changed a few . . . Anyway, I'm here at your disposal now."

She looked at him, hurt that her charms had been made to compete with those of Bucharest, and had only narrowly won. Or was it the call of duty that had won? "I understand—you changed your plans to please your uncle. How kind of you! But since no one has asked me, I'm afraid that you might be wasting your time. You see, *I'm not* sure that *I'll* be able to change *my* plans to go along with this," she said firmly.

A strange pallor came over his face, the brash confidence disappearing, his eyes going dark and still. He looked wounded. "You mean . . . you want me to leave?"

She felt an immediate pang of remorse. No, she did not want that. Not yet, anyway. "I didn't say that. I mean . . . this is Gran's show, after all, and so if she's decided that I'd be more effective with your help . . ."

A gleam, almost offensively knowing, came back into his eyes. She noticed it immediately. "Look, if I agree to let you join me, I'd like to make something perfectly clear right from the beginning. I didn't ask for help. I'm perfectly capable of doing this job on my own. And I won't agree to have anyone order me around or tell me what to do."

He took a step toward her, his face calm and serious. "I didn't doubt that for a minute. But I also want to make something perfectly clear. This wasn't your grandmother's idea, or my uncle's. It was mine." His large hands reached out, taking the cart from her.

She made no further objection, walking along silently beside him.

The car was a tiny red Peugeot 206, upholstered in the color of whitewashed jeans. Just looking at it made her feel like a college student off to drink beer and wear a bikini for a week. She waited as he loaded her suitcases, embarrassed by their weight and number and untraveled newness; wishing she were wearing jeans and carrying a duffel bag. Wishing she were not Francesca Abraham; that she could shed that staid, plodding person in some dressing room along with her stodgy outfits.

He asked her short, pleasant questions about her flight and the state of her stomach, and she murmured polite replies to set his mind at rest. She tried to seem offhand, but all the while she was vitally, almost uncomfortably, aware of the solid reality of his thighs inches from her own, the smooth tan skin of his neck disappearing beneath his shirt, and his thick dark hair.

There was a low fog in which the road disappeared, and a faintly lit mist, like some kind of stratosphere, took its place. Francesca had the feeling of being lost, or of having entered a mystery—a little dangerous and wickedly exciting.

"Do you have a hotel booked in Madrid?"

"Do you want to go to Madrid?" He looked at her in surprise.

She pulled out her day planner. "That's where I'm supposed to be going. I've got a list of book dealers to call, libraries and museums . . ."

"My dear Francesca. Please trust me. It's a waste of time. We've got a small window of opportunity here to find the person who's been selling off the manuscript. If we don't catch him soon, the manuscript might disappear again for another four hundred years."

She was shocked. "We're looking for a person? A 'him'? I mean, someone *has* the manuscript!? How do you know that?"

"The pages I sold your grandmother were sold to me in Barcelona by a rare-book dealer who is a close friend of mine. He told me he thinks there is a lot more where that came from, but that the source has suddenly disappeared. Apparently, he's run away."

"Why?"

"I don't know exactly, but it makes sense to think that if one runs, one runs *from* something, no? The danger may or may not be connected to the manuscript. But as I always say, '*Cherchez l'argent.*'"

"Isn't that '*cherchez la femme*'?"

"I've always found money a much more passionate motive than sex for most people," he said, grinning.

"But if they know someone wants the manuscript and is willing to pay almost any price, why should they run?"

"I can think of a few reasons."

"Give me one."

"If you're selling something that doesn't belong to you and certain authorities have found out about it . . ."

"We don't want to get mixed up in anything like that!"

"Don't we?"

"Well . . ." She stared at him. He looked very strong and confident behind the wheel, but a little reckless in the way he took turns and pressed down on the gas pedal, going barely within the speed limit.

"I have no intention of getting arrested, Marius."

It was the first time she'd said his name. It had a strange flavor in her mouth, like some tropical fruit full of seeds, delicious, yet complicated.

"Then where are we going?"

"Toledo."

She looked through her day planner. "It's not on my schedule at all. It's a very old city, isn't it?"

"Over two thousand years."

"Wow! That's amazing."

"You Americans find it so hard to comprehend anything that old, don't you? I mean, you think anything a hundred years old is ancient. Your whole country is only a little over two hundred. Don't misunderstand me. I love America. It's a fresh, lively, new country, like a young virgin. Rootless, in a way."

"It's not rootless," she said, wondering what kind of firsthand knowledge he had concerning young virgins. "It's just full of people who've been uprooted. They've brought their roots with them."

"And is the American soil a fertile place to plant them?"

"I don't know," she said honestly. "I've never thought about it before."

The fog began to lift. She looked out, disappointed, at tall brick apartment houses that reminded her of a neighborhood in Flushing, Queens, and road signs offering "Sprite" and "Muebles de decoración," and "Sofa-Expo."

And then, just as suddenly, the landscape changed again: There was a field of grazing sheep and whitewashed houses with flower-filled porches, thriving beneath a generous and benevolent sun. There were rolling green hills and old farmhouses. Flanking both sides of the road as far as the eye could see, there were olive trees whose gnarled branches and hunched appearance reminded Francesca of grandparents on park benches. There were fields of poplars and evergreens, and glimpses of the red-tiled roofs of exquisite Mediterranean villas. And there in the distance (could it be a mirage?), a giant black bull rose from the low plain.

Her heart began to sing.

It was a hum at first—low and simple—like a whistle in the dark. But then she felt her heart grow warmer, shooting up a flame of joyous abandon to her throat and lips.

The song grew more sonorous, less self-conscious—a singing in the strange summer showers of unknown gardens—louder and sweeter, the fear overtaken by a sense of pure, vital pleasure.

Being alive was an adventure, wasn't it?

How easy it was, she thought, astounded, to leap off the precipice of the nice, safe, familiar life! Lifting up one's feet—that was hard, almost impossible—and getting them up and over the guardrails. But the jump itself—lovely, like a bird sailing through cloudless skies, all the earth, the whole of it, stretched beneath you like of platter of delights waiting to be plucked and savored.

And what had this to do with briefcases, or duty-free carts, or the sound of adding machines totaling up the purchases of unnecessary watches, perfumes, and scarves?

"Olé!" she called out of the car window, snapping her fingers, wondering if she were going mad, and, if so, why she hadn't done it long ago, being that it felt so wonderful.

Marius stared at her, then threw his head back and bellowed with laughter.

But she didn't care. She wasn't Francesca Abraham, unemployed computer programmer with a pigeon coop on the Upper West Side. She was the descendant of Spanish royalty in a little red Peugeot with an overbearing but enticing stranger who was going to do her every bidding, she swore silently, boldly examining Marius's thick, dark brows and the sensuous way his hands slid over the steering wheel.

The road led straight into Toledo, which seemed at first a modern city of brick apartment buildings, whitewashed town houses, and busy shopping centers plastered with sale signs proclaiming *locas rebajas*. The people were attractive, well-dressed Europeans, and the kids wore jeans and T-shirts.

"Shouldn't we be looking for a hotel?" Francesca asked.

He didn't answer, making a sudden turn around a traffic circle. With a swift transition she found almost impossible to conceive of, she found herself face to face with one of the most remarkable sights she had ever seen in her life. "Stop the car, please!"

She got out and stared: a city on a hill, too old to be real, entirely surrounded by an ancient wall, set off by bridges and moats and gates over a swiftly flowing river. It was so very beautiful, she thought. But it was not that which left her breathless. It was that the mists of history had suddenly grown flesh.

Marius stood beside her, his arms crossed. " 'G-d fashioned Toledo before He made the world. Only then did He set the sun to shine above it, like a crown.' This is what it's like." He nodded toward the incredible view. "That moment when you climb into some attic covered with ash and dust and find a pile of exquisite books, wonderfully preserved, as if they'd been waiting patiently for hundreds of years just for you. Waiting to tell you some matchless secret."

She searched his face. The arrogance was gone, and there was a shyness she had not noticed before, like a mischievous young boy caught in some secret act of kindness. And then, without warning, a look of sadness spread over his features. "It almost makes me wish I didn't know," he said softly.

"Know what?"

"Never mind. It's getting late. We need to check into our hotel and make some phone calls."

She followed him silently, wondering.

It almost makes me wish I didn't know, she repeated to herself voicelessly, a sudden chill spreading down her spine.

The hotel had suits of armor in the lobby, and red carpets and coats of arms hung over a huge fireplace. It had a touristy feel to it, Francesca thought, but in a welcoming, Disneyland kind of way. It did not prepare her for her room, which was full of lovely, polished antiques and marvelous old Spanish prints. Best of all was the small wooden balcony off the bedroom, facing the back of the hotel. Francesca stepped out and took a deep breath. Below her were the ancient green-red tiles of Toledo's houses, the dark, fog-drenched valley and church spires, silent in the afternoon siesta. Here and there, she heard the soft hum of a distant car motor working its way along the modern highway back to Madrid. But aside from that, she seemed to have left the twentieth century behind.

It was two o'clock, the heat of the day. She drew the drapes and shed her sweaty clothes, walking naked through the room, feeling the sensuous comfort of an animal shedding its winter fur. The shower caressed her. She closed her eyes, giving herself up to the pleasure of it.

Without her quite understanding how it had happened, her body was no longer the enemy. She looked down with satisfaction at the womanly expanse of flesh, not wishing there were less or more, satisfied with the glowing youth of her skin, the healthy fullness of her limbs. Youth and health, she thought with gratitude, the image of her grandmother suddenly flitting through her consciousness.

How was it she had not regularly thanked G-d for both?

She lay down on the clean, soft sheets, carelessly letting her wet hair soak into the pillow. They were to meet in the lobby in a hour to set out for their first call: a Señor Luis Perez de Almazan.

I will wear something casual, she thought drowsily, something bold and summery that makes me look like a young girl, instead of a CEO. And in her mind, she could already see Marius's eyes lighting up with that same look of appreciative hunger men always managed to have when they looked at Suzanne.

What does she have that I don't? she mourned, dozing off before she found an answer.

"Uh-oh," Marius said when he saw her. "You look beautiful."

"Then why the 'uh-oh'?" She looked down at her form-fitting jeans and halter top.

"Francesca, we are in a very conservative Catholic city. We are going to be visiting a prominent professor, and perhaps some churches as well. Please put on a dress."

"American women don't take much bossing," she snapped.

"I wasn't trying to! Why can't Americans ever understand that when they travel, they have to adapt themselves to the places they visit, and not vice-versa?"

"And I suppose you look perfect," she challenged.

He looked down at himself, surprised. "What?"

"That beard . . ."

He caressed his face as if to protect the precious growth from imminent harm. "You don't like it?" He seemed stricken.

"Actually, it's none of my business. It's a personal choice, and it would be rude of me to demand you change your appearance for my sake."

"You mean you *do* like it?" he asked hopefully.

"That's not the point." She shook her head, exasperated. "I didn't say *that,* either, although it's not so bad. But it's . . . the point is . . ."

"Is the rest of me all right?" He looked down at himself, suddenly concerned.

"Well, you've got on a jacket, but no tie. . . ."

"I hate ties. They feel like a noose. But let's get back to the point. Are you going to change? Because there is no way we can go through Toledo with you dressed like that."

"Are you going to put on a tie?"

"I don't own a tie," he apologized. "Please, Francesca. I'm honestly not trying to be overbearing. It's simply necessary."

"Oh, all right," she relented, feeling suddenly foolish. "I guess I over-reacted. I'll be back in a few minutes."

She rummaged through her suitcases and found a pretty summer dress the color of golden topaz, and a matching wide-brimmed summer hat.

Not her style at all, she thought, wondering what in heaven's name had possessed her to buy it in the first place. It was the salesgirl, she suddenly remembered. She'd suggested it might be fun to buy something that wasn't "her" at all.

She held it against herself, looking into the mirror. Pretty, modest, and irresistibly feminine, with a tiny waist and a full skirt. It would have made her teeth ache if she'd seen it on another woman.

Slowly, she slipped it over her head, then stared at herself in the mirror. It was certainly not sensible Francesca Abraham, New York subway commuter and bank employee. More Scarlett O'Hara Abraham on her way to the barbecue, she thought sheepishly, pinning on the hat. Her eyes looked back at her, pleased, gleaming like amber out of her fair, narrow face.

He might laugh, she considered.

Whatever.

There was *no way* she was changing again.

When she got out of the elevator, he was sitting directly across from her. He got up slowly, his step hesitant.

"Francesca?"

His face lit up with a familiar look, an expression she recognized immediately: it was the one men had when they looked at her sister.

22

Something about him was different. The collar of his shirt was high and chafing against his tanned skin. He wore a pale blue tie.

"Gift shop," he mumbled.

She nodded, trying not to laugh out loud.

He offered her his arm with old-fashioned courtesy. She took it with a sudden shyness. Surprisingly, she did not feel the least absurd. He was very broad-shouldered, but not really that tall, she noted, looking up at him with satisfaction. She hated men who towered over her, putting her in their shadow.

It was surprisingly cooler in the shadowy old cobblestone streets that twisted into narrow walkways and quiet courtyards. They left the car in front of the hotel, deciding it would be almost impossible to navigate through these ancient labyrinths.

"Can you tell me who this person is and why we're going to see him?"

"Señor de Almazan is a professor of history at the local university. He also has a strange hobby. He makes ritual objects: menorahs, spice boxes, mezuzah holders. He has a store where he sells these things, and other rare objects, including manuscripts of Jewish interest."

"Is he Jewish?"

"I highly doubt it. But his interest isn't surprising, considering he's a Toledano—that is, a citizen of Toledo. Toledo had the oldest Jewish settlement on the Iberian peninsula."

She looked around at the old Moorish alleyways, the gloomy houses dark with age. A sudden inexplicable shiver ran down her spine despite the summer heat. "What happened here, Marius?"

He hesitated. "Where should I begin? With the Visigoths back in 305 A.D., those lovely barbarians who murdered men, beheaded women, kidnapped small children, and then declared everyone not of their religious persuasion slaves—all for the glory of Christ? Or with the Almohades, who did the same—and worse—for Mohammed? Or maybe we should start with the Inquisition, since that lasted the longest."

"Did they burn people here?"

"Of course. In the square near our hotel. But I've always thought the worst part of the Inquisition wasn't the burning, it was what happened before. Wives testifying against husbands, children condemning their own mothers and fathers, their own brothers and sisters."

"How is that possible?" She shook her head with disbelief.

He shrugged. "Let's not ruin a lovely day."

She didn't press him, wondering if she really wanted to know.

They walked quietly along the pleasant bustling streets filled with families and tourists licking ice cream cones and chattering in front of store windows. Then they turned off the main thoroughfares into the quiet alleyways of old stone buildings. Exquisite, wrought-iron railings held overflowing pots of red geraniums, which spilled over and down, brightening the old facades.

"*Calle de la sinagoga*" she read from the street sign, startled. "Can that mean what I think it does? 'Street of the Synagogue'?"

He nodded.

"Does that mean there are regular Saturday services?"

He smiled. "There hasn't been a Jewish community in Toledo for over five hundred years."

"Then why keep calling it the 'Street of the Synagogue'?" she asked, feeling inexplicably irritated.

"It's part of Toledo's history. They can't bear to part with their Jews after all. They say Franco himself was a descendant of *conversos*. He took a strange interest in restoring these buildings. This one especially was in great disrepair. It had been used as a barracks, an ammunition dump, and then a convent for fallen women."

She looked around, startled. "I don't see any building."

"Behind you."

Broken steps led to a narrow opening, almost hidden from the street. She stepped inside and was enveloped by a fragrant garden of roses and acacias. A row of cypresses led to the imposing doorway of an ancient building.

Francesca heard the creak of massive old wood beams as the door swung open. They stepped over the threshold. It was nearly pitch dark inside.

"*Uno momento,*" someone said. They heard scurrying footsteps. A few yellow lightbulbs suddenly went on.

The sight was startling: Dozens of octagonal columns, each graced by an intricate carved capital, crowded the huge space. Graceful Moorish arches spanned the room, leading one's eyes upward toward the ceiling paneled with carved rosettes, fleurs-de-lis, and medallions interwoven with the Star of David.

Francesca looked up with a dizzying sense of disbelief. It had a strange, ancient beauty that seemed to rise from the mists of imagination.

"What is this?"

"It is called the Church of Santa Maria la Blanca now. But it was originally built in 1259 by Yoseph Ibn Shushan as a synagogue."

Francesca wandered through the hall, reaching the Christian altar at the other end. Its gold leaf and statuary were clearly a foreign element in the Jewish-Moorish structure.

They stood before it.

"It's so hard to make sense of any of this. A synagogue that looks like a mosque and is now a church . . ."

"On the contrary, it makes perfect sense. For hundreds of years there was this apache dance: First, Christians, Jews, and Muslims danced cheek to cheek, and then bloodied heads were thrown against the walls. And it was always the same: forced baptisms, ultimatums. Convert or lose all your property, your homes, your jobs, your children, your freedom. The Christians did it to the Moors and Jews, and the Moors did it to the Christians and Jews. Whichever religion was in power made the other two suffer."

"But it makes no sense! Didn't they all believe in the same G-d, really? In loving your neighbor, in goodness? Where did all this hatred in the name of the G-d of love start?"

"It's even worse than that. All three monotheistic religions were founded by blood relatives. It was brother against brother."

"Really?"

"Well, Abraham was the founder of Judaism. His concubine, Hagar, gave him a son, Ishmael, who fathered the Muslims. And his grandson, Esau, fathered Edom, which is Rome and Christianity."

She sat quietly, reflecting on the story. There was something terribly wrong about the place. It was like one of those hybrid monsters in Greek mythology, with the tail of a fish and the head of an ox.

"Let's go, Marius."

"Sure?"

She nodded.

They walked farther up the street. "Here's the second one."

"Second what?"

"Synagogue."

"Was this one also converted to a church?"

"Yes, but it isn't used for services anymore. It's part of a Sephardic Jewish museum. It's called El Transito. It was the private family synagogue of the King's wealthy treasurer, Don Samuel HaLevi Abulafia. When he built it about six hundred years ago, he defied all the laws about synagogues being smaller and lower than churches, and plain of decoration. He put his whole soul into it. Poor man."

"Why? What happened to him?"

He sighed.

"Another horrible, depressing tale?"

"Are you sure you want to know?"

"No, I'm not," she murmured. "Okay. Tell me."

"King Pedro the Cruel was a fickle playboy. After Don Samuel had filled his coffers with collected taxes, the King accused him of treason, confiscating all his money and ordering him tortured. Don Samuel was so outraged at the injustice of his treatment that he never uttered another word, either to protest his innocence or to condemn the King. He died on the rack in silence."

She let out a deep breath. "I don't think I can stand going inside now that I know!"

"It's one of the most beautiful places you will ever see in your life."
She followed cautiously behind him.

There were guards, and modern lighting, and tickets to be purchased. She felt the sense of having entered some well-preserved work
of art, beautiful but without function. But when she passed the outer
doorways into the single-nave hall, all her listlessness left her.

It challenged all her previous conceptions of beauty. The workman-
ship, the symmetry, the exquisite design and execution of the most intricate patterns imaginable—everything pointed to man paying homage
to the glory of heaven. Even the walls seemed to sing with prayer.

The ceiling was hand-carved larch wood. Two bands ran across all
four walls. On the first were blind and open windows, covered with
magnificent latticework. Beneath was a band of intricate, carved lettering and floral motifs, intertwined with the shields of Castile and Leon.
Both bands were framed by Hebrew letters.

She studied the richness of the decoration, the foliate interlacings in
colors of red, green, blue, white, and black. The eastern wall was the
most magnificent of all. Stucco work of an endless pattern of rhom-
boids competed for the viewer's admiration. In the center was a carved-
out niche.

"That would have held the Torah scrolls," Marius pointed out. On
either side were carved inscriptions.

"What do they say?"

"'To Don Samuel, a man raised to the highest, may his G-d go with
him and extol him. He has found grace and mercy under the wings of
the mighty, great-winged eagle, warrior valiant among all others, the
great Monarch our King and master, the Great Don Pedro,'" Marius
translated from the Spanish museum guide.

She shook her head. "The great Don Pedro, indeed! And what about
those?" She pointed to the frieze of Hebrew letters that ran all around
the room.

"They're verses from Psalms, Chronicles, and Kings, about the joy
of serving G-d and the everlasting value of prayer."

It was unimaginably beautiful.

She thought of the kind of man who had conceived it and had possessed the power to oversee and finance its construction. What a remarkable human being was Don Samuel! Quick tears came to her eyes,

imagining his final days, the courage of his silent contempt for those who would degrade him.

On the south wall were great windows facing an overhanging balcony. She knew, instinctively, it must be the women's section.

She wandered up the steps and stared at the glass cases holding wedding rings and traditional Sephardic bridal robes. Suddenly, her mind filled with the strangely vivid image of pews filled with wives and grandmothers, aunts and sisters, prayer books in their hands as they looked through the latticework at their men. And there, in the place of honor at the eastern wall, she could see a great, dignified personage sitting next to the rabbi, holding the Scroll of Law.

She heard all the voices rising and mingling, one shout of joyous homage to their Maker. And then, as in a dream, someone whispered in her ear:

> *Pan y bino beo*
> *En la Ley de Muysen creo*
> *Dios no a benido, mas Dios bendra*
> *Dios que me hizo, Dios me salbara*

It was a woman's voice, husky with emotion, and she was practically singing.

Francesca turned, startled. But except for a few Japanese tourists and their guide at the other end, the gallery was empty.

Her face went white. She hurried down the steps.

Marius took her arm. "You look positively spooked! And what's all that gold stuff on your dress?"

Little gold threads clung to her sleeve. She stared at them. "Someone sang in my ear! But when I turned around, no one was there."

"It's all my stories! I'm upsetting you."

"This is not my imagination, I'm telling you! It was a woman. She sang in Spanish . . ."

He touched her shoulder lightly. "You're shouting."

She looked around, mortified, her fingers brushing off the gold threads. Silently, she followed Marius out. As they passed once again through the great prayer hall, she took one last look at its otherworldly beauty. These walls were built to echo with prayer, she thought with sudden, tragic clarity. And that would never happen again.

The thought was devastating.

She walked into the adjoining museum. There, behind glass cases, were silver spice boxes, Torah ornaments, charity boxes, menorahs, and Sabbath candlesticks. She touched the cold, protective glass, closing her eyes.

Once, long ago, she'd breathed in the magic fragrance of myrtle branches and mint, held to her nose in a silver box. "To have a sweet week!" someone had sung. Someone—she couldn't remember who, but someone very old—had held a tall, bright candle and told her to look at her own reflection flickering in the sweet wine of a silver goblet, a good charm against all harm.

She stared at her reflection in the cold glass. Museum pieces, she thought. Never again would they need to be polished against the acid and sweat of human hands; the accretions of dust and memories, both tragic and joyful, were ended now forever. They had been removed from time and life, made irrelevant and useless.

It was so sad, almost unbearable.

She opened the door and walked out, looking for the exit. Instead, she found herself in an outer courtyard enclosed on all sides. A light sweat suddenly broke out on her brow. Everywhere she looked were old tombstones.

"'They are old tombs from ancient times / In which some men sleep the endless rest / Inside them is neither hate nor envy, nor love, nor neighborly enmity / And I cannot know from looking at them, the difference between lords and slaves.' Moses Ibn Ezra, twelfth century," Marius said softly, standing beside her.

She held herself, shivering. "What is this?"

"They've been gathered from ancient Jewish cemeteries all over Spain. It's out of respect. A way of preserving them."

Almost as if someone were leading her by the hand, she found herself wandering around the courtyard until she came to a piece of dark gray granite whose chiseled letters were only barely visible beneath the greenish-black mold. It was hundreds of years old.

"Can you make out the words?" she asked Marius.

"The letters are Hebrew script. *'Chana, bat Yehuda ve Ester Nasi'.* Hannah, the daughter of Yuda and Esther Nasi."

She looked at it, shocked. "What's the date, and where did it come from?"

"Fourteen eighty-two, I think. Somewhere near Seville."

Her fingers traced the cold granite. Almost erased, she thought, tears suddenly streaming down her cheeks.

He reached out to her wonderingly, gently brushing her tear-dampened hair away from her face, smoothing away the tears with his thumb. "Come," he whispered, tucking her arm through his and leading her back into the street.

They sat side by side in silence in a quiet quadrangle by a waterless old fountain. From somewhere down the street, music suddenly filled the empty square. It was Vivaldi, she recognized, sweet beyond bearing with an edge of something so sadly beautiful, so exquisitely heartbreaking, it again brought tears to her eyes.

"That's my grandmother's family, you see. It's our family name." She wiped her eyes and blew her nose. "I feel so stupid! This is not like me at all. You don't know me well enough to judge, but really, it's nothing like me," she insisted, shaking her head, ashamed of losing control.

He put his arm around her, and she felt the warmth of his skin banish the cold chill of glass museum cases and tombstones. The dead past, she thought. If you got too close to it, it dragged you out of the daylight, into dark, sunless corridors better left unvisited.

"How can you stand it, Marius? All those graveyards of dead books, all those ghosts of the past?"

"Books never die! The moment you read them, they live again. As for ghosts, there are all kinds. Some are quite wise and very beautiful," he murmured against her ear.

She felt the tingle of his breath against her neck. I should pull away, she thought, trying to resist. To her surprise, her body paid no attention, content and joyful, almost suspended.

"The first time I went book hunting, it was here in Spain. I had taken off one summer during college to research the family tree. The things I learned . . . it was enthralling, devastating. It almost destroyed me!"

She looked up at him, surprised. "Why?"

"Trying to assimilate hundreds of years of life that came before me, to somehow fit my own existence into that. It was so complicated."

"Yes," she agreed, feeling a strange new connection to him. "Exactly."

The music rose, weaving lavender and pale lace into the golden light. Unearthly now in the fading light, it wound around the trees, filling the silent square. The church bells pealed, and a flock of birds rose skyward with a silken rustle.

"You can almost feel the spirits of those who lived in these houses hundreds of years ago hovering in the air, can't you? It's as if they can't bear to leave."

She suddenly sat up straight, clasping her hands tightly around her knees until the knuckles shone white. "What am I supposed to make of all of this?"

"Ah! The golden enigma. What is one supposed to do with one's history?" He smiled ruefully. "Come, Señor Almazan is waiting."

A distinguished older man, with the sharply defined features one saw in drawings of Spanish conquistadors, opened the door to let them in. Despite his courtesy, there was a dignity and firmness in his expression that made Francesca feel he was not a man to be trifled with, nor one who suffered fools gladly.

He seemed a bit impatient, too, Francesca thought. But soon she realized that it was simply eagerness.

"Come up to the study."

They followed him up an old staircase leading to a wooden gallery overlooking the high-ceilinged living room. On the walls were framed prints by El Greco, Murillo, and Velázquez—dark, moody scenes depicting a suffering Christ and saintly apostles in the throes of a passionate devotion to something Francesca couldn't begin to fathom. Beautifully carved wooden crosses were scattered everywhere.

"May I offer you some wine?" he asked. "Ah, no. Jews do not drink wine unsupervised by rabbis," he corrected himself.

"Well, actually . . ." Francesca began, about to enlighten him that keeping such religious laws and customs had long ago been lost to her, and to most others she knew. But somehow in this setting, surrounded by the evidence of this man's own deep, religious devotion, she felt suddenly ashamed to admit it.

"Please forgive me," Señor Almazan continued. "Here is some hazelnut liqueur, Frangelica. That, I believe, is all right, is it not?"

"Yes, perfect. How kind of you, señor, to take such trouble," Marius interceded.

"Would you like to see my latest creation, Mr. Serouya?"

"I'd be delighted."

He reached up to an open shelf and brought down a silver spice box in the shape of a windmill, decorated with the six-pointed Star of David. He held it up for inspection the way a parent pushes forward his child: proud, yet anxious and hypercritical. "I copied it from a very old one found in a book about Toledo's Jewish quarter."

Francesca looked at Almazan and at the spice box: "Don de Almazan, are you from a Jewish family originally?"

He seemed taken aback. "Not at all—at least we have no proof." He hesitated. "But who can tell, really, here in Spain? The whole history of the Jews in Spain is like Don Quixote tilting at windmills. First, threatening the whole Jewish population with expulsion if they didn't convert, then not believing them when they did! And finally, after all those tortures to verify who were sincere converts, deciding we didn't want converts after all; that what we really wanted was *limpieza,* 'purity of blood.' A strange desire, wouldn't you say, after baptizing thousands, intermarrying with them, and letting them rise up as priests and bishops, advisers to the King . . . ?! And meaning only well, of course, dreaming only the purest, most impossible dream!"

"It's very strange."

"There is something in the Spanish soul that aches for a passionate kind of spiritual purity. Christianity gives us that. But this longing also corrupted us. The Inquisition was supposed to be on the highest, spiritual level, a way to root out heresy and cleanse the nation of all foreign, destructive elements. That is why the priests kept such meticulous records of the trials and tortures they inflicted. Instead, it created a lust for money and for blood.

"Whoever denounced someone as a Judaizer got a share of all his money, the rest going to the Church and the King. So it became the money after a while, not the saving of souls. And the autos-da-fé themselves were huge, crowd-pleasing spectacles, no different from feeding Christians to lions." He shook his head. "Have you seen Santa Maria la Blanca?"

"Yes. It was magnificent."

"You have to imagine what Toledo was like back then. Teeming with young Christian scholars from beyond the Pyrenees, Jewish poets and philosophers, and Moorish nobles and scientists, and everyone mingling and learning from one another. The Jews had a gift for languages, and so they translated the works the Moslems had brought with them into Arabic, and then into Latin, so the Christian scholars could read them. Works on astronomy, botany, medicine. The whole world was frozen in this terrible black ice of superstition and ignorance, and Toledo was burning with creativity and scholarship, melting the ice, beginning the Renaissance."

She twined her fingers together nervously, thinking about another kind of burning.

As if he had read her mind, he went on. "And yet we destroyed that golden time with our own hands. And all because of a poor self-image."

Marius and Francesca exchanged bemused glances at the use of the modern psychological term to explain the passionate religious furies that raged during the Middle Ages.

"Yes, don't smile! If one is deeply convinced that one has found the true way, why would one feel the need to oppress others who hold different opinions?" He looked across at them, his face full of sorrow, anger, and something akin to a strange pride.

"We were just discussing this a little while ago. All this hatred in the name of the G-d of Love."

"Exactly. Have you ever heard the story of the three rings?"

"No, I haven't," Francesca admitted.

"It goes something like this: There once was a man who owned a priceless, magic ring, a gift from someone he deeply loved. It had a stone of rare opal that caught and reflected every color of the rainbow, bestowing on its owner a magic power: Whoever possessed it and believed in its power would be beloved by G-d and man.

"The ring never left the man's finger. On his deathbed, he willed it to his favorite child, and asked that each of his descendants do the same.

"Generations passed, and the ring came to be owned by a father with three children. They were all wonderful, and he loved each one equally. He just couldn't bring himself to choose among them. So, he took the ring to a jeweler and asked that two additional rings be fashioned to exactly duplicate the original. Before he died, he summoned each one of his children to him separately, giving each of them a ring and a blessing.

"Well, the father was hardly cold in the earth when all hell broke loose, each one of the children declaring themselves the owner of the only real ring and thus deserving of being looked upon as the unquestioned head of the family. But no one could prove it.

"Terrible jealousies began, and the family was torn apart, each child seeking to degrade the other to prove his natural superiority, to prove that he, and only he, had inherited the true ring.

"Bloodied and depressed, they submitted their dispute to a wise judge, who told them the following: "Each of you shall continue to believe he has the real ring. Compete to make the ring's power manifest by showing humility, tolerance, and piety. And if your children's children's children can achieve the love of G-d and man, then it makes no difference who has the real ring.""

He shook his head.

"Whenever I think of those hundreds of years in which Christianity was triumphant, there is this image I cannot erase: the hordes rampaging against the defenseless, holding the cross as their banner, and those who faced them wrapped in prayer shawls singing Psalms. It haunts me. And so, I make these objects. In homage, you might say. Or even envy."

"Envy?" Francesca repeated, bewildered.

"Yes. Envy. There is a mystery hidden in your people, a riddle mankind has pondered for centuries. So many times, you've been like a tree pulled out at the roots. Instead of withering and dying, you somehow replant yourself, flowering in another place, at another time. Many peoples have been uprooted and dispersed. They simply merged into whatever culture they found themselves. Only the Jews remain stubbornly Jews. Why? How?"

She looked at him, puzzled.

She was a New Yorker. An American. Until this moment, the heritage she had been born with had always seemed like delicate, old lace wrapped in tissue paper in the attic: lovely and useless and quite irrelevant. Perhaps, she thought, the power, whatever it was, had finally disappeared.

She suddenly heard herself say:

Pan y bino beo
En la Ley de Muysen creo
Dios no a benido, mas Dios bendra
Dios que me hizo, Dios me salbara

Marius gazed at her in astonishment.

"I'm sorry! I don't even know what it means."

"'Bread and wine my eyes do see/In the Law of Moses I do believe/The Messiah has not come but he will appear/And the Lord, my creator, this Lord will save me,'" Almazan translated. "It is a very old *converso* prayer. During the Inquisition, anyone heard uttering such words would have signed their death warrant."

Francesca turned white. "I heard someone whisper it in my ear in El Transito . . ."

"Impossible! Only the most erudite scholars have ever heard of it!"

"I heard it!" she said stubbornly. "How else? I'm not a scholar. I don't even know Spanish!"

Almazan stared at her curiously. "There was an old woman who worked for me as housekeeper. She said it was well-known that the souls of those burned at the stake often came back to Toledo to clothe themselves in corporeal bodies, to visit the places they knew and loved. El Transito, she always said, was full of such spirits."

Francesca's face turned pale as she picked the last gold threads off her dress.

Marius cleared his throat. "Don de Almazan, you are a remarkable man. And if I might say so, your city, Toledo, holds its history like a beautiful setting holds a fine jewel." He picked up the spice box and turned it over admiringly in his hands. "As you know, we are searching for the manuscript of Doña Gracia Mendes. Francesca Abraham is one of the last of her descendants. We have found part of it . . ."

Señor Almazan held up a hand. "Do not go on. The story is well known to me. And, I'm afraid, it is not a pretty one."

Marius looked startled. "In what way?"

"Please, sit down, both of you."

He offered them tall, straight-backed chairs upholstered with antique, tooled leather.

"The manuscript in question was not the property of the person who sold it to you. It was stolen from the library of a church in the Extremadura, a small town called Cáceres, a few miles from the Portuguese border."

"Stolen? And from Cáceres?" Marius exclaimed. "How would such an important document have wound up in a church in Cáceres? And more important, where is it now?"

Señor Almazan shook his head firmly. "I can tell you no more. I am a professor of history at the university. I am a respected antiques dealer. I can have nothing to do with such a dirty business. I'm sorry."

"You mean . . . that is . . . you won't help us?" Francesca said, devastated.

"Even were it in my possession, which it no longer is, I could not in good conscience have handed it over to you."

"No longer is . . ." Marius said in a strangled tone. "Do you mean to say that you've seen it, the whole thing? That the manuscript exists and was in your hands, here?"

He nodded. "Yes, I have seen it, although I cannot be certain that what I have seen is all of it. I was only permitted to examine it for a short time in order to appraise its value. The person who brought it to me was a stranger. When I began asking him questions, he disappeared. That is all I can tell you."

"Then how do you know it was from Cáceres?" Marius challenged.

"Ah, that is detective work! You are in rare manuscripts, are you not, Mr. Serouya? Then you know we are all quite a small family. Toward the evening of the very same day that the young man disappeared with the manuscript, I received a phone call from my colleague in Córdoba, Don Elonza, who wanted to consult with me over the value of a manuscript, being offered him. When he described it—the watermarks, the color of the ink, the language—it all fit. I realized it was the same one I had seen just a few hours earlier. He said the fellow seemed desperate, saying he needed to return with the money to Cáceres, or he would be in terrible trouble."

"What happened?" Francesca inquired anxiously.

"I preferred to refrain from asking too many questions. I merely stated that I thought the manuscript genuine and worth quite a bit of money."

"What happened to it, *señor?*" Francesca half rose out of her seat in excitement.

Marius placed a calming hand over her arm.

"I really can't say. That is, I don't know, not for sure."

"How long ago was this?" Marius asked.

"Last Thursday."

"So, it might still be in Córdoba, if it was purchased. Or perhaps . . ."

"It could be anywhere by now," Francesca groaned. She couldn't believe it! They'd been so close.

Marius rose. "Señor de Almazan, thank you so much. Would you be kind enough to give me your colleague's name and address in Córdoba?"

He wrote it down for them, and accompanied them to the door.

Francesca extended her hand politely. He took it warmly, pressing it to his lips. "What is the secret?" he whispered.

She lowered her eyes, ashamed.

23

Suzanne felt the sunlight on her back. She pulled the fragrant silk sheet around her shoulders, her arms warm and heavy with a kind of peace she had never known. She shifted slightly, resting her head on the clean skin of Gabriel's broad chest, breathing him in. He had a unique scent, a combination of musk and rosemary. At first, she'd thought she'd imagined it. But it had turned out to be a special soap he used. An old family recipe.

My love, my love, my love, she thought, with unending wonder.

How was it possible, this connection, immediate and without any peer? I have been in love before, she insisted to herself. At least, I thought . . .

It was too painful, the comparison to Renaldo.

Nothing was the same.

Even the world was different, she thought, touching his sleeping forehead, her fingers smoothing his thick, bright hair, pale gold in the morning light. She felt like some worshiper at the shrine of a Greek deity, helplessly overwhelmed by the sheer depth of her devotion and vulnerability.

She thought of the moment when he must wake and lift his head, put his feet to the floor, and his arms to his sides. The moment when he would go to the bathroom and brush his teeth and take a shower; when he would dress and go outside, away from her.

It was almost unbearable.

I felt my heart ache with loneliness at the thought that my body should soon be separated from his.

The words, unbidden, echoed in her mind. She wrapped her arms around him, listening to his quiet breathing and the sudden tightening of his long, gentle fingers around her naked waist as he pulled her toward him.

"*Flesh of my flesh, bone of my bone,*" she thought, understanding for the first time the meaning of the story of creation. One creature, divided into two. Man and woman. And reunited, a perfect whole.

Perfect, she thought, taking in the silk-covered walls—color of the Mediterranean sky—the matching damask drapes, and the dustless antique furnishings. It made no difference to her, really. We could be out in the grass in a tent. On a mountainside in the Himalayas. In Brooklyn. Place had no meaning. Nor time. She wasn't even sure what day it was anymore, or what week. Had it been only that, she thought, startled, just weeks since the chance meeting in the lobby of the Savoy? Such a long journey, in such a short time? How far she had come from her old life! So far that units of measure such as calendars and clocks seemed puny and hopelessly inadequate. She was traveling in light-years.

It cannot last. It never does. Not with me. Not with anyone, a small voice told her.

She felt frightened, but not panic-stricken. There was truth in it. Always other, competing passions had chipped away, demanding her devotion. Her work, her studies, her delicate sensibilities. Men never lived up to her expectations. Except . . .

She mouthed his name—R e n a l d o—then checked herself for damage. Nothing had happened, she realized, ashamed, exhilarated, and almost tearful with freedom. No wound had torn open. No blood gushed.

She thought of his big, dark, laughing face with a fondness that was almost nostalgic. With Renaldo there had been joy, and the endless stirring of frantic experience. There had been wonderful physical pleasure, and stimulating mental exercises.

But there had never been this; this peace, this overwhelming certainty.

Like hearing something you had always known was true, something that matched exactly all the information stored in your heart. There was no question of disagreeing, of finding reasons to resist.

It was Gran's voice, she suddenly realized, disturbed by its emergence, unbidden, into a private conversation. It made her want to resist. Perhaps you feel this way now because Renaldo is gone, she thought, because you were so lonely, so empty. Perhaps if you saw him again . . .

She felt Gabriel's hands move slowly down her back, a long stroke of love, almost fatherly in its infinite tenderness. She reached up, touching his ears, the warm place in the back of his neck, bringing his lips down to hers with a neediness she could not help. He accepted her passion with a startled smile of joy, as if she had offered him a great and undeserved gift, and his pure happiness dissolved any shame. There could be no shame in partaking of the great, blessed abundance now rightfully hers, she told herself. No shame in reaching across the fleshy abyss that separated their souls. The body, as Gabriel was fond of saying, was always servant to the spirit.

For an instant, she thought of all those loveless acts she had committed so half-heartedly in years past, because of physical temptation, or laziness, or just plain having had too much to drink. The faked intimacy of the good-bye kiss, the embarrassment of seeing each other dress in the light of morning, and wanting, really, for nothing more than to see them leave. Worst of all, the degradation of peering into the soul of a stranger and watching it blink back at you without recognition.

She did not believe in sin or punishment. But she understood all at once that such acts had been a crime, a deep violation, against the core of her being.

I will explain this to my daughter, she suddenly thought, then stopped as she felt her lover's body move once more in perfect rhythm with her own.

Eventually, he did get up, and so did she. It seemed almost impossible that such things as flossing and pouring milk into coffee still existed in the strange, exotic world they now inhabited.

They sat across from each other at the small, charming table, waiting for the maid to leave the covered tray with their breakfast: warm croissants and fresh strawberries, marmalade, and scones. A vase of fresh daffodils and freesia perfumed the air.

They had arrived late the evening before. Gabriel had dumped the luggage on the carpet and carried her up the stairs into a lovely suite.

She poured his coffee, measuring the milk exactly to give it the toasty-brown color she'd learned he liked best. He picked through the strawberries, choosing the largest and sweetest ones for her, touching her face as he handed her the plate.

"Gabriel, my love, can this go on forever?"

"We would both hate that, wouldn't we?" he replied.

"Well, okay, not forever. But a few years, or months?" She smiled a little anxiously.

That was their problem, the one they had been avoiding. How to plunge back into the real world they had rocketed out of with such startling and wonderful success.

"You know, my friend George is covering for me at the center until I get back. . . ."

"Darling, saintly George." She came around and sat on his lap, draping her arm around his neck and feeding him strawberries. She kissed the wet, sweet juice that ran down his chin.

"But there is my practice. My partner will take the emergencies, but I need to see my children soon." He shrugged.

My children. She loved the way he'd said that, the way he referred to his patients. It almost brought tears to her eyes, she loved it so much.

"So, what next?"

"I want you to meet my family."

She'd known that was coming. That it had to, eventually.

"And what if I said: No way. No families. That the family is the root of all trouble, all meddling and destructiveness. That family is what we leave behind when we bolt away with our lovers."

He stroked her forehead. "You will come meet my family, though, won't you, my love?"

"Are they like you?"

"Much nicer."

She sighed, leaning against his chest like a sleepy, contented child. "You're lying, of course."

He laughed. "You know I never lie."

"Everyone lies."

"No, they don't."

She seemed honestly surprised to hear this. "Do you mean that?"

"I know people who don't lie. You, for example."

"I am the biggest liar of all."

"No." His lips touched her forehead. "You always tell the truth, no matter how unpleasant. It is part of your charm."

"Gabriel, I'm afraid."

"Of what?"

"Of hating your family. Of having them hate me. Of not being able to bear sharing you with them."

"Suzanne, you will love my family. And they will love you as they love me. They're very special people."

"Yes, I suppose." She resigned herself to the inevitable. "There is only one condition."

"Yes?"

"That you don't insist on meeting mine."

"Are you ashamed of me?"

"Oh, no! The opposite."

"Are they bank robbers? Child molesters?"

"Worse," she groaned. "Social climbers who buy bad contemporary art. At least that describes my stepfather."

"And your real father?"

"Real father," she repeated. "An interesting term. I don't have a real father," she said curtly. "The man who was married to my mother and produced me left us for another woman; someone, I might add, just as silly as my mother."

"You don't see him at all?"

"I see him every time I can't get out of it," she said matter-of-factly. "He bores me. They all do. Their lives are one big void waiting to be filled with things that cost money. And it never will be. They will never be able to buy enough to fill that box. They will open it every morning of their lives, and it will always seem empty. They'll always be hungry."

She walked to the window and looked out at the lovely English countryside blooming with the rich fecundity of a cherished and cared for paradise. "It's so beautiful here. I wish we didn't have to leave."

"We can always come back here. Whenever you like."

"You swear?"

"I never swear. But I'll make you a conditional promise."

"What's the condition?"

"That you come back here with me."

She took his hand and kissed it, leaning her cheek against the knuckles that rubbed along her face.

"When do we leave?"

"An hour?"

"So soon?"

"It's a very short flight, but we need to get to the airport."

"Airport?"

"We're going to Gibraltar. It's a family celebration. Everyone will be there, and, of course, they're expecting me. It's a perfect opportunity for you to meet everyone."

She held her hand out to him, and he took it, kissing the palm and each knuckle, then holding it against his cheek.

Flesh of my flesh, bone of my bone.

The idea that he would want her to become part of his family, as close to him as his own blood, made her feel like weeping with gratitude.

"What kind of celebration is it?"

"A bar mitzvah."

She stared at him. "Fonseca," she said slowly. "What kind of name is Fonseca?"

"It was actually da Silva, until a maternal grandmother insisted her grandson use her maiden name. That was in 1750. Before that, the family lived in Spain for centuries, up until the Order of Expulsion. After that, they scattered. They wound up in Ferrara, because there was a duke there kindly disposed toward refugees. And in England, because so many were bankers. Others went to Amsterdam and Morocco, and from there several wound up in Gibraltar. It's a tiny place, and oddly beautiful. And the people are extraordinary. You'll see. A few months ago, my cousin married a boy from Rome who is a very serious student of Talmud. I think they plan to live in Jerusalem, at least for a while." He looked at her stunned face, puzzled.

"Suzanne, is something wrong?"

Across the room, on the wall behind him, Suzanne stared at the shadow of an old woman. She was doubled over, her shoulders shaking with glee. It took Suzanne several minutes until she realized that it was simply the shadow of the daffodils swaying in the breeze.

24

DEAREST GRAN: WONDERFUL NEWS! MARIUS AND I HAVE
FOUND SOME MORE PAGES HERE IN CORDOBA! WILL SEND
A COPY ON TO YOU AS SOON AS POSSIBLE. URGENT WE
CONTINUE ON AS QUICKLY AS POSSIBLE. WILL CONTACT
YOU SOON AS TO WHEREABOUTS.

LOVE, LOVE, LOVE
FRANCESCA

Unbound manuscript pages. 23 x 33. India ink on parchment. Circa
1570? Alonzo dos Remedios, Rare Books, Córdoba. Sold to Serouya
and Company, London. Provenance unknown.

*M**arriage, my father wrote to me the day before my wedding, is
the most singular friendship in the world. So drawn are
husband and wife to one another by love and choice and
experience, that what one desires the other also chooses; and what
one says the other upholds in silence, as if he had uttered it
himself. In true love, two persons share a single soul. And out of
that singleness, comes children.*
   He wrote further:

Do not view motherhood as the curse of Eve. It is woman's privilege, and her burden.

Do not follow the fashion and abandon your tender babes to the nutrix and cunabularia, those ignorant peasants who wet-nurse for a gold coin, letting their own babes starve. For how often are highborn babes delivered to such women in swaddling of the finest linen, only to be returned in coarsely woven shrouds? Hold your child not only in your womb, but also, from its earliest infancy, in your arms. Hear its cry, and nurse it from the milk that is the product of your own blood.

Obey the laws of marriage scrupulously, with modesty and sanctity. Watch for the signs of your flow and separate from your husband. Be punctilious in going to the ritual baths. And be modest and decent in your relations.

Respect your husband and be invariably amiable.

And expect that he honor you more than himself, and treat you always with tender consideration.

Live in a community, not isolated from others.

And even if you must beg alms to provide it, see that your children have a teacher to instruct them, so that their souls and their characters may be amply nourished.

Marry off your children as soon as their age is ripe, to members of respectable families.

Don't eat heavy meals.

Wear clean, nice clothes.

Keep your house tidy, for sickness and poverty are to be found in foul dwellings.

All this do, that G-d may love and honor you after the manner of your fathers.

These were my father's words, written in his fine hand, because, I imagine, my mother was not there to do it for him. Also, I suspect he understood that from my aunt I should receive advice of quite a different sort. And so I did.

"Remember, if you step on his foot during the ceremony, you will rule over him. But if he steps on yours, you will be his slave," she advised.

"I have no wish to rule or to be ruled!" I laughed scornfully, forgetting G-d's wish that we honor our elders. My punishment was swift and cruel.

"Then be prepared to suffer!" she declared, pressing her lips together in that knowing smile of spiteful pleasure older people have when relating bad news to the young. "Every man is a wanton. Did not even our wisest of kings, Solomon, keep a thousand wives and concubines? Your husband, too, will have his mistresses, and his little bastards. For this is the way of all men, especially at Court. Look the other way and be grateful. You will be mistress of his household, owner of his property, mother of his heirs. And he will rob another of her rest!"

Her words filled me with bottomless horror. "Never!" I cried.

"Alcavo de un anyo el moso toma las manya de su ami," she said hatefully. After a while, a servant grows used to his lord's manners.

My head spun.

From then on, I found myself untouched by the frenzy of those laboring to dower me and prepare my wedding feast. Like some errant knight's armor, a sadness encased me that nothing seemed to penetrate.

Could it be, my mind ceaselessly pondered, that Francisco, my Francisco, would ever long to touch another? The idea tortured me in a way I was helpless to counter.

My wedding ablutions I performed in the river, far from prying eyes. The bogo de baño *and* cafe de baño *were picnics on the grass, rather than the elegant affairs of our ancestors. Still, we feasted on* dulce de naranja *and* dulce de conja.

My wedding day dawned fair and mild. My maids bathed and dressed me in my velvet gown of richest scarlet with its jeweled girdle of tiny pearls, rubies, and emeralds. They brushed and coiled my hair, then covered it with a rete of silken gold entwined with tiny diamonds. And when they were finished, they took the diadem that was Francisco's gift out of its golden box and placed it on my head.

I stared at it in the looking-glass: intertwining ovals of tiny diamonds and emeralds surrounded ten magnificent rubies the size of hens' eggs, all set in gold. No queen's crown anywhere in Europe could rival it, I warranted. I fingered it thoughtfully. Surely a man who would bestow such a gift upon a woman would have no desire to search for another?

But it was of no use. I could not convince myself. Gifts were not what I needed. The only thing I would ever desire from him was his heart. Unlike fine jewels, it could not be lent to another and returned to me without losing its incomparable lustre.

We drove to the Cathedral São Vincente de Fora. The King, Queen, and Court were in attendance. Gowns and jewels glittered in the sun, blinding me as I stepped down, looking for Francisco.

He had come on horseback. I could see the black mare gleam with sweat as she cantered to a stop, her gold caparison dazzling in the morning light. I was almost afraid to look at him, my heart was so full of fears. And yet his unseen gaze compelled me.

Oh, my Francisco. My love. An emperor triumphant never sat so tall, nor commanded more honest homage from all he surveyed! But he was too far away for me to read the message in his eyes, to decipher the expression on his face. He quickly disappeared inside the great, wide doors.

Soon I would be his wife. A sudden stirring of confidence and joy replaced my dire imaginings. The love I would give him would so fill him to the brim that he would have neither desire, nor need, to seek another.

My father walked beside me as the mighty organ blasts stormed the air, filling the immense space with sound. Up ahead, beyond the sacristy, dressed in his finest sacred robes, the King's own confessor waited patiently to perform the marriage ceremony.

To another, the magnificent artistry and somber majesty of the cathedral would have been a precious gift, uplifting the spirit and ennobling the soul for the holy ceremony that was to follow. For myself, it could have been so only if I denied my blood and forgot my past.

Never had the duplicity of my double life been more vivid or more degrading than at that moment. I could feel neither the spirit of my grandmother, my mother, nor any one of my ancestors beside me as I walked toward my beloved down the long nave

beneath the vaulted cathedral transepts. I tried to focus on my
beloved, to erase the bejeweled altar with its great bronze
candlesticks, diamond-studded monstrance, and reliquary
triptych. To forget that it would be here, amid those graven images
that were an anathema to my heart and spirit, that I would pledge
my most sacred troth.

At last, I reached him. I felt his hand take mine and hold it. And
suddenly, I felt his finger trace my palm. At first it seemed a
random caress. But then he repeated it, more insistently, and I
realized he was writing letters. The more I concentrated, the
clearer those letters became: aleph, daled, nune *and* yud, *the*
Hebrew letters making up the name of the G-d of Abraham. The
G-d who had written in that tome delivered to Abraham's
descendants—those former slaves, that stubborn, desert-
wandering people: "For thou art a holy people unto G-d, thy G-d,
and thee hath G-d chosen to be a people belonging exclusively unto
Him, out of all the people that are on the face of the earth . . ."

Quick tears came to my eyes.

The voice of the priest was chanting above us:

Sanctificetur nomen tuum, in nobis: humilitatis, obedientiae et
charitatis tuae spiritu; et te in eucharistia cognosci, adorari at
amari ab omnibus faciamus humiles et devoti. . . .

I looked up at Francisco. Somewhere, sometime, our eyes vowed
to each other: We shall relive this day. We shall enter a synagogue,
and climb up to the tevah *and stand beneath the prayer shawl,*
and hear the hakham *say in the ancient language of our fathers:*
"Soon may you hear in the cities of Judah, and in the streets of
Jerusalem, the voice of joy and gladness, the voice of the
bridegroom and the voice of the bride. Blessed art Thou, O Lord,
who makes the bridegroom to rejoice with the bride."

My knees ached and the diadem that crowned my head felt as
sharp as thorns. And all at once I understood why my
grandparents had abandoned centuries of wealth and position,
accepting those dreadful and never-imagined horrors that are the
fate of the exile. Wealth without liberty is worthless. For the largest
castle surrounded by drawbridges and barbicans cannot give one

*sanctuary if one's heart melts with fear within. And even the rarest
and sweetest old wine becomes poison if poured down one's throat
with force. True wealth is freedom, the power to live in harmony
with the deepest desires of one's soul.*

*As the ceremony ended and the cathedral bells began to peal,
Francisco took my hand and we hurried down the long, dark
aisles. Swiftly, he lifted me into our carriage, closing the coach
door behind us.*

I wept.

*He called me "my bride of gladness," whispering the words
almost fiercely, and cupping my cheek with his palm to wipe away
my tears. "Now," he said, "you will understand my need for wealth.
It is not for gaudy baubles, or even vast estates. It is simply for
power, for us and for all* Gente da Nação. *Only wealth, and
nothing else, can keep us safe until we can shed this masquerade
and join our people openly. One day, Gracia, you and I and all our
children and their children shall pretend no more. Upon my life, I
swear it!"*

And I asked him: "When?"

*He looked at me with a strange smile and said: "It has already
begun."*

*It was only much later that I discovered the shocking truth
behind that smile.*

*Later, in the windowless passageways beneath his house, Father
quickly read the* ketuba, *drawn by the Hebrew scribe according to
the Law of Moses. And in that marriage contract, my name was
enscribed as Hannah Nasi and my husband's as Semach
Benveniste. My father read the seven benedictions. After each, we
answered, "Amen." I removed the jeweled ring that Francisco had
placed upon my finger just hours before. Peering into my eyes in
the shadows, Francisco murmured: "Haray at mekudeshet li
b'tabat zu ki daath Moshe V'Yisrael." And then he took the gold
band and slipped it once again upon my forefinger.*

*We took the cup and sipped the wine. How sweetly it went down
our throats! Then, to my surprise, and my father's clear approval,
Francisco smashed the empty glass upon the floor at our feet. "It is*

a reminder," my father explained, "of the destruction of our temple
and our exile."

I did not need to be reminded.

My marriage to Francisco Mendes began in the way of all good
fairy tales: with castles, and golden coaches, and jewels beyond
compare. The home to which he brought me was vast and
imposing, a fine stone castle rivaled only by the apartments of the
King himself. There were enough servants to have formed a small
army, should we have found ourselves under siege: porters and
packers, wheelbarrowers, reapers, coopers, tailors, furriers,
bakers, butchers, shoemakers, candlemakers, blacksmiths. Not to
mention a harem of ladies' maids, cooks, and serving girls.

"Francisco!" I begged him in dismay. "What am I to do all day?"

He laughed. "You, my dear, are the general of this army."

"Don't mock me! How shall they listen to me, and I half their
age?!"

He looked at me quite seriously, taking my hands in his.
"Gracia, my beloved. Do you remember what I told you? An
increase in wealth brings an increase in power. With your
vigilance, our properties shall increase in value and expand in
size. You must be sure there is no waste, and that our hand is ever
open to the needy, for the generous hand is not cut off. In all we do
we must commend G-d's blessing."

And so, I set to my tasks, grateful for once for my aunt's
tortures. It was my job to see that the house was in repair, the
bread baked, the corn grown and ground for meal. Meat needed to
be salted and stored, and the salt supply kept adequate. Clothing
for the household needed to be spun and sewed. And in Francisco's
absences, which were numerous, I had to be prepared to fight his
lawsuits, collect his taxes, and ransom him (G-d forfend!) should
the need arise.

For all these tasks, I found that I needed a cool head and a
clever tongue that knew how to caress as well as lash. And I began
to realize that while strength of body and natural power were
given to Adam, Eve's understanding and her careful eye gave her
equal power. There was more than one way to rule.

My husband's long absences were the bane of my existence. Each time he voyaged farther and farther. My heart was sorely tried as I endured the lonely nights. How great was my joy at his return, the sound of his footsteps running up the hard granite steps to our chamber were to me a gift of princely tribute.

I tried not to complain. I understood that he labored not simply to multiply castellanos *and gold doubloons, but to win us that secret, priceless gift for which our souls did yearn. Soon, the household was running like one of my husband's four-masted square rigs with the wind at its back.*

I was as hard as nails with the tradesmen who short-weighted our goods, and exacting with housemaids who neglected their duties. Yet, I remembered always to pay a man or a woman their wages on time and in good measure, and did not hold a tight fist around a just reward. And if anyone of my household fell ill, I tended to them as if they were my very kin. I won thereby their loyalty, if not their love.

Soon, the household was not enough for me.

"Please," I begged my husband, seeing how wearily he returned from his exhausting journeys to the East, "let me help you in your business as well."

Another man would have laughed. Francisco looked at me thoughtfully and closed the door of his study. He began to explain to me the intricacies of the pepper trade, which was about to make him the richest man in Europe.

He described the vast triangle of the central Indian Deccan Plateau that stretched from the Vindhya Mountains in the north to Cape Comorin in the south; the narrow, fertile lowlands along the coast, the rolling Ghat Mountains, whose rugged peaks rise to nine thousand feet. Between the mountains, streams and rivers flow down to the lush tropical forests, overflowing with rice and coconuts, that fringe the Arabian Sea.

How beautiful it was there! Francisco said quietly, describing the green and golden treetops, the flashes of brilliant, sunlit mist swirling down from the hillsides. It was the kingdom of Krishna Diva Raya, or as he was better known, the Pepper King, who ruled supreme over that wild coastal area. Just to reach the fields, one

had to have the permission of the rulers of the neighboring
fiefdoms, who demanded tributes in the form of foodstuffs, cloth,
and finely worked tools. And then there were the Jammkar: the
landowners, rajahs, and Brahmins who rented out the land to
small farmers for a sum of money and a two-thirds share of the
crop.

It was a pity, Francisco said. The farmers who did the work
were so poor that some were even forced to sell or barter their
entire share of the crop to middlemen for paltry sums or a bit of
cotton cloth.

They were a villainous group, these middlemen; Francisco
scowled. Even if the crop failed, they demanded to be paid in full,
asking not the price they paid, but the full price of the ripened
crop at its worth at the ports! And if the harvest was good, the
middlemen took it by cart or ox or riverboat to the coast and sold it
for a hundred times their cost. It was terrible how those men
fleeced the poor growers!

And I suddenly said, "Francisco, describe it to me!"

"What?"

"The pepper!" I demanded, needing to envision it.

He looked at me, curious and amused.

"Please!" I begged.

He laughed, stroking my brow. "It is a large vine with small,
sharply pointed leaves that burn like a betel. The berries grow in
small, green clusters, ripening ruby red. Inside, it is as limpid as
glass, a soft core surrounded by pulp. This is the red pepper. To
make black pepper, the whole, ripened berry is crushed and dried
in the sun. White pepper comes from the core only."

"And how do the farmers plant it?"

"First, they plant those trees on which to train the vines: areca
nuts, mangoes, or betel palms in orderly racks six to eight feet
apart. The pepper is grown from cuttings at the foot of the trees in
June, just before the heavy rains. They take three years to bear
fruit, twining around the trees like clasping arms. The first buds
appear in March, the first fruits in May. By December, the berries
change color, and soon after, they must be harvested. They are
delicate and easily harmed."

"How long may they be stored?"

"Months."

"And how many years is each plant fertile?"

"Ten to twelve," he said, shifting impatiently in his chair. "What are you getting at, my dear?"

"Francisco, would it not be more just and compassionate, as well as more profitable, for us to buy the unripened crops in March from the growers, then send our own porters to collect it in January, delivering it directly to our carracks? We could also provide the growers with new plants, easing their expense and expanding their produce. We could pay them less than we pay the middlemen, yet much more just a price than they now receive. Would this not both ease their burden and increase our profits?"

He looked at me oddly, shaking his head. At first I was ashamed, thinking he mocked my childish prattle, but then I saw his eyes. "My love! My Gracia. El mundo pertenese a los pasensiozos! Each day I waited for you was an investment of greatest profit!" He clasped my face in his hands and kissed me most tenderly. "My love, if only. . . ." He paced the room, his hands grasped behind his back as he always did when he was excited or thinking of solutions to difficult problems.

"The middlemen, they are a violent group. We would need soldiers to protect our porters. But I am sure the King would arrange that. And it would mean a great risk—buying the entire crop at fair prices before it ripens. If the crop should fail . . ."

"But if it should succeed! Just think, Francisco!"

"Yes, we would own it all, everything. All of Europe would have to wait for our ships, and all who longed for pepper would pay almost any price. The profits would be unimaginable! It would mean . . ."

It was I who voiced it, that wondrous word, that greatest desire of both our hearts and souls: "Freedom."

25

The worst thing, the very worst, Catherine thought, was the smell, that mixture of sour hospital antiseptic and cold machinery. A smell that made it impossible to pretend that one was simply suffering through a temporary inconvenience, like accommodations in a bad hotel.

She reached over for the crystal atomizer filled with her favorite perfume, spraying her hair, her throat, the backs of her wrists. She closed her eyes, breathing in the delicate, alluring fragrance, remembering evening gowns fresh from Bonwit's drifting over her head, and little jeweled purses holding tickets to the ballet. . . .

She wanted her life back. She wanted to go home. And the more the doctors and technicians sat on her bedside and smiled encouragingly, explaining the Inquisitorial tortures they expected her to undergo bravely, the more she wanted to flee.

Why prolong it? Why not, as the good doctor from the talk shows with his little "how-to" best-seller on self-destruction suggested, simply lie back in a warm bath and let the darkness cover you? Why not "go gently into that good night"?

Life had been so lovely, so very pleasant and easy so much of the time, she thought. Why ruin it all with a sad and tortured ending? Pills, injections, bedpans, pain. Terrible pain. That was all she had to look forward to.

Janice was coming this morning. Again.

She was trying to be helpful, Catherine sighed, wondering how much of her empty chatter (the intricacies of wallpaper selection, the difficulties of finding a decent carpet installer . . .) she would have to endure before sending Janice away with the feeling that she'd done her duty by her difficult old mother.

Janice, of course, wanted her to endure the tortures.

They all did.

She lifted up her hand and touched her still thick hair. Bald and sick and unable to eat—one of the few pleasures age still allowed one—for weeks, they said. And if she was lucky, the enemy would be routed for a little while. But he would be back, storming the barbicans. This, too, was clear.

If they could only assure her she'd live forever. You'd go through just about anything for that, wouldn't you? But a few extra weeks, a month or two. What was the point?

She'd known that her body was going to reach this state. But somehow, now that the moment had actually arrived, she felt cheated, angry, and a bit guilty—the irrational emotion of having done something wrong, of having erred, somehow. The wild goose chase to Europe had probably not helped her health. But she felt no regret. It had been so lovely to share those beautiful moments with the girls.

If only Suzanne hadn't . . .

That child!

She'd always been her secret favorite. How could one help it? Beautiful, daring, bright. She was everything I always wanted to be, Catherine thought. And now she's gone off with a man. And if that didn't work out, she'd go find Renaldo.

Oh, G-d. Renaldo. What she had held most against him, she realized, was neither his age, nor his bohemian appearance, nor even his unresolved marital status. It was simply the sense of his otherness: He belonged to another people, another faith, with its own rituals, its own G-d. If Suzanne joined him, she would join that world. She, and all her descendants, would be lost to her own family, her own history.

Oh, she knew that people viewed mixed marriages easily these days. Each would keep their own religion. Mutual respect. And the children? Christmas trees and Hanukkah menorahs, Easter eggs and Passover seders, all mixed up together. As wholesome, some claimed, as scrambled eggs for breakfast.

How little people understood how life really worked! As if the soul were some iron-sided garbage can instead of a delicate living digestive system! As if you could throw into it whatever you pleased, making no distinctions, requiring no explanations! They wouldn't expect their stomachs to survive a meal of Japanese, Hungarian, and French cuisine, and yet that was exactly what they expected from their souls.

You had to make a choice. Your lives were either a validation of your ancestors, or a rejection. "Or both," she could hear Suzanne protest. Sometimes. But it wasn't that easy. The modern idea that a consensus is always best didn't always work. Sometimes you can't compromise. You either use the past as a jumping-off point for the future, or you erase it and start from scratch. Worse, you erase it and start from someone else's past, destroying all that had nourished those genes, those bones, and that flesh that had given you life.

That rejection, awful and absolute, was what Catherine feared most. The image of Suzanne holding a child in her arms to be baptized, instead of circumcised . . .

And Francesca? Dear, positive, responsible little Francesca, who never took chances? She'd probably look back on this trip to Europe as a strange interlude, nothing to do with her real life. And when she came back, she'd forget all about it the moment she got a new job and her own office on a double-digit floor in some glass tower. She'd attend some peroxided version of a Jewish service in some space-age excuse for a house of worship, going once or twice a year, the way she went to the dentist, and with the same amount of joy and meaning. She'd drag whatever offspring she had through the same experiences until their bodies grew too big to bully and their intelligence saw through the silliness to the frightening emptiness at its core.

She thought of the lines from *Dr. Zhivago* that had stayed with her ever since she'd come across them years before: "Lara was not religious. She did not believe in ritual. But sometimes, to be able to bear life, she needed the accompaniment of an inner music. That music was G-d's word of life, and it was to weep over it that she went to church."

She was not afraid for Francesca the way she was for Suzanne. Something about Suzanne's impulsive, searching nature would lead her to crave that inner music. If she did not find it in her own faith, she would find it in another's.

Had she been asking the impossible? To transfer values that she herself had ignored or felt indifference toward? And maybe that's not what we should want. After all, look at the kind of people who did move through the ages unchangingly, son following father, daughter following mother in an unwavering devotion to ritual: African tribesmen, aborigines. Or the Amish or the Hasidim, who were sunk in a time warp, down to their socks. Or the Moslem fanatics who mutilated their daughters so they would never know the joy of making love.

But the good things, the valuable things, it was so important that they get passed down somehow! Love of freedom, compassion for the poor, the transcendent joy of true prayer, the respect for a kernel of holiness in all human life and human creation. It was so important that those things didn't get lost or disappear. Like beads strung on a necklace, it was all right for each generation to restring them, rearranging them into new patterns and adding a beautiful bead of their own design. And it didn't even matter, perhaps, if the necklace looked completely different, as long as all the beads were there, and the string didn't break, scattering them into the dust of time.

The important thing was that the necklace get handed down. And if your own children's hands weren't worthy or willing to accept it, then it had to be given to someone else's children, who'd been raised with more wisdom, or perhaps simply more luck, than your own.

It made sense. And yet, a cold chill crept through her heart as she remembered the verse from the Scroll of Esther: "If you will be silent at this time, deliverance will come to your people from another place, and you and your father's house shall perish."

The tree, she thought with horror. The last two leaves falling to the ground and decaying into dust.

She turned over and faced the wall. It would be better not to live to see it.

"Mrs. da Costa?"

"Leave me alone!" she moaned, not looking up.

"Now, now. I'm just here to help."

"You can help by showing yourself out and allowing me not to waste my precious breath!"

She felt a hand on her shoulder.

"What?" She sat up, enraged, shrugging it off.

It was a stranger dressed in that long-sleeved, mid-calf manner consistent with ultra-religious Muslim women, or Hasidic Jews. Her scalp was covered by a strange, old-fashioned snood that hid almost all her hair.

"What are you doing here?"

"I'm a volunteer."

"Well, thank you very much, but I don't need anything, particularly not a do-gooder with a cheerful smile who invades private rooms and . . ."

The woman settled herself calmly in the armchair beside the bed.

Catherine stared, dumbstruck. "Do you want me to call the nurse and have you thrown out?!"

"I can only stay a little while. I can see that you're feeling desolate, that you need to make a decision, perhaps the hardest and bravest one you've ever made."

Catherine leaned back, sighing. If you wanted to get some rest, the last place a sick person needed to be was a hospital. "Why is your hair covered like that? You aren't bald, are you? I mean, you're not from some chemotherapy support group, are you?"

She shook her head. "I'm not from any support group."

"Because, if you are, I want you to know that you're wasting your time. There is no way I'm going to . . ."

"I've come to take you somewhere. I'll be back in a minute."

To Catherine's astonishment, she returned with a wheelchair.

"And how, exactly, am I supposed to move with all these tubes and plastic containers trailing out of my arms?"

"Never mind. I know exactly what to do." She grasped Catherine's arm and helped her up, expertly arranging the bags on mobile poles beside the chair.

"You're not a nurse, are you?"

"No, not a nurse. But my father was a doctor and I spent much time with people who were ill. My husband . . ." Her voice caught.

Catherine, who was glad to be getting out of the room no matter where she was being taken, looked up with sudden interest. "Are you a widow?"

She nodded. "All these long years. I was so young when I lost him." Her voice cracked.

Catherine reached out and touched her with sudden, impulsive compassion. "Were there children?"

"Yes. A little girl. A precious, lovely child."

"And you never remarried?"

"No, never. Come."

"Wait, where are you taking me? Does my doctor know? Do you have permission?"

"I have permission from the highest authority. From the top one in charge," she answered.

"The head of the hospital? Does he even know I'm here?" Catherine asked, startled, but strangely exhilarated at the roll of the wheels beneath her, the sudden movement out of the stale, unmoving air. She wondered if he was someone she'd been on a charity board with.

"And what about you?" the woman asked as she wheeled her down the corridor. "Do you have children?"

"One daughter and two granddaughters."

"Do they visit you often?"

"Often enough. That is, my daughter does. My granddaughters are in Europe right now."

"Really? Where?"

"One is traveling in Spain, and the other . . . I'm not sure."

"Tell them not to miss Venice. Both of them. They mustn't miss Venice. Will you remember?"

"It's lovely in Venice." Catherine nodded, remembering the soft lap of the water against the elegant prows of gondolas outside her hotel window. "Very romantic."

"I never found it that way. But no matter, they should both go. Together."

Catherine turned to look at her, startled.

They got into the elevator and rode up.

"Wait, why are we going up? Why are we getting out here?"

The woman didn't answer, pushing the chair swiftly down the hall.

"Wait! I shouldn't be here, it doesn't make any sense. Stop!"

The wheelchair came to an abrupt halt.

Catherine leaned forward, trembling, her hands shaking as they touched the glass.

Babies. About twenty of them, their tiny faces perfect in repose or alive with need, fists flailing, mouths open with complaint. She looked at their exquisite, perfect skulls, the downy crown of black or blond begging to be caressed. Every single one, a new beginning, she thought, possessing a lifetime of still unspent minutes, hours, days, months.

She turned pale with rage. "WHY HAVE YOU BROUGHT ME HERE?!"

"Look," the woman insisted calmly. "You aren't really seeing anything. Your mind is elsewhere, wandering, dreaming. Look harder. The answer. It's staring you in the face."

"What answer?! GET ME OUT OF HERE, I TELL YOU, BEFORE I SCREAM . . . "

The woman sighed. "Shall I tell you, then?"

Catherine suddenly stopped struggling, her body freezing, motionless with tension. "Tell me what I'm supposed to see."

"The future."

No, Catherine thought. Not the future. The past.

Janice. There was a time when I needed nothing else but to feel her tender skin, to breathe her fragrance, to sink into the folds of fat on the back of her neck, her perfect, round shoulder.

She looked at the babies.

Had Janice been the extraordinarily beautiful infant she remembered? Or simply endowed with that miraculous loveliness possessed by every new creature freshly formed by the generous hand of the Creator? I cared so much . . . I wanted to give her so much. . . .

My baby, she thought, trying not to weep.

And then, Janice herself giving birth, her body a woman's, like my own. And I was so afraid for her. I didn't want her to hurt. I tried to pray, but couldn't concentrate, couldn't find the words. Please, G-d, help her deliver this child, my grandchild, flesh of my flesh, my genes, alive and well. Let my daughter be all right. The quiet hospital corridors full of doctors' tired footsteps. And then the news, breathtaking in its joyous revelation: a healthy birth. A girl. A granddaughter.

And she had thought then: A new life that will go on far into the future when I am dust. A part of me, taken into the future, further than even I could imagine. Vital, young, healthy in body, just as my own body is fading, wrinkling, breaking down.

Would you want to be young again, she asked herself? Go through all of that again?

She thought of her youth, those hot and fecund days filled with childbirth, swollen breasts, and a hungry infant that filled the world, reducing it to a small circle, almost intolerable in its intensity, and so rich with meaning nothing else ever came close.

Never. I couldn't, wouldn't want to.

I'm happy to be on the outside looking in, to watch the blossoming of those seeds I planted, the turning of the wheels I set in motion. Until the very last moment, she thought, with a clear sense of revelation, to see it all for as long as possible.

Babies again. Great-grandchildren. My flesh young again, beginning all over again. New hope. New chances. The formation of hands willing and eager to grasp the precious beads left behind. The future.

"Is it possible, for me?" she whispered, reaching back to feel the hand on the handles of the chair.

"I promise you," the woman said, grasping her hand warmly, like family. "If you just hang on. If you do everything you can to keep on living."

She put her hands in her lap and leaned back, exhaling long and hard. "Thank you," she whispered hoarsely. "And now, please, take me back. I need to have a word with my doctor."

Nothing happened.

She twisted around in her seat. Her mouth hung loose in surprise: pale light floated like a golden bubble until it burst and disappeared. The corridor was empty.

A very put-upon nurse from the maternity ward wheeled her back to her room.

Janice was waiting, her nails polished a striking peach, her eyes red.

"Mother!" she jumped up, wringing her hands. "The bed was empty. No one knew where you were. What happened to you?"

"It's all right, Jan, I'm fine, fine."

She allowed Janice to help her back into bed, arranging the tangle of tubes. Then suddenly, Catherine sat erect. "Jan?"

"Mother?"

"Come, let me hug you for a moment."

Janice walked stiffly into her mother's outstretched arms, surprised.

"My child," Catherine whispered. "I love you, Jan."

"*Madre!*" Janice collapsed inside her mother's arms, resting her head on Catherine's bony shoulder as if she were five years old.

Catherine stroked her soft, shiny hair. My little girl, she thought, aware of the sudden wetness on her daughter's smooth, made-up cheek.

"He's got another woman! He said he would give her up, but I know he hasn't. He doesn't love me anymore. I don't know what to do. . . ."

"Look to the future, child. There's always a future. I'll help you. I've decided I'm going to live a while yet after all." Catherine smiled ruefully. "Simply out of curiosity. . . ."

"Curiosity?" Janice wiped her eyes, looking up.

"Never mind. What's that you're holding?"

"It's another message from Francesca. I think it's just the news you've been waiting for."

26

"What are you thinking about, Francesca?"

They were on their way to Cáceres in a rented convertible. The wind was rummaging through her hair like gentle fingers. She closed her eyes and tilted her head back toward the sun. A field of red wildflowers burned their way through her eyelids.

"About Gracia. In the first chapter she calls herself a young widow. I'm wondering what happened to Francisco Mendes and how she could have possibly survived without him."

He shrugged. "Life goes on. People fall in love again."

"They were more than just lovers! They were partners in every sense. It wasn't just about passion. It was about friendship and respect and devotion to the same values," she said emotionally. "They were soul mates. You can have only one soul mate in your lifetime."

He looked at her, intrigued. He had never before heard her so stirred. She looked out dreamily at the enchanting shady grove, the quiet, blue waters lying at its back. Her face shone mysteriously.

"What?" He smiled.

"Oh, nothing. Everything. Wishing . . ."

"You? Wishing? For what?" he asked, surprised.

"That I could just . . . I don't know . . . forget everything and just get out here and spend a month swimming."

"Such frivolous thoughts from Francesca Abraham. I'm shocked!"

he said, wide-eyed with mock horror. "Do you really want to stop and get out?"

"No, of course not! I mean, I know we can't. We've got to get to Cáceres . . ."

He sighed. "Right."

"Do you think we'll make it before nightfall?" she asked, looking up at the suddenly overcast sky, the gray, gathering clouds. "It looks like the weather is turning."

He barely had time to agree when the rain began in earnest. He hurriedly put up the top. Wind-driven sheets of water dashed against the car, making it rock. Lightning split the sky and thunder crashed above them with explosions of menacing sound that made the ground tremble. The windshield wipers moved with useless fury to keep up with the deluge, to no avail. Visibility was almost nil.

"Marius, stop the car! This is too dangerous. Let's just wait it out."

"You're right," he agreed, turning off the road and shutting down the engine.

Mists rose in thickening darkness against the windows, giving them the feeling of being adrift together on a large silver sea. He sat watching her. Her face was soft in the fairy light of the forest, the eyes pensive and a little frightened. Her breasts rose and fell, stirred with quiet emotion as she contemplated the ghostly sway of the branches, the rustling song of the forest. She was an unknown creature to him, he realized. The essence of woman's otherness. Her beauty was all the more tantalizing, wrapped around the mystery that was the key to her nature, a mystery that had so far eluded him. He touched her shoulder lightly. "Francesca . . ."

She turned toward him, her lips slightly parted in surprise, her teeth a flash of gleaming white. The tender beauty of her features took his breath away.

"Frightened?"

She shook her head, drawing her sweater around her. He reached out to help her, his fingers brushing her soft, bare shoulder. "You had this same look after we visited the Cathedral of Toledo, right after leaving Señor de Almazan's. You never did tell me what happened to you in there."

She looked at him. "I came across this shrine. . . . It had a picture carved into beaten brass: weeping women holding infants; small children being dragged away; old men bent over their staffs. And on either side were these lovely stone angels with this look of serene happiness on their faces, you know, like models in a refrigerator commercial: 'Just look at this wonderful product we've created just for you!' I read the inscription. It was a shrine dedicated to Ferdinand and Isabella in honor of signing the Edict of Expulsion."

"Exactly what about it upset you?"

She was silent for a moment, her fingers pressing into her thighs. "How anyone could depict all this human misery and then praise those who'd caused it! But it was more than that . . ."

"What, then?"

"It was the picture itself; the idea of suddenly waking up one morning and finding yourself thrown out of your safe, happy life by forces you couldn't have predicted and had no control over." She stopped, looking out the window at the raging sheets of rain that had so suddenly transformed the world around them. "I went to work one morning and found myself out on the street just because some corporate president signed papers in lawyers' offices hundreds of miles away."

"Life is unpredictable." He nodded. "It's hard to lose a job you love. I'd hate to lose mine."

"But Marius, you don't really expect to go on doing this forever, do you? The constant traveling . . . and it's all so . . . so risky and unstable. What if you run out of leads? If you don't find anything valuable for years, then what?"

He shrugged. "Hasn't happened so far. But I'm realistic. I expect I'll have to make some changes over time. When I'm eighty, for example, I'll probably need someone with me to hold the ladder," he grinned, but his dark eyes went suddenly serious and searching. "What is it *you* really want, Francesca?"

"I'm not sure." She frowned. "A feeling of safety, maybe. Of being in control and secure. A feeling of being respected."

"Safety, control, security, respect. . . ." He shook his head, reaching out and running a finger along her elbow down to her wrist. "What about happiness, love, excitement, meaning. . . ."

She vibrated with unconscious pleasure, like a perfectly tuned note. She looked at his dark, handsome face, the beautiful tan flesh of his neck and strong arms.

If it were Suzanne, and not me, I know what would happen now, she thought, wanting to give in, to move toward the warm promise of his arms, hating the fact that she simply couldn't do it.

She pulled open the car door and dashed out into the warm rain, letting it fill her open mouth. She felt a sense of giddiness, a reckless freedom as she flew down the hill to the lake, sheets of rain soaking her to the skin.

"Francesca!" she heard him call. She ran faster, ducking the heavy branches of trees that swayed around her like dancers in some strangely choreographed dream. Only my part is improvised, she thought. I am the one who writes the program that controls all the actions of this little, defective machine. But, still, I'm in control, she told herself. I know exactly what I'm doing.

She plunged into the water. It was wonderfully cool and fragrant, with the smell of warm summer nights. She floated on her back, staring at the blurred faces of sleeping stars as the rain tickled her face. Everything seemed to float upward, lifted and borne away, turned ghostly and strange. The lights on the distant shore blinked in astonishment.

Then suddenly, he was there beside her, his wet chest solid against her own. She felt his arms encircle her waist and touch the small of her back. No, this was not under control, she thought. Not at all . . .

"Francesca," he murmured, his breath warm in her ear, his lips touching her forehead, her cheeks, the tip of her chin. Then, finally, her lips.

"Don't!" she moaned softly. "You don't understand. I can't. I'm not like that. Not like my sister."

He lifted her in his arms, nuzzling the soft skin of her chilled shoulder. "Who are you like?"

"Put me down!"

"But why?" He was loath to let her go.

The rain suddenly stopped, and yet he saw the rivulets streaming down her cheeks. He hugged her. She slapped him, hard.

Stunned, he released her, his hands hanging helplessly at his sides. "Francesca! Why?" his voice echoed in the forest.

She ran, wet branches cracking beneath her, filling the air with sound. Suddenly, she cried out in pain.

"Where are you! What's wrong?"

He found her in the thicket.

"It's my . . . ankle, I think."

He crouched down beside her, probing it gently. "It's not broken, but it's swelling up. Here, lie still." He covered it with cold, wet earth and damp leaves as a poultice.

"Mud?"

"An old hiking remedy. It's been around for ages. The point is to keep it cold."

She felt the gentleness in his hands as he touched her bruised skin. She looked up shyly. Everything seemed to glisten.

"Are you cold?" he whispered, rubbing her arms.

"A little. Marius?"

"Yes?"

"I'm sorry. I'm insane. I have been ever since I set foot in Spain. It's as if something's gotten inside me that I can't control."

"Why do you always have to be in control? Why not just . . . live? Moment to moment. Why does everything have to fit into your little planner, your little Bible of minutes and hours and days?" Suddenly, a gleam of understanding came into his eyes. His jaw flinched. "Someone—sometime—hurt you, didn't he, Francesca? Badly."

She leaned back silently, studying the darkening skies, the yellow and purple vapors rising across the moon.

"I want you to know that I'm not that kind of man. I would never, ever do anything to hurt you. I swear."

They sat unmoving in the growing shadows, listening to each other's soft breathing.

"Marius? Could you carry me back to the car, please?"

She felt his strong arms lift her off the ground and leaned into his chest. Her cheek tingled against the smooth, damp skin of his shoulder. A sudden, eerily sharp sense of déjà vu made her stir and look around for a presence that seemed to be hovering over her, watching her.

I stopped struggling, feeling a burning tingle that began in my forehead and streamed through my body. And as I peeked at the dark rim of his eyes,

the rich thickness of his manly beard, I felt a clap and a sharp, white-hot
wrench to my heart.

It was the moment where one's soul enters into another's and emerges,
dazzled.

The words went through her like alcohol, making her dizzy and
warm. She looked into his eyes and suddenly she felt as if she had
crossed some secret threshold, emerging into a brand-new world. For
a moment, her whole body suddenly gave up its resistance as she allowed herself to lean against him. For the first time in a very long time,
she felt absolutely safe.

27

Speeding down the Costa del Sol, the great palms waving in the distance, Suzanne saw the Mediterranean as a winking blue eye. She leaned over, her fingers burrowing through Gabriel's warm hair, caressing the smooth skin of his neck. "What do you say we dump the relatives, Gabriel, and hole up at the beach for about a month?"

He turned his head slightly, kissing her fingertips. "One day, I promise. Perhaps we'll spend a summer here, with our children."

She sat up straight, hands massaging each other tensely in her lap, the vision of romantic coastline and nude, warm flesh dissolving into the specter of thigh-heavy mothers carrying undiapered, wailing infants. "No way. You've got the wrong girl!"

His voice was deep and serious as he answered, "Isn't it natural for a man to want children from the woman he loves?"

A flash of joy went through her and the temptation to sink into the comfortable niche he was building became almost irresistible. And so, quite perversely, she decided on vigorous opposition. "What about overpopulation? What about jeopardizing the survival and quality of life for humanity out of selfishness and ignorance?"

"I love children," he said simply. "Don't you? And isn't that what we're both working so hard for, to make a better world for them?"

"Maybe," she admitted. "But I just think we have plenty of time to settle down to all that boring domesticity."

"Statistics for problem pregnancies go shooting up in older prima-paras," he said matter-of-factly.

What could you say to that? she thought sullenly, cornered.

"You are such an interesting woman, Suzanne! Most women adore it when men start talking babies, families . . ."

"That's because they're insecure about their ability to hold their men in sexual thralldom forever . . . ." she said, grinning.

"So, that is where you think your power lies, yes?"

"Don't you?"

"Quite the contrary."

Her forehead puckered. "Meaning?"

"It is your fascinating personality."

"And if I weighed two hundred pounds?"

"There'd be more of you to love," he answered gallantly, his hand fondling her slim arm. "But perhaps I might love you less per square inch."

"You!" She put her hand underneath his shirt to pinch him, but the delicious smooth warmth of him made it impossible.

"Please, Suzanne, I won't be able to concentrate on the road!"

She was about to say something suitably clever when she looked up. There it was, that great outcropping of rock extending with a sweeping majesty straight up to heaven.

"It looks exactly like those ads for the insurance company," she quipped, covering her confusion. It really *was* awesome.

"'Pillar of Hercules,' the ancients called it. There's another one in Morocco, Mount Abyla. They say Hercules split one great mountain in two to let the Mediterranean in. It was the medieval world's portal to the universe."

Seagulls circled high around the green-drenched mountain overlooking the bluest of seas. Just beyond was Morocco, Tangiers, Casablanca, Ceuta. . . . Suzanne stared at the great boats in the distance. "Refugees from the Inquisition must have sailed these waters. Perhaps even this ancestor of mine."

"Who?"

"Gracia Mendes, my fabulously wealthy, jewel-bedecked ancestress," she said lightly, unaccountably embarrassed for some reason at having thought of it.

"She was much, much more than that!"

She turned around. "You've actually heard of her?"

"My mother was a great admirer of Cecil Roth. He wrote an entire book about Gracia."

"So I've heard . . ."

"You mean you haven't read it!?"

"I've been meaning to." She bit her lower lip. "What did you mean by 'much, much more'?"

"She was a heroine, in every sense of the word."

Hiding her pleasure, she protested, "What's heroic about cornering the pepper trade and making a king's ransom?"

"The trade wasn't the point! According to Roth, her company operated a secret underground network that snatched hundreds of people out of the fires of the Inquisition."

"How?"

"Read the book!"

She tapped her foot listlessly, offended.

"Darling!" He kissed her fingertips. "It will be good for you to do a little research. It was an unbelievably daring and wonderful system. But the risk was enormous: slow torture, certain death, and the confiscation of everything she owned. She was so brave."

She caressed his face, touched by the sincerity of his admiration, wishing she were the object. Smoothing back a thick, honey-colored lock from his brow, she vowed to do a little more reading.

Cars had come to a halt, inching their way to the border crossing.

"How long will it take?"

"Hard to tell. Twenty minutes, two hours! A few years ago, you couldn't cross this border at all. The Spanish were so incensed at the English for insisting on keeping Gibraltar one of their colonies that they closed it. You'd have to fly or sail in!" Gabriel whispered, as a guard approached them to check their passports.

But once across the border, the time it took to reach the center of town was unbelievably swift. One moment they seemed to be facing an endless expanse of sparkling sea, the next the bustle of a port city. Celebrating sailors, long-skirted Moroccan women jangling with silver jewelry, young Jewish boys in black skullcaps, and tourists of every description crowded the duty-free shops, which lined the main street in either direction as far as the eye could see.

"Is this it?" she said, a bit appalled at the transition. "Is that what people do here, shop?"

"No. Sell. At least, my relatives. Gibraltar's a duty-free zone. They sell perfumes, leather goods, liquor, electronics. I think among them, my relatives own over a dozen shops. It's quite profitable."

"Which street are their shops on?"

He waved his hands, grinning. "There are only two streets in Gibraltar."

"Tiny as that?"

He nodded. "Tiny and wonderful. Either the *muezzin* is calling the faithful to prayer, or the church bells are ringing, or the streets are full of people walking to and from the synagogues! And everyone interacts and gets along."

"Sounds just like New York," she said dryly.

"Except that the whole of Gibraltar could fit on a few avenue blocks in Manhattan! That's what makes it so special. Everyone's on top of everyone else, and yet there is so much tolerance!"

"No one feels threatened?"

"On the contrary, they reinforce one another's values: close-knit families, religious instruction for the children, early marriages among their own kind, prayer, charity, honesty . . ."

"You're right. They're such close neighbors that they have no choice but to get along."

He took her hand and kissed it. "Maybe one day everyone will feel that way about the planet!"

"But isn't it ironic to find such a place at the tip of Spain, I mean, with its history of intolerance."

"Be fair! The Inquisition happened, but for hundreds of years, Jews, Christians, and Moslems all lived side by side in Spain with incredible tolerance. Gibraltar is the clock turned back to the Golden Age."

"How long has your family lived here?"

"Actually, my Great-Aunt Claudina, my grandmother's sister, married into a Gibraltan family. Her husband's family has been here for hundreds of years. The first Jews came right after the Expulsion, but a

British ban forbade them to settle. So they sailed just beyond, to Morocco and North Africa, trickling back little by little, opening up businesses. The English sort of closed their eyes to it. They've been here ever since."

"Where are we going to be staying, Gabriel?"

"With Auntie Claudina, of course."

"Wouldn't it be better for us to go to a hotel?" She panicked, picturing an elderly chaperone checking on their sleeping arrangements. "And how are you going to introduce me?"

"As my dear friend." He stroked her cheek, smiling.

"Really, Gab. I don't know about this."

"Trust me, darling. You'll love them. And they'll love you."

"Well, here goes."

"Where?"

"To your great-aunt's of course."

"We're here."

She looked around at the teeming main street, then stared at him, stunned. "She lives here?! On top of the shops?"

"Everyone here does, because they all want to live in walking distance of each other and of the two main synagogues. Orthodox Jews don't drive on the Sabbath."

"But . . . over the shops?" She looked around, appalled.

"Don't jump to conclusions, darling."

He rang the bell. A uniformed maid opened the door.

"*Buenos tardes, María.*"

"*Señor Gabriel! Como esta usted?*"

"*Muy bien, gracias. María, Señorita Suzanne.*"

"*Mucho gusto!*"

Suzanne stepped over the threshold, amazed.

It was like the interior of some stunning English mansion, all dark mahogany wainscotting and dusky-rose, damask wallpaper. A gracious staircase curved upward beside a private elevator.

"Come." Gabriel smiled, taking her hand and enfolding it in his.

Upstairs, numerous rooms led off a long hall lit by bright crystal chandeliers. She followed Gabriel into a huge sitting room. It was wondrous, she thought. Like stumbling through a time warp into the private salon of some Victorian queen. In the center, ensconced on an overstuffed and probably enormously costly antique sofa, was a tiny, quite elderly woman dressed entirely in white.

"Auntie!" Gabriel said reverently, bending his head and kissing her twice on both cheeks.

The woman clasped him with her gnarled and wrinkled hands, whose fingers were weighted down by many large and heavy rings.

"My lovely nephew! G-d bless you! And who is it you bring me?"

"My friend, Suzanne Nasi da Costa Abraham."

The old woman's face lit up, her faded blue eyes studying Suzanne with alert pleasure. "Lovely to meet you, my child," she said with a broad smile, holding out both hands. Suzanne grasped them, surprised at their unexpected strength and eagerness as she bent to accept the touch of the old cheeks on her young ones. They felt like dry parchment.

"A Nasi *and* a da Costa!" Claudina exclaimed with glee. "My dear boy, wherever did you find such a treasure?"

He was amused! Suzanne noted, annoyed, feeling like some dusty auction find. Of all things to impress people with! Your family! Still, she could not stop the tiny smile that found its way to her lips as she tried to imagine any one among her New York acquaintances desiring her for her lineage.

So what? she argued with herself, attempting to still that growingly strident voice that had taken to complaining nonstop about her unrepentant happiness. What difference did it make if it was her family's money, or her body, or her mind that made people smile at her with welcome? The bottom line was that this was Gabriel's family and they were happy to see her.

Yet, she couldn't completely shake off the unbelievable ignominy of being in love with someone whose family not only approved of her, but whose approval would be reciprocated in spades by her own. The image of Gran and Claudina sinking into the sofa cushions side by side, sighing with contentment, beaming down blessings and cheek-kissing into the next century, was more than she could bear.

"Maria will show you to your room, my dear," Claudina told her. "The maids will bring you whatever you need. We dine at eight. Gabriel, the cousins will be coming, and Uncle Serge and Auntie Orvieda and Uncle Joseph and Auntie Esther. I'm afraid we tend to be a bit traditional here, especially Friday nights. I hope you won't find it too terrible," she said, smiling at Suzanne.

Suzanne, suddenly acutely aware of the fraying rips in her faded jeans, smiled back in confusion, wishing she'd brought a few more suitcases.

Not only weren't their rooms next to each other, they weren't even on the same floor! Suzanne groaned, pouring out the contents of her bag onto the bed. But it was one stunning room. The dark, polished wood was full of intricate inlays, finely carved and finished with a luminous richness that spoke of an age when craftsmen lingered over their work with pride. The bedspread and canopy were extravagant creations consisting of yards and yards of sumptuous fabrics in shades of cream and royal blue.

She glanced toward the heavily curtained windows. There was nothing but the busy street to look out at here, she thought, leaving the curtains drawn. She felt detached from the world and from time, in a magical location where the disappearing ozone layer, the endangered whales, desertification, Ebola, and date rape didn't exist. A place where blissful and perfect happiness would be allowed to sing its song aloud without being asked to turn down the volume out of respect for those less fortunate.

She laid down, pulling the featherbed blissfully around her shoulders and dozing off. When she awoke, she wondered not only where she was, but who. She blinked, looking around the room. Fresh towels had appeared on the washstand and a small covered tray on the night table held a Limoges teapot and a silver salver of petit fours. Hanging by the full-length mirror, was her freshly ironed Chinese silk dress.

She stared at it. She had intended wearing it that evening. But having it selected for her this way was unbearably annoying. With a firm and deliberate motion, she hung it back inside the closet, taking out a wrinkled white cotton blouse and a long, crush-pleated Indian skirt. She showered and dressed quickly, determined to have a word with Gabriel.

Servants in black uniforms with white aprons stopped scurrying as she passed, nodding and greeting her with a curtsy and a friendly "*Buenas noches, Señorita Abraham.*"

How many were there, she began to wonder in dismay. Didn't these people do *anything* for themselves? But the help all looked content and

well-fed. Creating employment was also a virtue, she admitted grudg-
ingly.

She wandered though the house until she reached the dining room.
The table had been exquisitely set. Crystal, porcelain, and silver—spot-
lessly clean and polished to perfection—created the feeling of a royal
banqueting table from a different age. The centerpiece was a huge silver candelabra.

"My dear!" Auntie Claudina suddenly appeared, her gracious and
friendly glance betraying only the most imperceptible surprise as she
took in Suzanne's wrinkled outfit. She herself was dressed in a black
suit of silk brocade straight from the couture houses of Paris.

"I'm sorry about the clothes," Suzanne stammered, filled with a sudden, sharp regret. "I didn't realize . . ."

"Never mind," Claudina patted her arm. "It takes a while to get used
to us, I know. But we didn't invite your clothes, we invited you!" She
looked tiny and elflike as she leaned on her cane. "I was just about to
light my candles. Won't you join me?"

Suzanne hesitated.

She hated mumbo-jumbo, the repetition of meaningless rituals
performed to satisfy some bullying invisible power—call it "custom,"
or "G-d," or "family tradition." But then she thought of the consequences. She wasn't, after all, at home now. She was a guest. And this
was someone else's party.

To her surprise, Claudina walked past the candelabra into an alcove
near the fireplace. A small card table was set up in the corner. They
weren't Sabbath candles at all, Suzanne realized, but small glass dishes
filled with oil and floating wicks.

"I thought you meant the Sabbath candles."

"Ah, that, too, soon. But first these. Have you never seen them before?"

"I . . . I don't really remember."

"Your grandmother, perhaps?"

No. Not Gran. She was certain of that. "My grandmother is rather,
well, nontraditional in some ways. What are they for?"

"Oh, everything. And everyone. This one I light for my niece who is
having an ultrasound on Sunday. They fear something might be wrong
with the baby. And this one is for my brother's boy, who took his law ex-

ams today. These are for the souls of my father and mother and my husband, and this for the child I lost in the womb. And this is for the Jews of Salonika who lie in unmarked graves. There were fourteen thousand Jews in Salonika before the war. Twelve thousand were killed. Many were from my mother's family. Did you know that eighty-nine percent of Ladino-speaking Jews in the world died at Hitler's hands, many of them in Auschwitz? We are all that is left." She spread out her hands, including Suzanne. "A tiny, precious few. And this one is for Gabriel. And this one is for you."

"For me?"

"Yes, to light your way in the world, that you might find your true path home."

What could she mean by that? Suzanne wondered, staring at the candles. "Lights for the living, and for the dead?"

"The dead are with us always no less than the living. The flame gives them pleasure. They know that we think of them."

Suzanne studied her old hand as it held a lit taper to the wicks. One after another, they burst into flame, hovering like floating gold in the pale, dusky room. Wordlessly, Suzanne took the taper, lighting a wick of her own.

In the pale, golden light, she studied Claudina.

There was something ageless and regal in the lift of her head and the way her eyes smiled with the serene mystery of a Buddha. She seemed to be contemplating some truth that transcended time, a vision both wise and unexplainable.

Suzanne stared at the tiny, leaping flame, thinking of Renaldo.

Your family is right. You will find someone better for you. Someone who deserves you and can truly make you happy. . . .

His dark brown eyes had been full of pain.

And now she'd betrayed him. Betrayed their love.

She'd proven him right.

"And now, the Sabbath candles. These are the most powerful ones of all. They bring perfect peace. Even the souls of the suffering sinners in *gehinnom* are released on the Sabbath."

She watched Claudina light the wicks in the beautiful silver candelabra, waving her hands over them, then touching her fingertips to her closed eyelids, whispering the incantation:

Baruch ata Adonai Elohenu melech haolam,
asher kiddishanu be mitzvotav vetzevanu
l'hadlik nar shel Shabbat

She imitated clumsily, repeating the strange words. A warmth came over her, and in the distance she heard music, like the murmur of tiny bells.

"And now you must add a prayer, one of your own choosing, and in your own words."

"I can't . . . I've never . . ."

"Then listen: G-d of my fathers and mothers before me, who has sweetened my life and given me blessings beyond measure, hear my prayer. Bless my children and grandchildren with good health and peace of mind. May they want for nothing, and may they please You always with deeds of kindness and charity. Help my cousin Orvieda find a good bride for her son. Please don't let the Hassan brothers open a successful store next door to my son Serge's. Let my psoriasis heal. And may the rains not flood Gibraltar this winter as it did last. Amen."

Suzanne smiled at the mixture of sublime and ridiculous. She closed her eyes and waved her hands over the kindled lights. "G-d of my fathers and mothers before me, hear my prayer," she repeated silently. "Bless Gabriel Fonseca, the man I love. Let nothing ever part us. Bring your healing grace to my grandmother in her hour of need, so that her soul find ease. Give me wisdom to help all those who come to me in need. Direct my steps toward good in the world all the days of my life."

She opened her eyes and stared into the flickering flames, which blurred like watercolors through her brimming eyes. "Excuse me, Auntie. I'll be right back."

She walked to her room, closing the door behind her and leaning against it. Slowly, she pulled off her clothing, changing into the green silk dress and twisting her hair into an elegant French braid. She stared at herself in the mirror. "Leave me alone," she said, shrugging, her mouth twisting in irony.

The lively mixture of adult voices, squealing children, and deep male laughter drifted down to her as she walked back toward the dining room.

"You look exquisite!" Gabriel exclaimed, taking her in his arms. "Your whole face is glowing."

She touched her flushed cheeks. "Is it?"

He was dressed as she had never seen him before: a dark, beautifully tailored suit, a dazzlingly white shirt, and a blue paisley tie. There was a gleam about him, a wondrous aura of light.

"The whole family is here. The children, especially, adore being together. But I have to warn you, it gets a bit loud."

"Do they do this often?"

"Every Friday night."

"And I thought my family was bad getting together once a year for Passover!" she groaned.

"You will like it," he said with completely unwarranted confidence.

About as much as a root canal, she thought, wondering how she was going to extract him from all this.

"Here, child, sit by me."

Suzanne followed Claudina dutifully to the head of the table. To her great relief, Gabriel sat down on her left. The room began to fill. Claudina's son, Serge, and his wife, Orvieda; Orvieda's sister, Esther, and her husband, Joseph; Claudina's daughter, Rachel, and her husband, Moses; and numerous children of all ages.

The men wore impeccable, bespoke Savile Row suits, the women equally English fashions straight out of Harrod's or Sloan Square. The women, though they looked well-to-do, had nothing in common with the spoiled, nail-wrapped women of her mother's set. Their faces were more serious, and their clothes expensive, but practical and subtle. They looked, she thought, like the successful, hardworking businesswomen most of them surely were. These busy shops did not run themselves.

And the children: She simply lost count after a while. There were quite a few redheads and blonds, beautifully dressed little girls wearing frilly Laura Ashley–style dresses, bows in their hair, and patent-leather shoes. The boys ranged in size from stringy, shy adolescents to a toddling two-year-old hell-raiser bent on overturning the crystal vases. They wore their holiday best: white shirts and jackets and well-pressed dress pants. A few, but not all, wore black skullcaps.

"*Buenas entradas de Saba!*" they greeted one another.

"What does that mean?" Suzanne whispered to Gabriel.

"'Happy entry into the Sabbath,'" he whispered back. "And the proper response is, '*Shabbat shalom umevorach.*' But don't worry about it! No one will mind if you don't join in."

It was true. Everyone had beautiful manners, even the children, who were curiously friendly, but in a diffident, sweetly shy manner that seemed from a different era. What a well-behaved, happy, self-confident bunch they were! she thought with grudging admiration. Was it growing up in these big, extended families that gave that to them? Being led by their parents' hands to and from a house of worship every week? These big, festive, holiday meals?

Or were they simply normal kids with punishments hanging over their heads compelling them to put on their best behavior to impress the company?

They probably all hate each other and are just afraid not to show up here, her inner voice lectured. Get to them one by one and they'll tell you how this one cheated that one, and how they all can't stand Claudina, who runs roughshod over them, batting them into place with her wealth or her other devious powers.

There is no such thing as one big, happy family.

But it was hard to find any real evidence backing up these silent allegations. Claudina looked as fragile as the pages of an old manuscript, and far too full of simple happiness to harbor Machiavellian plots. And as the family slowly took their places around the table, and Suzanne's senses took in the scene in its entirety, it seemed even more unlikely.

There was a glow of warmth, a feeling of riches, she thought. Not the material kind, but something else: the sense of growth, of something flourishing and healthy. Like a plant with abundant new leaves ready to unfurl. Alive, vibrant.

And then, without warning, everyone began to sing: It sounded like some Spanish *cancionero,* something very authentic and old. Even the smallest children seemed to know the words. And the volume! Suzanne thought, shaking her head. Something tribal!

That's what had always been missing from her family's holiday meals, she thought. The loud voices of children. It had always been just her and Francesca surrounded by plodding adults with bad bodies and strange hairdos making terrible jokes and strained attempts to encourage an intimacy they hadn't earned. And even the younger uncles, the ones she wouldn't have minded knowing, lived too far away to really be part of her life, or she theirs. It was no one's fault. Once a family spread out like that all over the world, you ceased to really be a family, except in name.

She watched Gabriel take a small, dark skullcap from his pocket and place it on his head.

"Why?" she whispered, surprised and confused.

"Respect, tradition." He shrugged. "Does it bother you?"

"No, not at all," she lied.

The maids brought in platters of food. Different kinds of fish, vegetables, and olives prepared a dozen ways. And each time one plate was passed around, another took its place.

"So much food!" Suzanne exclaimed, changing the subject with a little too much haste.

"Too much food? Is that what you said?" Serge, a charming, distinguished older man graying at the temples, leaned over and winked at her with a mischievous smile.

"It wasn't meant as a . . . that is . . . I didn't mean to . . . " Suzanne stammered.

Serge snorted with amusement. "My dear Suzanne. The meal hasn't even begun yet!"

Everyone laughed, but in a friendly, almost self-deprecating way. "We Sephardim have a custom of saying a hundred blessings a day. On the Sabbath, since we don't have the chance to say our usual number, we have to make up for the loss by saying extra blessings over food. That's why we add all these extra dishes at the beginning," Joseph explained with the air of the Talmud student he obviously once was.

She nodded, surprised. She'd assumed it was just the usual family stuff-fest. But knowing this made it seem less a meal than an orchestrated ceremony, with its own choreography and score.

Ritual followed ritual. First, Serge rose at the head of the table and poured wine into a magnificent silver beaker that he held in the palm of his hand. Everyone at the table rose up with him in respect, and even the children were silent as he recited the prayer sanctifying the day as a special one: *Baruch ata Adonai . . .*

"What do the words mean?" she questioned Gabriel in a whisper.

"'Blessed be You, G-d, our G-d, King of the Universe, Who has sanctified us by His commandments and taken pleasure in us, and, in love and favor, given us His holy Sabbath as an inheritance,'" he whispered back.

"An inheritance," she mused, looking around the table at the rapt, intent faces. Something to pass down, to give, like a gift.

When Serge was finished, the children responded like little soldiers to some unspoken command, walking to the head of the table and bending their heads. One by one, Serge laid his hands upon their bright hair, murmuring blessings over them.

Grandpa Carl, his big fingers warming her scalp as he recited magic incantations to protect her from all harm, Suzanne suddenly remembered. Her turn, then Francesca's. She'd made him stop, of course, when she got into junior high, embarrassed, not wanting anyone— even Grandpa—to touch her. And then the last time, his breathing so heavy at the end. . . .

She reached up and dabbed her eyes, wondering if the mascara was going to run, feeling like a fool. She was thankful that no one seemed to notice. They were busy again, rising and pouring water over their hands from a silver cup into a porcelain basin, then reciting more blessings over shiny, braided loaves torn into small pieces and dipped in salt.

Bread and wine, she thought. Renaldo would say it's just like the Sacrament.

Rituals, and more rituals.

Did it really give you anything? she wondered. Or was it just more useless baggage you dragged around until you had the guts to unload it? Like Francesca's suitcases. She smiled. But then, one never knew, did one, just when such seemingly useless baggage was going to come in handy. She looked down at her dress, wondering what she was going to wear tomorrow.

She looked across the table at Orvieda sitting next to her husband, leaning over to talk to her sister Esther. Further down were their children, all sitting together, the older ones watching the younger, straightening bows and wiping chins.

Francesca and me, she thought. A few years from now, sitting side by side, our kids like brothers and sisters. Everyone helping one another, the table groaning from food, the room filled with voices. Beginning our own family tree all over again.

She looked at Gabriel. He was smiling, relaxed, leaning over to tease the children, especially the smaller ones. There was a marked family resemblance.

He belonged in that picture, she thought. It was his perfect place.

But did she? Or was this exactly what she had been running from her whole life?

She thought about it with a growing sense of panic. And then the food began to arrive in earnest. Platters of roast meats, chicken in wine, large bowls of fresh and cooked vegetables delicately seasoned with olive oil and fresh spices. Meat-stuffed grape leaves, and delicate filled squares of puff pastry. There were platters of vegetables stuffed and baked with meat and rice—tomatoes, squash, and green peppers—and numerous dips made of eggplant and red peppers. Everything was incredibly delicious. She ate what she thought were enormous amounts, but the platters kept coming back to her, with a general admonition to do them justice. She tried, until she thought she might actually burst something.

"We have been trying for ages to find someone for Gabriel. How did you two meet?" Orvieda asked. She was a small, elegant woman with the bearing of a true aristocrat. Her question was neither coy nor intrusive, simply the friendly curiosity of an ally.

"Fate?" Suzanne answered, leaning lightly against him.

"What does it matter if she chased him or he chased her," Serge said wickedly. "You women always have it your own way!"

"Our own way?" Orvieda huffed, frowning at her husband. "I suppose I had it my own way!"

"Now, now."

"Orvieda could have had any man she wanted, any man at all!" said Esther—a tall, dark beauty—rushing to her sister's defense, although Suzanne couldn't understand what needed defending here.

"I just didn't want to marry on the rebound," Orvieda explained sorely, obviously assuming Suzanne knew all kinds of things she didn't know.

"My son Serge just couldn't make up his mind," Claudina announced authoritatively. "He was opening one store after the next, making too much money for his own good, and he didn't see any reason to get married."

"Now, *Madre*," Serge said mildly, leaning back easily in his chair. He turned to Suzanne, his eyes amused. "I had everything I needed. A fine, small apartment with a maid and a cook. I spent plenty of time with my nieces and nephews, what did I need to rush into marriage for? Wives just rule over you!" He nodded conspiratorially at Gabriel.

"And I wasn't waiting for him," Orvieda sniffed. "I went to Israel for a year to study, and then to Paris. I had ten offers of marriage a year."

"Oh, yes!" all the women chimed in protectively, nodding their agreement. "She was the most beautiful girl you ever saw!"

"Men couldn't take their eyes away from her. "

"She was so intelligent and educated."

"I kept going to school, waiting and waiting for . . . him!" she accused.

"And we kept saying to him: When will you settle down, have a family of your own, children of your own? Without that, you may be as rich as King Carlos. What does it matter? Who will you leave it to?"

"We kept telling him: Orvieda is still waiting for you. But she won't wait forever."

"Finally, thank G-d, he woke up and went to her to beg her to forgive him and to marry him."

"Yes," Serge admitted. "I did. Flew to Paris bearing gifts. Sending a certain persistent Mr. Levi on his way."

Orvieda dimpled with pleasure.

"Yes. Finally, he came to his senses!" Claudina exclaimed, reaching over to touch a few of her grandchildren—a stunning blonde beauty of about ten, a six-year-old redhead with a mass of wonderful curls, and a delicate, sensitive boy of about thirteen, whom Suzanne immediately realized, was the reason for the celebration. His name was Isaac, she remembered, and he was the bar mitzvah boy.

"Foolish men!" Claudina wagged her finger at the entire male sex. "But our Gabriel is smarter. He doesn't wait until he is almost forty to begin his family. He understands the true meaning of life is not to make more money and more money." She turned curtly to Serge. "To open another store and another store. To keep it open even on the Sabbath."

"That again, *Madre!*" he groaned, turning to Suzanne. "Years ago, everyone kept their shops open, and the employees were Christian or Muslim, they wanted Sundays or Fridays off anyway. They didn't care. But now we have returned to our roots. We keep the store closed Saturdays as well as Sundays. We Sephardim are like reeds," he said with charming insouciance. "We bow to the wind. When it blows hard, we bend instead of breaking. When it passes, we stand up straight again and go on, until the next wind."

There was a short, uncomfortable silence.

"The Ashkenazi Jews always hold that against us. When they were asked to convert, they killed themselves."

"And we pretended and survived! The dead are no use to Him."

"Not all pretended," Claudina chided him. "The Sephardim produced more than their share of apostates, who became our people's worst enemies. We destroy ourselves through our own hands." She glanced at Gabriel, who seemed to freeze.

Suzanne caught the exchange and wondered at its meaning until she was distracted by the maids bringing in beautiful silver dessert trays. Chocolates and sugar biscuits fried in oil, and almond cakes and all kinds of sweet jams.

"*Biscochos,*" Claudine explained, pointing to the cookies, and then to the various jellies: "*Dulce de naranja*—made from orange peels, *dulce de rosas*—rose petals, *dulce de bimbrio*—quince."

It was eerie. The very same foods mentioned in the manuscript! Suddenly, five hundred years didn't seem that long ago. Only seven or eight generations. And everything that had happened between the age of Gracia Mendes and Claudina was simply a series of errant blips—the conversions, the intermarriages, the abandonment of religious traditions, the crass modern world—all of it an aberration that had passed, leaving the descendants closer than ever to their roots. The same rituals, the same language, the same values, even the same foods!

Reeds, bending in the wind.

Was it inescapable? she wondered.

And did she really want to escape?

Saturday morning, a small knock on her door woke her, and a breakfast tray was set upon her night table.

"*Churros con chocolate.*" The maid nodded pleasantly.

Hot chocolate and fried sugar doughnuts, Suzanne discovered on investigation, lifting the clean white napkin that covered the delicate china.

Although after dinner she'd sworn never to eat again, here she was, ravenous! She finished breakfast off with what she thought was indecent haste, then leaned back with a sigh, licking the sugar from her fingers.

There was another knock on the door.

It was Gabriel.

He sat by her bedside, brushing the sugar crystals from her lips with his long, elegant fingers. She leaned toward him, and he drew her closer, slipping the straps of her gown down over her shoulders, burrowing his head into her bare, smooth neck.

"Gabriel," she whispered, pulling him down. But he resisted her gently.

"How I wish!" he groaned, taking her head between his hands and kissing her lips with the perfect mixture of passion and tenderness she so loved in him.

"This is torture!" she moaned.

"You have to be at the synagogue in half an hour. I'm leaving now with the men. The women always come later, but you don't want to miss Isaac being called up to read the Torah."

"I don't?" she said skeptically.

He was silent. "They'd be most distressed and insulted if you did, Suzanne."

"Well, we wouldn't want to do that." She shrugged, feeling a sudden resentment she couldn't really justify.

"Thanks. I'll see you later? And Suzanne," he hesitated, "the women dress fairly conservatively when they go to synagogue."

The powerful morning sun pierced through the grillwork, throwing strange patterns of light over his hair and features. He seemed different: older, more severe.

A shiver ran through all her limbs. He was suddenly a mystery, almost a stranger to her.

How much more of this was she going to have to endure? she thought, nodding obediently.

And then he was gone.

She closed her eyes and leaned back, envisioning getting into the car and driving to the beach. Then she rose reluctantly and put on a long blue skirt with a matching sweater, the most dowdy and presentable outfit she owned. She surveyed the results in the mirror, unsatisfied. It needed a scarf, some jewelry.

She rummaged through her bag and found a little package wrapped in tissue paper.

Renaldo's bracelet. She had taken it off the night she'd run away with Gabriel. She wiped it off gently. It looked neglected, she thought, the bright, intricate design gathering dark tarnish here and there. But it was still quite beautiful. She snapped it around her wrist, feeling guilty and somewhat defiant.

Arm in arm, she walked with Claudina through the lively streets, stopping every two steps for Claudina to receive and bestow kisses on an endless stream of friends, relatives, and acquaintances. Their progress was excruciatingly slow.

When they finally arrived at the synagogue, they walked through a small courtyard bordered with trees. The women's gallery was a flight up, overlooking the men's.

It was breathtaking.

A carved frieze of intricate pattern ran the whole length of the room. Silver candelabrum, modernized with electric lights, hung from the ceiling. The wooden pews had been polished by the backs of many generations. Each seat bore a brass name plate: Esther Abecasiss, Miriam Abergel, Esther Benzaquen, Rivka Abuelo, Claudina Benador. . . .

"Why are so many named Esther?" Suzanne asked in a whisper.

"Because she is the heroine of the *conversos*. She was forced to marry the King of Persia and 'did not reveal her family or her people.' She was the first secret Jew. Her silence led to salvation. She foiled the plot to eradicate the Jews of Persia by intervening with her husband, the King. It is an honor to name our daughters Esther."

Suzanne looked around. The place, as old and beautiful as one of those architectural treasures the British were so keen to turn into lifeless museums, vibrated with life. It was packed with families, reverberating with the chanting of communal prayers.

She stared down at the graying men and their middle-aged sons; the rows of lively teenagers and children barely out of diapers traipsing up and down the aisles with irreverent familiarity. There was nothing artificial, nothing staged. It was as natural and comfortable to the participants as being at a party at the house of a good friend.

The women's section was emptier, but it, too, filled eventually. Like their men, the women were all ages, and singularly friendly. As each entered, they kissed the others, beginning a buzz of whispers that never really subsided.

Suzanne found this annoying. She was surprisingly anxious to hear and see everything that was going on.

It was so different from the service she remembered from the Reform Temple in Manhattan: those slow, orchestrated, wordy parodies of prayer, led by some fair-haired singer-entertainer trying to keep the bored participants from dozing off. Here, the entire congregation chanted the prayers together with the exotic tunes of cultures far from New York City's assimilated Sephardic remnant.

The thickly accented Hebrew, almost indistinguishable from Spanish or Arabic, filled the vast halls with a vital energy.

Claudina handed Suzanne a prayer book, opening the page to the correct spot. But it was hopeless: Hebrew on one side and Ladino on the other. She held it out of courtesy, but barely glanced at it, her attention captivated by the happenings on the raised platform before the carved wooden doors holding the sacred Torah scrolls.

It was almost a stage, she thought, feeling as if she had good seats to a particularly unique performance.

She saw the little bar mitzvah boy rise and walk to the front of the room, climbing the steps to the *tevah*. He was soon followed by his father, grandfather, and uncles. A smaller child of about five or six, whose red hair gave him away as a member of Gabriel's clan, pulled back the velvet curtain. The rabbi opened the ark and handed the Torah scroll in its large, exquisitely painted wooden box to the oldest man present. He in turn passed it to his son, and so on until it reached Serge.

He turned to his son Isaac, chanting a blessing. Then he held out the heavy parchment scroll to the boy.

For a moment, the child hesitated. Suzanne held her breath, watching him brace his thin body. Finally, he held out his thin arms to receive it.

"What if he drops it!" she whispered.

Claudina turned to face her, shocked. *"Hashem Yishmor,"* she murmured, whispering an incantation. "It would be a curse on the whole congregation. But don't worry. He won't."

He was so young, so small, and the scroll so old and so heavy! Yet she saw his thin arms enfold it, displaying a confident strength that seemed to Suzanne as strangely wonderful as it was improbable.

The box was laid flat on the reading table and opened. The boy, surrounded by relatives, the rabbi, and others, stood on his toes and began to read. His voice, a sweet childish soprano, took up the strange melody with an ease that startled her.

It was a chant that had in it the sound of the synagogue, the Muslim *muezzin,* and the Spanish *cancionero.* Sung in his young voice, it took on a wonderful freshness.

He didn't look unhappy, Suzanne had to admit. Simply dwarfed by the weightiness of symbols and the insistent presence of the older men who hovered over him in anxious, prideful silence.

Something must have happened, she thought, as Claudina gave out that high-pitched, vibrating scream with which women of the East have for centuries marked joyous occasions. The other women joined in immediately, and the whole congregation suddenly transformed into some huge ululating tribe, centuries melting, Western veneers dissolving. Small candies were rained down about the child's head, landing in the collars of the men's white prayer shawls, scooped up from the floors by active little boys who descended upon the loot like locusts.

A clapping began, and the shrill, birdlike warble of the *hellulah* continued, as the bar mitzvah boy stepped down to shake the hands of the men in the congregation. To her amazement, Suzanne sensed a little swagger in his stride, as if he had pressed some claim and been victorious. And unless he did something unforgivable, that claim would always be valid, reserving him a place among his people.

No, this place would not be a museum. Let the millennium come and go. There were enough children here who would claim their place, who would fill the empty spots created by death and unexpected desertions.

And what of her section, the women's gallery? She glanced around the room. Young matrons with babies, young girls in their bright dresses, matriarchs in exquisitely tailored suits, their faces happy and satisfied, as after a job well done. They, too, knew the joy of place, of fitting into a world made for them, and preserved by them.

Suzanne felt an unwilling surge of joy that she couldn't explain. In its own terms, it was a real accomplishment. And yet, by the same token, she found something about it simply appalling: the iron-fisted parental control, the boring sameness of the rigid steps that led the child to emulate the parent. The predictability and perhaps, too, the narrow-mindedness that allowed for such consistent and unwavering steps forward in the same direction as those who had come before.

And where had it led? To this last small outpost of an empire in which they had almost entirely disappeared. For five hundred years since the Expulsion, Sephardic Jews had wandered to North Africa, South America, Bulgaria, England, America, Salonika, and places too numerous to mention. And what had been the result: *Eighty-nine percent of Ladino-speaking Jews in the world had died at Hitler's hands, many of them in Auschwitz.*

She remembered a passage that Boris Pasternak had written in *Dr. Zhivago* about Jewish leaders: "Why have they not—even if at the risk of bursting like boilers with the pressure of their duty—disbanded this army which keeps on fighting and being massacred, nobody knows for what? Why don't they say to them: 'Come to your senses. Stop. Don't hold on to your identity. Don't stick together. Disperse. Be with all the rest.'"

Lemmings or survivors? she wondered.

Or simply, very simply, a family.

She wiped away an honest tear drawn up from a well of ties long ignored or forgotten. A tear of bitterness and compassion, of rage and unwilling pride.

28

F A X

TO: CATHERINE DA COSTA
FROM: FRANCESCA ABRAHAM

Dear Gran,

We reached Cáceres just as the afternoon light was fading. It was like being transported back in time. The houses, the churches, the old synagogue, all left exactly the way they must have been five hundred years ago. Marius says it is a well-known tourist spot for that reason. I don't think that many tourists find their way here very often, though.

The streets are a rough, hard cobblestone that would make any jogger's teeth bang together like castanets. I swear I could almost hear the echoing clack of hooves. In general, the place seems riddled with ghosts. They peek out at you from the dark, gray granite houses, hiding behind the immense, metal-studded wooden gates and shutters. Despite the intense Spanish sun, the streets are quite dark, leaning over you and whispering conspiratorially behind your back.

From the hilltop, you can see the snow-capped Sierra de Gredos shining in the distance, touching the thick, low clouds. Looking down at the clustered houses, you can still see the smoke rising

from chimneys and the ivy overlapping green moss on garden walls.
Up in the church spires, I saw a nesting stork, and below I glimpsed
this strange hidden garden with an old stone sculpture of an open
book.

The former synagogue (for hundreds of years a church, it is
unnecessary to add, since there hasn't been a Jew in Cáceres since the
Inquisition) has hardly been touched. There are no crosses on the
original building, or any carved images. You can see where the
women's section was, and where the Ark must have stood. How
strange it must have been for the new converts, especially the
unwilling ones, to suddenly find themselves in their old house of
worship, everything so familiar, yet so utterly changed: monstrances
instead of Torah scrolls, altars and crucifixes instead of the *tevah* and
Star of David.

We arrived full of expectations, but have so far been sorely
disappointed. The person who has been selling off the manuscript is
a local boy named Juan Martinez Ortega. He had a job working in the
church archives—a favor the priest did for his widowed mother.
Apparently, he has been stealing for some time to pay his gambling
debts. He brought a page from the manuscript to a rare-book dealer
almost two years ago, but the dealer wasn't interested. Then when the
international rare-book grapevine starting throbbing with the news
that such a manuscript was worth big bucks to some crazy
Americans, the dealer remembered the boy and contacted him.
That's where the pages we got in England came from. The boy, either
because he was afraid of being caught or was getting wise to the
worth of his merchandise, decided to check out its value with dealers
in Toledo and Córdoba. Again, he sold only part of it and
disappeared with the rest—at least that's what the dealer in Córdoba
says, although he admits it's just a hunch. There's no way to know
how much of the manuscript was actually available to him in the first
place, and how many pages—if any—he's got left.

How the manuscript made its way to the archives of the Church
of San Mateo in Cáceres is anybody's guess. Local folklore says it was
in a suitcase left by a refugee at a border crossing at the base of the
Pyrenees. A truckdriver on his way to Cáceres to deliver meat picked

it up and was very disappointed to find it full of old books and yellowing papers. He just left it behind him at the inn before starting back to Madrid.

It was the innkeeper who turned it over to the local priest, an educated and very righteous person with an extensive library. Until the priest's death five years ago, no one had access to his collection. The new priest, also a very decent fellow, has been trying to catalogue the vast collection.

Ortega's job was to carry piles of the material from the storeroom to the priest's study, and back again. It was his habit to quietly filch a few pages here and there from things that looked old and valuable. His decision to steal an entire manuscript—that is, whatever pages there were, the priest hadn't catalogued it yet, so there is no way of knowing—was probably a result of the good price he'd been offered for the pages he'd showed the dealer. (Note: The dangers of announcing you'll pay any price for a manuscript!)

Anyhow, the final point of it all is that young Mr. Ortega, having filled his coffers with ill-gotten gains, has vanished. Father Serrano says the boy did contact his mother once or twice, but even that has stopped.

We are sort of dancing around each other: Father Serrano is trying not to mind that we have in our possession property stolen from his church archives. He is also gently probing what we plan to do to young Ortega, if and when we get our hands on him (he's a local boy, after all). We have hinted that we have no claim against the church for not turning over the material to international authorities after the war, and that the young thief doesn't interest us, only his booty.

I think the priest would like to be done with this, and with us, as soon as possible. And who can blame him? In the meantime, he's promised to pump the boy's mother for clues.

As you can see, a bit sticky.

So, we will wait a few days, then decide where next.

I find that I am quite depressed about it all. It's not like me to be wandering around impulsively in strange countries where I do not speak the language. I'm ignoring your itinerary (but it's for your own good). For the very first time since I began this, Gran, I am wondering if it is all doomed to failure, and if the manuscript will slip through our fingers once again for another few hundred years.

This is painful to think about, especially since I know the next part is a really important one. I'm afraid it's the part where something happens to Francisco. Gracia, after all, called herself a "young widow." I think I was dreading reading this part, as much as I am curious to know what happened to him.

I will write you soon, hopefully with better news.

My love,
Francesca

P.S. Still not a word from Suzanne?

Catherine put down the letter and closed her eyes, feeling the tubes in her arm fill her veins with the medicinal poison they promised would not kill her. Yet.

I don't need to read the manuscript to know that part of Gracia's life, she thought.

I can see her as if she is sitting here across the room. A pale, fractured light comes through the wooden grilles that shade her windows from the harsh Portuguese summers. It falls on her hands, gripped in her lap; hands that are smooth with youth and yet wrinkled with the tension of a grief that startles her body and numbs her mind.

Her eyes are vacant, staring across to where her husband's body lies draped in black, surrounded by a hundred small candles whose wax drips like solid tears, accumulating on the cold, gray granite. She is waiting for the inevitable steps of the men who will come to carry him down that wide stone staircase and out of the house, never again to enter there or any part of that world of which she is still—to her heartbreak—an unsevered part.

She will wait this way, keening the melodies of mourning remembered from her mother's passing, and then her father's, until the other women join her and the keening becomes the shrill scream of grief, its rising volume a kind of homage.

And when they arrive, she will defy them, those learned men who insist she must not come to the cemetery to see his precious body receive the thudding shovels of earth. Oh, the horror of that first heavy clod that lands just above his breast! She will take a step of rage toward the shoveler, until she remembers it is Diogo, her husband's own beloved brother, whose eyes shift, catching her own in a moment of terrible acknowledgment.

She would have closed her eyes then, reliving the rituals performed to honor the dead, remembering how his tall, beautiful body was purified seven times with clean water mixed with myrtle leaves; how his soft black hair was washed and left gleaming. And her thoughts, the only way she can still be near him, will not wander until once again everything is erased by the outrageous sound of the earth falling from the shovels, a sound that grips her heart with brutal fingers, until that last thud—that last terrible, unbelievable, unbearable thud—finishes the growing mound.

Francisco.

Carl.

I can see her reach for the lace of her collar, the embroidered velvet of her overmantle, ripping both in grief.

It is only the child who will keep her sane, reminding her that there is still something of him left in the world. She will feel a fresh spasm of grief thinking of Reyna, remembering that because of her youth she did not kiss her father's hand nor feel it rest upon her head; neither did she recite the prayer for the dead. And her love for the child will burn in her like a slow, warming fire, reminding her of her duty, demanding she must rise up in the morning, and open her blouse and give her warm breast to her baby's sweet, demanding mouth.

For a moment, she will feel confusion, thinking of the child's warmth and the cold grave wherein her husband lies. Only when she sits by the grave and talks earnestly with Francisco will she hear his voice explain so clearly what it is she must now do.

Does she plead with him, or accept? I think she pleads. Her strength comes later. There, with the scent of the newly turned earth still fresh in her nostrils, she longs for that moment she can join him, wishing away the long years that are ahead.

But soon she will find the years cannot be wished away. That they are slow. Oh, how inexorably slow!

Afterward, there will be the *seudat hav'ra ah,* and she will have the strange sensation of sitting on the floor eating eggs, olives, and bread while the mourner's candle burns in front of her, and the visitors come in an endless stream, whispering: "May you know no further sorrow. May the deceased have eternal peace and may he pray on behalf of the mourners that they have good health and patience."

The *meldados,* the sacred learning sessions in honor of the dead, would begin: *corte de mes, corte de siete meses, corte de nueve meses,* and at the beginning of each, a candle would have been lit, helping the soul to rise higher and higher. She would have seen food was served to the poor, and that the old, bearded men whose chanting filled the house were given raisins, drinks, and *biscochatas.*

Diogo would have said kaddish secretly. There was no one else. And she would have mourned that she herself was not permitted to say it for him herself. Mourned, but not raged. She would have bowed her head in obedience to all the customs and rituals demanded by her true faith, despite the heartbreak, the dangers, the pairs of curious eyes among the mourners who would have taken in the unChristian rites, along with the enormous wealth of the young widow and her baby daughter.

And soon the Grand Inquisitor of Portugal would have been notified of the rich pickings to be had, and the many witnesses to be called, and the easy case to be made. Like locusts, they would have been upon her, depriving her of everything she owned, including her only child, including her very life.

But that did not happen. She survived. She escaped.

She had to. She had a child to protect, didn't she? And all that her husband had worked for, given his life for, the wealth to buy their freedom?

She was twenty-six years old when he died. The same year the Inquisition was established in Portugal.

Catherine opened her eyes, filled with nausea and a growing sense of anguished discomfort.

How had she survived?

29

It was an ancient garden, the kind that seemed to have been there always, with man and woman arriving much later and being of little importance. The palms, like bearded old men, touched the broken clouds, and the majestic eucalyptus peered down with the indifferent calm of fairy-tale giants. The sea, empty and calm as a wise blue eye, winked.

Gabriel held Suzanne's hand in both of his as they sat looking out at the wide horizon, watching the moments pass through the changing light and color of the sky. And as they sat, people turned their heads to look at them.

Wherever they went, people stared. They were the kind of couple that made you smile and secretly feel a bit desolate, so perfectly were they matched: the height, the slim, angular beauty, the flawless features. They seemed like a kind of natural aristocracy selected by forces that couldn't be argued with. Even their hair—his dark blond, hers coppery gold—seemed touched by mythic crowns.

He smoothed back her hair and kissed her at the temple, his warm lips making the sound of her beating heart suddenly loud and real in her ears.

"Suzanne, marry me!"

She reached up, holding her palms against his cheeks, staring into his eyes. And then she turned away from him.

"When I was a little kid, I had a garden," she began, leaning her back against his chest, the top of her head touching his chin. "It was just a small patch of ground in front of the house. But the soil was good and I watered it well and almost everything I planted grew.

"I remember the seed packets—all kinds of strange and exotic plants from Australia and Africa and South America. I used to just open them up and fling them on the ground like dust, without digging any kind of neat furrows or sticking in little signs. And every spring I would see strange little green heads cutting through the earth, and I never knew if it was the beginning of something wonderful or just weeds, so I couldn't bear to tear anything out of the ground. I kept waiting and watering, hoping they'd bloom. Sometimes I was disappointed, but mostly not. The colors of the flowers were unimaginable: periwinkle blue, deep apricot, mauve, scarlet, wild plum. And every single one that bloomed was a surprise and a gift.

"Eventually, of course, the weeds just got out of hand. They choked the old plants, and wouldn't let the new ones root deeply enough."

He touched her face, turning it toward him. His eyes were troubled.

She took a deep breath. "There have been so many beginnings in my life. Things sprouting and full of promise. So many of them have turned out to be weeds."

His eyes were touched with fear. "What is it?"

"I just don't know . . . I don't know if I can do this. If I can be the person to fill that place at the table and in the front pews of the women's section . . ."

"You don't like my family?"

"I do! I do like them all! But that doesn't matter. Don't you see? I've been fighting this my whole life. I don't want to sink into some little round hole that's been dug out for me. I can't just commit myself to doing things out of a love for you. It has to be real. To be me."

"You have to know I would never force you to do anything you didn't want to! But I can't change who I am, or the things that matter to me. Suzanne, Suzanne, what are you afraid of?"

I don't know, she thought. Not really. Except that everything was moving so fast in a direction she had long ago rejected.

She pictured her apartment in the village; the faces of the different men she had known over the past year; Oreo cookies and ratty bathrobes. None of it made sense if she attached Gabriel to the picture.

"I don't want to be a rich Jewish doctor's wife who shops at Harrod's! I don't know if I want children! And if I do, I'm not sure I'd want them dressed up in white shirts and skullcaps, standing at the front of the synagogue getting a heavy scroll of law dropped on them."

"And if nothing at all is demanded of a child, if nothing at all is handed to him, is he better off?" he asked her quietly.

She dropped his hands and stood up tensely. "Look, you know exactly what I'm talking about."

He stretched his legs and put his hands in his pockets, looking down at the ground. "I was never handed anything, except maybe tennis rackets and croquet sticks! Sports. Now that was important! Every child gets something thrown at him. At home, we behaved like lapsed Anglicans. I didn't even know I was Jewish until after my mother's death and meeting Aunt Claudina. My parents thought it was irrelevant—more—embarrassing.

"The week after my mother died, my father took me to Gibraltar to be with her family. We sat on the floor, we lit candles and had study sessions for her soul. It was like being pulled down into some quicksand of primitive emotion. I felt as if I was going to suffocate. But then something happened to me. It wasn't so much participating in the rituals themselves as it was the feeling of being part of a tribe; of feeling for the first time that I was involved in something authentic, instead of all this outward posturing at being the perfect Etonian, English gentleman. This was my place. These were my people. My culture. Who I really was. I want my . . . our . . . children to have that."

She turned to him, and his solid reality almost broke her. It was laughable, really, the audacity of thinking she still had a real choice. She couldn't imagine being parted from him. But just at the moment when her whole being was ready to give in, something deeper took hold: a stubbornness that screamed "foul" like an enraged and discarded mistress.

She walked away, looking out at the sea. Then, suddenly, she turned to face him: "Gabriel, why isn't your father here?"

"My father," he swallowed hard, "is not welcome here."

There was a short, stunned silence.

"Why not?"

"After my mother died, he remarried. The woman was of a different faith. To please her, he converted."

She shrugged. "What difference does that make?"

He stared at her, and for the first time in their relationship, his eyes were cool.

"What difference does it make if the few remaining bald eagles mate with swans and die out? Read the statistics. We're a dying breed."

She didn't know what to say.

"I knew about your mother's intermarriage," he continued, "and about your upbringing when Marius suggested setting us up to meet. It worried me. But Suzanne, I saw you this weekend. You're as much a part of all this as I am. If you'd just stop fighting it . . ."

She stood stock-still, the color draining from her face.

"Marius set us up?" she said dully, her eyes glassy with shock.

"Well, indirectly. It was actually your grandmother's and Alex Serouya's idea."

"My grandmother. . . . You mean, none of this was an accident? That night when you came to our restaurant . . . ?"

"I thought you knew," he said, his tone taking on a slight edge of caution as he watched color suddenly flood her pale face.

No! she thought. No, no, no, no, no. . . . She looked across at him, her eyes full of tears. Then she laughed, almost hysterically. "And I thought it was destiny, a ghost!"

"Suzanne, don't!" He tried to gather her in his arms.

"NO!" She shrugged him off.

"I don't understand. Why are you so offended? This is very usual among Sephardic families. Everyone in Gibraltar gets married this way. Is it so uncommon in your country?"

In my country, she thought. In New York City, in the Village, where the phrase "Sephardic family" gave off the same musty, anachronistic odor as "Plains Indian." Oh, yes. All the time. "Did the matchmaker get his fee already? I hope you paid him well. After all, what a find!" she said with frozen contempt, "Not only a Nasi, but also a da Costa!"

"Suzanne! You're being foolish! There was no question of that after we'd met! It would have made no difference to me who your family was. Suzanne!"

But she was already halfway down the road, hailing a taxi.

"Suzanne!" he called, disbelieving, unable to move. He could see her stiff back flinch as she climbed into the backseat, slamming the door behind her.

30

Loose manuscript pages, wrapped in newspaper, inside an old leather backpack filled with tangerines carried by Juan Martinez Ortega as he crosses the border to Portugal on his way to the docks of Lisbon to await an outward-bound freighter.

W*e had seen* conversos *butchered in Gouvea, Alemtejo, and throughout the land of Portugal after the earthquake that hit Lisbon in 1521, destroying the city of Santarem. The priests had blamed it on those who continued to Judaize, and King João had seized the unrest to press his purpose: the introduction of the Inquisition into Portugal.*

I saw the handwriting on the wall. The time had come to keep the sacred oath I had made to Francisco as he lay dying. Nothing but G-d's Almighty hand itself would stay me from my purpose.

It was no simple task. Royal decree forbade us to leave the country if our destination be some land where the hand of the Church held no power. Sea captains risked losing their lives, as well as their ships, if New Christians were found aboard heading for the lands of the Moors, or those parts of Italy outside the Holy Roman Empire.

We gathered our belongings—those treasure chests of jewels and gold that were the fair profits of the House of Mendes in Lisbon. The rest—our great household—we left behind, intending to

transfer it at a later date. Passage was duly booked for myself,
Reyna, my sister, Brianda, my nephew Joseph, and several
servants.

My sister was included in our party not because of any mutual
desire on either of our parts. She'd agreed to come simply because
she disliked her life in my brother's household, with its many
children and chores. I agreed to take her because I understood my
duty: Brianda was still of marriageable age. It was my obligation
to save her from some disastrous Old Christian attachment that
might come about were she left to her own devices.

More important, I had a duty to the family. Like wolves,
Inquisitors would invariably pounce upon a New Christian family's
most vulnerable member, in the hope of easily frightening them
into a betrayal of all the family secrets. What might Brianda reveal
at just the mere sight of the rack?

And I must admit, I harbored some soft, foolish hope that under
more positive influences, Brianda might yet be redeemed from that
disastrous tutoring that had made her the most selfish, foolish,
and gold-loving of young women.

For good or ill, Brianda was my family. Her worthiness or lack
of it did not come into play. What I did for her, I did for my own
flesh, my own blood. Even when she turned on me like the bitterest
enemy, endangering my child, my life, and everything I owned
with her cruel and foolish deeds, I always tried to remember that.

Diogo had been living in Antwerp for many years, managing a
branch of the House of Mendes. And it being a Christian country,
and I having recently inherited half the House of Mendes, it was
both expedient and natural for me to join him there as a first step
toward achieving my goal.

How strange a light time casts upon our memories, transforming
them with the translucence of knowledge. I cannot look back and
see my nephew Joseph as the thin young boy he must surely have
been when my brother, Miguel, entrusted him to my care. Even in
memory, he seems a tall and comely lad of graceful features and
handsome form, someone upon whom I leaned rather than a child I
must surely have embraced with my support.

I was only twenty-six years old when I left my birthplace and the only life I had ever known; a sheltered, pampered daughter who had become the adored bride of a wealthy, generous man. Little did I suspect what harshness lay in the world, what cruel and insidious dangers. And as I look back and see myself waving good-bye, I feel a great wave of pity and of pride in the foolish courage that allowed me to dream that I might actually succeed.

The Antwerp branch of the Mendes trading house had long overtaken its mother branch both in activity and in profits. This success was entirely due to Diogo's remarkable abilities. His brilliant strategy was to establish a number of alliances. The first was with the great mercantile House of Affaitati in Cremona, Italy, through whom our spices were marketed throughout Europe. Soon, company agents were operating in England, Italy, France, and Germany, and the spices that had once graced only royal tables became part of every prosperous burgher's household. This partnership soon allowed the House of Mendes to buy entire consignments of spices from the King of Portugal: six, eight, or even twelve hundred thousand ducats' worth a year, and to dispose of them throughout northern Europe.

The profits were so enormous that even now I would surely awaken the Evil Eye were I merely to describe them. Thus, I will say but this alone: G-d, in His Infinite Mercy, saw fit to bless the House of Mendes with such wealth that Diogo could not possibly employ more than a mere fraction of his capital in the firm's own mercantile business. To put the profits to best use, he concluded another alliance with Fugger of Ausburg, the greatest banking house in Europe. Through Fugger, Diogo loaned out his profits to the money-hungry and profligate rulers of the world.

Charles V, Holy Roman Emperor, ruler of Spain, the Netherlands, Naples, Sicily, Sardinia, and Austria was by far his greatest customer. Calling himself "G-d's standard bearer," his motto was "plus ultra." Unfortunately, this was how the Emperor handled his debts.

In those endless wars to gain dominion over the Moslem Turks and the Protestant rebels, his coffers were always bare. Indeed, less than a decade before I reached Antwerp, his army, furious at

having received no pay, sacked Rome! Diogo loaned Charles
200,000 florins to conduct the Turkish war, and soon was asked to
loan him more. Until the day he retired to his house in Spain to
stare at works by Tintoretto, tinker with old clocks, and eat
gluttonously, the Holy Roman Emperor was often deeply indebted
to the House of Mendes for the very bread he ate.

This, my children, was a most dangerous situation. For a
borrower soon becomes an enemy whose only desire is to be free of
both debt and lender! In 1532, just four years before we left to join
him, Diogo had been arrested on charges of lèse-majesté. Had not
a tremendous outcry gone up all over Europe, with the King of
Portugal and Henry VIII demanding his release because his arrest
would cause them bankruptcy, it might have ended very badly for
the House of Mendes.

As you can see, solid ground did not exist for our feet, and even
as we walked upon it, it trembled. And thus, when I embarked
upon my journey, it was not the last time I threw myself
impetuously into G-d's hands, as my fathers did when they plunged
into the Red Sea, the Egyptians at their backs.

The passage took several months, and included a stopover in
England in which our ship was boarded by envoys from Henry
bearing gifts, and a foppish Duke who had heard of my
inheritance and sought to convince me of his instant and
everlasting love. I thanked him for his attentions, but told him I
had not yet concluded my year of mourning for my husband.
When he returned the next day to plead his case anew, he found
our ship had already sailed.

When we finally arrived safely in Antwerp, I was overwhelmed
with joy! What a city it was, sparkling with rare commodities
hardly seen elsewhere: figs and raisins, ivory and Brazil wood,
cotton, oil, and wine. Precious gems were being honed in little
workshops, diamonds cut to unheard of brilliance. Everyone was
prospering.

Diogo's mansion in Antwerp, where we took up residence, was
striking in its outer appearance. But its true beauty lay within. I do
not, my children, speak of furnishings. For a house is just a shell—
no more—to be filled with the lives of its inhabitants, colored by all

they do. Diogo Mendes's home was a meeting place for anyone possessing some extraordinary quality of mind and heart.

Joos van Cleve had come in from King Francis's court at Fontainebleau and was painting the most delicate portraits. Antonio Moro, Hans Holbein, and Pieter Jansz Pourbus often met and argued about their art in front of the hearth. The unfortunate Mr. Tyndale was there, busy with his Protestant translations of the Bible until he was arrested and executed for heresy. His command of Hebrew was such that we asked him to tutor Joseph.

But most of all, we found much happy companionship amongst the numerous Spanish and Portuguese conversos who shared our language, culture, and religious loyalties. What scholars they were! What brilliant writers, essayists, playwrights, physicians, and poets! Damião de Góis, Martin Lopez de Villanueva, whose even more brilliant nephew, Michel de Montaigne, was the golden diadem of French essayists.

Our physician, young João Rodríguez of Castel-Branco who later became the most famous medical writer of his day, under the pen name of Amatus Lusitanus, was my dearest, dearest friend. He and his colleague, Dr. Pires, who wrote wonderful Latin poetry, calling himself Pyrrhus Lusitanus, became frequent visitors to the lively salon that served as our own royal court in Antwerp. In later wanderings, too, we often crossed paths.

Although we did not dare to practice our religion openly, we rested on the Sabbath, did not eat prohibited food or leavened bread on Passover, and always kept fast days scrupulously. Moreover, our home often hosted secret prayer assemblies in which we allowed ourselves the indescribable comfort and joy of entering G-d's mansions through the sacred portals of our ancestors, which no tyrant could force us to keep locked for long.

Along with this, we nevertheless were forced to attend mass regularly, to be shriven and to act the part of good Christians, for anything less would have seen us all arrested and charged with heresy.

Why did we risk so much, my children, for things that seemed so small? A word, a song, a meal, a prayer? And I answer you thus: What would not a man wandering in the desert do for tiny drops of

water? The thirst of our souls was no different. It gave us no peace
until we quenched it. But the more we drank, the more our thirst
grew, until we dreamed of great pools of water in which to splash
and laugh and swim and bathe.

We dreamed of freedom without boundaries.

As I said, my plan was to stop over in Antwerp, and from there
to seek refuge in those places where we could finally throw off the
oppressive yoke of tyranny and fear. After six months had passed, I
grew anxious to continue my journey. I proposed to Diogo that he
join us.

"A shroud has no pockets, Diogo," I said with great self-
righteousness. "Surely the profits of the House of Mendes shall
stand us in good stead all of our days!"

"Ah!" he sighed deeply. "If only it were so simple! It is impossible,
especially now."

It was then that I learned the terrible news: All those rich bribes
lavished on King and Pope to stay the Inquisition at the Portuguese
border had finally failed. As the days blackened with the growing
shadow of that dark death moving inexorably from Spain to
Portugal, there was only one way to save the intended victims: to
move as many as possible secretly out of harm's path.

The escape route, I learned to my surprise, had long been in
operation, with Francisco an active participant. This is how it
worked: Our Portuguese spice ships would dock at Plymouth or
Southampton with refugees, there to be boarded by a company
agent who would describe the safest route in which to proceed to
the Low Countries and from there to Turkey or Italy. Another agent
would give them bills of exchange for their goods, which they
could redeem at once from the company offices at their
destination.

It was not a fixed route. For every day, new decrees closed
borders or filled others with the Inquisition's spies. Every day, the
latest information had to be passed on to those refugees still in the
middle of their precarious journey. Even as we helped smuggle
people over borders, we renewed our efforts to turn back the
Pope's black knights through the fabulous bribes that had so often
worked in the past. New negotiations were already under way,

Diogo informed me. If we succeeded, the wealth of the House of Mendes would be needed to save our brethren.

I looked at my brother-in-law. He had never married. His fair hair was touched with gray now, and his once gay, youthful face clouded with care, the skin crisscrossed with lines of heavy thought. I knew I could not leave him to face these burdens alone.

I touched his shoulder. "We are partners now. I will not leave."

A strange look of longing passed over his face, and he rose, taking my hand and kissing it.

We became partners in every sense of the word, our lives fused with the oneness of purpose that comes to kindred spirits embarked on a great and noble enterprise. I tried to enter into the daily running of the House of Mendes, to understand where to cajole and where to bribe, where to be yielding and when not to bend. The House of Mendes was an empire, and for all purposes, Diogo and I were its king and queen. Our decisions affected our profits, and our profits the lives of thousands of our people. I dedicated myself heart, soul, and mind to making all our enterprises successful.

On the surface we negotiated ever more profitable business ventures, overseeing the daily workings of our vast trading empire with meticulous care. But our true task was unseen. We plotted endlessly, bribing officials and magistrates, kings and members of the church to loosen the bands of tyranny growing ever tighter around our people's throats. Within the year, we achieved a stunning success. It was decreed that New Christians might settle in Antwerp freely, with full rights, and with full immunity from prosecution for offenses committed elsewhere.

I remember how we celebrated: The whole converso colony was there in Diogo's pink marble salon, the great fire leaping on the hearth, the dazzling crystal chandeliers dancing on the walls like a shimmering rainbow, a Divine promise to end all destruction. We toasted to our victory.

And when the guests had gone, we walked through the gardens side by side with only the faint light from the curtained windows to guide our way. The smell of jasmine and honeysuckle suddenly made me feel faint with longing. I steadied myself against Diogo, a sudden sharp feeling going through me, leaving me breathless.

Marriage between us was impossible, forbidden by Mosaic laws. One brother could never marry another brother's wife, with one exception: if she had been widowed and left childless. Then he was obligated to marry her.

Reyna's birth stood between us like an angel's blazing sword.

As we gazed at each other in the moonlight, I saw that his heart keened with mine for the union we would never know, which might have brought us so much happiness.

Words never passed between us.

But less than a fortnight later, Diogo asked my permission to marry Brianda.

I did not know what to say, torn as I was between my sister's immense good fortune and my knowledge of the failings of character which would make such a union disastrous. Also, I could not be sure that my heart was pure in wanting to prevent it. And so I held my tongue except to wish them both every happiness.

Brianda was an ecstatic bride-to-be. Although she asked me to help her choose her trousseau, I saw that my presence and my advice were to be ignored. She chose the stones for her betrothal jewelry and gowns by size, rather than quality or taste, always picking the largest and most gaudy. She fretted that her gowns were to be made by local seamstresses, and insisted on compensating by choosing the most elaborate designs and the most showy, costly fabrics. She began to walk about the mansion with the airs of a mistress, disturbing the cook with demands, and upbraiding the housemaids with shrill commands until I was sorely tempted to wring her silly neck.

I could see Diogo's eyes grow tense as he received more and more complaints from his staff. But he said nothing to Brianda, simply contriving to be home less and less of the time.

I finally confronted her.

She tossed her head and told me that as she would soon be mistress of this house, the staff might as well grow used to her ways. As for me, she assured me that as long as we could continue to live together amiably she would have no objection to my staying on with Reyna after her wedding. But if there was to be quarreling, then it would be best for us to find our separate accommodations.

"If I say but one word to Diogo of all I know about you, there won't be a wedding," I told her curtly.

I could see my words hit the mark. After that and until her wedding night, she was as docile as a lamb, and as sweet-tempered as a good little girl. Nevertheless, I arranged for separate lodgings for myself and my staff as soon as I could.

I must say that for a time, Diogo seemed genuinely happy.

But slowly, almost imperceptibly, I saw the light fade in his eyes, whether from his marriage, or the dangers constantly eroding the foundations of our lives, I could not say.

There was no stopping the Inquisition. The Holy Office was officially established in Portugal in 1539, and by 1542, the smoke from the first auto-da-fé began to char the bodies of my people. The stream of immigrants turned into a flood, the numbers reaching such proportions that in 1540, a commission was set up in Milan, which was under Spanish rule, to investigate the matter. As a result, mass arrests were made of New Christians en route to Ancona and Salonika, and the New Christian colony in Milan was imprisoned.

Diogo and myself called an emergency meeting, attended by the leading New Christian merchants of Antwerp and our London agents. It was decided to raise a large sum to persuade the Milanese royal magistrates to suspend their investigation and activities. In addition, a sum of 2,000 ducats was sent to our agent in Milan, to try to ransom the prisoners, and to see to their food and clothing.

During that time, one of our employees, Gaspar Lopes, was sent to Italy on business where he was promptly arrested. To save his own skin, he betrayed everything he knew. When the Emperor heard these reports, I suppose he saw the opportunity he had been looking for to free himself from repaying his loans. He immediately ordered his officials to investigate the New Christian community of Antwerp, especially Diogo Mendes.

Diogo went into hiding. He had already been arrested once. It was just a matter of time before he would be caught again. In the face of such evidence, nothing would save him, or us, or the House of Mendes.

I begged him to arrange for all of us to leave at once, finally convincing him that we could do no good to anyone were we to find ourselves penniless in the dungeons of the Inquisition.

For many weeks, he hesitated. But then an event occurred that finally changed his mind.

Brianda was with child.

At long last, he agreed.

We began to wind up our affairs, deciding that in twelve months' time, we should find ourselves on the road again, this time toward true freedom.

In due course, Brianda was delivered of a lovely baby girl, who brought great joy to all our hearts. At Diogo's insistence, she was named Gracia.

It was only a few weeks later that Diogo came down with that same strange fever that had killed his brother. He burned for three days and three nights, as Brianda and I took turns wetting his forehead with cool linens dipped in ice water. On the fourth, he seemed to improve. He sat up in bed and sipped a bowl of sweet almond broth. But as night fell, the fever returned and a swelling began in all his limbs, turning the joints blue.

He was dead before the morning sun broke through the clouds again.

May G-d spread wings of comfort over him, and may the Garden of Eden be his everlasting reward.

There are many moments in a person's life when he feels the great hand of destiny has slapped him down, but only a few when the great heel of fortune uses its full weight to grind his body and spirit utterly into the dust.

This was such a moment. For within six years I had lost both husband and dearest friend, my only helpmates and shields from the terrors of a world suddenly revealed to me in all its poisonous horror; a world closing in on me and all those I loved.

How I wanted to take to my bed, to weep and refuse to be consoled! Never in my life did I wish more to be allowed the womanly liberty of nervous collapse, of using the excuse of my sex to claim the right of incompetence. I wanted some protector to rise like a mythic hero from the dark shadows, surprising me with his strength and intelligence, the brilliance of his ability to rebuild from the splintering shards of my life something whole and firm.

I could not comfort Brianda. I could not even stand to be in the same room with her, so panic-stricken and hysterical was she, moaning to all who would listen that the King's Imperial Guard would at any moment knock on our doors and drag us off to the Inquisition.

And then Diogo's will was read.

He left a startling amount for charity, the income of which was to be distributed yearly in three equal parts to dower orphans, help prisoners, and clothe the naked. To Brianda, he left the return of her dowry and whatever allowance I thought best.

As for the rest, he left it all to me, in trust for his daughter, Little Gracia. Since half the company was already mine because of Francisco's will, I was now solely in charge.

And thus, I became the administrator of the greatest fortune in Europe.

It was the exact opposite of all I wanted.

And yet, I could not but hear the voices of Francisco and Diogo urging me on, flinging over me the great mantle of their work to save our people through our wealth. I straightened my slim, womanly shoulders, and walked out of the great pink marble hall to my carriage. All the ride home, I clasped my hands and prayed, asking for the wisdom and guidance of my G-d and my ancestors.

Time heals no wounds. On the contrary, the longer the days stretch between the last living contact with one's beloved, the more the longing to see him grows. And yet, I could not but feel that all that had happened, that great turning of the wheels of fate, had done all it could to prepare me for the greatest task any woman had ever been asked to undertake.

I knew I was ready.

31

Roth, Cecil, Doña Gracia of the House of Nasi,
The Jewish Publication Society of America,
Philadelphia, Pennsylvania,1948; 1977.

*Fresh proceedings against Diogo for heresy had perhaps been in
contemplation at the time of his death, being delayed only in order to
collect overwhelming evidence. From the point of view of the imperial
treasury, they would obviously have been lucrative, for a
condemnation on this charge entailed automatically the confiscation of
a man's entire property. . . .*

*It did not seem equitable that his death should involve the emperor
in loss; and posthumous proceedings were therefore opened against
him. Doña [Gracia] fought courageously against the danger, piling up
evidence of his unimpeachable orthodoxy, bringing witnesses to prove
his Christian zeal, placating the officials with gifts of money, using
every possible expedient and sparing no reasonable expense; there was
obviously no other course that could be taken, save to accept defeat
and confiscation. . . .*

Manuscript pages, unbound, circa 1610–1620. Hidden in the
binding of a book taken from Caceres to Venice.

W*hat else could I do? I paid. One hundred thousand florins. A loan without interest to the Emperor, they called it.*

All charges were dropped.

There was no question, of course, of my leaving Antwerp now, with so much to be arranged, so much to oversee. But G-d in his mercy prepares the cure before He creates the illness. Just when I began to truly despair, I looked across the dinner table to find the solution smiling at me. Joseph.

He had grown from a gangling, shy, sweet-tempered young boy to a tall, handsome man of acute intelligence and immeasurable charm. He had long been involved in helping Diogo administer the House of Mendes and was not only completely versed in our commercial dealings, but privy to the complex secret dealings upon which so many lives depended.

Realizing that our relations to the royal family must be sweetened, I sent him to live at Queen Mary's court in Brussels. He soon became adept at jousting, hunting, swordsmanship, and courtly dancing. He and the Queen's nephew, Maximilian, soon became boon companions. Having prepared the ground, I then joined him.

How can I make you envision my arrival in Brussels to the resplendence of the royal court? I was still young, still greatly admired for my enormous wealth and not unpleasing person. They paid me court, those endless stream of royal cousins, untitled and titled noblemen, men who saw in me a womanly body, larger houses, and lesser thrift. I accepted their gifts; the poorly worked jewels, the illuminated manuscript of the Book of Matthew; the awful poetry and the endless bunches of dying flora! I smiled. I served tea. I flattered them enough to have them leave in good spirits, yet not enough to encourage their imminent return. It was like a fencing match, I told Joseph. The object was to neither mortally wound, nor jump back in defense over the castle parapet.

And just as I began feeling the smugness of victory, I realized that the enemy had changed the rules of the battle and the object of victory. Before I realized what was happening, the light of avid interest began to shine on my daughter, my Reyna.

She was like some rare flower, her graceful head blooming on the gleaming white stem of her fresh, lovely body. People remarked that her blue eyes were like the sky over the deep blue Mediterranean. Others compared her golden-red hair to that of Isabella, little realizing my revulsion at the thought of any connection, however flimsy, between my child and the Catholic Queen who had caused our people so much grief.

Her charming smile, her little ivory hands, the smoothness of her alabaster brow . . . the praise was endless. I was confused at first, as perhaps a mother with a daughter so newly emerged from childhood can claim her right to be. I allowed myself to savor the praise as a sculptor savors gushings over the form released from stone by his skillful chisel. But soon I awoke, understanding how all this flattery once again placed us in mortal danger.

It was not unheard of for monarchs to simply take charge of the promising, wealthy offspring of members of court, bringing them up and disposing of their matrimonial futures as they would gifts at their disposal, to be conferred at will upon anyone who had gained their favor. Through my contacts and Joseph's, we were able to convey in the strongest possible terms that any such attempt would be viewed with extreme disfavor, backed by the considerable resources of the House of Mendes.

Thus, tactics changed again. It was decided to allow the maiden to be wooed.

I see her now in my mind's eye, seated demurely in our salon, her dainty hands twisting the folds of her blue gown as the men lean in toward her with cunning smiles. Her face, confused, already glowing with the reflected light of male approval. For I am sure among the dozens were several honestly smitten, who gave no thought to the rich wrappings that would accompany such a prize, even if their parents did.

It was, and is, my great fortune to have been blessed with a child of great good humor and calm nerves. She did not complain, taking it in with the wonder of Columbus gazing at the sudden appearance of a world he had hitherto not known existed.

Some were honest, handsome of face and form; kindly and possessing great wealth and position of their own. Still, as I explained to her, marriage to any Old Christian was out of the question. *Reyna, having received at my hands the same education my mother had given me, did not have to be told why.*

Gradually, the ranks thinned. Only one would not be put off. His name was Don Francisco d'Aragon, a bastard of the Aragonese royal house. He was in good favor with Queen Mary and the entire royal house, having distinguished himself in his zeal in investigating the crimes of New Christians. Indeed, years before (for he was a man of an age more fitting to be my father than my daughter's husband) he had accompanied the Empress Isabella herself on some state journey.

You might imagine, my children, my joy in contemplating such a match for my only daughter! I nevertheless was forced to entertain him on a number of occasions, though I made sure Reyna, who found him odious in the extreme, was spared such ignominy. When his persistence forced me to stretch my ingenuity to the extreme, I decided to return to Antwerp in great haste, putting as much distance between us as possible.

When d'Aragon found himself unable to breach our gates at will, he went directly to Charles to press his suit. Through Joseph and his well-placed spies, I learned that he had proposed the following: 200,000 ducats to our impecunious Emperor from my daughter's wealth if the marriage took place!

Charles wrote immediately to Queen Mary, insisting that she arrange it, promising her a quarter of the spoils for her own needs.

Then began a series of meetings I shall not forget. Queen Mary, Regent of the Netherlands, deputy to the Emperor, driving up to our home in Antwerp and seating herself in our salon.

"A little refreshment, Your Majesty?"

The golden plates, the rich cakes, the hot brew. Her smile, her words of praise for Reyna, her desire, as one who was as fond of her as her own mother, to see her settled well. The wonderful opportunity to marry with such royal favor a man of such impeccable renown.

"Sugar, Your Majesty?"

"What is your answer then, Doña Beatrice? Shall this wonderful match not be immediately taken advantage of?"

"My dearest Queen, may our close relationship allow me to speak with candor?"

A gracious incline of the royal head.

"Your Majesty, permit me to say that I would truly prefer to see my child dead and buried than married to an opportunistic, elderly vagabond who is old enough to be her grandfather!"

It was a shame, the next day, that urgent business called the Queen from our company and back to court.

The letters from Charles to the Queen Regent, and d'Aragon to Charles, continued, full of eager suggestions. The mother's consent, d'Aragon advised, was of no importance whatsoever. Why not simply choose the day and time and send the Imperial Guard to accompany the bride there safely?

Do so and the merchant class of Antwerp, whose taxes fill your coffers, will rise and leave as one man, the Queen's advisers pointed out to her, an impression that Joseph no doubt had some part in creating.

Perhaps then, a ball. Invite the Mendes women to court here in Brussels, where they shall be my honored guests until such time as I shall find it in their best interests to permit them to leave. . . .

Unfortunately—as I explained to my Queen in letters written on parchment and sealed with wax—my health did not permit me to accept her gracious invitation. Indeed, as the invitations mounted, I realized my health would never permit a journey in that direction.

I held out as long as I could.

The next time the royal messengers arrived at our door in Antwerp, they found the house empty of its inhabitants.

I had begun my next journey, escaping with Reyna, Brianda, and Little Gracia to Venice.

32

"Good news?" Janice looked up from the brilliant pages of her glossy magazine into her mother's distant smile.

"Wonderful!" Catherine said hoarsely. "Can you bring me a drink of water, please?"

Janice hurried to pour some into a tall glass, cradling her mother's head as she drank in long, painful gulps. She finished less than half before impatiently waving Janice away.

"It seems that the suitcase which held the manuscript pages in Cáceres held some old books as well. One of them had a name and address: Elizabeta Bomberg, Venice."

"What kind of book was it?"

"An old Christian theology text. Absolutely worthless, Marius says. But the priest has given it to Francesca and Marius as a kind of good-bye-and-good-riddance present."

"So," said Janice, "they're off to Venice. Wonderful shopping there. Too bad they missed carnival," she mused, turning the pages of her magazine.

"Janice. We must find Suzanne!"

"Really, mother," Janice said calmly, examining a fashion layout from Armani, "when are you going to come to terms with Suzanne? She'll appear when she's run out of money, not before. It's hopeless to try to track her down."

Catherine sat bolt upright, resting her whole weight on one frail elbow. "Nothing is hopeless, isn't that what you and my doctors keep telling me?"

Janice looked up, the magazine suspended in midair. "You're upsetting yourself!"

"Promise me you'll talk to Marius and get him to call this young man, this Gabriel! He's a doctor, he must have an answering service that knows his whereabouts."

"A Jewish doctor, isn't that what you said, English or something? It sounds wonderful, Mother. Maybe we shouldn't interfere. Let nature take its course."

"I tell you, you must find her!"

"And let's say we do, then what?"

"I want her to go to Venice. She must go to Venice!" Catherine slammed her fist down on the bed, rattling the plastic coils, the tubes, and metal hooks.

"*Madre*, please! I'm going to have to call the doctor if you don't lie down!"

"Write it down!" Catherine demanded.

Janice took out a lapis blue fountain pen trimmed in eighteen-karat gold, but discovered she had nothing to write on, except her checkbook. She tore out one of the accounting pages and turned it over. "I'm writing, *Madre*."

"Call Marius or Alex Serouya and tell them to contact Gabriel and find Suzanne. Get word to Suzanne that she must meet Francesca in Venice right away."

Janice kept writing.

"Have you got all that?"

"Of course. Can I ask why?"

"You won't understand, but I'll tell you anyway. I had a visitor a while back. She told me that the girls mustn't miss Venice. Both of them."

"A visitor? Who?"

"A woman. She took me upstairs to see the babies, remember? That time I disappeared?"

"That deranged volunteer!"

"She wasn't deranged and she wasn't a volunteer. She was my *memuneh*."

"Your what!?"

"My guardian angel, if you'd prefer."

"Did this person ask you for money, by any chance?" Janice asked tensely, her eyes narrowing.

Catherine chuckled. "It isn't a usable currency where she comes from. Besides, ghosts don't really shop."

"You frighten me when you talk this way! Do you want me to call the doctor and ask him about your medication?"

"Never mind my medication! I'm not hallucinating, I tell you! Look, Janice, even if you don't care to believe a word I say, think about it: What possible harm could come from telling Suzanne to meet Francesca in Venice? Call it an old woman's whim."

"Why is it so important to you?"

"The woman said specifically that both of them shouldn't miss Venice. Don't you see? Venice wasn't even on the itinerary for them, and now, suddenly Francesca is going there! I just know something is going to happen there to both of them that will change their lives for the better."

"Be realistic! They've never gotten along! Can you really imagine anything lasting and positive coming out of forcing them to be together? Some people are better off apart," Janice said tearfully.

The divorce papers had already been drawn up. The inelegant wrestling match over money had begun.

Catherine lay back, exhausted, turning her face to the window. "I've always loved summer. When I was a little girl, we had a house on the beach. I used to watch the sun make this shining pathway on the water, like some golden road to heaven. And there were always these quiet old men in soft cotton shirts listening to the waves, their eyes closed, content."

She turned to look at Janice, her voice faint, but stirring with strange emotion. "Do you remember that summer you discovered you had a lovely voice and you sang all day? That was the summer I thought: This is going to be the most wonderful year, yes, the most beautiful year of my life."

Janice stared at her, transfixed.

"You were a darling child. In my mother's and grandmother's day, you would have been considered the perfect daughter—pretty, docile, sweet-natured. But your father and I, we considered ourselves modern, progressive. We wanted you to succeed, to be accomplished, to contribute. That was it! To make some *contribution* to mankind.

"You weren't a scholar, even though you did manage to pass all your courses. Nothing much interested you, though, but young men and real estate. Oh, that's unkind! You wanted a husband and a home. You were all right. It was the world that changed.

"But that summer, listening to you singing all over the house, I felt such a breaking out of happiness. And then suddenly, I got depressed. I got strange aches and pains, sometimes sharp ones right over my heart. I felt anxious. I couldn't sleep. I overate. And then I felt sluggish and sleepy. All day, all I wanted to do was sleep.

"This went on until I finally understood what was wrong with me: Everything in my life was suddenly perfect. I was terrified I wouldn't be able to hold on to it. So I made myself miserable. I couldn't trust the future. I didn't believe it would be kind, even though it had brought me that lovely summer, so unexpectedly. Do you understand what I'm saying, Janice?"

Catherine did not hear her answer, the sudden blackening into unconsciousness taking her unawares. She felt a sudden sliding beneath her, as noiseless as a swan, and smelled the weathered wood of the gondola. She lay back, the sunlight warm on her face as someone competently manned the oars, singing with great happiness as they drifted toward some pleasant, unknown goal. It would be so easy to get there, she thought, wondering why she had been resisting, why she had been so afraid. True, she had not planned it this way, but what did that matter? The important thing was . . .

And suddenly, she couldn't remember. Nothing seemed important anymore, just peace, perfect peace. That was the goal in the end. Those old men, their eyes closed, had found it with less trouble than she.

Madre!

Unpleasantly louder, the voices, a shout, not a song. A scream of alarm, and the shaking boat dashed recklessly against the pier.

The harsh light. Janice's tearful, frightened face. Concern, pain, noise, needles, flashing red lights.

Not yet, she thought, full of regret and a small hope. Not yet, but soon.

Janice closed the door and bought a cup of bad coffee from a hospital machine, more to hold than to drink. Her hands shook.

A fainting spell, not a heart attack, they said. She wiped her sweating brow, leaning back and trying to gain her composure.

She remembered that summer. She'd been thirteen years old. And all summer long, the disc jockeys had been wearing out records of Arlo Guthrie, Bob Dylan, Pete Seeger, and the incomparable Joan Baez, whose lovely voice filled you with a longing so painful that your whole body ached with joy. She'd spent that entire August with a Joan Baez song book and a guitar, sitting on her bed singing about lost maidens and drowned sailors and unfaithful true loves, feeling as lonely and lost as she'd ever felt in her life.

Lovely singing voice!

She'd never even been able to carry a tune! And it had made *Madre* so happy! What could that mean? Living in the same house at the same time with someone, and yet not even having your memories vaguely intersect? Had they been part of each other's lives at all? And were they now, and would they ever be?

She downed the coffee in one long, lukewarm sip of displeasure, wondering if Kenny's lawyer had responded to her lawyer's latest proposal. Wondering if she could take an hour or two off to go down to Bendel's to walk through the perfume counters, to shake off the smell of hospital antiseptic. Wondering how much longer this was going to take. . . .

She reached into her handbag for a tissue, and pulled out the note she'd written. Call, do, tell. *Memunehs* and guardian angels! Foolish, all of it. But *Madre* wouldn't forget. She'd ask about it later, fainting spell or no. *I'd better get to it immediately.*

Trust the future, she thought, wondering what in heaven's name that could possibly mean.

33

The fog rose from the water like steam, hiding the houses in a fairy-tale mist that made you feel you were walking open-eyed through a dream.

"It can't be real!" Francesca murmured.

"Come!" Marius took her arm, guiding her to the *vaporetto.*

"A boat?"

"There aren't any streets. Think of it as the local bus."

She felt disoriented looking around at the flooded spaces, reminiscent only of places declared "disaster areas" on American television news. "The suitcases?"

"I've arranged for a porter to bring them around to the hotel. Relax."

She did. It was really nice having him take care of the luggage, she thought, standing beside him on the prow. It was true that everything he did for her she could have accomplished pretty easily by herself, but how lovely not to have to! Not to have to struggle and be self-sufficient all the time. To simply *lean.*

She leaned. She could feel his muscles brace, accepting her weight. She felt protected and cushioned as her ear rested against his arm and her soft curls brushed his shoulder. Since the incident on the road to Cáceres, he had been careful not to touch her, even casually. She looked up at him. He was smiling down at her with a look of perfect contentment. She smiled back. Suddenly, strongly, she felt a wave of happiness.

The boat moved slowly through the water. Francesca gazed, enchanted, at the magnificent old palaces and charming bridges that appeared and vanished, ghostlike, in and out of the fog. Venice and Cáceres, she thought. Places that wear their history neither as shroud nor costume, but simply as a fine old gown lovingly preserved. Yet, as much as she wanted to be absolutely charmed, she found she couldn't ignore the patches and tears: the polluted smell of the gray-green water, the peeling shutters and crumbling stonework, the way the entire dreamscape seemed to be sinking like a rotting tug into oblivion.

Why do you always have to do this? she complained to herself bitterly. Why do you have to examine everything under a microscope until the little, swarming microbes appear, ruining everything? Why do you have to constantly talk yourself out of feeling joy?

The image came to her of a child in a sporting-goods store being outfitted for Rollerblading by his anxious mother: the crash helmet, the chest protector, knee guards, elbow guards.

When had she acquired all this protective gear?

After Peter? Or was it even before? Daddy walking out?

Or was it Darren Stockwell?

She shivered.

"Are you cold?"

She shook her head. Still, he took off his light summer jacket and draped it around her shoulders.

Put it out of your mind!

But it wouldn't go. It sat there, as if once again the door were locked and the big football jock, whose father had worked with Kenneth Barren, were standing in front of it.

It had been her first big date for her first Homecoming weekend. They'd both had too many beers and she'd invited him up to her dorm for a minute. He'd been so nice. A senior, pre-med, beautifully built. Rich. Courteous. Up until the moment he'd locked the door of her dorm room and put his hands around her throat.

Getting "carried away" is what he called it before leaving her. And she hadn't corrected him, hadn't called it by its rightful name, the name the police would have used, had she not been too hurt, too confused, and too ashamed to call them.

The only person she'd ever told was Suzanne, years later, and more as a warning than a plea for comfort and protection. She'd found ways of protecting herself.

The first step was not to connect: to turn down the pages of the newspaper, to turn off the radio and TV news; to live in a building with security guards, where you didn't know anyone, and no one knew you. To concentrate all your efforts not on saving the world, but on saving yourself.

So far, she'd succeeded, she thought, straightening up.

The boat made regular stops, docking to take on and leave off passengers, just like a normal, wheeled vehicle of public transportation. They got off at Piazza San Marco. It was only a short walk to their hotel.

Even from the outside, Francesca knew this couldn't be the one on her itinerary.

"The Gritti Palace? There's got to be a mistake."

He patted her arm and slipped it through his. "Nothing less will do for the descendant of Doña Gracia Mendes."

"I don't have a budget for this, Marius!"

"Tut, tut. My treat. I insist."

It seemed more like the private home of fabulously wealthy aristocrats than a place that accepted Visa and MasterCard.

"A perfectly restored fifteenth-century Gothic palace," Marius murmured, taking her into the lobby.

It was lavish. Yet, the sumptuous overstuffed period furniture seemed intimate and cosseting. Porcelain vases held huge, fresh flower arrangements reflected in ornately gilt-framed mirrors. Through tall, heavy, wooden doors, she glimpsed a charming crowd of well-dressed strangers basking in the magical light of dazzling crystal chandeliers. That and the staff, so diffident and spoiling, really did make her feel like traveling royalty.

"Shall we have lunch after we freshen up? The Club Del Doge is one of the finest restaurants in the world."

She looked at him curiously. He never spoke about money. He didn't dress or act like a wealthy man. But if he was offering to pick up the tab for all of this . . . ? She didn't know what to think.

Her bags were already in her room. She pulled back the heavy drapes and looked down into the sea. The soft sound of the anchored gondolas tapping their pointed prows against each other drifted up to her. It was a sound that would forever bring back to her this particular place, this particular time, she thought.

They sat facing each other in the exquisite dining room, sipping tall, cool drinks in lovely colors, watching the boats drift by on the Grand Canal. She ran her fingers through her curly hair, realizing that it had grown since she'd left home. It was past her neck, almost touching her shoulders in a thick mass of uncontrolled curls.

He reached across the table, taking the lock from between her fingers, rubbing it tenderly.

"I'm not good at this. I take these things seriously," she said, shaking her head.

"I mean it and have meant it seriously from the very beginning. From the first moment I looked at you. Francesca, you must know how I feel." He leaned back, looking away from her out to where the sun had begun its slow, golden fall into the sea. Then he leaned across the table, taking her palm tenderly in his. "I think I'm in love."

The words went through her like a crack of thunder from a clear sky. Could this really be happening, she wondered, their palms electric and warming against each other. Or was it simply a strange dream? "But why me? We're such opposites!"

He shook his head and began to protest. She covered his mouth with her hand. "Don't deny it! Of course it's true! I was meant to have the kind of life where the most exciting thing that happens is that my treasury bonds go down two percentage points. I'm a homebody. If I ever did travel along with you, all I'd ever do is hold the ladder and scream: 'Be careful! Be careful!' Trust me, you don't want me."

He looked at her, enclosing her hands in both of his. "Oh yes," he said. "I do."

"But why?"

He grinned. "Because I think you'll do a very good job holding the ladder."

"Seriously!"

He stretched out his legs and put both hands into his pockets, his gaze shifting from her face to the fading light blushing over the horizon. "A few years ago, the day I decided to break up with my first love . . . "

Francesca swallowed. "You had a first love?"

"Oh, yes, indeed. She was a doctoral candidate, studying archaeology at Oxford. She was dark, like you. But she was very adventurous. She liked to jet off weekends and disappear, joining digs in Iraq or Turkey. Summers were always spent in the hottest climates, in the worst possible conditions. She took her work very seriously.

"With her schedule and mine, we could never make plans—and there was this constant competition. She constantly asked me to prove things to her, and I don't think I ever did. She wanted the kind of freedom I knew I could never give her, not if I wanted a family."

"Do you? Want one?" A surge of strange warmth passed through her stomach.

"Of course. Anyway, one weekend we went away together to a lovely old hotel in the Lake District. I'd gone down to breakfast and she'd decided to sleep late. I was sitting there with my coffee and hot rolls and marmalade, feeling forlorn, when I looked across the room. There was this couple, a man and his wife. The man had gray hair and looked about fifty, and the wife was pretty and small, about the same age. And as I was watching them, I saw her reach across to him and smooth down his hair. You could sense they belonged together. And in that instant I just knew that Christina and I didn't."

"So," she said, exhaling deeply, as if having surfaced from beneath the sea, "what next?"

"It's up to you, Francesca. It's all up to you."

She didn't protest.

She had wanted this to happen, she realized. But now that it had, she immediately felt herself backing away, filled with doubts. Could she really envision a life together with this man? The "what do you want for breakfast, have a nice day, 'bye honey, don't forget to pick up the dress at the cleaners" kind of life?

Nothing about their relationship had been ordinary. It had all been a kind of magic: exotic places, hotels, foreign languages. Was there really a place with an address on the firm landscape of the reality she knew that would take them both in? And when it did, how long before either one of them began to feel like moving?

She waited for him to press her for some kind of answer or declaration, and wondered—almost frightened—what she would say.

He didn't.

Instead, they ate in almost palpable silence. When they had finished, he took her by the hand and led her down the winding old stone steps to where the gondoliers had gathered to wait patiently for tourists.

They climbed in. *"Lentamente,"* Francesca heard Marius whisper to the gondolier.

They sat side by side in the softly rocking boat as the gondolier swept the immense oar slowly through the water, sending them into the lazy current of the Grand Canal. The fog had lifted, and in its place was the softly glowing reflection of the pink and lavender sky.

The light, Francesca thought, was like a stage set in a Christmas matinee of *The Nutcracker;* a wondrous pink glow that turned even the most ordinary prop into a thing of enchantment. Even I, she thought, must look enchanting.

She turned around, leaning back into his arms, and felt the brush of his lips against her forehead, so sweet it could have been almost fatherly if her own body had not responded with such unfilial passion.

"Marius . . ." Francesca began, but the gondolier began to sing a lively Italian song with much more enthusiasm than skill, winking and grinning at them in pure delight.

"Amore, amore, amore," he sang.

"Amore, amore, amore," Marius repeated in a whisper she could almost feel entering her ear and mind and heart.

Slowly, like some fragile plant seeking out the sun, she turned her body toward his. Trembling with fear as she felt the cast-iron shields encasing her melt, she placed one hand on his shoulder and the other into his thick, dark hair. Looking deep into his startled and delighted eyes, she kissed him.

His whole body moved up to meet hers, his arms catching and holding her close to him, creating a magic circle of connectedness that she had never before experienced, nor even imagined possible. All her senses suddenly woke up and laughed with a vigorous new joy of life. His body, his smell, the texture of his warm skin against hers, it was all so precious, so new, and yet so very familiar. It was as if she had always known him, and he had always been a part of her.

Because an old woman had changed her mind at the last minute, Suzanne had gotten a seat on standby on the first available flight out of

Malaga. It happened to be going to Rome. It was as good as any other place, she'd told herself.

Listless and with no real plan in mind, she spent a few days wandering around the Colosseum, the Roman Forum, and the Vatican Museums, detaching herself from the Italian guide who spoke three languages, all incomprehensibly. There was a sinister echo in the silent stone seats of the great amphitheater, and the irradicable sense of cruelty, blood, and pain, both human and animal. If she closed her eyes, she could almost hear the echo of long silent screams.

The Forum, with its broken stone reminders of the fleeting nature of power, was even more depressing. Rulers of the world! Reigning now over a landscape of crumbling old marble, their heirs purveyors of fashionable leather goods and well-designed furniture.

Feeding Christians to the lions, burning Jews at the stake. There was no place in Europe you could wander joyously once your ears insisted on hearing the echoes, and your eyes persisted in seeing ghosts. Depressed, she abandoned the idea that had flitted briefly across her mind of retracing her epiphanous college trek with Renaldo. It all seemed so different now, so changed. On the spur of the moment, she decided to take a train to Florence, to the one exhibit she and Renaldo had missed that summer, either because it had been closed for renovations or on tour—she couldn't recall which. Only the image of Renaldo's disappointed face as he stared at the locked gates was clear in her mind. "We'll come back here many times," he'd promised. A promise he hadn't kept.

Galleria dell'Accademia. She walked through the gates into the vast room.

And there it was: Michelangelo's statue of David.

She staggered to a spot where she could sit down, shocked by the otherworldly, almost crushing immensity of the encounter. Whatever reproduction or photograph of it she'd seen had done nothing to prepare her for it; quite the opposite. They had been outright lies that made the revelation of truth that much more astonishing.

You *could* believe in G-d, she suddenly realized. For here, truly, she thought, was proof positive that man was created in His image. How else could you explain the touch of Divine in Michelangelo's hands that had allowed him to release such incredible warm beauty from the cold stuff of marble?

She tried to analyze its power. It was not classically beautiful. The proportions were off, the powerful arms and shoulders far too large for the boyish, short legs. The neck and the face, the epitome of male beauty, were filled with courage, fear, and doubt.

Michelangelo had been twenty-six when the Cathedral Works Committee tossed him a ruined piece of marble abandoned by another artist, she'd read. As she looked into David's face, she could see clearly reflected the young sculptor's own courage and doubt as he flung his masterpiece in the face of the Goliath of established powers like some slingshot stone.

That night, she dreamed of David, his hard, cold body suddenly thawed into flesh, the blank, stone eyes warming as they looked at her, all fear and hope gone, replaced by longing. And suddenly she felt herself enveloped by the strange creature, part stone, part man, whose icy-cool cheek she touched with warm hands.

She awoke in the dark and cried until daybreak.

In the morning she called Paris. Renaldo wasn't there, they told her. Professor Barrie had unexpectedly received an award and flown to America, and Renaldo had taken over his graduate seminar in Venice.

Venice.

Can I stand it? she wondered.

34

They walked arm in arm back into the lobby, lost in each other's eyes. Francesca looked at the elevator that would take them upstairs, wondering how and where they would spend the rest of the night. It seemed to her that now a decision had to be made. She felt on the verge of making it.

"*Signor.*" A clerk respectfully cleared his throat.

Marius looked up, dazed, his eyes moving from Francesca's face and back into the everyday world.

"There are some messages for you," he said, handing Marius some white envelopes.

Francesca wondered at the sudden rush of color that bathed his face as he read them.

"I knew my hunch would pay off!" he kissed her hand hurriedly. "I've got to go."

"What?!" she caught his arm and shook her head in disbelief. "You're leaving me? Now? After everything that we've . . . "

"You don't understand, my love! They've found it! Part of the manuscript! In the Bodleian Library, mistakenly attached to a fifteenth-century manuscript of de Camoes *The Lusiads*! Imagine! It's taken months for my graduate student to go through this stuff, but I didn't give up!"

"That's fantastic! But, Marius, why can't he just copy the material and fax it?"

He looked pained: "Francesca, they don't let you photocopy rare fifteenth-century original manuscripts. And there's something else, some notes in the margin, hardly readable. I've got to see it before anyone else does."

"When do we leave?" She shrugged.

He touched her shoulder gently: "Listen to me, my love! I've got to leave immediately. And you're going to stay behind and follow up the lead from Caceres."

"But, Marius, all I've got is a name and an address! We don't even know if the person is alive anymore. And even if she is, how will I speak to her? I don't know Italian!" she protested.

He kissed her. "You'll do just fine! Besides, I'll be back in a few days." He took her suddenly cold hands, warming them between his own. "Trust me?"

"What's a few days?"

"Two. Four. Maybe less."

She sat down heavily, sinking into the down pillows of the sofa in the lobby. They sucked her in like quicksand. Her eyes darted to the elevators, dull with disappointment. She felt immobilized. "I can't believe that tonight, of all nights, you're going to abandon me!"

"Darling Francesca, I'm doing this for you, for your family!"

"For your own unmatched reputation," she added sullenly.

He grinned, holding her chin in his palm, caressing her cheek lovingly with his thumb. "Actually, I'm afraid you'll take advantage of me in this romantic setting. I don't want to be seduced in the moonlight only to be abandoned in the sensible light of day over bran flakes and the *International Herald Tribune*. I want to give you time to think about all this." His eyes grew serious as he laced his fingers through hers. "But when I come back, I want an answer."

"What's the question?" she said flippantly, scared.

"You know," he whispered, rubbing his knuckle along her cheek.

What he was saying was not only right, but admirably sensible, she tried to convince herself as she watched him pack, ride down the elevator, and climb into the *vaporetto*. But as she lifted her arm to wave goodbye, she felt a sense of stunned disbelief that bordered on physical injury.

He was gone.

That night, sleep felt like a deep, dark hole. She awoke feeling heavily drugged, or like someone who'd spent too many hours on the beach. She literally dragged herself out of bed, struggling with the unbearable idea that her life had finally returned to normal.

Breakfast for one.

The stock page.

Bran flakes.

She pulled back the curtains. The fog had vanished, taking with it all mysteries, leaving behind the mundane light of day. She took out her day planner, checking her schedule, feeling the day stretch out before her like a long, hard road.

She looked through the phone book, but could find no one by the name of Elizabeta Bomberg listed. She felt inexplicably relieved, wondering what she was doing anyway initiating a telephone conversation in a language she neither spoke nor understood. She opened the old book and looked again at the address: 12 Rio della Misericordia.

The concierge, a charming older man who spoke decent English, was delighted to help her locate it on the map. She wrote down his directions carefully, all the while looking over his beautifully cut hair, the way the black color gradually turned to gray at his temples. Old age didn't have to be a jump off a cliff, she mused, just a walk down a gently sloping hill. Until, of course, illness gave you that grand push.

She thought of her grandmother, wondering if all was well. The maid or the answering machine always answered her calls these days, and when Gran phoned back, her tone was overly cheerful, as were her faxes and letters. She seemed delighted at the progress they were making, and there was never a word of criticism. Considering it was Gran, that was extremely suspicious, as were the ever increasing gaps of late between their contacts. It worried her.

On the map, Rio della Misericordia didn't seem far.

She walked around the corner to the Piazza San Marco. Times Square, Venetian style, she thought, gazing into the windows of lovely little pastry shops whose enticing displays of cakes and chocolates made her mouth water. Later, she promised herself, her pace slackening as she passed shops selling beautiful porcelain collectors' dolls, unique, hand-painted face masks, luxurious furs, and gorgeous glazed ceramics. There was nothing for sale you couldn't live without. But why, in heaven's name, would you want to?

Everything was so beautiful, arousing a desire for possession that was almost irresistible. One became irrational, she thought, amazed at the almost physical desire she felt to take out her credit card. As if under a spell, she was lured into a doll store. She fingered the smooth porcelain heads, the gold-lamé clown outfits, the fool's cap with tiny bells, the ruff of lace trimmed in gold thread. Each one was lovelier than the next. But you couldn't possibly buy just one, she realized. Buying one would mean rejecting all the others, a virtual impossibility. You'd have to buy the whole store—or at least a good portion of it—to satisfy yourself.

You could go mad, she thought, fleeing. Really. You could turn into one of those tabloid horrors that shoot their parents to get their hands on loot for shopping sprees. Venice, she began to realize, was a dangerous place.

The streets were narrow, winding and short. She found that she never walked very far in a straight line before coming upon a *campo*, those charming little squares from which alleys led off in all directions, multiplying your chances for getting lost.

How quickly one could get used to getting places by foot, she thought, watching the Venetians pulling their shopping carts after them along the bustling streets. How clean, quiet, and charmingly Old World it all was!

It was the absence of cars, she realized. The noise of honks, the exhaust fumes, the harried pace of people traveling at inhuman speeds gave a certain character to modern life everywhere. Without wheels, life seemed to slow down to a more human pace.

She bought a *vaporetto* ticket. The ghosts were gone, she thought, climbing up to the prow and watching the bright spring light sparkle on the eddies of water that slapped against the seaweed-green foundations of Venetian *palazzi* lining the route. Imagine, living in one of them! The most romantic thing in the world, even if their plumbing was rotting and there was no central heating.

And, of course, churches, churches everywhere.

She got off at San Marcuola and asked directions. It was surprisingly easy to find. She rang the bell once and waited, not wishing to be appear rude or demanding. Five minutes later, she rang again. She was just about to leave when she heard the shushing noise of slippers rubbing against the floor. The door opened narrowly, with a creak.

A beautiful woman of indeterminate age stood looking through the crack. She wore a well-cut suit of heavy blue brocade whose skirt fell well past her calves. It was an outfit that seemed very expensive, yet at the same time strangely worn, like those clothes one sometimes found in genteel secondhand shops catering to the castoffs of spoiled, rich women. Her hair was drawn back and hidden in an elaborate head-dress, the kind worn by women artists to match their flowing caftans.

"*Si?*"

"*Per favore,*" Francesca floundered, unable to stop staring. "Are you Elizabeta Bomberg?" She switched to English, rattled.

The woman stared as if she'd seen a ghost. "And you are?" Her accent was slight and charming.

"Francesca Abraham."

"And what do you want?"

"I'm sorry. I don't know exactly. I . . . that is, we, found this book in Cáceres with your name and address . . ."

"Cáceres? Books?" She opened the door wider.

"Yes. Someone left it at the Spanish border during the war."

"Is that one of them?" The woman's voice rose in excitement as she looked at the volume in Francesca's hand. "*Per favore!* Come in, come in!" The door was suddenly flung open. Francesca hurried over the threshold.

The rooms were long and narrow, leading off a central hall. It seemed expensive, but gloomy and a bit musty. Like the clothes, Francesca thought, imagining that the windows had not been opened for quite some time. She shivered as she followed the woman into the dark hallway, beginning to feel a bit queasy. "I'd appreciate any help you can offer. Thank you."

"Please, may I look at it?" the woman suddenly pleaded, staring hungrily at the book.

"Of course," Francesca responded quickly. But a sudden unease compelled her to add: "My friend—he's a rare-book dealer—says it's not worth much."

"Ah!" She took it. "Does he?" She walked to the windows and drew back the thick, velvet drapes. A sudden burst of light flooded the rooms. Francesca caught a small gasp of surprise before it burst from her throat. All around the room there were giant bookcases holding hundreds, even thousands, of volumes.

Francesca glanced at the woman once again. In the clear light, it was easy to see that she was extremely old, her face lined like those Afghani mountain people claiming to be one hundred thirty.

How could I have missed that at the door, Francesca thought, shocked. Even with the poor lighting, it was so obvious!

"Light is very destructive to parchment and paper. So we live like moles. Have you ever heard of the Bombergs?"

Francesca shook her head no, following the woman's slow, halting steps across the living room to the gilded, period furniture grouped around an old stone fireplace.

"Please, take a seat," the woman said graciously but with unmistakable authority. Francesca sank down, breathing deeply. There was the scent of cold ashes and fresh roses . . . and something else . . . something spicy and pungent and unfamiliar.

The woman's heavy but graceful body settled itself comfortably amid the thick cushions. "You have never heard of the Bombergs? Ah, then we must begin at the beginning. It is a long story. Would you join me in some Madeira? Or coffee perhaps? Nothing? Are you comfortable? Good. Tell me something about yourself."

Francesca looked at her, flustered. "What would you like to know?"

"Who you are. What you're doing wandering around with a rare book from Cáceres looking for Elizabeta Bomberg in Venice."

"I've been sent by my grandmother to locate a family heirloom, the memoirs of one of our Spanish ancestors."

"And do you have any real interest in your ancestors, your history, or do you do this to please your grandmother?"

She paused, taken aback by the probing, almost rude frankness of the question. But that's the way old people are sometimes. She tried to shrug it off.

"At first, I saw it as a job. But along the way, I learned many things of interest that made me see that time really can't be divided into these neat compartments—past, present, future. That sometimes it spills over and the present looks and feels like the past, and the past seems like an omen for the future," she heard herself say, to her surprise.

"And do you admire what you've learned about your ancestors, or not?" the woman interrogated.

"I don't know. Certain things were admirable and romantic. Others, appalling and incomprehensible."

"Appalling? What do you mean?"

"The way people betrayed each other during the Inquisition. Children testifying against their own parents."

"And you judge them? You think you would have acted differently?"

"I can't imagine turning in my own mother!"

"Let me help your imagination, then," she said, settling back and staring out the window. "You are fourteen years old—a sweet little thing. Maybe you've just been let in on the family secrets of why, unlike your neighbors, you light candles Friday nights, keep pork out of the menu, avoid lighting fires on Saturdays. You know, nothing major, quaint customs here and there. This is what our ancestors did, Mother tells you, and we try to keep it going. Or maybe you and your family have been good, loyal Christians for generations with all those customs as strange to you as to the next person.

"And one day the soldiers and the priest show up at your door. Someone's turned you in. Maybe one of the neighbors who didn't like your dog, or a serving girl who coveted the family silver. No explanation, no warning. Mother's weeping and begging, but they drag you away and throw you into this dungeon and lock you up. Now your cell is about the size of a broom closet and it's got this wet straw on the floor. They throw you your food. No one is allowed to see you. And you can't talk to anyone. Weeks go by."

Francesca rubbed her temples.

"Do you wish me to stop?"

"No! Please! Go on."

"They come to get you. A man who looks eight feet tall in a white sheet, with only his eyes showing through the slits; a priest; a notary. They lead you down damp, wet corridors into the *casa santa*."

"The what?"

She looked at Francesca with pity. "The torture cell." She paused. "They open the door. The place smells of blood and vomit. The walls are pitted, like people clawed at them. You're standing there and you see the *garrucha,* the pulley attached to the ceiling where they will hoist you up and tie your wrists and ankles, the wheels tightening the ropes in opposite directions until your joints are loosened from their sockets. You see the rack with the ropes that they will tie around your wrists, breasts, and waist, squeezing you until you pass out. Maybe they'll turn the wheel around once just so you can hear it squeak and grate."

Francesca shuddered. "My G-d!"

"Then they start asking you questions: 'Sister in Christ,' the one in the friar's robes starts, 'confess your sins and be reconciled to the Church.' Yes, you're thinking. Anything. But you don't know what sins they're talking about, you see. You explain this to them. But they will not even give you a hint. No, they tell you. It's got to come from you. You plead and beg and cry, and protest your innocence. Well, they finally say, in that case, we have no choice but to refresh your memory.

"The giant grabs you and strips you naked, tying the ropes around you. Already you feel it cutting into your flesh. One more chance, they say, looking at you expectantly. 'I don't know what you want me to say,' you weep and beg. They begin turning the pulleys. You have never felt this kind of pain before. . . . "

"Please!! Really . . . this is . . . " Francesca protested, beginning to feel frightened. The woman seemed almost possessed.

"I asked you if you wanted me to stop. Do you?"

"Yes! No. I don't know. It's horrible."

"Yes." The woman looked out at the pale light coming through the window. "Horrible. And you are only a child, really. You have only known kindness."

Almost against her will, Francesca found herself asking: "What happened when you didn't give them the right answers?"

"They give the wheel a few more turns. By now you are screaming in the worst pain you have ever felt. You will say anything, anything, to make it stop. 'Yes,' you confess, 'I am guilty. I have done everything, everything you suspect me of. List them,' you beg, 'and I will acknowledge.' But that isn't enough for them. They'll keep turning and turning until you come up with a few ideas of your own, which may or may not have been on their original list, in which case they'll say, oh, we didn't know about that one, let's add it!' But maybe they have other things to

do that day, so they start asking questions: 'Have you ever believed another faith to be true other than that the Roman Church believes to be
true?'"

"'Oh, no!' you protest.

"'Then what are you confessing to?' They turn the rack again.

"'Oh, yes,' you agree, when the pressure goes slack. 'Anything, say
anything.'

"'Did you observe the Sabbath day on Saturday instead of Sunday?'

"'Yes.'

"'Did you eat meat during Lent? Did you eat unleavened bread during the Easter season? Did you cook food on Friday for Saturday? Were
the words *Adonai* and *Merciful One* contained in books in your home,
and not Jesus Christ?'"

Francesca looked up with a sense of shock. "I've read this, heard this
somewhere, these questions . . . I don't remember exactly . . . But go
on. Then what?"

"Well, you've confessed. And by then you're hoping to die. You just
don't care anymore. But they're not finished. 'Now,' they tell you, 'tell us
about your family.'"

Francesca looked up, transfigured by horror.

"That's it, you think. I'll never do that. I'll never betray my own family. Then they show you something else: It's a metal instrument, pear-
shaped with sharp prongs. There are three of them: one for the rectum,
one for the vagina, and one for the throat."

"Please," Francesca begged, wiping her eyes.

The woman got up slowly and bent over, putting motherly arms
around Francesca. "Forgive me. But this is the truth. Otherwise, you
can't understand anything about your people, your past, the danger
that forced such terrible choices. Whole families were betrayed and
condemned as a result; burned alive. It was a popular thing, the auto-
da-fé, like bullfights or parades. First, they marched you through the
streets in this yellow robe with depictions of demons all over it, called
a *sanbenito*. All your neighbors and friends came out to jeer. Then you
reached the pyre. All around you, it was set up like a royal festival:
grandstands, banners, nobles, and the town's elite. It wasn't just an execution—it was an occasion, a way to honor coronations, or national
celebrations.

"If you repented, they garroted you before the flames reached you. If you insisted on your innocence, or declared with pride you were a Jew and proud of it, you were burned alive." She walked painfully back to her chair.

"Please, who was Elizabeta Bomberg?" Francesca asked weakly, her throat dry.

"Daniel Bomberg settled here in Venice in the early 1500s. He had a printing house. Just by chance, he made the acquaintance of Felix Pratensis, a converted Jew, who convinced him of the great need to print Hebrew books. He became one of the most important Hebrew publishing houses in the world. Hebrew books are still printed copying his typeface and page layouts."

"He himself wasn't . . . "

"Jewish?" She smiled. "No. He wasn't. But Jews always say that they owe him the greatest of debts."

"And Elizabeta?"

"Elizabeta Bomberg was one of his descendants. She was a dealer in rare books. So what she did was natural, even though many think she was a heroine."

"What did she do?"

"You mean you *really* don't know?!"

Francesca shook her head.

The woman peered at her quizzically, as if deciding whether or not to believe her. Then she turned her attention to the book, turning it over in her hands, then opening it. Slowly, with infinite care, she began to scrape along the binding with her fingernail.

"I think I'll be going now. Thank you." Francesca rose abruptly, snatching it back and checking it for damage. She walked quickly to the door.

"Please," the woman begged, following her, placing a cool, restraining hand over Francesca's. "You don't understand!! Don't go!! Let me explain. I think I can help you find your manuscript, the memoirs of Gracia Mendes."

Francesca turned back, staring. "How did you know?"

"Please, you needn't be afraid of me. Please sit down. I'll explain everything."

*   *   *

Suzanne took off her shoes and stockings, wading into the Rio di San Francisco with the matter-of-factness of Venetians used to dealing with high tides. The water was pleasantly cool on her hot, tired feet. She had been walking around for hours through the Accademia Gallery, the Museo Correr, the Museo Marciano, and countless other repositories of Venetian art treasures, retracing all the steps she'd taken when Renaldo was her teacher and she his brightest seminar student.

It was as if she were searching for a lost piece of a puzzle, an answer to a question, a tiny but indispensable part that would make the whole machine hum and buzz again the minute you plugged it in. She didn't know its color, or shape, or how she would recognize it. But the same strange faith that had set her searching, comforted her that she would know it when she found it.

Or perhaps, perhaps, she was just torturing herself.

She couldn't help it. She felt like a rag, twisted and twisted, all its loose fibers compressed into one simple, hard knot of longing.

She walked through endless *campi* and over lovely little stone bridges. And then, as suddenly and profoundly as coming across a loved one's face in a crowd of strangers, she saw it in the distance.

The Church of San Zaccaria.

It was a masterpiece of Renaissance architecture, its symmetry and balance so inhuman in its perfection, it left you yearning for something that nothing human could satisfy.

She walked up to the heavy wooden doors and opened them, walking in slowly. Her footsteps echoed and drowned in the cold, vast space of the great nave. At the far end, she saw the students gathered, their rapt faces turned toward the first altar on the left side.

And then, suddenly, there he was.

Renaldo.

She felt his presence like a hard blow straight to the stomach.

Nothing had changed. The same dark, unruly hair, the same clean, blue cotton shirt open at the collar. The same voice, too. She listened— that rough baritone, interspersed with snorts of laughter that slid so unexpectedly into soaring emotion full of hidden promises and sworn vows. It was a voice that had always hooked her like a drug.

Nothing had changed, she repeated. And yet, everything was different. She stared at him, feeling a strange sense of detachment. So many promises not kept. So many vows shattered like flung-down tablets of stone.

And suddenly all the excuses with which she'd comforted herself up until this very instant turned meaningless. For there was no way to belie the evidence of her own eyes. He was where he wanted to be, undamaged, going on joyfully with his life.

Her family had interfered. But it had been Renaldo's choice to pick himself up and run. Something inside her, as weighted and immovable as thousands of tons of grain, suddenly shifted and groaned.

Why?

The answer to that was there, too, she realized, looking beyond him to the art he was describing. It was Bellini's altarpiece. She studied the painting: the simple, elegant setting; the enthroned Madonna and child bathed in light; the serenity of wisdom from the standing figures of the saints. It was impressive. A fine example of Italian Renaissance art.

But nothing more. Not for her.

But for him, it was much more.

She looked at the deep, tender devotion in his eyes, at his cheeks and forehead flushed with feeling. For him, it was a sacred icon infused with holiness that sang to his soul.

She had never been able to hear that music. Both of them knew that. And until now, she had always been secretly ashamed of her deafness. But watching him now in this setting, she suddenly understood the truth: They were simply tuned to different wavelengths, created by their own unique histories.

She had finally heard the music meant for her own soul.

She had heard it in Gibraltar.

His students leaned toward him. How young they were! she thought, staring at a young woman's supple back, her long, shining hair. The girl was holding a pen and notebook ready, not writing anything, but watching Renaldo's every move as if he were performing some sacred ritual.

Suzanne withdrew into the shadows, transfixed by the girl's face. It had a light in it, she thought, as beautiful as the light Bellini had shed on his Madonna and child. She was in love. All his students were. And all of them, she knew too well, thought it was with Renaldo.

It wasn't. He was simply the receptacle. They were in love with beauty, with the passion of human creativity. It would take them a while to figure that out. But they would, sooner or later.

It had been the same with her own seminar class.

It had been the same with her.

She saw Renaldo glance at the girl with a swift, hidden smile and a flash of the intimacy she had once known so well.

She wiped the sudden tears from her eyes, then turned and walked quietly out the doors, closing them gently, but firmly, behind her.

35

Francesca walked out into the street, her eyes adjusting slowly and painfully to the flooding light. A sense of confusion and exhilaration overwhelmed her as she half-walked, half-danced over bridges and across canals. Finally exhausted, she sank down to rest.

Could the woman's story possibly be true?

It had to be. No one could make up a story like that!

A cool breeze came off the water, carrying with it a gentle spray that anointed her flushed face. She sat there, breathing deeply, feeling washed by the light. She wasn't tired anymore, she realized. On the contrary, she felt charged and almost voiceless with excitement as she reviewed all she'd learned.

She sprang up with nervous energy and began to walk again, savoring the magic of Baroque churches, fifteenth-century bridges, Gothic palaces, and sweet, hidden cloisters. Venice. It all felt like a dream, she thought, suddenly missing Marius terribly, wanting to share with him everything she'd learned; wanting to listen to all the odd and interesting facts he'd surely add. She wanted to let herself wander at his side on unbeaten paths toward hidden wonders everywhere.

She was surprised and inexplicably disappointed at how quickly she reached her hotel. She felt too restless to take a shower or rest, or even eat, almost afraid the moment she touched real life the magic would vanish, like a genie diving back inside his bottle.

For there was no question that the meeting with the woman in the blue dress had been nothing short of supernatural. The woman had to be a sorceress, Francesca thought. How else could one explain her uncanny ability to resurrect the pale ghosts of the past?

It had all seemed so real! The young girl in the dark torture chamber, the story of the manuscript—and of Elizabeta herself! Even now she wasn't entirely free of the spell. She looked around her, almost expecting to see Nazis, to hear the vicious, hard stamp of goose-stepping marchers against the pavement.

She walked around the corner. There was St. Mark's Basilica. The angels over the entryway seemed to wave their wings at her, beckoning her inside. She stared, dumbfounded, rubbing her eyes and blinking. The spell, she thought, wandering over the threshold as if compelled by some strange, irresistible force.

A vast chamber of amber light enveloped her. The incalculable riches of decoration, the indescribable artistry in every detail seemed to slap her down like an enormous wave. Like all medieval churches, it simply crushed you with its vaultingly ambitious but doomed attempts to contain the uncontainable: a concept of G-d.

She wandered, lost, trying to find some meaning, some reason for having entered. A group of people were waiting in line to see something called the *Pala d'Oro*. Not even sure what it was, she nevertheless felt a strange compulsion to join them.

She stood there, her confusion growing. Why am I here? she wondered, almost angry at her helplessness, her inability to simply leave. She looked toward the head of the line. A sudden shaft of light illuminated someone's hair, turning it to reddish gold.

She stepped out, taking hesitant steps forward, trying to satisfy herself that it couldn't possibly be . . .

"Suzanne?"

"Francesca?"

They stared at each other, until pushed forward by the line they found themselves in front of a mesmerizing tenth-century altarpiece. Their faces gleamed, touched by the golden, bejeweled glow of the *Pala d'Oro*. They reached out, needing the reassurance of each other's solid, warm flesh, proof that they both weren't dreaming.

"How is it . . . when did you . . ."

"My G-d, Suzanne! It's you! You're really here!"

"I wasn't even going to come inside here! I had this strange vision, something almost dragged me."

"Me, too!" Francesca exclaimed, flabbergasted. "You didn't see angels' wings moving, by any chance?"

"Huh?"

"Never mind. Isn't this amazing, I mean, us finding each other like this! Did you know I was here? Did Gran tell you? This can't be a coincidence, can it?"

Suzanne gazed at her. "I could have gone anywhere in Europe, and so could you . . . And yet both of us wound up coming to Venice and going into this place, just at this time. It's . . . it's like we were both guided here." She shook her head. "What did Gran call it, a *memuneh?*"

"It won't be the first spirit I've met on this trip! You wouldn't believe the kind of day I've had. The kind of month! If something supernatural isn't going on, then I'd like to know what is! It's confusing and scary."

The line behind them began shifting restlessly. A few Italian phrases, aggressively intoned, drifted their way.

"Let's sit down somewhere and talk."

They walked out into the light and the bustling crowds, stopping at a little coffee house with lovely pastries in the window.

"Florian. Isn't that where Casanova hung out and seduced his women?" Suzanne said.

Francesca looked over the elderly, satisfied crowd of cream-cake eaters, none of whom looked remotely seduceable. "If it is, I'm sure it was a long time ago."

They ordered cappuccino and a chocolate confection of obscene caloric content, then eyed each other carefully.

"What in heaven's name are you doing here, Suzanne?"

"I could ask you the same question."

"*I'm* still looking for the manuscript," Francesca said stiffly. "Tell me the truth. Did Gran tell you where I was? Did she threaten to cut off your funding unless you caught up with me? Really, Suzanne, of all the incredibly selfish things you've done to the family, dumping Gran and me, leaving us sitting like idiots in that restaurant waiting for you to come back ... it took the cake. You should really learn to practice your promiscuity on your own time. How could you?"

"Didn't you read my letter?" Suzanne countered, shocked at her accusations.

"Yes, I read it! And so what? You admit you're better with helping strangers than helping your own family. Like admitting it somehow makes it all right!"

"Look, let's get something straight: this whole family thing is a myth, as far as I'm concerned. Just because you've got some biological link with someone doesn't mean you have to have anything to do with them if you don't want to! If people treat each other badly, or simply don't interest each other, why should their lives have to touch just because they have some genetic link they had no control over? At some point, you have to be together for the same reasons you choose to be together with your friends: because you enrich each other's lives with love, caring, consideration. Otherwise, spending time with family becomes some miserable obligation you fulfill because some bully is holding a club of guilt over your head ready to clobber you."

"Is that how you feel about me? About all of us?" Francesca said levelly, her throat aching, tears springing to her eyes.

"No! I don't! I've always cared, enormously. Not because I have to, but because I *want* to. That doesn't mean that I can always give you what you want, because in my opinion, it's not always good for you."

"The big expert on what's good for people! You with your sponging and your alley-cat morals!"

"And you with your vision of life as an FDA–approved drug! Take two green ones twice a day and your life will be safe and perfect. Nothing spontaneous, nothing that forces her to feel will ever happen to Francesca Abraham, G-d forbid! She'll sit up on her high bench in her black robes judging the rest of us according to her warped standards, no matter how miserable they make her!"

Francesca's eyes widened. "Answer me this, Miss Spontaneity. How do you justify copping out of your commitment to Gran and me to shack up with some one-night stand!"

"Oh, Francesca, it wasn't like that!"

"Tell me the truth for once. You were in it for the money, weren't you, right from the start?"

"I don't know." Suzanne hesitated. "I thought about the inheritance, about staying on Gran's good side so that some of the money would go to good causes. It also crossed my mind that Renaldo was in Europe, and this was a way of finding him."

Francesca shook her head slowly.

"But all that changed somehow once I got involved. I *am* just as committed as you are. Just not in the same way. I'm committed to fulfilling Gran's real need, which isn't the same at all as looking for an old manuscript."

"What are you talking about?"

"You just don't get it, do you? This quest has a secret agenda, one we're not supposed to know about. It's a way for Gran to expiate her sins with us."

"Sins?"

"Yes! Don't you see? We're the last links in the golden chain, and both of us are utter failures. We aren't interested in the family's past or religion. Worst of all, neither of us is married or even engaged to the 'right' kind of boy. What we are really supposed to be doing here is giving ourselves the good education Gran feels she failed to pass on. Culture, religion, heritage . . . The manuscript isn't really the point."

"When did you figure this out?"

"I think I understood all about it right from the beginning. For me, it was never just the money or Renaldo. I felt Gran's need. It didn't make any sense to me at first, but I looked at her and realized she was, I don't know, so frail. And she was asking this of me."

"Even if I believe you—which I'm not sure I do—how does any of this connect with what you did!?"

"I had no choice, really!" she blurted out. "I mean, I *did*, of course, but . . ." She stopped, swallowing hard. "Do you remember what Gran said that night, about hearing something you had always known was true, something that matched exactly all the information stored in your heart so that there was no question of disagreeing, of finding reasons to resist?" She reached out and took her sister's hand. "Please, Francesca, try to understand . . . this wasn't the same as the other times. This was really, really different. It was overwhelming."

Francesca looked at her thoughtfully. "If it was really so different this time with you and . . . What's his name?"

"Gabriel," Suzanne whispered, growing paler still.

"Gabriel. If it was the grand, once-in-a-lifetime passion Gran was talking about, then what in heaven's name are you doing here looking up Renaldo?"

Suzanne stared at her, stricken. "Please, Francesca. Don't make me answer you now. Please don't . . . I'm begging you . . ."

"Okay, okay! What's wrong with you? You look positively ill!"

"And you look lovely," Suzanne said hoarsely, pressing the palms of her hands into her eyes.

"My hair needs to be cut," Francesca murmured, running her fingers self-consciously through her hair, strangely pleased.

"Don't you dare touch it! You look like an angel. Actually, I've never seen you so . . . relaxed? Happy?"

"Really? Do I really look different?" A slow smile spread across her face.

"Is it Marius, Francesca?"

She nodded. "But nothing's settled, of course. So many things are up in the air. We're so . . . different."

Suzanne reached out for her hand and squeezed it. "Where is he?"

"Back in London examining something at the Bodleian Library he thinks might be useful."

"And what have you heard from Gran?"

"I'm scared, Suzanne. There are all these too cheerful phone calls, but she's never at home when I call her. . . . " She shrugged.

"She's never home?"

"Not for the last few weeks."

"You don't think that means . . . ? G-d! Someone would have told us if it was serious, if she'd been hospitalized or anything. I mean, Mom would have let us know, right?"

"When was the last time you spoke to Mom?"

"Well, actually, not since we left New York."

"Mom would know. We should call her." Francesca shook her head.

"Mom might know, but she won't necessarily tell us. They might be in cahoots," Suzanne pointed out.

This shocked Francesca. "But why? Why keep her illness a secret?"

"Because she doesn't want us to abandon this quest and come running home to be with her."

"But you've already abandoned the quest and run off!"

"I did exactly what Gran wanted me to do!"

Francesca stared. "What are you talking about?"

"Gabriel and me. Even my running off. It was all part of Gran's plan, the real purpose of this trip."

Francesca looked flabbergasted.

"She set us up, Fran. That is, she set *me* up. With Gabriel. She was *hoping* I'd run off. I'm not sure about you and Marius, though. But it wouldn't surprise me. You see, it's time we two were married to nice, Sephardic boys and got some leaves growing on the bare-branched bough."

"Don't be ridiculous!"

"I'm telling you it was no accident that Marius and Gabriel were at the River Room the night we were. I know, because Gabriel told me all about it."

They sat across from each other in silence.

"He told you himself that Gran arranged for the two of you to meet?"

Suzanne nodded.

"My G-d!" Francesca chewed her lip, remembering her grand-mother's odd behavior in the restaurant after Suzanne's disappearance: her radiant face, her laughter. It all made perfect sense now. "Do you think . . . did she . . . Gran . . . make some arrangement? With Marius, I mean. Did she promise him . . . them . . . something like . . . like . . ." Her voice grew low and horrified. "Dowries?"

Suzanne, to whom such a thought had never occurred until now, turned ashen. She stretched out her legs and moved down low in her chair, staring at her spoon with stony-eyed malevolence. "Who knows?"

"I wish," Francesca said in a low groan, "that I had never been born."

Suzanne rubbed her forearm, feeling the goosebumps rise. "Yes," she said. "Exactly."

They walked slowly into the fading daylight and sat wharfside, look-ing down into the swirling, dark eddies of water. Now and again, the laughter of holidaymakers drifted back to them, sounding hollow and unreal. The wind blowing off the canal turned rude, whipping their clothes and disheveling their hair, destroying any attempts to pat things neatly back into place.

"Suzanne, did you find Renaldo?"

"Yes," she answered softly. "I did."

"So, what happened?"

"He was standing in a church. He looked happy. And there was a girl, a student, very young and pretty. She was smiling up at him and he was smiling back, giving her his special smile, *my* smile." She swallowed. "But it was all right, you know? I realized, then, that it was never meant to be."

They listened to the slap of the water against the wooden sides of the boats.

"And Gabriel?"

"I left him standing on the quay in Gibraltar. I feel like part of my body is missing," she whispered. "I've never felt this kind of pain before." Her chin quivered. "What are you going to do about Marius?"

Francesca hugged herself. "He . . . he made me believe that he cared. That it was me . . . " She choked, devastated. "The heiress. That's what Peter used to call me, remember? I *trusted* Marius, Suzanne. And I haven't done that with a man in a very, very long . . ." She suddenly sobbed.

"Don't," Suzanne said, holding her tight, ignoring the stares of the sympathetic and interested drama-seekers among the passersby.

36

"Come, Francesca."

She looked up, bleary-eyed. It was almost dark. "Where?"

"I don't know. Your hotel, I guess."

A certain cool light came into Francesca's eyes as she wiped them dry. "Yes. And I'll tell you what else we're going to do. First, we're going to check you into the largest suite they've got, Suzanne. And then we're going to have the most extravagant meal in the most expensive restaurant. And after we charge it all to Gran, we're going to call her and . . ."

"Yes?"

"Make her tell us the truth!"

"Is there any hope she would?"

"She has to! You just can't do these things to people, no matter how good your intentions are. You can't manipulate lives like this! My life!"

"But we can't even be mad at her, can we? Not now. Not with her condition."

"All I know is if she promised Marius something, if this whole thing was some sort of scheme, I'll never forgive her for as long as I live."

"Yes." Suzanne nodded. "Exactly."

"Oh!"

"What?"

"I just remembered. I've got to go out this evening. I promised someone. That is, someone promised *me*. There's a costume party, and she was going to give me a tour of Venice . . . all kinds of places tourists never get to see."

"Who is this person?"

"It's this woman I went to see this morning about the manuscript. I think her name is Elizabeta Bomberg. She never really said. I haven't decided if she's real or a ghost, a sorceress or a good fairy!" Francesca shook her head.

"I can't believe my sensible sister is going to put herself in the hands of some weird stranger. Where's your New York smarts?"

Francesca hesitated. "Do you remember those books by Carlos Castaneda?"

"The ones where this college student doing research finds this old Indian who becomes his spirit guide in Mexico and he has all these out-of-body experiences? Didn't that all turn out to be a fake?"

"I can't explain it, Suzanne. I know it doesn't sound rational, but there really is something magical about this woman. She's an aristocrat, but from another age. Someone who doesn't seem to belong to this world anymore. And she has this grasp of things—history, human nature. A kind of wisdom, I guess you'd call it. The things she told me were awesome. You must meet her!"

Suzanne eyed her skeptically. "This doesn't sound like you at all. What did she do, cast a spell over you? My friend from Haiti says that witch doctors can do that. How did you meet her, anyway?"

"Her name and address were in a book we found, together with the manuscript pages in Cáceres."

"Does she know anything about the manuscript?"

"You wouldn't believe what she told me! I'm still in shock! Come to my hotel room. We'll order some drinks, and I'll tell you everything."

They sat on the bed in their slips, drinking expensive champagne brought in a silver ice bucket by room service. Between them, they finished the bottle.

"This is the story: David Montezinos was a famous book collector who lived in Amsterdam. He was a rabbi's son, and a teacher at a famous Talmudic academy founded in 1616 called Etz Hayyim—which means 'tree of life.' Anyhow, there were more than twenty thousand books and manuscripts—mostly in Spanish and Portuguese, having to do with the Sephardic Jewish community—in his collection when he died in 1916. Including, most probably, the Gracia Mendes memoirs. He bequeathed the collection to the academy.

"When it began looking likely that the Nazis were going to take over Europe, the curators at Etz Hayyim were afraid the Nazis would either steal the collection or, worse, just burn down the whole building. Actually, the Nazis did steal another famous Jewish book collection in Amsterdam called the Biblioteca Rosenthaliana. They sent the whole thing back to Germany."

"What does any of this have to do with—"

"I'm getting to it. Elizabeta Bomberg was a well-known book dealer in Venice. She offered to help hide the Montezinos collection until the war was over. Bit by bit, couriers took out some of the most valuable books and manuscripts and delivered them to her. But then it got very dangerous. One of the couriers got caught and others panicked, just abandoning suitcases full of books and manuscripts wherever they happened to be. Under torture, one of them talked, and Elizabeta was arrested."

"What happened to her?"

"The Nazis tortured her, but she wouldn't tell them anything. She had powerful friends who got her released. But she suffered tremendously."

"What happened to the collection?"

"Elizabeta returned it after the war. But she was heartbroken about the losses. She was especially upset about the Gracia Mendes memoirs. It seems she had a great interest in our ancestor and had done a great deal of research into her life and history. This woman I met said she wanted to share that with me."

"Wait a minute—this woman, the one you met, the one who's coming over tonight, is she or isn't she this Elizabeta Bomberg?"

"I don't really know!"

"That all happened half a century ago. If that's who she is, then she must be ancient!"

"It's so strange. When I first saw her, she seemed, I don't know, youngish. But when I looked closer, I realized she was very old. She could hardly walk."

"And she's taking you on a guided tour of Venice?"

"You know what, I'm not sure of anything anymore," Francesca answered, throwing back her head and draining the last drops from the glass. "But I have this feeling"—she pressed her fist into the center of her body—"that she knows something really important, and that she'll tell me what it is tonight. I've simply got to go. Please, Suzanne, you've got to come with me!"

"You don't think I'd let you wander off with this nut-case alone, do you?" Suzanne muttered.

Francesca ran her hand over her sister's lovely hair. "Don't call her that. We'll need costumes."

"What kind?"

"I think it's a Renaissance festival, or something."

Suzanne cocked her head. "What about this for a compromise? Let's get the most expensive costumes there are and charge those to Gran!"

Francesca opened her door, answering Suzanne's knock.

She sucked in her breath and whistled. The wig, the Lucrezia Borgia gown of beaded deep green velvet, the low, low neckline. . . . "Sumptuous, my dear. Simply sumptuous," Francesca said.

"And you! Turn around."

Francesca did a dutifully slow turn. She was dressed in a deep crimson gown with a high ruff collar and an elaborate headdress, loaded down with gold chains. Her pale skin and dark hair made her look almost otherworldly.

"Isabella herself!" Suzanne exclaimed.

"Don't say that! Even in jest."

"Why?"

"I went through Spain. I've learned a few things now. You have no idea how much suffering she caused."

"It's history!"

"It's family."

They stared at each other.

The phone rang. "Okay, we'll be right down. Well, she's here. Ready?"

Suzanne slipped her arm through Francesca's and winked. "To take on the town."

37

They saw her as soon as the elevator doors opened. She sat in the center of the lobby, wearing a magnificent paisley gown of russet, black, and cream brocade. A thick net of gold braid covered her shoulders on either side of her long white neck, and a matching gold hairnet restrained hair (a wig?) that was thick, curly reddish brown. She wore enormous drop-pearl earrings and two strands of the largest pearls either sister had ever seen. A beautiful painted mask hid her face.

"Elizabeta?" Francesca asked.

"Francesca!" she rose, holding out both arms, which shook a little (age? emotion?). "And this must be your sister, Suzanne."

Francesca was dumbstruck. "How did you know?"

"You told me, didn't you? How else?"

"I don't remember." Francesca squeezed Suzanne's hand. It was ice-cold. "What?" She looked at her, surprised.

Suzanne stood transfixed, a look of wonder akin to horror passing over her features. "Who are you?" she asked with a tense calm that was almost belligerent.

"I'm dressed as Leonora of Toledo from the famous portrait by Bronzino."

"I didn't mean the costume! You were in my dream! I saw you!"

"Suzanne!" Francesca squeezed her elbow, mortified. "Please, forgive my sister. She's had a long day."

"In your dream, were we properly introduced?" the woman asked.

They stood motionless, facing each other, until finally the woman slipped one arm through Francesca's and the other through Suzanne's, leading them through the lobby with queenly grace. "Come, daughters. The gondolier is waiting! There is so much I want to show you and so little time!"

Her arm was almost weightless, but with a firm grip that guided them purposefully toward the bobbing boat. They climbed down shakily, one after the other, reaching up to help Elizabeta make her way down.

"I can still manage." She smiled, ignoring their offered hands. With a light and youthful grace that made them both stare at her in wonder, she hopped down beside them.

They didn't stare long, distracted by the bustle of activity all around them. They leaned forward to catch a better look. Boats, lined up as if at the beginning of a regatta, were charmingly decorated, their silken banners fluttering like glowing exclamation points over the dark water. Everyone seemed to be in costume.

"Isn't Carnival in February?" Suzanne asked.

"Of course. This is a special day. An anniversary of sorts . . ." the woman began, but her voice was drowned in the sounds of singing that began to rise up from the gondolas and *vaporetti* like a burst of steam, filling the clear night air.

They floated, feeling the full enchantment of the glittering fairy-tale palaces which, in the magic of starlight, had shed their aging decrepitude, reverting to the glory of their youth.

"What a relief it was to finally arrive!" the woman suddenly said, breaking the dreamy silence. "The escape from Antwerp took months. And every step, one had to look over one's shoulder, to listen for the hooves of the Emperor's guards bearing down, racing to catch up . . ."

"Excuse me?" Francesca said politely, wondering if she was missing something.

"Ah. Gracia, Brianda, Reyna, and Little Gracia. They arrived in Venice on this day, four hundred and fifty-two years ago."

"How do you know the exact day?" Francesca exclaimed.

The woman's masked face turned to her inscrutably in the darkness.

"Certain things one never forgets. It was vital not to raise suspicions until safe conduct could be guaranteed out of Charles's clutches," the woman continued, ignoring the interruption. "So there was this plan. First to cross over into France, as if to take the healing waters at Aix-la-Chapelle, and then, from there, to trek slowly across Italy. If you run, your enemies only chase after you. So it was important to walk with dignity. Besides, with all the servants, the household goods, everything that could be carried in coaches trailing behind, one couldn't exactly gallop!"

"They took everything with them?" Suzanne interjected.

"But of course! To leave it behind in Antwerp was to make a gift of it to Church and Emperor. Neither deserved any gifts. Thieves never do."

"You've done so much research! Please, go on."

"Joseph came, too, but later. I can imagine he wasn't happy about being left behind in Antwerp to settle affairs. He was in love, you see. Already, in Queen Mary's court, he had started looking at his young cousin Reyna differently. Who could blame him? She was so beautiful, surrounded by admirers. He was mad with jealousy. But the mother saw nothing. Mothers never do." She sighed.

"It's genetic," Suzanne murmured.

"She was too busy scouring the world for a son-in-law from a noble Spanish-Jewish lineage, someone faithful to his heritage, intelligent, handsome, wise. When all along . . ." The woman snorted with strange laughter.

"What happened when they got to Venice?" Francesca pressed.

"I do not have to tell you. You can see!" She waved her arms expansively. "Venice was built on profit, not Divine Rights. The *pallazi*. The works of artists like Titian, Veronese, and Tintoretto. The rare woods of Africa, the spices of the East, the wares of Arabia, China, and the New World . . . everything was for sale to those whom the gods had favored with profits. They were welcomed like royalty."

"But didn't Gracia write about being thrown into a dungeon in Venice?" Suzanne said doubtfully.

"Yes! And almost losing her child," Francesca added.

"As I said, Venice is a city that worships the Prince of Mammon. Ducats and crowns, gold, and precious stones—all those things that create masks and costumes. But underneath all the glitter, death was there, waiting patiently for the fools who believed in the show, who thought it was real."

Her voice, sonorous and full of meaning, stirred them both with strange emotion.

It was the voice of the woman in El Transito, Francesca realized, stiffening with shock. It was the voice of the woman in my dream, Suzanne remembered, shaken. They felt the sudden cold chill of night run through their bodies as they stared at the masked figure who sat facing them in the darkness.

It was all like some dream, they thought, shaken from their solid sense of reality, made receptive to all that was to come, the way dreamers accept the visions and voices of the night.

The wet, gray stones glistened like liquid silver in the moonlight as the gondola slid up to the docking quay of the large *palazzo*. The gondolier's swarthy, firm hand grasped theirs, helping them to shore. From above, the faint sound of a string quartet playing Mozart's *Eine kleine Nachtmusik* drifted down to them. They turned their eyes in the direction of the music, fascinated by the glow of lights and the shadows of moving bodies behind the drawn drapes.

An endless stream of boats pulled up, revelers disembarking one by one, dressed in elaborate costumes of brocaded silks, satins, velvets, and silk damasks, with plunging necklines and hair piled high, or braided with pearls or feathers.

Suzanne and Francesca looked at each other in wonder. Even for New Yorkers who had seen it all, it was an astonishing spectacle.

"You think it's beautiful, don't you? Beautiful enough to drive one mad! And you are right. This is what happened to Brianda in the end. The beaded silk, the ostrich plumes, the gorgeous palaces!"

"I almost went raving mad in a doll store," Francesca admitted. "I don't think you can ever have enough money to spend in Venice."

The woman slowly turned her masked face in her direction. "And do you understand how someone, because they want to buy things, can betray all that is sacred, their own family, their very own child?"

"Is that what she did?"

"She wouldn't listen to reason. She was ready to settle down in

Venice, to install herself in a grand *palazzo,* to marry some fawning Old Christian aristocrat, down on his luck, who filled her silly ears with flattery. To live a life of ease and luxury. In order to do that, she needed money. Lots of money." Her voice turned low and ominous. "She was willing to do anything to get it."

The laughing crowds of costumed revelers pressed them forward.

"Wait! I know this place! Look! There's the winged lion, and the guardian angels of Charity, Prudence, Temperance and Fortitude," Suzanne said excitedly, pointing to the carved pillars. "This is the Porta della Carta. The main gate to the Doge's palace! I can't believe they're letting us in at this hour!" Suzanne exclaimed.

"Come, daughters."

They walked inside the portal toward the enormous statues of bearded Neptune and belligerent Mars that guarded either side of the wide staircase leading to the inner chambers and the loggia.

"What did Brianda want?" Francesca asked.

"She wanted Little Gracia's inheritance turned over to her to dispose of as she pleased. Gracia, of course, refused. She had been given a sacred trust. She could not agree to let her niece be beggared by her foolish mother. She owed that to Diogo."

"What did Brianda do?"

"She was advised by her new friends to take her sister to court, to show that Gracia wasn't a fit guardian."

"On what grounds?" Francesca scoffed.

"On the grounds of Judaizing. She denounced Gracia to the Inquisition."

"My G-d!" Francesca groped the banister.

Suzanne leaned against the wall, hugging herself tightly. "She did that? To her own sister?"

The woman nodded, climbing up slowly. She paused on the landing, touching stone faces set into the wall. They had bushy brows, cruel, cunning eyes, and open mouths.

"Into these slits were dropped the secret letters of accusation, letters that went straight to the Inquisitors. The Inquistors took action. Here they stood, by these stairs, watching Gracia, Brianda, and the two children walk up, accompanied by armed guards. With each step the sisters took, the accusing mouths opened wider to devour them."

Suzanne felt uncomfortably hot, then suddenly chilled. "All of them were arrested?"

"Not at first. They walked up the stairs separately, Gracia the accused, Brianda the accuser."

"And then?" Suzanne asked with a feeling of dread.

The masked face turned slowly in her direction. "Do you really want to know?"

"Why wouldn't I . . . we . . . ?" Suzanne stammered, feeling somehow accused.

"Because knowledge transforms. It obligates." The dark eyes behind the mask glittered.

"Yes, we want to know." Francesca stepped forward, holding Suzanne's arm. "We want you to tell us."

"Come, then, and I will show you!"

She walked slowly down the hall, her footsteps ringing ominously on the cold marble floors. "Here it began." She opened the wide doors and stepped inside the great chamber: The Hall of the Three Chiefs of the Council of Ten.

Suzanne and Francesca stepped in after her. They shuddered as their eyes met the painting on the wall, studying the helpless, naked flesh of the vulnerable young woman threatened by the upswept dagger.

"There they sat in their black and crimson robes. The most feared men in Venice, controlling a network of spies that respected no office, no power. Can't you hear it, see it? Brianda's loud, braying whine of accusation, her pointing finger. And Gracia, her head bowed helplessly, betrayed by the very thing she loved most—her family."

They looked around the empty room, hearing faint whispers and seeing shadows, feeling betrayed by their eyes and ears. This could not be happening, could it?

"Look, can't you see the Inquisitors looking at the two sisters, their eyes almost amused and filled with cunning?" the woman continued. "Here, the largest fortune in Europe had fallen into their laps. And if Brianda was telling the truth, then Gracia Mendes planned to take it out of the country to Turkey, where she would revert to her Judaizing ways openly. Why find her innocent, when there was such profit to be gained by finding her guilty?

"See the Judges bending toward one another, and then toward the

Chief Inquisitor? They will converse for a moment before announcing their judgment: to jail both sisters, and to tear both girls from their mothers' arms."

"Oh, no! Not the children!" Francesca cried.

"They jailed Brianda as well? But she wasn't even on trial!"

"Of course. What profit would there have been in confiscating the fortune of one sister simply to hand it over to the other? Much better, they thought, to rid themselves of both and pocket the fortune of the Mendes banking house themselves."

"What a fool Brianda was!" Francesca exclaimed.

"The greedy always are. A shroud, after all, has no pockets. Come!"

She opened a side door. The passageway was rough and narrow, the walls damp and unfinished on either side of the winding staircase leading down into the dark chambers beneath the palace apartments.

"I can't!" Suzanne said with sudden fear.

"You must!" The woman pulled her along.

The bars were high and sharply pointed, made with thick, forbiddingly cold metal. The gate screeched in protest as it was pushed open.

It was the smell of the Colosseum, Suzanne realized. The scent of the true malice of humankind, the only species that tortures its own. She ran her fingers over the rough, cold walls, feeling the nail scratches, perceiving the staining dark brown splatters of human blood. It was the breakdown of all human feeling, when the family of man loses all compassion, turning into monsters in human form. It was the essence of pure evil.

"I feel like I'm choking! There's no air," Francesca cried, feeling a sudden, irrational sense of panic. She sank to the floor, resting her back against the rough granite. Above, a small, barred opening let the moonlit night stream in like a guilty secret, its faint light swallowed by the thick gloom. She could see the waters of the canal and the ancient Bridge of Sighs, named by the suffering prisoners who gazed up at it from this hell below.

"Imagine sitting here listening to the screams from the torture chamber and from the other cells, not knowing . . . wondering if it was your own little girl." Francesca's eyes filled with anguished tears.

"Robbery, murder, rape, and torture in the name of some holy ideal. Inquisitors, Nazis, corrupt governments, terrorists. The names change, but the result is the same," the woman told them.

"And it never ends. It never, never ends," Suzanne agreed, shaking her head. "But Gracia survived it." She nodded with bitter satisfaction. "I don't think I could have."

"Yes, you would have! Because you must! Every human being, sooner or later, sinks to a moment of absolute despair," the woman's voice said with deep conviction. "A moment when one feels absolute detachment from all succor, at the mercy of that black evil whose hands hold all power. There is a secret to survival. A weapon stronger than any they can bring against you. Something so powerful it is beyond their comprehension."

The sisters looked at each other in wonder. Slowly, they turned their eyes toward the masked stranger, a slow dawning of recognition breaking over them like a wave of light.

"Take off the mask!" Suzanne demanded.

"Who are you? Please! And what is the secret?" Francesca begged.

The woman lifted her arms and undid the mask. In the darkness, her skin shone like pale milk, almost translucent. Her voice took on a strange, almost bell-like timbre that was not quite human: "The secret, my daughters, is the awareness of G-d's presence."

> The Lord is my light and my salvation
> Whom shall I fear?
> The Lord is the source of my life's strength, of whom then
> shall I be afraid?

"Bodies may be tortured. They may even die. But the spirit goes on. And if a person is part of a family, the spirit is housed anew in another body each time a child builds his home as a branch of his parents'. In this way, every father and every mother, every grandfather and every grandmother, goes on living in children and grandchildren.

"And this is the secret of the everlasting, blossoming stem."

Francesca clutched Suzanne's cold hands, pulling her to her feet. They stood staring at the glowing form, which seemed to float upward in the dark room.

"It was you in El Transito, wasn't it? You taught me your prayer!" Francesca exclaimed.

"And I wasn't dreaming either, that night in my room, when you came to me, was I?" Suzanne called out, her whole body trembling with emotion. "Tell us what happened to you! Were you tortured? Did you manage to escape? Did you take your child with you?"

"And what happened to Brianda? Did you ever forgive her?" Francesca cried out.

All light in the room suddenly faded. They stared into the darkness. "Where are you! Please, don't leave us! Help us!" they begged.

A small shaft of light suddenly came through the barred window, creating a path of light. Francesca reached out and took her sister's hand, pulling her forward. They crept along the dark passageway together, following it up the staircase and out into the upper salons.

A sudden crush of revelers swept up the Giant's Staircase, separating them and pressing them forward.

"Suzanne!"

"Francesca!"

They lost sight of each other, surrounded by the swirl of strangers in masks painted with expressions of unchanging emotion, a solid wall of strange indifference that they couldn't penetrate.

Swept up to the top, Francesca found herself caught in the swiftly flowing human stream. Her ears picked up a strain of the music she had heard outside. She followed it down the corridors, crowds pressing her forward. All at once, the playing got louder. The streaming crowds swirled past her, pushing open the doors to a vast hall.

She felt her waist encircled by strong male arms.

"What!" she protested, wriggling to free herself, but his grip was too strong.

"*Buon giorno!*" He laughed, his teeth milky white against his swarthy skin, his dark hair curled like a sea god's over his ears and forehead. He smelled of good men's cologne, the kind that made a woman feel powerless. And suddenly, to her surprise, she felt her body stop struggling.

Abandon, Francesca thought with strange recklessness. And why not? Why not? Life wasn't an FDA–approved drug, after all. Suzanne was right. Was not this night all a dream? Was not all of life simply shadows and muffled voices dancing in the darkness against a palette of colors, real and imagined? Who knew what was real anymore? Marius, his love, Elizabeta? Suzanne was right. It was better to feel, to give in to the moment, before your time slipped away altogether.

The music grew faster, and the exciting warmth of the charming stranger pressed against her, feeling like love. He was here, now, without any hidden agendas, promises that needed to be made or kept, asking of her only what she was willing to give. So why not? Why not open herself to the world? Why not try to be Suzanne for just one night?

She felt herself twirled away into the crowd, her feet almost off the ground. He pressed against her, his cheek warm against her own, his hands massaging her back. Francesca felt herself moved toward the exit, the stranger's arm decisively around her waist as he led her down the stairs.

"Francesca, where are you going?" It was Suzanne.

"*Piacere, signorina,*" the dark stranger said gaily, looking at Suzanne with a wide, sensuous smile.

"Get lost, *per favore!* Francesca, please, don't!"

"Leave me alone! Why is it good for you but not for me?"

"This is no good! Not for anyone!"

"I can take care of myself. Go away!"

"I won't! I can't! You're my sister."

"Since when have you cared about that?"

"Cared!" Suzanne stamped the floor furiously. "What do you think got me interested in the women's center, date rape . . ."

"Date rape," Francesca repeated, shuddering, looking into the stranger's dark male eyes as if suddenly awakening. She recoiled, waving him away. Suzanne dragged her up the staircase.

"Why did you have to come to Venice! Why did you have to tell me that Gran paid Marius off?" Francesca shrugged her off.

"I never told you that!"

"Yes, you did!"

"Do you love him?"

Francesca looked at her, astonished. "How can you ask me that!" she screamed, furious, pushing her away. "After what you've told me!"

Suzanne pushed her back. "I never told you anything about Marius. I don't know anything!"

"Yes, you do!" Francesca slapped her.

"Gabriel said *we* were set up. Not you and Marius!" she shouted, returning the slap with interest.

"So what are you saying, what are you saying?" she screamed, punctuating her words with little sharp jabs to Suzanne's shoulder blade. "That Gran did it to you but not to me? You but not me, huh? Does that make any sense . . . ? I'm the SHORT, PLAIN, BORING ONE who never has a boyfriend, not you! I'm the one who NEEDS TO HAVE A MAN PAID OFF in order for him to show any interest in her. . . . !"

Suzanne stamped her foot down on Francesca's toes. "Yes, it does make sense! PERFECT SENSE!! I'm the problem child. Not YOU!! I'm the one who CAN'T BE RELIED ON TO MAKE THE RIGHT CHOICES. Who has to have a husband PICKED OUT FOR HER LIKE A GOOD MELON! My G-d! I think I'm going to be sick!" She ran down the hall to the nearest window overlooking the canal.

Francesca followed her, limping.

Suzanne heaved dryly, then wiped her mouth and closed her eyes, leaning against the wall. "And the thing is . . . the worst thing is . . . Gabriel *is* the perfect choice for me! G-ddamnit to hell! I love him! I can't imagine living without him! It kills me!"

Francesca held her breath, astonished. "What?"

Suzanne leaned once again over the banister: "If you laugh, I'll kill you!"

"Perfect for you? And Gran picked him out, like a melon, you say?" Francesca roared.

"I can't believe you think this is funny." Suzanne heaved, but instead of vomiting, she giggled. "It was supposed to be a blind date! And I ran off with him!! Oh my G-d. Perfect," she howled. "And . . . and all the time . . . all the time I was thinking . . ." She choked, holding her shaking stomach. "I tell you, I was thinking: To hell with the family! To hell with Gran!"

They laughed until their bellies hurt and their throats ached, and their palms were soaked from wiping away the tears. . . .

"So, what do we do now?" Francesca asked.

"We get out of here," Suzanne answered, slipping her arm around her sister's waist.

38

"Want a stiff drink?"

"Please," Francesca said gratefully, her feet on the floor, the rest of her body lying flat on the bed. She flung her arm over her eyes, exhausted.

"Want to talk about it?" Suzanne asked hesitantly, handing her a rum-and-Coke.

She sat up wearily. "Whew! I don't even . . . can't even . . . guess. Can you?"

"That was really weird. Maybe it was all that champagne we had before we left. I mean, you don't really think that it was"—she lowered her voice to a whisper—"*her* . . . do you?"

"I don't know what to think! If it was just this one time, well, maybe. But I've been sober as a judge this entire trip, and it hasn't stopped one strange coincidence and event after the next from happening to me! And certain things I *know* really happened. I didn't dream them. Like that woman who whispered a Spanish prayer in my ear in the El Transito synagogue, and finding you in that church! It was a very special prayer known only to scholars. And I had no intention of going into that church!"

"I know what you mean. Like that dream I had. I'm telling you, Francesca, I saw that woman! She was in my hotel room. She even left a gold thread from her shoes on my carpet." Suzanne hugged herself.

"There's got to be some simple explanation. I don't believe in ghosts, Suzanne. At least I never did until now."

"Well, maybe *one* believes in *us* and is following us around! Unless you can come up with a more reasonable explanation."

Francesca shrugged helplessly. "Could she have been an actress hired by Gran, to teach us a lesson? There has to be a logical explanation, right? But I can't think now. I'm absolutely exhausted. I'm just going to read my phone messages and go to sleep. I'm sure in the morning, when all the alcohol has worn off, we'll both come up with something perfectly reasonable." She yawned, flipping through the white notes.

"Who are they from?"

"This one's from Marius. He wants me to call him back. One from Mom. Hey, this one's from Gran! And it's addressed to both of us!"

Suzanne sat up straight. "But no one knows I'm here!"

They studied each other.

"This really *is* spooky! Unless she was just taking a shot in the dark. Suzanne, look!"

"What?" she turned, confused.

"The night table! The book!"

It was full of torn paper.

"My G-d! Someone's destroyed it! How did they get in here? Why would anyone do that! I don't believe this!" Francesca ran to the table and picked up the volume. Large tears had been made in the inner binding. "Just destroying it like that, for no reason! Criminal, insane." Her face changed colors. "Elizabeta!"

"Why would you say that?"

"She was trying to tear it when I was at her house! I snatched it away."

"Let me see that."

"Maybe I could tape it up, or take it to a book bindery. . . ."

"*No!* Look at this." Suzanne peeled off some more pieces of paper.

"Are you crazy, Suzanne?!"

"Francesca, look!"

A small slit had been opened on the inside of the binding from which off-white parchment stuck out.

"There's something inside the binding."

"You're right." Slowly, she continued peeling away the paper until the folded pages slid out.

It smelled of ambergris.

"My G-d! What is it!?" Suzanne exclaimed.

But before Francesca could examine it, the phone rang.

"Mom?" Francesca said, staring at the floor and listening until finally she lifted her head and looked at Suzanne, wide-eyed in pain.

Letter to Marius Serouya, left with the concierge at The Gritti Palace, Venice

Dear Marius:

A miracle has happened: We've found another piece of the manuscript. It was hidden inside the binding of the book from Cáceres.

I tried to call. You weren't in. I don't have much time. As you can see, we are gone. I say "we," because Suzanne has joined me, quite by accident, or the hand of fate (which I'm beginning to really wonder about . . .).

My grandmother is very ill.

I contacted Elizabeta Bomberg. Or someone who lived at the address written in the book. I still can't decide what part of her was real, and what part I imagined. In any case, the whole experience was very strange. Please follow up. Ask her why she disappeared. Tell her we found the manuscript pages and thank her for opening the binding and revealing them to us. We are bringing them back to New York and will have them translated.

As I said, I'm out the door. But even if I had more time, I don't know what I'd say to you. Suzanne tells me that your friend Gabriel met her by design, not chance. And I can't help wondering if your romantic interest in me is based on the same old-fashioned horse-trading that has been going on in our families for centuries when it comes to arranged marriages.

I have to know. Whatever else I believe or don't believe, I somehow trust that you will tell me the truth about this.

I'll be waiting,
Francesca

39

"Are you dreading this as much as I am?" Suzanne murmured to Francesca as they walked through the hospital corridors.

"How are you feeling? Stomach any better?"

Suzanne shook her head. She had spent the plane ride throwing up into barf bags and the entire morning in the bathroom. She walked with gingerly care, as if every footstep loosened the plug keeping her insides down. "I can't stand hospitals!"

"Do you have the manuscript pages?"

"Yes."

"I wish I knew what they said."

"The translator's coming by this afternoon. But I thought Gran would want to see the original, anyway."

Francesca nodded. "Any long-distance calls?"

Suzanne pursed her lips and shook her head. "What about you?"

"Nothing," Francesca said dejectedly. "Well, here goes."

They pushed open the green hospital door.

NO! they thought.

Catherine lay against the white pillows, eyes closed, with a stillness that could not be mistaken for rest. Her skin was the pale, dull color of parchment, wrinkled and dry. A few thin strands sprouting at odd intervals were the only remnant of her pride—the beautifully coiffed hair. Her lips were cracked, and black-and-blue marks from needles and infusions covered her arms.

The girls stood motionless.

Janice rose and hugged them, trying not to cry. "I'm so glad you're here! You have no idea how awful it's been. *Madre,* the girls are here!" she whispered.

Catherine opened her eyes, taking a few moments to focus. So young! she thought, feeling as if roses had bloomed and filled the room with spring. Granddaughters. Two of them. Her heart leaped up in pleasure. Why had she felt so alone, so forlorn? She held out her dry, veined hands.

Francesca moved forward hesitantly, reaching out to take the of-fered hand. Suzanne stood motionless at the foot of the bed, her eyes brimming, her mouth defiant.

"Don't cry!" Catherine murmured hoarsely, struggling painfully to sit up. "Roll this thing up!" she demanded with something like her old imperiousness. Janice hurried to crank the bed to a sitting position.

"That's what your mother does. Comes here and sits and weeps! I know she can't help it, but I hate it! I'm not as bad as I look." She tried to smile, smoothing the pitiful thin strands with her pale, almost ghostly fingers. "But the treatments are a horror. They promised . . . the doctors. A little extra time, they said." She looked at them. "But maybe now I'm glad I did it anyhow."

"*Abuela,* look!" Suzanne held out the manuscript pages.

"What! Really?" Catherine reached out, touching them, a new light brightening her weary eyes. "I can't believe it! Where?"

"Inside the binding of an old book that we found in Caceres," Francesca explained, handing them to her.

Catherine held them for a moment. "You found them in Venice, didn't you?"

The girls nodded, startled.

"Ah, yes, of course. Never mind. I can't explain. You must tell me all about everything you did! But not now. Now I want to ask you some-thing else. How are you? How was it, the journey?"

"Magic," Francesca said, closing her eyes for a moment, a lump in her throat. "The places I saw in Spain and Venice made the past seem like the next town instead of some distant planet covered with clouds and barely visible through a telescope. Yet, in a strange way, everywhere I went, I felt like I'd been there before."

"And Marius? Was he helpful to have along?"

She shrugged warily, studying her grandmother for clues. "I suppose."

"Suzanne?"

She stared at her grandmother, a terrible struggle taking place in her soul that was reflected in her eyes and the corners of her mouth. Pity, gratitude, hostility, and love dashed against one another like waves in a punishing sea.

How am I? she pondered. Did I discover the truth and find my eternal love? Or did I learn just enough about myself to destroy the value of everything I have, without finding any replacements? "Excuse me, I feel a bit . . ." She rushed off to the bathroom.

"Stomach flu." Francesca shrugged. "I think she caught it in Venice."

Suzanne walked back in, paler still. She groped through the room, sliding into a chair next to her mother's.

"Have you seen a doctor? You really should find out what it is. All those strange foods, and the unsanitary water in Europe. It might be something serious," Janice lectured.

"I don't need a doctor. I know what it is. And it has nothing to do with unsanitary food and drink in foreign lands . . ." Suzanne winced.

"Well, then, what is it, dear?" Catherine asked with a hesitant smile.

"Morning sickness."

"No!" Francesca exclaimed.

"A bastard!" Janice wailed.

"The child has a father and a mother!"

"But not married. You are not married!"

"What difference does that make?" Suzanne was shaking.

"Suzanne, are you sure?" Francesca flung her arms protectively around her sister's shoulders. "Are you sure, Suzanne?"

She nodded, surprised by the sympathy. "Yes."

"What are you going to do?"

"I'll tell you what's she's going to do! She's going to get married! Now! What's his phone number?" Janice demanded.

"Silence!" Catherine da Costa said suddenly, her voice hoarse with insistence.

Everyone froze. Then slowly, in petrified silence, they turned to look at her. Her expression was unreadable.

"Suzanne, come here."

Suzanne walked toward her with heavy, reluctant steps. When she reached the head of the bed, Catherine laid her hand above the warm, taut skin of her rounding abdomen. "Can it be true?" she whispered, her face suddenly breaking out into a joyful radiance that caught them all unaware. "A baby?"

The work of creation, of new lifeblood, flowing forward. The bough breaking out in fine, fresh leaf. Not dead! Not dead at all!

Suzanne suddenly knelt, her head burrowing into the white, starched sheets smelling of the potions and elixirs that were holding death so lightly at bay. *"Abuela,"* she wept, the words echoing in her mind: *And this is the secret of the everlasting, blossoming stem. . . .*

Catherine ran her fingers through the bright, warm, clean hair. Lovely color, she thought. Sunsets. Ripe peaches. Early mornings. A lovely color to pass down.

English translation of manuscript pages, circa 1568, collection of David Montezinos, Etz Hayyim Academy Library, Amsterdam. Stained and water-damaged. Several pages illegible.

. . . And so Reyna and I were reunited at last. Whether it was the magnificence of our bribes, or the threats of the Turkish Sultan—who so kindly took up our cause after Joseph explained the matter to the court physician, a pious Jew of Spanish ancestry called Joseph Hamos—I do not know. But the Venetians surely could not have ignored Sultan Suleiman's threat that should any harm befall us, he would retain Venetian trading vessels in Constantinople until our safe release.

As much as I admired the Sultan's kindness, I had no wish to so publicly put myself (and all my worldly goods!) in his debt. And so it was that I journeyed to Ferrara, there to join the large converso community under the protection of the benevolent Duke Ercole II of the House of Este.

And what, you ask, of my sister, Brianda, and Little Gracia?

I do not know what turnings of the heart befell my sister in her dark, cold confinement. But I would like to think that no one is immune to salvation, and that each heart, however twisted with evil desires, may be straightened and bleached by suffering, and purified and softened by repentance.

Brianda was released soon after myself. I expected her to take up the glittering life she had spared no ignominy and treachery to gain: to seek a husband for herself, and for her lovely child, from among the vain, strutting patricians whose company she had found so much to her liking upon our arrival. True, her claim to fortune had vanished, but her allowance was still ample enough to assure her continued attractiveness to a certain type of opportunist. I expected her to seize the first opportunity that came her way.

Instead, I found her on my doorstep, bags packed, holding Little Gracia's hand. Her heart, she declared, was truly shattered. She begged to be allowed to join me on my journey back to the religion of our forefathers, and to put Venice as far behind us as possible.

What did I do?

The only thing I could, of course.

Was not Little Gracia my own dear niece, the child of Diogo? Could I refuse to keep her near me and oversee her welfare? And Brianda, was she not, after all, my sister? Did not the blood of our blessed parents flow in her veins?

The whole family left for Ferrara, together.

Much may be learned from this, my children.

In Ferrara I began to breathe the air of freedom. I also met a woman who taught me much, and whom I loved: Señora Benvenida Abrabanel. She dowered orphans, ransomed a thousand prisoners, and endowed houses of learning. She encouraged me to support our Hebrew scholars by providing livelihoods for those involved in the translation of our prayer books, our Bible, and other works into Spanish and Portuguese, so that those who had forgotten their faith might rediscover it.

Many beautiful works resulted from this. But one was, and remains, my most beloved: The Consolation for the Tribulations of

Israel. *The author, Samuel Usque, expounds that which my heart already knew: that the countless sufferings of our people point to the great truth of our faith, rather than deny it. For all that has happened G-d's prophets foretold, even to the starving mothers who ate their own tender babes. And if that is so, may not we trust that His prophecies of redemption may also be fulfilled?*

And so it was that my heart turned toward the Holy Land, which sat in desolate waste, awaiting our efforts to prepare it for the final coming of the Messiah. It was then that I understood, at long last, just where my journey would finally end.

(Illegible. Water damage.)

40

The apartment was a wreck, Suzanne noticed vaguely. The smell of marijuana lingered in the air, along with sour laundry and a million cigarette butts in plastic cups. There was a note from Jean apologizing like mad and promising a thorough cleanup as soon as she got off work. There was a CD of Haitian music in the stereo, a man's pants hanging in the bathroom, and a toilet seat that showed signs that no effort had been made to lift it when it should have been lifted.

There was also no food in the house. Did she have any money? she wondered. Something left over from Gran's largesse? A little bit would do. Tomorrow, she'd sign up for unemployment again. And maybe the center had gotten some grants, enough for back salary.

She sat down on the threadbare couch, her sudden weight sending minions of dust mites floating into the pale city light. Joke's on me, she thought. Not a molecule of her carefully constructed life had been swept away in her absence. In fact, not a damn thing had been swept, washed, or cleaned at all!

She grinned, enjoying the miserable irony of it all. What was I so worried about losing? she thought in astonishment. What was I so afraid of leaving behind?

With her last strength, she stripped the sheets off the bed, found the two cleanest pieces of linen, made it up, then crawled gratefully inside.

She'd called him, but only a machine had picked up. She'd left him a message. From the corner of her eye she studied the little red light on her answering machine, willing it to flicker with the joyful notice of new messages.

It did not.

That was the thing about slamming doors in people's faces. Sometimes they took it seriously, especially if they themselves were serious people.

She lay down and wept, her whole soul pouring out in an agony of longing and regret and most of all fright. She was more frightened than she had ever been in all her life; terrified of the idea that certain acts were irrevocable.

When she got up, the house was dark and someone was pressing the buzzer.

"A minute!" she said hoarsely, groping her way out of bed.

The moment she sat up, the nausea began again. Worse this time, she thought, feeling the underpinnings of a ravenous hunger she couldn't have imagined, let alone remember experiencing. It was as if she had been brutally and deliberately starved for a week.

Food, she thought. Anything.

The buzz gave way to a bang, somehow less angry, but more insistent than ever.

"One second! Jeez!" she called out, desperate for something to eat. Who could it be, anyhow? The landlord? Jean? Watchtower people . . . ? She suddenly couldn't think of a single person she really wanted to talk to, or would be particularly happy to see.

"I'm going to look through the peephole, and if I don't open the door it means I don't want you, so get lost!" she shouted, remembering the old line that worked so well.

There was a carton of half-eaten cottage cheese, and an elderly orange. She peeled it greedily, pressing the soft, dry sections between her teeth, savoring the imperfect flavor. Then she opened the cottage cheese. Green mold stared back at her. Was it harmful? she wondered, pushing it aside with a spoon and searching for the white underneath. Antibiotics were all molds, weren't they? She stopped, shaking her head in disbelief and tossing it into the trash.

Chinese, she thought. Succulent, spicy, with lots of stir-fried vegetables and those long, delicious noodles, piping hot. Three or four bowls, at least. Only after she'd finished imagining it down to the last detail did she realize that the knocking had finally stopped.

Good. She grabbed her purse and checked out her cash. Enough for one meal at least, she thought gratefully, opening up the front door. But at the threshold, something stopped her. She stepped out, searching in all directions, feeling a sense of palpable loss together with a strange, nameless kind of hope.

She leaned back against her door, closing her eyes and breathing deeply. The scent of musk and rosemary seemed to drift down over her.

Imagination, she told herself. Wishful thinking.

She locked the door and walked thoughtfully down the steps toward Mulberry Street, her head spinning and her heart pounding as if inside her some red arrow were moving up toward the exploding point.

She searched the crowds. Sometimes she thought she saw someone who looked like him, but as she neared, the hair turned the wrong shade of blond, or the height was not right.

Lost.

Get lost.

Groping her way to the stoop of an old brownstone, she sat and watched the crowds swirl around her, thickening. The Festival of San Gennaro, she realized, looking at the sidewalk vendors, the colorful floats full of sacred icons, and the people following behind, chanting prayers. All at once, she saw the years of her life swirl past, full of sound and color and movement, lacking in all meaning. Depthless. The chance, one in a million, to find her true soul mate, gone forever.

Lost . . .

"G-d of my fathers and mothers before me, who has sweetened my life and given me blessings beyond measure, hear my prayer," she heard herself say. "Help me."

"Food?" a vendor offered her. "Ham, and blood sausages."

"I'm a vegetarian." She shook her head.

"There's this Buddhist-vegetarian restaurant around the corner. Why don't you go there?" the woman said helpfully. "That is, if you're hungry."

"I'm starving," she said.

"Well, what are you waiting for, then?"

What am I waiting for? she thought.

There it was. The pickle barrel. The fringes of the red lanterns, a bit more frayed now. She ordered large bowls of steaming food and ate slowly, tasting nothing, simply anxious to feel some relief from the craving for sustenance.

She left with the ache of hunger gone, but feeling emptier than ever. She wanted to crawl back into bed and cover her head with a pillow and weep for all the vanished riches of a life that had almost been hers; for the rough, dark clouds hovering above her that would never part. Reluctantly, she climbed the steps back to her apartment.

There he was, sitting with his back up against her door, his elbows on his knees, palms over ears, fingers pressing into his scalp in an attitude of utter desolation.

She dropped to her knees and sat back on her ankles, resting her hands softly on his shoulders. His arms were around her, filling the emptiness, overflowing with an abundance that made her want to laugh, to cry out that it was too much, too much. And when he looked up at her, she saw the clouds part and the shining beauty of the world come through again.

41

"Well, how does she look?" Francesca fluffed the stiff netting of the white veil over Suzanne's shoulders and spread the long satin train in a perfect arc.

Janice, a little weepy, stood on one side of Suzanne, their father, Craig Abraham, on the other. "Beautiful!" they chorused.

Catherine da Costa sat up in her wheelchair. She looked at her blossoming granddaughter, touching her rosy cheek and drinking in the whiteness of her smile. "More than that! She looks . . ." Catherine caught her breath, watching Suzanne straighten her shoulders and lift her chin with the calm dignity of a young queen about to be crowned. ". . . like a true descendant of the House of Nasi."

Suzanne knelt, putting her fragrant young arms around her grandmother's frail, thin waist. "Gran, Gran. Thank you," she whispered, her voice breaking. Catherine leaned into her granddaughter's warm, full breasts. When they parted, both felt as if some great secret had passed between them.

"There is something we need to do. Carlotta!"

"Here, missus." She put a tooled-leather case into Catherine's hand.

"And here is the pen and ink. Come. Let's begin."

She opened the case and carefully removed the family Bible. With trembling fingers, she turned the pages until she reached the tree with its golden boughs. "Janice, your hand is steadier than mine. Write it in."

Janice took the pen and dipped it into the peacock-blue ink. Beside her daughter's name she wrote in carefully: "Gabriel Fonseca, m., 8.6.96."

Catherine looked at it, her eyes brimming. "And when the baby comes, don't forget to fill it in. And when Francesca marries . . . "

Suzanne put her hand gently on her grandmother's shoulder. "You'll be here to remind us, *Abuela.*"

Catherine patted her hand and smiled. No, she thought. I won't.

From inside the synagogue came the faint strains of the band beginning to tune its instruments.

"You'd better go in, *Madre,*" Janice urged.

Carlotta pushed the wheelchair toward the front, positioning it in a spot right near the wedding canopy.

The great central chamber of the old Spanish and Portuguese synagogue in Manhattan was filled with lilacs, hyacinths, and roses of every hue. The polished wooden pews gleamed with a warm, homey light. The music began: Mozart and Beethoven, some Hebrew melodies, and finally, when the family began the long procession down the aisle toward the wedding canopy, traditional Ladino melodies.

Gabriel entered first. Tall, golden-haired, wearing a black tuxedo beneath which a gold embroidered Spanish vest flashed with little bursts of light as he walked. His face was light, filled with such utter and complete happiness that it could not be mistaken for anything else, anything less.

A group of Gabriel's cousins came next, the little girls in apricot organza with lacy collars and wide puffed sleeves, their shining hair crowned with wildflowers.

Then came Francesca and Marius (who had arrived from London two hours before), the maid of honor and best man. In a tiny-waisted dark peach dress with a full skirt and puffed sleeves, her hair falling to her shoulders in a mass of lovely curls, she looked like an older version of the children. Or like the sweetest angel Botticelli ever conceived, Marius thought as he kept pace with her. He looked very distinguished in a formal black tuxedo and striped cravat, which every now and again he picked at as if it were choking him.

And then came Suzanne.

There was a hush in the room, like a collective inheld breath. Oh, the shine about her! Catherine exulted. A light like a golden sphere. It sparkled and blurred and finally divided, becoming a number of golden spheres that hovered on the ground and in the air.

Catherine closed her eyes, pressing her fingertips gently to the lids, hoping to clear her vision. But when she opened her eyes, the spheres had multiplied, filling the entire synagogue, thousands and thousands of them, hovering points of light containing in each the figure of a man, woman, or child.

The synagogue was packed now, she saw, as the rabbi read out the seven blessings. Relatives, friends, living and dead, some she remembered, and many more she had never met joined one another in the pews, up on the ceiling and over the doorways, bathing the young couple in a warm glow as they stood giving and receiving those ancient, sacred vows of fidelity and honest love that bring mankind its truest blessings.

There was her Grandmother Nasi, wearing her flowered synagogue dress; and her mother, Elizabeth, her kind, patient face full of thoughtful happiness. There was Carl's young niece, and Carl's parents. And there was Carl himself, waiting by the door, handsome in his favorite sweater, his pipe in his hand as he waved to her.

She let out a soft moan.

"Gran?" Francesca turned, looking at her in concern.

"I'm fine. Fine." She patted her granddaughter's smooth, young hand.

And now, another contingent of spheres blew in, their light glowing with a richer patina. They wore sandals and togas, pointed yellow hats and farthingales. In the middle were Gracia and Francisco Mendes.

They moved slowly down the aisle until they stood on either side of the bride and groom. Catherine saw all four climb up together to the *tevah* until they stood beneath the prayer shawl.

The rabbi began: *"Soon may you hear in the cities of Judah, and in the streets of Jerusalem, the voice of joy and gladness, the voice of the bridegroom and the voice of the bride. Blessed art Thou, O Lord, who makes the bridegroom to rejoice with the bride."*

She watched Gracia and Francisco repeat the blessings and sip the wine as if they, too, were getting married again. And when the glass was broken, and the cries of *mazel tov* rose up like incense, Catherine found Gracia standing beside her.

"You've done well, Rivka. Everyone's quite pleased. They're all waiting to welcome you. Are you ready?"

Catherine looked at her granddaughter, resplendent in the regal white gown. And what of the baby, her great-grandchild? She wanted so much to hold it in her arms, to be at the celebration of its birth. To know if it was a boy or a girl. And then she looked at Francesca. The contours of her young face were sensitive and vulnerable as she looked at her young man sitting in the front pew waiting for her.

Marius and Francesca. She laughed to herself, shaking her head. But opposites often made the best partners, forming the strongest bonds of completion. They would have their chance, anyway, which was the most anyone can hope for. How she wanted to know if they would marry, to attend their wedding, to see their children.

How she wanted to live forever!

She gasped. The pain, both terrible and familiar, hit her full in the stomach with the punishing force of an instrument of torture. Her face turned white as she clutched herself against it, waiting for it to pass. When it did, she smiled wanly.

No, not forever. Not this way, she thought, tugging on the ugly tubes that stretched from her arms to the metal post. Not another minute, this way.

The spheres moved and floated and danced around her. She watched them, fascinated. They were corpuscles, she realized. Some remnant of each one of these men and women flowed through her veins, just as some part of her flowed through her granddaughters'. And each time a family celebration took place, something of her would be there, too, encased in her own golden sphere.

"I'm ready now," she said out loud.

"*Madre?*" Janice bent down to her. "Did you say you were ready?"

She looked at Janice, startled. "Yes. I'm ready to leave. You and Craig go on to the party. Carlotta and that Fredericks nurse will take good care of me. I'll see you all in the morning."

Janice bent over her, her face puckered with concern. "Sure?"

Catherine reached up and touched her daughter's face. Craig was also in the middle of a divorce. Maybe they'd get together again. Who knew? "*Mazel tov.* Now it's your turn to become a grandmother."

"Never!" Janice cringed.

"Wait. You'll love it more than anything else in the whole world, Janice. You'll see."

"Gran, let me drop you off. I don't mind," Francesca urged.

"Francesca, I think there's a young man waiting over there to talk to you. Go to him! I've always liked Marius."

"He'll wait," Francesca said. "*El mundo pertenese a los pasensiozos.* Isn't that what you always told us?"

She winked. "Who says I always know what I'm talking about! Now, go, go." She smiled, blowing them all a kiss as the competent Mrs. Fredericks wheeled her toward the exit.

"When did you get in?"

"Just in time to make it to the ceremony. I've got so many frequent flyer miles, they don't allow the plane to take off until I arrive. . . . Brings back memories, no?" he said, glancing around at the Spanish-inspired decor.

She nodded dreamily. "Toledo. Córdoba. I guess you can take a Sephardic Jew out of Spain, but you can't take Spain out of a Sephardic Jew. Wherever the Jews of Spain wound up, they brought with them a little of the world they'd left behind."

"Marry me," Marius murmured.

"What?"

He took her hands eagerly into his. "I tried calling you in Venice. But you'd already left."

"Why did you leave me in Venice?"

"Because I had to see the notes in the margin of that manuscript myself."

"Were they important?"

He whistled. "You might say that. They were in Hebrew. I think it means the whole manuscript might have been translated into Hebrew. It might be in some collection of medieval Hebrew manuscripts."

"You're impossible! That's all you think about! You shouldn't have left me in Venice. It was our moment."

"All the moments can be our moments," he said softly.

"Did you go see Elizabeta?" she said, changing the subject.

"There was no one at that address but an elderly caretaker who didn't have a clue as to what I was talking about. But a professor friend of mine told me Elizabeta Bomberg of Venice died fifty years ago. Apparently, she'd been working for the Italian underground and was caught and tortured by the Nazis."

"What? That's impossible. Elizabeta Bomberg took us to a costume party! Sh . . . she . . ." She stopped. Cold chills ran up her spine.

"I think someone said, though, that she had a niece with the same name, a professor of history in Venice. . . . Let's not talk about that, though. I want an answer!"

"I also want an answer! About the other things, the things I asked you in my letter."

"You mean about marrying you for your money . . . ? You can't be serious!" He shrugged, amused.

"Yes, I am," she said stubbornly. "I have to know! Were we set up? Did Gran discuss dowries and who knows what else with you behind my back? Don't lie, Marius. Gabriel already told Suzanne he didn't meet her by accident."

"Of course he didn't. Your grandmother approached my uncle, who approached me. It was my idea to introduce my best friend to your lovely sister. Although when your grandmother first saw Gab, she was ready to execute us both," he chuckled. "I guess he didn't have that settled, Semitic look about him. So what? I think it turned out rather well, don't you?"

"Can you answer me?"

"The answer is yes. I discussed the idea of forming a relationship with you with my uncle and asked him to intercede with your grandmother and gain her permission. I did this the first day we met, out of respect for tradition and for your family. Because this is the way things are done. Your grandmother was all for it, by the way. But Uncle thought it was a terrible idea. . . ."

"He did?" she said, swallowing hard.

"Yes, indeed. You struck him as a very fine, sensible girl. He thought I'd be very bad for you." He grinned.

"Well . . . then . . ." she sputtered, beginning to feel embarrassed and foolish. "And you never once . . . I mean . . . Gran never once told

you that you'd get something if you and I . . . if we . . . wound up . . ."
She took a deep breath.

"Actually, it wasn't your money I was after," he deadpanned. "It was your grandfather's book collection."

"This isn't funny! At least not to me."

"My dearest Francesca—you look so ravishing! Have I mentioned that? Promise me you'll wear this dress on our honeymoon? Ah, yes. You're waiting for an answer. Let me think of how to put it best. Hmm . . . Okay. It is true that I will go into Brazilian rainforests, climb Carpathian mountains in January, and sneak through secret police roadblocks to get my hands on something I want. But there are certain things even I won't do, because they're much too dangerous. Marrying you, if I didn't love you, is one of them."

He put his arms around her and pulled her close.

She hesitated. "Can we sit down a minute?"

"What's wrong?"

"Marius, how would we live?"

"Happily ever after." He shrugged.

"No. Seriously. I mean, where, for one thing. I suppose I could get a job in London, but I don't know if I'd want to leave the States. And . . . and . . ." This was hard. But it had to be said. She couldn't start out a life together with him without saying it. "How long do you plan to keep running around the world like some pirate, or treasure hunter? What are your plans for the future?"

"You mean, what am I going to be when I grow up?" He wasn't smiling.

"No. I mean . . . Yes. Exactly."

His face went ominously dark.

"I think I could help," she said hurriedly. "We could open up a store in Manhattan, something similar to your uncle's. I mean, I could crunch some numbers, and call some real estate friends . . ."

"Francesca . . ." He got up and put his hands into his pockets. She could see the outlines of his tightly squeezed knuckles bulge through the material.

"I'm not a shopkeeper. I earn a very respectable living at what I do. And I'm good at it. I'm the best. Do you think Picasso should have given up painting and opened a nice little shop selling framed clown prints? Home by six, supper at six-thirty? That's not who I am."

"But I think . . . I know . . . that is who *I* am."

They stared at each other across the empty pews, the sound of celebration suddenly gone, replaced by an eerie silence.

"Can't I change your mind?"

"I don't know," she said honestly.

42

Letter, found on the desk of Catherine da Costa on the morning after her death, addressed: To All My Children. Read, together with her last will, in the presence of her family in the offices of Schnader, Lipton, Morrison, and Siegel, Attorneys at Law.

It is late. The wedding was beautiful, worth everything I did to keep me alive a little while longer.

Tell that suicide doctor I think he's an ass.

I'm sitting in my living room; my music is playing and there's a good fire on the grate. I've had a lovely glass of wine, and some of those chocolates I adore but haven't eaten in ages. I think I've eaten four or five. I've lost count.

Gracia's with me, of course. She calls me Rivka and tells me to call her Hannah now, as that was always her true name. She wore the name Beatrice like clothing; Gracia like skin. Hannah was the name that echoed in her soul; the name she heard G-d call her. She's sitting on the couch keeping me company, supplying me with words when I need them, ideas when I can't think.

I have my pen and paper ready. I think I understand Gracia at last. I, too, wish to leave behind something to keep you all safe and happy forever. I don't have her noble, exciting history, but I have certain things I know, and others I've learned. I have a history that I, too, would like to share.

My mother, Elizabeth Nasi, valued family and education. She raised her husband's nephew. In addition, she had living in her home her unmarried sister (who was a school principal, and later the head of an academy that trained many fine teachers) and her father, who was crippled in a railroad accident. She supported many other family members in a quiet way.

Recently, someone told me that she slipped money to a Sunday-school student for him to donate to charity, as the child was embarrassed not to have anything to give. A refugee from Hitler's Germany told me she taught him English, and a neighbor said she came daily to read to a dying child to amuse him and relieve the family.

She taught Sunday school, and each year the highlight was a model Seder, which she made as beautiful as possible by bringing all of her finest dishes, silver, and the most delicious food.

I think she inherited a wonderful character. A wonderful goodness. And it has made me think that I understand something I never did before.

We are all part of something, something truly great, a oneness that encompasses everything. The important thing is not to fight that. To understand your place in it. Once you see yourself as a part of that whole, a clear ingredient in the universe, a partner with the G-d who created you, you will stop fighting so many things, accepting them and being enriched by them.

Accept the past.

Learn from the good that was part of your history, that which ennobled and raised your people ever higher. Don't battle it, don't insist you were born rootless. It will take so many years of your life to fight, and in the end you will lose, because the truth can't be overcome. Only when the legacy of one's ancestors corrupts and enslaves the human spirit should one pick oneself up and walk away, forging a different path. That is the legacy of Abraham.

Accept that there is within you an eternal part that cannot be destroyed. There is no reason to fear death, no reason to fear the future. You will always be part of it in some way. While you live, create your own beautiful bead, the jewel of a life intelligently and generously lived, so that you may leave it behind to be strung on the necklace that adorns mankind, time, and history.

There is also no reason to battle mankind, other cultures, other races. All of mankind is one, each contributing a unique and matchless truth. There is no need for one truth, for one contribution, to negate the others. We are all endangered species, all cultures, all religions, as mankind marches into the future with jeans and Rollerblades and bad T-shirts and Walkmans. There is no danger in our differences; but in the overwhelming tedium of the damning sameness that is drowning out what each of us has learned, what each of us can contribute. A sameness that is turning the necklace of mankind into a string of cheap plastic beads of dull and even color, which jangles around our necks like a noose, cutting off our oxygen, choking us like the detergent-fed plankton of a dying sea.

Fight the degradation of your culture, of your environment, of your nation and community. Dust off the jewels in the attic, shake out the skeletons—stare them in the face.

Stop being afraid.

Wisdom will be yours, because you have earned it.

Peace will be yours, because G-d will be yours, as you rest in His fathering care, His mothering spirit of good.

> G-d bless you all,
> Catherine da Costa,
> of the House of Nasi

43

Eighteen months later.

The phone rang.

Francesca rolled over in bed, groping for it. It was Paul Chorman, her new supervisor. She listened in dismay as he outlined another ten changes he wanted to the presentation she had to give that morning on the client-server current account reconciliation system.

"No, no problem at all," she lied. "Oh, don't worry about it. I'm usually up this early. Of course. I'll take care of it. See you at work."

She lay on her back a few moments looking at the shadows on the ceiling. They were big and gray with uncertain edges, something like storm clouds in a dull, wintry sky. If they'd just listened to her and gone in the direction she'd wanted to in the first place—an integrated PC network—there wouldn't be any of these problems!

She dragged herself out from under her warm covers, taking the eight hundred pages of specifications from her attaché case. She looked at the bulky document. It was the old story. Big, solid males wrapped up in big IBM mainframes. She penciled in notes frantically.

It had been fairly simple to find a new job in another big bank. People at the office were friendly, although most of them were already living with someone. Her social life was the usual blank: She'd gone out with a dentist Janice had sent her way, who'd talked about his sailboat all evening. And then there'd been the owner of a shoe store she'd met at the gym—a congenial and sensible fellow who spoke in measured, calm tones about financial strategies, new plays, workout techniques, and summer vacations. Before her trip, she would have considered him pleasant company. Now, she was excruciatingly bored.

She exercised, showered, then went to her closet to find something to wear. It was uncomfortably stuffed. Clothes had been her one indulgence since her inheritance. She'd paid off her mortgage and invested the remainder—almost half a million dollars—in treasury bonds, a sensible stock portfolio, and money market funds.

Along with the cash, she'd inherited Grandpa's book collection (except for the family Bible and Gracia's manuscript), some beautiful jewelry, expensive sets of dishes, and half of the heirloom silver. Suzanne had gotten her equal share of everything, and vowed she was actually using the silver ritual objects, particularly the candlesticks.

According to the will, neither she nor Suzanne was allowed to sell the heirlooms. But if they chose, they could donate them to a museum collection in their grandparents' name. The Bible and Gracia's manuscript were with Mother, to be passed down to the eldest great-grandchild with the stipulation that they be kept forever in the family.

She looked around. She could certainly afford a larger place now, she thought. But the idea of uprooting all that lovely cash from where it was growing like pretty little plants in the sun was painful.

Besides, she was in no hurry. She had everything she needed, really, didn't she? Life would go on, calm and serene. She need never get her feet wet again, she thought, with a strange absence of satisfaction.

She looked out at the cold, pale city sky, the indifferent glass eyes of the brick towers. Red geraniums, she thought, spilling out of window boxes in Córdoba; the smell of orange blossoms in Seville; the sound of gondolas in Venice.

Restlessly, she paced around the room, stopping finally at the coffee table. She picked up a photograph. Little Hannah in Suzanne's arms, holding a tiny flag that read "Save the Whales," a mass of red-gold curls tumbling over her tiny shoulders. Gabriel was standing next to them, one arm around them both, the other resting on Suzanne's rounding stomach. In the background was the new Women's Health Center, which Suzanne had used a considerable amount of her organizational powers—and her inheritance—to help create.

They all looked so happy.

She put it down, discomfited.

Gran had left considerable amounts to charity—all her usual causes, as well as a few surprisingly large bequests to Suzanne's center and Greenpeace.

I really *should* give some money to charity, she thought, ashamed.

For the last year she'd been volunteering at the center twice a week, manning the phone lines. But giving money away . . . That was different. If she found it hard to spend it on herself, even considering donating it was pure torture.

She'd have to work on herself, she sighed.

She picked up another photo: Mom, her plastic claws gone, holding little Hannah in soft, grandmotherly arms as if it were the most natural state in the world. Who would have imagined it? Janice, archetypical grandmother, with the fold-out brag book and the shopping trips to Baby Gap? She was installed in Gran's apartment on Fifth, happily, now that she'd gotten over the fact that Gran hadn't left it to her outright, but in trust for the great-grandchildren. Since Hannah's birth she'd come to peaceable terms with the arrangement, feeling it far more natural and less insulting.

Janice had taken up life alone with surprising grace. She'd been the one to organize the Passover seder this past year, presiding over the rituals with a commendable authority. She was dating some man she'd met in the Catskills, a retired history professor, and seemed content and more serene than she'd been in years.

Francesca put the picture down and picked up the next one, holding it in both hands and studying it carefully. He was standing in the fading afternoon light, in front of the waterless old fountain in Toledo, his eyes smiling, his blue shirt cool against his warm, tanned skin. Her thumb caressed the glass. Marius . . .

He'd come to Gran's funeral, asking Francesca once again to marry him and move to London.

And she'd said something hedging and polite with "more time" in it. He'd taken it as no, and returned home.

He'd called her several times during the past eighteen months, mostly updates on his research on the Gracia memoirs. The last conversation had something to do with the Guenzburg Library in Moscow.

Sometimes the conversation had spilled over into their personal lives: he, probing hers delicately, as if it were an old book; and she, dancing around his without touching, without actually knowing what it was she wanted to ask. And now, for the past three months, there had been silence. She'd tried calling him, but had only gotten through to machines.

But then, that was the problem, wasn't it? He never was in one place for very long. But even that wasn't the most insurmountable difficulty in their relationship. Her biggest problem with him, she had to admit, was simply one of imagination: She couldn't imagine life as the wife of Marius Serouya.

She was afraid, terrified, really, of so many things:

Of marrying the wrong man.

Of never finding the right one.

Of never having children.

Of having a husband who wouldn't be a good father; who wouldn't be home for them; who would find domestic life boring.

Of getting divorced.

Of creeping age and of death from sudden accidents and/or a long, painful illness.

Of losing her job, of being left behind at promotion time, of being less than appreciated.

The list went on and on.

She replaced the picture carefully, then glanced at her watch and panicked. Stuffing the specifications back into her attaché, grabbing the unread *New York Times* and a high-fiber bran muffin, she dashed toward the subway.

The platform was packed, smelling of old, damp wool and grime.. Bodies pressed up against her rudely, throwing her petite body off balance. She felt like a piece of not-quite-fresh meat swaying on a hook in some butcher's window. She made a valiant effort to balance her briefcase between her ankles, opening the paper and turning to the business section. She had just checked the stock prices and was about to glance through the ads when a small article caught her eye:

Serouya Rare Books and Manuscripts, Ltd.
Honored by International Antiquarian Booksellers Association

Alex Serouya, recently retired director of the hundred-year-old firm of
Serouya and Company, Dealers in Rare Books and Manuscripts, one of
Europe's premier dealers, has been selected as this year's honoree at the
International Antiquarian Booksellers Association's annual book fair,
to be held this week in London.

Newly appointed successor, nephew Marius Serouya, is highly re-
garded among his peers and has been responsible for several spectac-
ular finds, most recently a handwritten copy of the New Testament,
thought to predate all existing copies, discovered in a cave in Ethiopia.

Francesca put down the paper and hugged herself. She was suddenly freezing.

Marius.

The train stopped. She watched the doors open, then, with a dull
sense of hopelessness, watched them slowly close again. She got off
three stops later, walking briskly down the platform toward the exit
and the huge glass tower waiting to swallow her in its elevator banks,
when, suddenly, someone rammed into her, sending her attaché case
flying.

"Why don't you watch where you're going!?" she shouted at the
woman who had pushed her, realizing too late it was some mental case
wrapped up in rags, wearing torn gold-lamé house slippers and haul-
ing fifteen filthy shopping bags.

The woman turned around, looking at her in hostile disgust. "And
why don't you get yourself a life, girlie?" she snarled.

Helplessly, Francesca knelt, frantically gathering together the pages
that had spilled all over the platform. Suddenly, she had an intense
awareness of the dozens of feet rushing by. She stared, mesmerized, at
clicking, high-heeled instruments of torture; badly polished, narrow
loafers run down at the heels; highly polished, expensive designer im-
ports that squeezed the toes; and comfortable, clean New Balance
cross-trainers.

She stood up, studying her own feet.

Getting up in the morning. Suffering through rush hour on the subway. Dashing to some tedious job. It wasn't some sacred duty. It was simply for the money. People did it simply because they needed money.

But I don't.

So why am I doing this?

Get yourself a life, girlie!

She felt her whole body tremble as the platform rumbled and the cool breeze of an approaching train washed over her. She turned to look at it, her face radiant with sudden revelation. In a swift and deliberate motion, she turned the attaché upside down and watched as the white papers blackened and shredded beneath the wheels of the oncoming train. Then she took out her day planner. One by one, she tore out the pages filled with frantic scheduling and demands, balling them up and scattering them like confetti.

She ran up the steps and out into the street.

There she was.

"Here, add this to your designer collection." Francesca laughed, handing the old bag lady her attaché. "And something else." She took out two fifty-dollar bills and pressed them into her chapped and bandaged hands. "For shoes."

"G-d bless you!" the woman shouted, shoving the money into her pocket, waving at her.

"You too, Gran," Francesca whispered, looking after her with odd recognition, just before hailing the taxi that would take her to Kennedy Airport.

To: Paul Chorman, V.P. of Information Services, Metrocorp
From: Francesca Abraham
Sent from Kennedy airport's business client's lounge

Dear Mr. Chorman:

Francesca Abraham DEEPLY REGRETS her inability to continue offering you her services as a VALUED EMPLOYEE. On behalf of Ms. Abraham, please accept DEEPEST THANKS AND BEST WISHES on finding someone else to match her HIGH LEVEL OF ABILITY AND PERFORMANCE.

To: Marius Serouya
From: Francesca Abraham

ARRIVING HEATHROW FLIGHT BA428. WILLING TO HOLD
LADDER.

She walked out into the waiting room at Heathrow, her stomach
lurching with a sudden wallop of fear as she scanned the crowd of unfamiliar faces all waiting for someone else.

Maybe he hadn't even gotten the fax. Maybe he was in the Cayman
Islands or Istanbul. Maybe he was in love with somebody else. . . .

"Francesca!"

She turned toward him in a kind of dream, terrified at every single
step. Whatever was going to happen was going to happen, she understood, giving in. For good or evil, for better or worse, this was her life.
Her *mazel.* The thought that through ignorance, stubbornness, or simple cowardice she might have missed it was suddenly the most frightening idea of all.

He was wearing his light blue tie. She loosened it, unbuttoning his
collar, then slipped it off his neck.

"We will be happy, Marius, won't we?"

"Deliriously," he swore.

44

Marius turned off the motor, paddling the small boat to the dock, then tying it securely. He got out first, giving Francesca his hand. It was early, and the blue Mediterranean sky was still flushed with the pink flourishes of sunrise.

They walked up the banks of the beautiful Sea of Galilee, just west of the old Roman ruins of Tiberias. They had packed a wooden hamper with wine, warm pita breads, olives, hummus, fresh tomatoes, and cucumbers. They had two perfect peaches and two perfect croissants, and a thermos of coffee.

They laid the feast out on the checkered tablecloth and ate slowly, relishing the cool breezes that wafted through the tall eucalyptus trees, and the tantalizing smell of the delicious food.

He took her in his arms and held her close to him, running his fingers through her dark curls. "You're never going to cut out again, are you?" he pleaded softly, pressing his lips to hers.

"Never," she murmured, smiling, closing her eyes and feeling little vibrations, like electric shocks, run through her body. She turned, her head snuggled against his chest, her arms folding over his. "It's so beautiful here, Marius!"

He lifted her hair and kissed the warm spot on the back of her neck. "I'm glad. I wanted to bring you right after we got married, but then that manuscript in Cyprus turned up."

"What's a year?" She shrugged, grinning. "We're here, and it's lovely. Thank you, darling." She kissed his fingertips. "And to think, I suspected you had ulterior motives."

"What?"

"You know, when you suggested this spot for a belated honeymoon. I thought you'd be working the whole time we were here."

"Francesca, really! Is that what you think of me? I promised you we'd get away from everything, didn't I?"

"Jerusalem was fabulous, wasn't it? That wall around the Old City, built by Gracia's old friend Suleiman the Magnificent! Reminded me of Toledo, no? In fact, Israel looks so much like Spain: the olive groves, the herds of sheep . . . I can see why my ancestors fell madly in love with Spain when they were forced to leave here. It must have seemed like home. This part, the Galilee, is the most beautiful of all, isn't it?"

He nodded.

They sat wordlessly in each other's arms, watching the sun's slow climb and listening to the quiet murmur of the calm waters lapping against the side of the boat.

"Marius?"

"Hmm?"

"You know, in that book by Cecil Roth, he says Gracia bought some land from Suleiman and that she was headed there on her final journey."

"Really? I'd forgotten."

"He says that the land was right here, in Tiberias, overlooking the Sea of Galilee. Quite a coincidence, wouldn't you say?" she murmured sweetly.

He shifted, as if trying to find a more comfortable position. "Hmm . . . I guess."

"Apparently, she wanted to create a colony here for other *conversos,* a safe haven where they'd be free to live and practice their religion openly. I wonder if she succeeded, if she ever got here."

"The history books don't really say. But then, you know how it goes. Scholars poke around and poke around and suddenly all this new information suddenly turns up and answers all the unanswered questions. We may not know for a few hundred years."

"But if she did make it, wouldn't it be logical to think that a copy of the whole manuscript would be around here somewhere? After all, there were those notes in the margins in Hebrew, remember? And she would have finished writing it here. Maybe some scribe translated it into Hebrew. Maybe he wrote out a few copies and stashed them somewhere nearby."

He grinned, shrugging. "Pure speculation! And coming from you!"

"Say, isn't that a building of some kind?"

"Where?" He turned to look.

She stood up, peering inland toward a grove of date palms. "Right down there, see! Over by the right. A church or synagogue, maybe? Wonder how old it is?"

"I'm on vacation. I'm absolutely not interested!"

She got up and pulled him after her. "Race you?" she challenged, not waiting for an answer. With a great show of reluctance, he got up and ran after her.

But it wasn't fair. She was carrying two, and he already knew the way, having marked it off on his map long ago.

EPILOGUE

Mŭhimme Deftri, vol. 6, no. 2354, Register of Public Affairs, Ottoman Treasury, Wakf, December 1565–May 1566, Istanbul, Turkey.

Document One

To the General Governor of Damascus and to Mustapha, the administrator, the following order:

> *. . . A Jewish woman by the name of Gracia has agreed to pay a thousand golden ducats a year on condition that all the income of the area known as Tiberias belong to her. In addition, she has agreed to supply the cost, labor, and materials to rebuild the fallen walls around the city of Tiberias that it may once again become a safe place of habitation and trade for all its inhabitants. She proposes building a water pipe to bring the waters into the city, and will undertake this cost as well. It is my command that she be given all due cooperation.*

Document Two

A Jewish woman by the name of Gracia, who has been granted by the Munificent One the land known as Tiberias—an area near a great lake and healing hot springs, full of palms, and good for silkworms and sugarcane—has written to complain that some of the gatekeepers who guard the walls of the city, by Your Honor's orders, have been negligent and irresponsible in carrying out their duties.

This Gracia, who has built a large and benevolent home on the shores of the great lake, has contributed much to the land and its inhabitants, whom she gathers from many places across the seas.

She further complains that the janissaries and officers of the local governor are exploiting the farmers, causing them pain and misery by illegally exacting high penalties and collecting extra taxes. These farmers, according to this Gracia, are in her domain, and she will not tolerate their exploitation. She asks Your Excellency to intervene to warn these janissaries to desist or to face the consequences of their illegal actions.

And so, I respectfully order that this matter be looked into immediately. I ask that you find upright men in Damascus to replace them.

Consolaçam às Tribulaçoens de Israel. Composito por Samuel Usque. Emprello en Ferrara 5313.

DEDICATION

To

The Very Illustrious Lady,

Doña Gracia Nasi

The Lord has sent to you in these trying days, a soul from the highest ranks of His armies, placing it in the most proper womanly body of the fortunate Jewess Nasi.

It is she who greatly helps your needy sons at the beginning of their journey, helping those who cannot save themselves from the pyre and undertake so long a road because of their poverty, her hope giving them strength.

As for those who have already left and arrived in Flanders and elsewhere, who are overcome by poverty, or stand forlorn by the sea in danger of being unable to venture farther, she reaches out to them with a most liberal hand, with money and many other aids and comforts. *It is she who shows them favor in the bleakness of the stormy German Alps and many other lands, when the extreme misery and many horrors and misfortunes of the long voyage overtake them, succoring them willingly.*

It is she who . . . helps the multitude of necessitous and miserable poor, refusing no favor even to those who were her enemies and sending boatloads of bread and necessities to all, reviving them from the grave which threatened them in those waters. In this way, with her golden arm and heavenly grasp, she has raised [our] people from the depths of . . . infinite travail in which they were kept enthralled in Europe by poverty and sin, bringing them to safe lands and . . . guiding them [back] to the obedience and precepts of their G-d of old. . . .

Thus has she been . . . a bank where the weary rest; a fountain of clear water where the parched drink; a fruit-laden shady tree where the hungry eat and the desolate find rest. . . .

The End

ACKNOWLEDGMENTS

I am deeply indebted to the late, great historian Sir Cecil Roth, whose wonderful book, *Doña Gracia of the House of Nasi*, first brought the story of Gracia Mendes to my attention. I would like to thank the Jewish Publication Society for granting their permission to use material from this work, both verbatim and as background material, for the historical sections in this book.

The full text of the Edict of Expulsion, along with de Gois's description and other accounts of the misfortunes of the Jews in Portugal, can be found in the excellent anthology *The Expulsion 1492 Chronicles*, edited by David Raphael and published by Carmi House Press, P.O. Box 28104, Seattle, Washington 98118.

Information about the medieval pepper trade, used in Chapter Twenty-four, was found in Anthony Disney's *Twilight of the Pepper Empire*. *A Medieval Home Companion* by Tania Bayard—an authentic list of instructions written by an elderly medieval husband to his inexperienced young bride—was the source of the medieval recipes and housekeeping hints in Chapter Fourteen. The *converso* prayer in Chapter Twenty-one was taken from Professor Haim Beinart's wonderful article, "The *Conversos* in Spain and Portugal in the 16th to 18th Centuries," included in his anthology *The Sephardic Legacy*.

In addition, I would like to thank:

Rabbi Mitchell Silverstein of Hebrew University; Dr. Steven Harvey, professor of medieval Jewish and Islamic philosophy at Bar Ilan University; and Dr. Abraham David, senior researcher of the Jewish National and University Library in Jerusalem, for sharing with me many scholarly insights into how rare manuscripts have been hidden and discovered.

M.B.E.R., the mysterious manuscript hunter (who, true to character, has asked to remain anonymous), for allowing me the unforgettable glimpse into the real world of rare-book hunting I could never have seen without him.

Dr. M. Orfali, professor of Spanish Jewry and the Sephardic Diaspora at Bar Ilan University, for his invaluable help in sorting out the Spanish, Ladino, and Portuguese words in this book.

Mrs. Betty Weil, a descendant of Gracia Mendes, for sharing with me her inspiring family history.

Mr. Kyle Shulman, for many insightful comments.

Ms. Laurie Bernstein, my talented editor at Simon and Schuster, for advice and guidance each step of the way.

Ms. Annie O'Connor for her invaluable editorial direction.

Lisa Bankoff, my agent at ICM, for her enthusiasm and support.

My thanks and my love to my husband, Alex, who was never less than immeasurably helpful at every turn; and to my children, Bracha, Asher, Rachel, and Akiva, who cheerfully listened to this story as many times as I told it, and were always enthusiastically receptive.

I welcome the comments of my readers, and can be contacted at P.O. Box 23004, Jerusalem, Israel; or E-mail address: nragen@netmedia.net.il

Naomi Ragen
Jerusalem
1998